SHERIFF SKINNER AND

THE MAN FROM
THE PAST

Sheriff Skinner and the Man from the Past
Published by: Primer Cap Pistol Publishing
October 2004

Cover Design: Joey Wu

ISBN: 0-9715542-3-4

To Eileen

Thanks to:

Glenna Goulet – *Transcriber*
Maurie Klimcheck – *Editor*
Helen McCormick – *Proofreader*
Archetype Book Composition – *Typographer*

CHAPTER 1

"You're not going back to your office now, are you?" scolded the small, dark-haired woman. She put aside her embroidery, glaring, as her tall husband slipped off his carpet slippers to stomp his feet into boots.

"Sorry, Gen—I got to. Sam has made town patrol with Cletus for the last ten days while I was laid up." The tall sheriff fastened his gunbelt and reached for his black frock coat.

"I thought Mr. Giles was the night marshal. The doctor said you needed your rest. It's not two weeks since you were shot in your head; or did you forget?"

"Now don't exaggerate. I wasn't hurt that bad and Happy is also the night jailer. He's got too many prisoners up in that cell to leave them alone and go checking on saloons. That's why Sam was filling in. It's my turn tonight."

"You need more deputies, Sylvester. They can't expect you to work day and night." Gen would not let the subject die.

"You're right. But hopefully, it's only temporary. If it continues—I promise I'll ask the commissioners for another deputy. Does that satisfy you?"

"I guess it will have to," complained Mrs. Skinner. "Why you ever came to this Godforsaken, dusty hell-hole in Arizona—I'll never know. And you with a good hardware business in Rochester."

"It wasn't all that good, Genevieve, and I heard that all before. Just drop it—please."

1

"Go on, Sylvester Skinner," she answered in her martyr's voice. "Go out and arrest a bunch of drunken miners. Just try not to get hurt again in that hard head of yours."

"I promise not to get hit in the head—how's that? I'll be home in a couple of hours at the most." He blew her a kiss and slipped out into the night. True to his word, he was back to their bed close to two hours later, at midnight.

The blast's shock wave rattled their bedroom window and was followed, almost immediately, by the noise from the explosion.

Skinner scratched a match to light the bedstand oil lamp. "Four-oh-five," he intoned groggily after checking his watch—laid out by the lamp.

"Is that from a mine?" asked Gen, bolt upright in bed.

"Don't know yet," grunted the sheriff, pulling on trousers and stuffing his bare feet into boots. "Keep an eye open in case it's a fire."

"How could I go back to sleep? I was practically thrown out of my bed. Should I make coffee for you?"

"No time." The sheriff buttoned his coat over gunbelt and galluses.

"You don't have a shirt on, Sylvester. What kind of a sheriff is that?"

"The in-a-hurry-kind. Take care," . . . and he was out of the house.

"Why, Sylvester? Dammit—why?" she said bitterly and got up to see if she could see anything from the windows.

******

The sheriff lived on Chestnut Street, two blocks from Main Street. The blast seemed to come from beyond his house toward Elevator Row, six blocks from Main Street. But the explosion did not come from one of the dozen large and small mines that bored into the subterranean silver-bearing reef that brought fortune to Green Falls, Arizona.

The blast happened on Elm Street where a single-story residence stood wounded by a large, jagged hole from roof to mudsill—that still spewed dust and smoke. A cowed crowd of neighbors was warily peering into the ruptured maw of what seemed to have been a bedroom.

"Make way for the law!" roared Skinner, startling the spectators into making access for him.

"I need light here. Who can fetch lanterns?" Several men volunteered to bring their lanterns, dashing off to secure them.

"Now—whose house is this?" demanded Skinner, voice harsh with authority.

"It's mine," said a tall, nightshirted man, who was supported by sympathetic neighbors.

"And your name?" demanded Skinner.

"He's Theodore Ostenhaven," put in a large ill-clad woman, holding onto the evidently shocked man.

"You are Mrs. Ostenhaven?"

"Certainly not," she retorted. "That's the trouble. He can't find Anna."

"Anna—being Mrs. Ostenhaven?"

"Yeah, she's missing," offered the small man at Ostenhaven's other elbow.

"When did you see your wife last, Mr. Ostenhaven?" Skinner had to shout over the clamor of the crowd.

"I can't find her, you know." He was shaking from his ordeal.

"He told us, before—that he went out to the backhouse and the explosion came," said the small man, starting to tremble, also.

"Yes," confirmed Ostenhaven. "In the outhouse."

Sam, Skinner's chief deputy, came through the crowd, elbowing people aside with his muscular body. "Sam," yelled the sheriff. "Find a rope or something to keep these vultures back." Sam grabbed a man, giving him instructions.

"I got Ames to find a rope. What's going on here?" asked the stocky deputy.

"This man's wife seems to be missing. I got lanterns coming. Then we'll go in and look."

"How come he's alive?"

"Says he was in the outhouse when the bomb went off."

"Bomb?" questioned Sam.

"You can smell the dynamite, if you get away from this crowd," said Skinner.

"That figures—the bomb, I mean."

"What does that . . ." Skinner was interrupted by a man with a lantern, who pushed it at the sheriff.

"I got it," the man panted, triumphantly.

"Keep the crowd back for now, Sam. I'll check out the bedroom." The sheriff advanced on the gaping hole, holding the lantern at arm's length.

The blast shredded the shiplap siding and had completely blown out a window—for glass shards were everywhere, even embedded in the inside walls and ceiling. The flooring was ripped from the joists, which were dislodged and amputated by the explosion.

The bed was dashed against the far inside wall. The bedstead was splintered—its canopy rent and tattered. The woman's bloody body, a victim of a hundred separate wounds, was jammed against the wall.

Another figure climbed into the shattered room, bringing another halo of lantern light. This was Deputy Cletus McCoyne, the former Army scout and mountain man.

"Holy jumping Jehoshaphat," gasped the big deputy. "Somebody sure didn't like somebody in this house."

"'Fraid so, Cletus," grunted Skinner. "I'd like to get her body out of here. Can you pull that door off its hinges? We can set her on it and carry her out."

A few minutes later they gingerly threaded their way out of the blasted bedroom; pulling, pushing and finally carrying the door with Mrs. Ostenhaven's body on it.

Once outside, the sheriff sent a bystander to wake up Marks, the undertaker. He was to bring his wagon and collect the body.

Leaving Cletus to watch over the body, the sheriff went back to the husband. Someone had brought him a blanket and he was sitting propped against one of the spindly elm trees that were prescripted by the city fathers. The blanket was wound tight against his thin body.

"Feeling better, Mr. Ostenhaven?" asked Skinner.

"A bit. Somebody gave me a drink of whiskey. I'm not really a drinker. I can't believe my wife is dead."

"I want to go over, again, where you were at the time of the blast. I believe it was deliberate. A dynamite bomb, I think."

"A bomb—my God—why?" Ostenhaven shook his head feebly.

"We'll find that out later. Now tell me about where you were at the time of the blast."

"I have a weak stomach. If any little thing in what I eat is the least bit bad—spoiled, I mean—I get diarrhea. Last night it was probably those little pickled sausages my wife liked so much. They're made in Tucson. Spicy, though. Too spicy for me, I guess."

"Go on. Don't get lost on sausages," directed Skinner.

"I won't. I had to evacuate my bowels about midnight. So I lit a candle and went to the outhouse."

"Wait a minute—the blast was a little after four."

"That was the second time I had to go. The first time was around twelve o'clock."

"The second time you were out there, how long were you sitting there before the blast went off?"

"Not long. Frankly, Sheriff, I had to run like hell to get out there in time. Before I fouled myself, you know."

"Assuming this was a bomb, do you know of anyone who could wish you ill?"

"I'm a mine manager now; took over the Stella's Stake two months ago. Came down from Denver. Too cold there in the winter. As a mine manager, you have to make hard decisions. Fire people, dock their wages, sometimes. Can't be lovey-dovey or nothing gets done, you know. I guess somebody out there could be angry at me . . . I don't know."

"I'm going to need a statement when you're up to it," said the sheriff. "Come down to my office and myself or my chief deputy will help you."

"Are you through with me? And Anna—what about her? She should be properly buried. She was very churchgoing."

"I'm finished with you for now. I want the doc to look at your wife. Marks, he's the undertaker, will contact you, when the doctor is finished. I'm sorry this happened, Mr. Osten-haven. I'll try my best to get to the bottom of your wife's death. That's a promise."

"It wouldn't bring Anna back, but thank you anyway." Skinner left the man against the stunted tree and went to Marks, who had come up in his closed van.

******

The sheriff had gone home for a wash and shave and a clean shirt. Breakfast found him mumbling vague answers to old Mr. Hansen, their perennial boarder, who had taken over the woodshed as his bedroom after building the Skinner's house.

"Lost your appetite, huh?" asked Hansen. "I could find room for them sausage patties of yours."

"Be my guest," said Skinner morosely. "In your case, I guess I said that one time too many."

"That's all right—I'm thick-skinned." He reached for the sausage patties.

At the Sheriff's Office, Sam was pouring coffee from the big pot. "I saddled your horse already. Doc Seevers wants us down at the undertaker's by 7:30."

"So early?" Skinner commented.

"He says he's got to reset a bone at 8:30. It's on the Macreedy kid. The little girl. But I got to talk to you before we go down there."

"Talk? What about? I'm not at my best this morning. Can it wait?"

"No. This is important. It's about last night."

"What about last night?" Skinner was querulous.

"Ostenhaven isn't Ostenhaven."

"What! Who the hell is he, then?"

"He was called Captain Theodore Eckhardt when I knew him."

"You knew him—when?"

"Too damn well—I'm sorry to say. He was prison commandant at Camp Brooklyn."

"Camp Brooklyn?"

"It was the hulks. Six old, rotten, wooden, former warships, anchored in the East River. One hundred yards off the Brooklyn shore, in New York City."

"And you were there, Sam?"

"Myself and fifteen thousand other Confederate prisoners of war—crammed in those damn boats. Starving always. Dying of disease and sweating in the summer and freezing in the winter. I was lucky, I guess; I was only in the hulks for six months or so. That's why I'm still alive today. You captured my men and me on April Fools Day outside Richmond, remember?"

"I had forgotten it was April Fools Day," said Skinner.

"It was . . . and the joke was on my men and me. It took four days on the train to get to Hoboken and we were put on a barge while a steam tug pushed it to the East River and the hulks. Once there we were put on a smaller hulk. That's the first time I saw Eckhardt. He gave us a welcoming speech that was mostly threats."

"You mean Ostenhaven?"

"That's what he calls himself now, I guess. He's got a beard now and is greyer—but it was Eckhardt. His face is burned in my brain."

"He was cruel—or was he just strict?" asked Skinner. "I remember, toward war's end there was a policy against paroles."

"Way past strict. He was wicked. Ran the hulks like he was an Oriental potentate of some kind. I'll tell you how the hulks worked."

"Let me have some coffee while you enlighten me." The sheriff recovered his cup from a desk drawer.

"After us new prisoners had our indoctrination period, they split us up, sending us on the barge to other, bigger, hulks to fill up the ranks of the centuries—taking the places of those that died."

"Centuries?"

"That's what they called each group. Each was in a thousand square foot cell—one hundred prisoners made up a century."

"Sounds crowded," Skinner commented.

"It was. The gun decks on those old hulks had only five foot of headroom under the beams. But let me continue. Eckhardt and his superiors made their money by sending the centuries out to work—every day."

"What kind of work?"

"Unloading and loading ships, shoveling out the coal cars at the gas works, every lousy job that people would pay for—Eckhardt had the centuries doing it. He had contracts with everybody. But that's not the worst."

"No?"

"No. The employer would figure, for instance, that a century should load 5,000 bags of grain on a ship in five hours. If the century only loaded 4,000 bags in that period, that would mean the century worked at only eighty percent efficiency and the century's ration was cut accordingly. The thing you have to remember is that every century had a number of men that were unable to work; too weak to even crawl out of the cell. They were dying. Most of the time the century was lucky to scare up eighty men for work detail. The ration that night would reflect the production. Instead of half a pound of groats or barley, it would be six ounces or so per man for the day."

"And Eckhardt—I mean Ostenhaven—profited from this?"

"Him and his superiors. Rumor had it that Secretary Stanton, even, made money on us. They didn't care about us. They wanted revenge for Libby Prison and that prison camp in Georgia. An eye for an eye."

"But the war ended—when? The twenty-sixth of April, wasn't it?" questioned Skinner. "You should have been released by the end of April."

"More like the end of October," answered Sam. "And damn glad we were, too. It was starting to get cold. The centuries were all down to eighty or seventy-five men at most 'cause we weren't getting replacements—with the war over."

"How could they possibly hold you? I mean with the war over."

"Claimed we all committed criminal offenses. Said we were under arrest and investigation. And they kept working us and pocketing their money."

"So how . . . I mean why—did they let you out?"

"Some of the prisoners were British citizens. The British ambassador raised holy hell to President Johnson and he ordered Stanton to release us. They gave us five dollars and a railway voucher good for a thousand miles. I got as far as

Galveston, Texas. And that's the story about Captain Eckhardt—except I didn't mention Sergeant-Major Finsen."

"Finsen? Who's he? This is quite a tale."

"He was, and still is, Eckhardt's right-hand man."

"Whatcha mean—still is?" asked the sheriff.

"Just what I said," continued Sam. "He's Eckhardt's assistant at the Stella's Stake. Does all the book work, from what I hear. He's unmarried and lives in the Congress Hotel. Fancy dresser with a Van Dyke beard. He's short-like; wears a top hat to make himself look taller."

"Think I've seen him at the Congress bar. Carries a silver-headed stick?"

"That's him—the weasel," confirmed Sam.

"So—Mr. Chief Deputy," observed the sheriff, with an edge to his voice, "how come you know so much about Eckhardt, or Ostenhaven, and his pal? It almost makes you a suspect."

"I recognized them—the day they got off Sweeney's stagecoach. I'm a lawman, remember. It's my job to keep track of people, especially people I don't like."

"Question number two, Deputy Buller. If you're such an eagle-eyed lawman, how many of your old friends, the Confederate prisoners on those hulks, have you spotted around Green Falls?"

"Two—that I know of. And I'll tell you now, because you're bound to find out sooner or later; Eckhardt had my brother whipped for failing to hand over suitable coal. His wounds became infected and he died of fever."

"Failure to what—with coal?" asked the startled sheriff.

"The prisoners were allowed to steal coal for our stoves—for cooking and heat. Every century cell had a cookstove to boil our gruel. The guards looked the other way at the gas works and when coaling steamships. But at night every prisoner had to come up to the barge and pass by the provost sergeant. A large clump of coal had to be in each hand of the prisoner and he had to drop one in a wheeled-barrow there, beside the sergeant. My brother, foolishly, tried to palm off a small piece of coal and was made an example."

"How old was he?"

"Seventeen and a half—always laughing and full of mischief."

"And getting back to my question about others in Green Falls?"

"Like I said, two—that I know of. Could be others I haven't seen. And I didn't know all the prisoners in all the hulks."

"And who are those two gentlemen?" asked Skinner.

"One is Mike Birnby. He's a dealer in the New Orleans Belle, your pal Caudelet's place. He got bad lungs from the hulks—coughs too much. Tall, skinny, prematurely white hair and mustache."

"And the other?"

"Otto Floss, a blacksmith with Busby Number Two. Big, blond hair going grey; droopy mustache, sorta like yours," Sam smiled. "A tic in one eye—forget which; walks with a limp from an old wound to his hip; hard-drinker and tough on the woman he lives with. You could say he's a mean one."

"Is that all, Sam?"

"That's it and if we don't leave soon, Doc will be mad as hell."

"Wouldn't want that, would we?" said the sheriff. "Go up and tell Happy we won't be long. Hate for him to lose too much sleep."

CHAPTER 2

"**H**ere come the two sleepyheads now," greeted the caustic old former cavalry surgeon. He and Marks, the undertaker, were playing checkers on a board resting on the bloody bosom of Mrs. Anna Ostenhaven. Marks carried the board, careful not to dislodge the checkers, to a wooden pail and placed the checkerboard over it, saving the game for another day.

"Whew," said Skinner, "she looks worse in the daylight."

"A real mess," agreed the doctor. "I counted one hundred thirty penetrating wounds and then I quit counting. Eleven in her head, alone."

"That was the glass, Doc?" asked Skinner. "I mean that made the wounds. It was all over the room."

"Nope—not even half was glass. Most were caused by this little lethal beauty." He held up, between two fingers, a triangular piece of rough cut iron—the size of a postage stamp cut diagonally into a right triangle. "These are what did the damage. The glass helped, but was probably incidental."

"You mean some kind of manufactured shrapnel?" quizzed Sam.

"That's it, Mr. Brains," said the doctor sarcastically. "Like a bomb."

"Can you dig me out some more?" asked Skinner. "Say half a dozen. I'd like to compare them."

"To what?" objected the doctor.

"Just get five more out, will you please, without the bull-shit, Doc," ordered the sheriff. "You're getting paid for this examination."

"Damn tooting, I'm getting paid for this. Marks, what did you do with that probe and forceps of mine?"

"You put 'em in your bag, Doc," explained the undertaker. "To make room for the checkerboard."

"Oh yeah—let me find some easy ones in her arm or leg."

It took time, but finally the surgeon had six of the mur-derous triangles in a pile in one of the undertaker's enam-eled-iron bowls.

"There, hope that satisfies you, Sheriff. My report will say that death was instantaneous due to multiple wounds to thorax and brain. Now—can Marks have the cadaver for burial?"

"Go ahead—bury her," agreed Skinner. "When would the funeral be?"

"Not sure; haven't talked with the bereaved yet. Maybe tomorrow; not sure until I see if he wants embalming, you know."

"Let me know, Marks. I like to see who shows up to funerals. Come on Sam, the jelly buns are on me."

But the sheriff had to pass up the jelly-filled buns for apple tarts. The jelly buns, with their little ooze of red jelly, looked too much like Mrs. Ostenhaven's riddled body for any enjoyable eating.

The sheriff and Sam had just tied off their horses outside the Sheriff's Office when a Negro man in a dirty apron ran up to them.

"A shooting!" he cried, gasping for breath. "At the Emerald Sea Oyster Bar." Another gasp, then, ". . . killed the cook . . . shot him dead."

"Here," said Skinner. "Take this package inside and give it to Mr. Giles. Tell him we've gone to investigate a shooting."

The Emerald Sea Oyster Bar had never had a fresh oyster cross its threshold, and truthfully, not too many canned oysters either, due to their cost. The shooter was still sitting at the lunch counter, his none-too-clean right forefinger searching about the inside of his mouth.

The shootee—or is it "the shot"—was lying down inside the counter on the duckboards which normally keep the filth of the floor from interfering with foot traffic. This reclining man had a hole in the middle of his forehead that was red in color and ringed with a powder burn.

Sam collected the shooter's pistol, smelled the barrel and nodded, overstatedly, to the sheriff.

"Got it!" mumbled the shooter, pulling out part of a broken molar and laying it regretfully and tenderly on the lunch counter.

"Would you have an explanation for your behavior?" asked the sheriff.

"Most certainly," said the shooter. "What kind of a fellow do you take me for? As you can see by my collar," he turned toward the lawmen, "I am a clergyman. A man of peace, mostly. Possibly not at this particular time—but mostly."

"You were attacked, maybe?" prompted Sam—hopeful of an explanation.

"Not quite—in a direct manner—one would say." The cleric shook his head as if to second himself.

"You were insulted, reviled?" It was Skinner's turn.

"Yes—sociologically speaking. Society was abused by this man. He's the cook here, by the way."

"Aha," said Skinner. "That's your excuse—abusing society, is it?"

"More like violating social mores, I'd say," explained the clergyman. "I was a victim today. You could be one tomorrow."

"How were you victimized, sir?" asked Sam.

"He broke my tooth; that's part of it there. The other half is still in my gum."

"He hit you in the mouth and broke your tooth?" was Skinner's next question.

"Not with his fist. More like with his omission," said the clergyman.

"What's an omission?" asked Sam. "Some kind of a kitchen tool?"

"An omission, my dear man, is an apparent failure to commit an action that one's duty requires. In this particular instance the cook, there," (he pointed to the duckboards), "was charged with preparing a pot of chili beans to some historically accurate representation of said dish throughout the Southwest."

"He was—all that?" said Sam.

"Certainly," confirmed the shooter. "Look at the menu board. Do you not see 'chili beans, bowl, 50 cents'? That establishes the standard."

"And he missed it?"

"For certain—as my tooth will bear witness. He neglected to inspect the beans for stones. One of which broke my tooth. As any cook will testify, the beans must be checked for stones before cooking. It is a prerequisite for chili bean cookery."

"I think we're getting to the heart of this matter," observed the sheriff. "Now, sir, what transpired after you broke your tooth?"

"I asked to speak to the cook. He came out—fairly belligerently, I should add—saying, 'what's your problem, dude?' I stated that a rock in his beans broke my tooth."

"He said, 'Bad luck, dude.' To which I asked whether he inspected his beans for rocks? 'Naw,' he says, 'Too much trouble.'

"At that point I asked the man what he was going to do about the injury to my tooth. I said at the very least he should apologize. Perhaps even pay for the removal of the shattered tooth.

"He said—this is a quote now, 'I'm just going to laugh like hell at you, dude.' So I shot him to protect society from any more of his omissions."

"Just like that," said Sam.

"Exactly like that," said the clergyman.

"Sam," ordered the sheriff, "take this man up to the prosecutor's office and have him tell Mr. Rose his story. Personally, I think it's justifiable homicide. Tell Rose that. But he's the prosecutor; let him make the decision. And remind Rose this is Arizona, not Boston. Go along, now. I'll get someone to take care of this cook. Marks is making money today."

******

Theodore Ostenhaven had risen from his despair and desolation by the stunted elm tree to go about his life. He had always prided himself on his pragmatic attitude toward life's vicissitudes. He had never allowed himself to overly applaud his successes; just as he never permitted setback or stoppage to deter him from his course. The terrible death of his beloved wife, he rationalized, was a disappointment to be overcome on the path to success.

Had not unfortunate circumstances tried to trip him up in his Army career? Had he not lined the pockets of his superiors with the lucrative prison labor contracts? Those very superiors had turned on him when a new political breeze had blown over Camp Brooklyn. But fortitude, nerve and a very complete listing of the financial "favors" disbursed to those turncoat superiors helped him to escape serious court-martial proceedings. An expeditious name change allowed Eckhardt, now Ostenhaven, a newly-immigrated Swiss gentleman of means, to disappear into the limitless western United States.

Ostenhaven packed a small valise, leaving his blast-damaged home for new quarters in the Congress Hotel. A good wash with hot water, a relaxing shave by the hotel barber and a tasty, filling, breakfast elevated his spirits immeasurably.

As he re-entered the hotel's lobby, he encountered his supposed assistant, the former Sergeant-Major Franklin Finsen. In actuality, Mr. Finsen was a full partner in his and Ostenhaven's outside business enterprise. At the Stella's Stake Mine, though, the fashionably-clad Finsen was engaged as chief bookkeeper and managerial assistant.

Finsen's talent was a predilection for the many minutiae of business and commerce. No small detail escaped his nimble mind. No half-penny lay lost and uncounted or not cross-registered in his ledgers. It was Finsen who devised the century's production percentile system—that logically, arithmetically, reduced the prisoners' ration, putting thousands in the pockets of the greedy officers and politicians.

"I must see you immediately, Franklin. Trouble has reared its ugly head." Ostenhaven betrayed no emotion.

"My room," replied Finsen. "The maid won't come in for at least an hour."

When the room door was closed and locked, Ostenhaven's stony facade collapsed. "My wife was murdered last night," he said, tears welling up in his eyes.

"Wh . . . what?" Finsen seemed shocked. "How did it happen? Was she shot?"

"It was a bomb of some sort. Didn't you hear the blast? Around four o'clock."

"I thought it was an over-large shot from some mine," explained Finsen. "I just went back to sleep."

"You know what this means, don't you?" said Ostenhaven. "Someone from the hulks has recognized us."

"Us? They didn't bomb me," retorted Finsen.

"You'll be next, no doubt. I think we should hire a bodyguard. Do you know of such a person, Franklin?"

Finsen thought a moment, eyes narrowing to aid mental activity. "Jack Sprague," he whispered as though to mask the thought.

"You mean, Sergeant Sprague? The chief guard of the hulk 'Champlain'? I heard he fled to Canada when that Johnson man started nosing around."

"He did, but he's back in Missouri now, I think. A railroad guard—of some type."

"I'd hate to meet him on the roof of some freight car on a dark night."

"He's an imposing presence, surely," agreed Finsen. "Did an excellent job of keeping the lid on the prisoners. They learned that to their sorrow—the Rebels, I mean."

"Is it possible to contact him to see if he would take this position? I don't want to pay him from my personal funds. Is there a way the company could put him on the payroll? As a guard, perhaps?"

"All the guarding is done by the Association's police. I think though, I could find him a place on the payroll as a timekeeper. Of course it doesn't pay what Sprague would be worth."

"Perhaps, Franklin, you could promise him more—in the future when this other business starts showing a profit."

"I could, indeed," said the smaller man, taking a yellowish cigar from a box atop the dresser. "And talking about the other business—we hit a snag."

"What! No more trouble—please."

"Maybe just a setback, then." The smaller man fired the cigar, after neatly cutting a vee in its head.

"That's what I've been telling myself—that my wife's death was a setback," sighed Ostenhaven. "But don't let me interrupt you."

"A snag, I said," repeated Finsen. "But a delay all the same, I'm afraid. Tent-Peg Pete passed away while Mr. Hurst was questioning him."

"Died?"

"I'm afraid so. Mr. Hurst thinks it was his liver. The old man was quite a drinker, from what I'm told. Mr. Hurst admitted, in hindsight I might add, that perhaps he should have given the old man water. But that's all water over the dam." The smaller man laughed at his pun—until he started choking on the cigar.

"I'm glad you are able to be comedic, Franklin; I surely am not. One disaster after another."

"Setbacks—remember. And don't be discouraged; we know the general whereabouts of the mine. Hurst followed him that last time almost to where the mine should be.

"Who would have thought an old geezer like that could sneak out of his camp in the middle of the night?" Finsen added.

"Certainly not your Mr. Hurst," said Ostenhaven.

"Now that's unfair, Theodore. You had an opportunity to turn down Hurst's proposition. But that big nose of yours sniffed gold and off you bounded after Hurst. Hurst is just as much your man as he's my man."

"You're right, Franklin. It is this damn bombing that has upset me. Tell Mr. Bowers I'll be late today. Have him check out that cribbing we were discussing yesterday, by himself. And start the repairs. I had trouble with my stomach last night and should not have had anything greasy for breakfast. I also have to meet with the undertaker—about Anna."

"Just relax, Theodore. I'll handle everything. Come in when you feel up to it."

"Do you think Hurst can find this mine, now—what with the old man dead?"

"It might take time. But as long as we keep paying Hurst, he'll keep looking. It should only be a month or so."

"God—I hope so. We need a victory, Franklin."

"Yes, Theodore. We need a victory," echoed the smaller man, watching the ash on his cigar.

******

"Go on, you stupid lump of fleas!" yelled the bearded man, yanking on the mule's lead. Charlie Hurst was attempting to enlist Tent-peg Pete's jackass into finding the former owner's gold mine. For the greater part of the morning Hurst had dragged the mule up and down the blind canyons of this section of the Santa Catalinas known as Apache Heights. A torrid piece of high desert, dissimilar to most of the mountain range.

Hurst was just about to shoot the recalcitrant mule when it suddenly brayed smugly and scampered off up a narrow animal track to finally stop at a small, trickling spring. The spring had been improved with the addition of a mud and stone catch basin. This, evidently, was Tent-Peg Pete's water supply.

"Go ahead, flea bag, drink your fill," rasped Hurst. "You found it. I'll take seconds." After they all had their fill, including Charlie's horse, the canteen and water bag were filled and the horses were led out of the hidden grotto. The mule was again given its head as Charlie Hurst hoped "Flea Bag" would strike gold next, rather than water.

******

Sam came back without the clergyman in tow. "Where's the apple tarts?" questioned Sam.

"Where's the chili bean killer?" countered Skinner.

"I asked first," said Sam. "My lips are sealed until pried open by pastry.

"Your sweet tooth will be the death of you. However, I rescued two from Happy's jowls." Skinner passed an apple tart to Sam.

"You said two."

"One for you and one for me—think I'd cheat you?"

"Yes—about pastry, I do. And to answer your first question, the chili bean killer, alias Dr. Parkham, posted bail and is now visiting with Mrs. Mosely. He will no doubt visit there for several days. He, believe it or not, is the new Episcopal Bishop of Tucson."

"Bail for killing the cook?"

"Not for the killing—that was justifiable. Rose liked your idea. The bail was for firing a weapon with reckless disregard. Ten dollars."

"He got off easy. Surprised at Rose, though. What happened to his Boston upbringing?"

"Turns out the bishop went to Harvard. Was chaplain in some Massachusetts regiment that Rose's uncle was in. Old home week—there in the Prosecutor's Office. And by the way, Rose said to tell you they got beans in Boston, too. Boston baked beans—and the cooks there have to check for stones, also."

"Isn't that wonderful," said Skinner, pushing his skinny butt to a more comfortable position in his chair. "Our country joined together by a fraternity of bean eaters—eating and making bodily odors all in perfect harmony."

"Only if there's no stones," added Sam.

******

The two grimy children sat on the dirty, warped porch, playing by the shack's open doorway. They were playing store. The blonde girl was the shopkeeper; the different sized stones, which were her wares, were lined before her tattered dress as she played. Her brother, no less dirty, was haggling over a commodity, represented by a smooth rock. At last the price was agreed on and the boy counted out his money on the filthy floor.

Their father came banging up the porch steps, the makeshift iron and leather boot on his crippled foot announcing his arrival. His children looked up, anxiously, from their play

"Whatcha got there, boy?"

"We're playing store, Pa. "I jes bought me a bag of potatoes."

"Wish they was," growled the man. "What's that yur using fer money?"

"Jes them iron pieces you wuz making before, Pa. Found 'em in the dirt by the chopping block—see?" He held out a handful of small iron triangles.

"Gimme them damn pieces," yelled the father, throwing a punch, which the boy dodged with practiced ease. "Any more of those out there by the block, that I missed?"

"I dunno, Pa. They was flying every-which-way when you was a cutting them off. Maybes I could find some more. Iff'n I looked real hard."

"You jes do that, boy, 'n' giv'em to me. 'N' you forget you ever saw them pieces—remember." The father banged his way into the hovel, yelling for his wife. The children looked at each other, disappointed at their game's sudden ending.

"Maw said it were the war," explained the girl. "When he got his foot hurt an' all. Weren't like that before, she said."

"I didn't know Pa before," replied the boy, throwing the girl's wares at the chopping block in the front yard. "I wuz too little."

CHAPTER 3

M r. Gompers, of the Gompers' Department Store, was waiting for the sheriff when he returned from dinner. Gompers, a full-bodied, balding, fifty-year-old was visibly agitated, jumping up from the chair Deputy Sam had put at his disposal.

"Well, at last—I've been waiting almost a half-hour for you, Skinner," griped Gompers.

The sheriff shot a look at Sam, who made an eloquent shrug. "Sorry, Mr. Gompers," said Skinner. "Didn't know you were waiting. Couldn't Sam help you?"

"I wanted to deal with the boss," stated the department store owner. "This is extremely important." Sam was nodding deprecatingly behind Gompers' back.

"I found this in my post office box this morning." Gompers handed Skinner a sheet of paper, folded to make its own envelope. Skinner opened the letter to read:

> Gompers—this is yur one an only warnon. I want $500 bucks or yur store gets blowed up just like that house. Put the money in a cigar box and give it to the bartender at the Belle. A man will come pick it up. If somebody follers him I will shoot within a good rifle.
>
> Love Mr. No Name

"At least," said the sheriff, "he sent his love." Skinner passed the note to Sam.

23

"Levity has no place in this situation," lectured Gompers heatedly. "Is this a serious threat? What should I do? Five hundred is a lot of money. This could be a hoax—and I'd be out the money."

The sheriff took some time framing his answer, time he used to fill his pipe bowl. He looked at Sam, who gave an almost imperceptible sign of assent.

"Get the money ready in the cigar box and tie it with cord. Don't try anything stupid—like cutting up newspaper instead of greenbacks." Skinner paused to light his pipe, blowing a cloud of blue smoke up at the ceiling.

"Give a damn extortionist what he demands?" argued Gompers angrily.

"Bait for the trap, Mr. Gompers. You don't begrudge putting the cheese on the rat trap, do you?"

"A piece of cheese isn't $500, if I may be permitted to point out."

"Hopefully, you'll get the money back," encouraged Deputy Sam, backing the sheriff's play.

"And then what?" asked the department store owner. "Take the box to the New Orleans Belle?"

"At eleven tonight, on the dot. And now," continued Skinner, "we must put on a small exhibition—in case Mr. No Name has followed you to this office and thinks you're asking for our help."

"I never thought of that. He might kill me for seeking the law," confessed Gompers, suddenly frightened.

"Don't worry about that. He wants the money, first. Now, here's what we have to do . . ."

A few minutes later the sheriff's door was wrenched open by a red-faced Gompers, who stomped out angrily on the porch, then turned around to hurl harsh words at the sheriff.

"You go to hell, Skinner! I'm not losing my store just because you got a great big damn stubborn streak up your back when it comes to crooks! It's my hard-earned money and I'll give it to anybody I want to. Forget I ever came here, you long-legged ass-hole!" He walked back to the door to slam it, loudly.

"Goodbye, Mr. Gompers," whispered Sam, choking with laughter. "Long-legged ass-hole—that's wonderful. I can just picture that—walking down the street, carrying a bag of jelly-buns."

"A rectum has no hands, and don't be so gleeful when your boss is slandered," put in Skinner.

"Could be hemorrhoids holding the buns," theorized Sam. "Anyway, it's how I imagine it."

"Instead of imagining parts of the digestive system, perhaps you could sit down and draw up a scene that shows which buildings Mr. No Name could use to fire down upon me when I follow the messenger with the box of money."

"You're going to follow the messenger?" asked Sam, suddenly mirthless.

"And you and Cletus will, hopefully, shoot Mr. No Name."

"Maybe you better wear a piece of iron inside your shirt."

"Why—so I could clang like a bell every time he shot a hole through it? I want you to shoot him first, thank you."

"That puts a lot of load on me and Cletus," observed Sam.

"That is why I hired you two as deputies; not for good looks, most certainly."

"Well, thank you, Sheriff Skinner. For that I should let you clang at least a couple of times, but as it's your turn to buy at the bakery tomorrow I'll have to try to save your—what did Gompers call it?—your long-legged ass-hole."

"There you go again," answered Skinner. "You completely forgot that I bought today—but you showed marvelous memory for Gompers' remarks—which were play-acting, by the way."

"Says you," said Sam, digging out paper and pen.

******

There were eight Indians but only seven badly used horses. Two of the Apache braves shared a horse, taking turns riding or running alongside, holding on to the rider's lance loop as a help. This was a band of renegades, White Mountain Apaches, who had quit their sub-tribe, seeking adventure and spoils.

Three of the braves were young and on their first real raid. This, though, was not a juvenile night foray to steal a few horses from a neighboring tribe. This was a war party, for was it not led by Slit-Nose, the fearsome and experienced warrior; he of song and legend? Did not Slit-Nose carry the white man's rifle that could carry fifteen of the shiny bullets in its stomach quiver, ready to spit their fire at any enemy?

Small Bear had no firearm, being too young and untried to be trusted with a firestick. He was armed with a bow and a handful of long arrows. The bow and the arrows were easier to carry, the boy told himself, especially when he had to share his horse with Beaver Tooth, who had stupidly ridden his own horse to death.

Beaver Tooth suddenly reined in the horse, almost causing Small Bear to stumble. Slit-Nose was signaling the band to advance at the walk, quietly. Small Bear's heart, already beating rapidly from his run, smoothed to what they called the warrior's breath as the anticipation of the battle swept over him.

Slit-Nose pointed to Small Bear with his lance and then pointed to a jagged rock, high on the flank. Small Bear raised his bow, hastily strung, to signal his receipt of the order and then ran the half mile to the rocky lookout.

Once on the rock, Small Bear crawled on his stomach across the boulder's burning surface, flattened from any enemy's sight. Inching himself forward, he saw what had caused Slit-Nose's horse to warn the leader. Down in a shallow valley, two of the moving tepees pulled by horses, of the white people, were slowly making their way along the valley floor. One of the moving tepees must have had a bad spirit imprisoned in its ring of sticks that walks, for it screeched and screamed to be let out.

As Small Bear watched, a white man on a horse came up to the first of the moving tepees. He had a black, extra scalp below his mouth that wiggled strangely when he made talk with the white who stayed in the round tepee opening. The second white man had no extra scalp on his chin.

The bad spirit had quieted when the moving tepee stopped and Small Bear saw the man climb down and bring food to the bad devil who must have lived in the ring of sticks upon which the white man's tepee moved. The white man took a stick and gave food to the devil. Then he shook the ring of sticks, scolding the devil. The white man returned to the tepee opening and struck the horses with his long quirt. They moved forward, pulling the tepee on the rings of sticks. The devil, now fed, lay quiet within the ring of sticks.

Suddenly Small Bear remembered. He was not sent here to observe the devil in the ring of sticks. He was to scout the enemy's strength. How many fighting men were there and how many firesticks to fear? Carefully he made his count. Then he backed off the lookout rock and ran back to report his findings to his leader.

******

"I've got to go out tonight, later on—about 10:30," Skinner told his wife at the supper table.

"I thought you took your turn last night," complained Gen. "Now it's tonight, again."

"This isn't the saloon patrol. It's something different. Sam's got the saloon patrol tonight."

"When are you supposed to sleep, Sylvester? The doctor said you should have rest with that head wound. But you just blithesomely ignore everyone's warnings."

"I'll take a little nap after supper, how's that?"

"Oh, thank you so much, Sylvester. That will fix everything. A nice nap."

"Excuse me, Mrs.," interrupted Hansen. "Can I have some more pea soup and do you have any more of them biscuits? Sure is good."

"You certainly may, Mr. Hansen. At least you aren't afraid to drop a crumb of a compliment, once in awhile."

"I'll try to watch them crumbs, Mrs. Skinner. I don't have the best table manners, I'm afraid. I was brought up by the Wolfs, you know. That's why."

"Wolves, Hansen?" asked Skinner, suddenly stimulated. "Like Romulus and Remus? Nursed by the wolves with the milk of the wolf bitch."

"I'd never call Aunt Gracie that. She'd have knocked me plumb overboard. You see, Uncle Thomas Wolf had a riverboat. Not one of them steamboats. This was a pole boat, only thirty foot long. Never had a table to eat at. Just sat on the deck and spooned your food from Aunt Gracie's big iron pot. Mostly fish chowder or eel stew. Boat always had a fish line or two trailing behind. That's why I appreciate your grub so much, Mrs. Skinner—never any fish."

"My sentiments, exactly, Gen," said Skinner, getting up to seek his nap. "Wake me up, please—about ten, will you?"

******

Skinner checked his watch. It was almost eleven. Suddenly he saw Gompers coming down the street and he ducked further into the darkness of the fetid alley. Gompers stopped, checking to his right and left, furtive in his fear and then stepped inside the New Orleans Belle Saloon. The cigar box was clutched tightly under a thick arm.

The seconds ticked off to minutes as the sheriff stifled impatience and the first whisperings of panic. Had the box of money already been spirited from the saloon? Sweat broke out across Skinner's chest. Then he saw Gompers leaving the

Belle, hurrying, looking neither to left nor right, fleeing down the street to a safer place.

Again the minutes dragged by, each tick of time scolding the sheriff for *his* plan, mocking his forbearance. All at once, a young urchin dashed nimbly through the foot traffic of the New Orleans Belle's portal, the cigar box clutched protectively between his grimy hands.

Skinner, caught by surprise, pushed off on his long legs after the boy, trying to keep the slight form in sight. The boy, dressed in a too-long man's corduroy coat with the sleeves hacked off, set a zig-zag pace, dodging around the street's many boisterous pedestrians.

"Splang! Blang!" Suddenly Skinner was being fired on, the bullets zipping past him to ricochet against the adobe wall of another saloon. He tried to crouch lower as he ran after the boy, a burning jolt to his buttock slowing the running. Then the firing increased up the street, to stop as quickly as it began.

"Up here, Sheriff!" It was Cletus's booming hail. "We got him!"

The boy, up ahead, gave a cry and ran up an outside stairway that led to a landing with a ladder to the building's roof. Skinner caught up with the boy at the roof's edge. Sam was right behind him on the ladder.

Cletus helped the sheriff up on the tarred canvas roof and pointed to the dark lump of the dead sniper crouched immobile against the false front of the building.

"Pa," screamed the boy, rushing over to the dead man. "Pa—oh Pa! I told you it wouldn't work. I knowed they'd find out. Dammit, Pa—why'd you have to go and get kilt?"

"Sorry it took so long, Sheriff," Cletus whispered, trying not to interrupt the boy's grief. "I had three buildings to watch and Sam had four. Took a while to figure out which building he was shooting from."

"Fast enough, Cletus," said Skinner. "I ended up getting a round on the bounce." He turned to Sam. "Sam, better get that money back and bring the boy over to the jail for now. Right now I'm gonna go find Doc and get this bullet out of my butt." Skinner limped over to the ladder and painfully made his way down to the street.

******

The whites and their tepees that moved on the rings of sticks moved south with Slit-Nose's party shadowing them surreptitiously. The whites came across an unexpected stand of grass and stopped there to graze their animals and make their night camp. Once camped, all the whites came out from the tepees and could be better counted.

They were six males: the bigger man with the long chin scalp and two other white men, without the chin scalps. There was also three male children of different sizes. The women numbered five, with three of them fully grown and two girl children. The three men were armed with belt fire-sticks while chin scalp also carried a long firestick with him at all times.

The horses that pulled the moving tepees were untied from the iron ropes-that-make-happy-noises and they were hobbled to feed upon the long yellow grasses. The women worked together to fix three long iron sticks into the ground and then hung a shiny metal cooking pot from the iron sticks, building a greasewood fire under the pot.

Slit-Nose laughed at the smokey fire, pointing out how stupid the whites were to announce their presence with such a fire. Small Bear had to agree. His aunt, Warming Sun, who had raised him, always made a fire with little smoke, except of course when she tended the fire that smoked the meat for the winter.

"Rest and tend to your weapons," commanded Slit-Nose to his band. "We will attack at the time when the Mother Moon has gone to its rest and Father Sun has not yet risen. No brave shall take food or drink from this moment—so that his mind and body shall be alert to the night and to the enemy."

"Never forget," the war-tested leader said, "that the whites have many fire-sticks with many fire-mouths on each stick—that can kill again and again. The whites have superior weapons. We Apaches have the dark, our stealth and our patience.

"You—Small Bear—I make you a boon, a prize to you for sharing your horse with Beaver Tooth. You will silence the night guard so that we may attack with little loss. Do this killing quietly and we shall kill the whites easily. If you fail . . . and the guard should rouse the whites . . . some of our brothers here shall die." He opened his blanket in the same way as the horned owl raises his feathered wings to stop his slaughter-swoop upon his prey. His thin, sinewy arms reached out to embrace the circle of his intent followers; the blanket represented the band's presence within the harsh world of their spirits.

"I understand you—worthy leader," stammered Small Bear, his heart so full that his tongue was almost blocked. Then he thought of his mind picture, comparing Slit-Nose to the horned owl and he used the picture for the acceptance that custom required.

"As the horned owl rules the night, oh honorable leader, so shall I swoop silently on the night guard of the white. And as the horned owl takes his strength from his kill, so shall I, Small Bear—son of Sees-in-Darkness, killer of Paiutes—take my foe's strength to aid me in this fight. His scalp shall drip crimson on my arms as I exult in my glory. I swear this to you, my friends, and you, my leader; Small Bear shall not fail you."

"Good," praised Slit-Nose. "Paint your face and body for war—all of you. Each man go alone into the light of the dying sun to prepare yourself for tomorrow's battle."

******

Thankfully, Doc Seevers was at the Drovers Rest Saloon, sitting at his favorite table and swapping tall tales of when the West was wild and the women were either bad or absent. Normally, the old Army surgeon hung out his shingle at the table from 10 A.M. until 1 P.M., with a break for dinner and a nap until 4 or 5 P.M. From that hour until midnight or alcoholic stupefaction (whichever arrived first), he occupied his table, writing prescriptions most illegibly on various scraps of paper and sometimes attempting minor surgical chores.

This night it was Skinner's turn to submit his bare behind to the still-sitting surgeon—fairly upright for this late hour, it could be said in the good doctor's behalf.

"Pull them trousers down, my dear Sheriff," said the good surgeon, smiling through slightly glazed eyes. (The doctor was at the hail-fellow-well-met stage of intoxication.) "And let the world watch a miracle worker at his best."

"The drawers, too?" asked Skinner, eyeing the throng of interested spectators.

"Most certainly, Sheriff," purred the old practitioner, pouring himself another drink from the table's centerpiece. "Modesty has no place in the operating theater. This rump of yours looks fine to me, Skinner."

"It's the other side, Doc. The side with the blood," intoned Skinner patiently, wishing he had waited until morning and tried the French doctor at the Mine Association.

"Ah-ha!" exclaimed the doctor gleefully. "I found it and it's the biggest love bite I've seen on anybody's butt."

"Please, Doc," pleaded the sheriff, "just dig it out and sew it up—or whatever."

"Nothing to probe for; nothing to suture, dear Sheriff. The bullet evidently was flattened before it struck your hindquarters. All you've got is a bruise the size of a saucer. A most beautiful contusion, I might add. Black in the middle with blue and then purple rings about it—fading into a magenta sunset by your innominate bone."

"That's it—no surgery?" asked the relieved sheriff, quickly pulling up his trousers.

"No, it's not it," said the good doctor, now sliding into his grouchy stage. "You've completely forgotten the most important part of a doctor's visit—the fee."

"Send it to me, Doc—line of duty. The County will pay it, eventually."

"And that's it?" snapped the surgeon. "No thanks? No little goodnight glass of cheer—just walk out on the old doc?"

"Not really *walk*, Doc," explained Skinner reaching over to take a gulp from the centerpiece. "It's more like half walk and half hop"—as he demonstrated, limping to the door.

CHAPTER 4

Small Bear was alerted to his leader's presence more by intuition than by sound, as Slit-Nose made no noise as he came through the sparse brush. The old warrior moved like a silent apparition; not even his soft Apache boots making as much as a whisper against the sand.

"The Mother Moon has gone to her sleep, young warrior. Now is the time for you to strike. Are you ready? Do you wish my war club?" He brought out the obsidian-studded cudgel from beneath his blanket.

"No, my leader," spoke Small Bear. "I am sure that your war club would bring me a portion of your power and luck. But I had a vision when the light from Mother Moon still was in the heavens. I looked into the dark sky and saw a star fall from the roof of the world. The star's tail was green and blue like the stone that we prize. Suddenly this falling star stopped, there in the black sky."

"Stopped?" questioned the leader.

"Yes, great warrior," went on the youth. "The star moved not—but the star's tail widened and became more bright at its edges. And . . ." Small Bear fell silent as he remembered the phenomenon with awe.

"Tell me, young warrior, so that we both may understand this wonder the spirits have given you."

"It . . . the star's tail . . . turned into the form of a knife. My knife, with the stag's horn handle that droops at the butt and the bump where an antler point was severed and then smoothed. It was my knife, oh leader."

"I am sure it was. What happened next?"

"Then the horned owl made a great cry and the knife picture ran, like water, back into the star's tail. The star fell to a hand's breadth of the earth and died—its light gone out as when you would plunge a blazing stick into a river. No burning ash or afterglow."

"I see," stated the old warrior, "that the spirits wish you to slay this white guard with your knife. Not to do so would be to displease and ridicule the spirits that guide our lives. Go now with your knife that has been honored by the spirits. Slay this guard in silence, young warrior, and this night will be forever remembered in the songs of our tribe."

Small Bear rolled his blanket into a flat tube, placing it on his left shoulder and fastening the ends under his braided horsehair girdle. Then, stringing his bow and setting his quiver on the right shoulder, he jogged quietly off into the night, guided by the white man's campfire.

The whites had drawn up their moving tepees side by side with a space between them for the women to perform their camp duties. Their horses were tethered to the big staffs which were used to pull the moving tepees. The big staffs were tied together at their tips with the musical iron ropes. The campfire, which foolishly was kept burning after the cooking was finished, was behind the open space between the moving tepees.

That was where the night guard sat, his back against the rings of sticks on which the tepee walked. He had a firestick on his lap. The firestick that has two mouths and kills with small balls the size of rabbit droppings.

Small Bear circled far around the horses, afraid that they might smell him and become nervous, alerting the whites.

When he crawled close to the white, Small Bear saw that he was asleep.

At this the young warrior smiled, for every Indian knew of the fire devil who lay in wait for the sleepy and unwary person that would stare into a flickering fire. A large, roaring and bursting fire held no danger—but the small fire with its lazy, dancing flame was the home of the make-sleep devil. Watch that flame twist and turn in its dance and even the most vigilant warrior would soon be transfixed and senseless.

The sleeping white made it easy for Small Bear to kill him, but killing a sleeping foe was without honor. No honorable warrior could count coup on a sleeping foe.

The young warrior solved his problem by probing the sleeping guard to wakefulness with his bow. The white jerked awake, grabbing for his firestick as Small Bear plunged his knife straight into his throat. The white tried to open his mouth but the Apache pushed his fist, already on the knife hilt, against the dying man's jaw, forcing the death scream to die within the man's throat. Suddenly the man was dead and Small Bear could pull out the knife, now soaked in the white's blood. He could raise his bloody fist and knife and watch the dark streams race down his arms. He was happy. He was a warrior. He was now Owl-Who-Kills-At-Night.

******

Gen was in the kitchen punching out biscuits with a water glass when she heard her husband cussing in their bedroom. She shook her head, for she allowed no swearing in her home. No spitting, no swearing were her prohibitions. She went to the bedroom, dough-clotted hands held away from her bosom.

"What *is* the matter with you, Sylvester? You know I do not countenance filthy language in this house. Why are you prancing around like that? You'll fall on your hurt head if you keep that up."

"Dang it, Gen. I'm not prancing—nor am I dancing. I'm trying to stuff a bum leg in a trouser leg."

"That's your best trousers—from Martha's funeral. You're not wearing your best trousers today—are you?"

"Have to. Got sort of a hole in my regular trousers," admitted the sheriff, finally snagging the trouser leg on his immovable leg.

"Let me see the damaged trousers, Sylvester," said Gen unhappily.

"They're over there, on the chair. You'll have to get them yourself, I'm afraid."

"You're injured again—is that it? Lamed?"

"Just stopped a little ricochet with my rear end. Doc says it'll be all right in a few days. A contusion, he calls it. I'll put some liniment on it when I get to the office. Sam has a bottle he bought for his horse. Good stuff, he says."

"I'm sure," Gen snapped, "that if it's good for horses it should be fine for your backside, Sylvester; because sometimes you are a complete horse's rear end."

"That's an unkind remark, Genevieve, to make to a person in pain—like me, for instance." He finally managed to pull up the trousers and secure his galluses.

"Pain!" she snorted. "Every day in this place is pain for me. This place killed our Martha and it's killing you—a piece of you at a time.

"Go get shaved. You have lots of time—I've been standing here commiserating over your bruised derrière when I should have been getting the biscuits in the oven, letting sympathy get in my way." She fled back to the kitchen, leaving Skinner clutching the bedpost and trying to figure how to put on his stockings and boots.

"Thank you so much, Genevieve—for all your sympathy," he muttered to the empty doorway. "It's a big help."

******

The cavalry patrol was fairly strong, twelve troopers under Sergeant White, along with two pack horses. Generally the Santa Catalina patrol would have consisted only of a corporal, four troopers and one pack animal. But Fort Lowell had learned that Apaches had been sighted crossing the San Pedro and had beefed up the patrol in case it encountered the hostiles. Headquarters, in its unaccountable reasoning, now thought the increased patrol needed an officer leading and had assigned Second Lieutenant Jersie, a recent graduate of West Point.

This was the sixth day of the ten-day patrol; any good feeling or boisterousness had long evaporated in the harshness of the patrol routine and the hardness of the McClellan saddle. The few luxuries the troopers had brought with them, such as tinned clams and cheeses, had been consumed. Only the regulation bacon, hard biscuits, coffee and a bag of weevil-dotted flour remained to see them home.

It was nine o'clock by Lieutenant Jersie's turnip-shaped, solid-silver, graduation present watch, which meant that they had been on the march almost two and a half hours. In thirty minutes Sergeant White would, no doubt, ride forward and point to the sun, asking for permission to stop for the morning rest.

"Lieutenant sir," Corporal Sanchez, who rode next to the lieutenant at the small column's head, broke into Jersie's daydreaming.

"What's that, Corporal?" Jersie came back from lethargic introspection.

"Private Daniels, sir, I think he found something." Daniels was the patrol's advance rider. He came from Tennessee and was a born scout. At the present time he was galloping toward the column, waving his campaign hat over his head to attract attention.

"Troo-op halt!" yelled Jersie. "Sergeant White to the front!"

Sergeant White rode up to the lieutenant, looked at Daniels' racing figure and shook his head in reproach at the interruption of the so-far peaceful patrol. He spit out his chew, elaborately and expertly, and made a comment to the fact that if Private Daniels was ever caught hurrying, something unpleasant was about to happen.

Daniels slid his horse to a stop, made an attempt at a salute and blurted, "Over yonder—past the rise. A burnt up wagon 'n' what looks like bodies."

"Say 'sir', stupid," broke in Sergeant White.

"Sir stupid," parroted the excited young trooper.

"Thank you, Daniels, for my knighthood," said Jersie, tittering nervously. "Are there any hostiles about?"

"Didn't see nary a one." He glanced at the ham-fisted sergeant to add a belated, "sir."

"Corporal Sanchez," ordered the lieutenant, "take the first set of fours and check out the wagon and any possible ambush site. We'll follow in support."

When they arrived at the sad spot, they found two wagons had been burned. The dead numbered ten, evidently all members of a large family. They had all been scalped. One man, evidently the father, had his lower lip cut away and wounds to his eyes. The women—at least the older two women and the older girl, who looked to be about ten—were ravaged before being killed. The other children seemed to have been herded together and clubbed down. A younger man was killed by a knife or lance wound to his throat. Another man looked to have been captured and then used for target practice. He had been tied, head-down, to a wagon wheel and had a number of charred arrows sticking haphazardly from his crisp, diminutive body.

"Form a burial detail, Sergeant White," barked Lieutenant Jersie, trying not to retch and embarrass himself. "And have someone write down a description of each one of them."

When Sergeant White came back from assigning the unpleasant duty, he said, "I set old man Smith to making coffee. We'll be here a while. We've only the one shovel—and all theirs is burnt."

"What do we do next, Sarge?" asked the young lieutenant.

"It would look bad, sir, if we didn't try to catch them. At least—*try* to catch them. They're a slippery lot. And armed pretty good now. I didn't see any firearms left here. They probably got half a dozen guns from this bunch."

"And their horses," added the lieutenant.

"And food. Them devils know what to do with flour and grain. They're sitting pretty, compared to us. We'll be hungry after three more days."

"Can we salvage anything from this mess?" The lieutenant pointed to the smoldering wreckage.

"I'll have Smith check after he gets the coffee going, sir. Won't be much, if anything. Too bad they didn't kill a horse. That would have kept us going for quite a while."

"So—how many days can we chase them? The very maximum."

Sergeant White started counting on his sausage-sized fingers. "Two and a half—maybe three days. Then we got to high-tail it back to the fort. That's figgering on two-thirds rations."

"Could we get an extra day if we went to half rations?" asked Jersie.

"Not if we have to fight them devils. Won't have enough push to do any decent fighting. To tell you the truth, Lieutenant, the full ration ain't much to march on. Hell—I'm hungry all the time on these damn patrols."

"All right, Sergeant. I just hate to see them get away scot-free."

"I *can* send out Daniels. Let him start trailing the hostiles. That'll save some time—hopefully."

"Do it—but don't let him get too far ahead of us. Don't want him to look like that fellow over there." He nodded toward the arrow-riddled body.

******

"What's the galoot trying to do?" exclaimed Mr. Hansen, the Skinners' boarder, when he arrived for breakfast. The galoot was the sheriff, who was eating off the four-legged stool from Gen's wash kitchen. The stool, oddly, was placed on the top of the kitchen table, thus allowing the very immobile sheriff to eat without having to sit, bend or otherwise irritate his terribly painful rump.

"Pretty smart, huh?" bragged Skinner. "I might just eat this way for the rest of my life."

"Am I supposed to sit at my regular place with you hanging over me—like some kind of a vulture or something?" asked Hansen, hesitant to sit.

"Does it affect your appetite—I hope?"

"Well—I'm not sure. Let me sit and try to eat." Hansen sat, to soon devour his meal, as always.

"Looks like it didn't bother you a bit," commented Skinner. "Cleaned your plate in two minutes flat."

"Might give me dyspepsia, later on. You looming over me like that. A lot of animals, you know, don't like to be stared at whilst they eat. Something left over from when they was in the wild."

"Please note, friend Hansen, that I curb my natural impulse to compare you to some prehistoric carnivore," smirked the sheriff, being careful not to laugh and antagonize his condition.

"I'll leave it toward your painful fanny. Perhaps I could have another biscuit, Mrs., and some more of that tasty coffee."

"Certainly, Mr. Hansen," replied Gen. "I think Sylvester has a favor to ask of you."

"Fire away, oh lamed legionnaire of the law. I'm at my most complacent after eating."

"He wants you to help him get to his office. Why, I'll never know. He should stay in bed."

"I must go to the office today. We had an incident last night that must be cleared up," Skinner explained. "Can you push me down to the office in Gen's garden cart?"

"Well, let's see." Hansen took another biscuit to help his thinking process. "I was to be picked up here by Manny Ortiz, the builder. We was going over to that fellow's house that got blowed up. Osterhausen's the name."

"Ostenhaven," corrected Skinner.

"Haven, Hausen—his house has a hole in it. Manny is making a bid to fix it up. He wants me along because I would do the window and piece in the new flooring. Say—wait a minute. He's coming with his ox cart. You can ride on it. Just like a king in his carriage."

"Only it's an ox cart," observed Skinner.

"Full of bricks," added Hansen, reaching for more coffee.

******

The man wiped his mouth with a grimy hand, sighed and put his lunch pail back together. Once assembled, he stuck it in a vacant corner of his workbench and made his way out of the long repair shed. He usually tried not to walk much; the amputation to his foot pained him when he walked. But this noon it was a short walk, less than five hundred feet from Busby No. 2 to Stella's Stake. Then it was clump, clump up the stairs to the business office. The office was almost empty, it being the dinner hour. Only one man was present.

"Dammit!" hissed Finsen. "Jones, I told you never to come up here. We don't want to advertise our association."

"Easy for you to say, Mr. Finsen," said the cripple. "You ain't hurting for want of money. I got two hundred bucks coming. That'll buy me a lot of relief and sweet dreams."

"That damn bomb killed Mrs. Ostenhaven, not Theodore. She was a splendid woman. Warm, full-bodied, always thinking positive."

"A bomb ain't got eyes, Finsen. You light it—and it explodes. That's all. Most times it's enough. I didn't know the captain had the shits and wasn't in bed. I figure you owe me two hundred bucks. I want it. I need it. God dammit, Finsen, I gotta have the damn laudanum now—before the pain drives me crazy. Do you hear?"

"Jerry, Jerry. Settle down. Relax. It's me—Franklin. Haven't I always befriended you? Remember when you were in the hulks and I saw that you got a doctor for your foot and extra food and an easy job in the N.C.O. mess."

"It weren't for nothin', Mr. Finsen. I tipped you off to plenty. How many men died, swinging, from what I told you. A dozen, if it was a one. I bought my life in the deaths of a lot of good Dixie boys."

"But that's water gone over the dam, Jerry," Finsen soothed. "This is Arizona, not the Brooklyn shore. We're onto big things and you're right with me, Jerry. Here, I'll give you fifty—right now. That should tide you over until I can find more. How's that?"

"That'll help," conceded Jones. "I'm sorry about the captain. Should I make another bomb?"

"Not now, Jerry. He's on his guard. In fact he had me send for Sergeant Sprague—to be his bodyguard."

"God almighty! Sprague. That's all we need for this piece of hell—the devil. I'm not sure if I want to see him here or not, Mr. Finsen."

"My sentiments, exactly, Jerry. But Theodore insists and I can't reveal my hand at this hour. You had better leave now, before my clerks come back from their dinner."

******

"Your bottle of liniment, quick—please, Sam," gasped Skinner, once he was in the Sheriff's Office. He had been propelled from the ox cart's bed of bricks by Manny and Hansen, who pushed and dragged his statue-stiff form up the stairs, across the porch and then into the office. They left him hanging to the chained rifles on the rack, wet with the perspiration of his painful ordeal.

Sam came back from the stable with a flat-sided brown bottle of equine liniment. "It says, 'work under the coat thoroughly, keep away from eyes and mucous tissue.' Don't say nothing about trousers—only your coat."

"I am not amused, Chief Deputy. Stop the joking and apply the liniment," Skinner said coldly, letting his best trousers fall to the less-than-pristine floor.

"Do you know you have a hole in your drawers, or is that a special opening for applying the liniment?"

"Dammit, Sam! Use the back door flap. Get that stuff on so I can sit down."

"Here it comes." Sam poured the liniment on a gun-cleaning cloth and, passing it through the rear flap, rubbed it stiffly into the bruised skin of the hip.

"Aw—wa!" yelled the very upright man. "God, that stings. First it was cold—now it's on fire."

"Takes longer on a horse. Then they generally stamp. Good time to get out of the stall. Want your trousers pulled up?"

"Yes—starting to get numb. Still awful hot. What does it say about future applications?"

"Mm—'twice daily unless hide shows extreme hair loss.' Oh, wait a minute—you ain't in foal or oestrus, are you? 'Use is not recommended.'"

"Oh, how quick we forget," scolded Skinner. "Last summer you were hopping around with a bad foot, where that mule stepped on you. And I was the soul of sympathy toward you."

"You're absolutely right. I will bide my tongue. I will probably not even tell you about our child prisoner of last night."

"Let me try to get in my chair and I'll let you blab all you want," grunted Skinner, lowering himself slowly into the chair.

"There—thank God—I'm sitting. Go ahead. Is the boy upstairs in the cell?"

"The boy—mon sheriff—is not a boy. She is a girl. A very dirty girl, about ten years old."

"Oh gosh," groaned Skinner, lurching in his chair. "Get her, she or whatever out of that cell before we're up to our necks in angry women."

"Fear not. Your fine, upstanding, (which *you* aren't, by the way,) Chief Deputy Sheriff has ensconced the girl prisoner with Mrs. Kipp—in her boarding house. Mrs. Kipp, though, told me she could only do this temporarily as a favor to you. She says she's too busy to keep an eye on a ten-year-old and still run a boarding house for twenty elite lodgers."

"I bet she didn't say 'elite'," said Skinner. "I'll talk to Gen. Maybe we could put her up for a while in Martha's room. I'll have to see how she feels about it—the room, I mean. Might be good for both of them. The girl got any relatives—anywhere?"

"She wasn't talking much. Her father's death, you know. Guess she really was attached to him."

"Did she say what he did? For a living, I mean."

"Said something about him being a gambler. Street games, like shell games and three-card Monte. He had his fingers broke up by some unhappy customers in Tucson and they moved here, one step ahead of being tarred and feathered. Are you able to watch over this place while I go for the buns?"

"Watching—I can handle. Doing—I can't. But go anyway. But please, pour me some coffee before you go."

Mr. Gompers came in as Sam was pouring the sheriff's coffee. "Isn't this a nice domestic scene," he growled. "The chief deputy pouring the sheriff's coffee. All the comforts of home."

"Mr. Gompers," said Sam quite respectfully, "I know you're a county commissioner and owner of a nice, big department store; but sir, sometimes you're a horse's ass. The sheriff got a slug in his hip last night, chasing after your money and here you're making bad jokes about his invalidism. Shame on you, sir."

Gompers visibly reddened. He mumbled a perfunctory apology, to continue on in his brusque manner. "That's what I'm here for. To pick up my money. Not making interest here."

"Sam?" spoke the sheriff, still clutching his coffee cup as if afraid to put it down and irritate his body.

"It's in the safe. Locked it up last night. I'll get it for you if you promise to go away and quit insulting us." Sam unlocked the big safe and retrieved the twine-tied cigar box.

"Hmpf," said Gompers testily, and left, closing the door noisily to restore his self-esteem.

CHAPTER 5

"**W**ell, I'll be damned." Sergeant White was surprised when Trooper Daniels came back to the column to report that the hostiles were camped in a draw past the next hill. It was the evening of the second day of the chase.

"They're either awful dumb or awful confident," guessed the crusty non-com.

"What's the drill now, Sergeant?" asked Lieutenant Jersie tiredly. "Wait until it's full dark before we go in?"

"More like wait until the crack of first light," White answered. "We need rest—both men and horses. How far do you think we're from them, Daniels?"

"Near a mile, but we're upwind. Any closer 'n' they'd catch our scent."

"At a mile?" questioned the young lieutenant.

"They got good noses, sir," rasped the old sergeant, painfully swinging down from his drooping mount. "No fires, no tobacco smoking and half of us awake at any time tonight."

"When do we go after them?"

"You got the silver watch, Lieutenant. Pass the word at five. That should give us an hour to circle around and come up against the wind—in case it don't turn during the night. Now, lets find a spot where the horses can forage and we'll hobble them and get some grub, ourselves.

They left in the inky blackness and the chilling cold of the pre-dawn darkness—Trooper Daniels leading; the men leaving it to their mounts to follow. The wind had shifted 90 degrees, if you could call it a wind. Actually, it was a very slight, soft breeze, drawn to the colder mountains.

The troopers had to wait half an hour for the darkness to lighten; thirty minutes in their saddles, motionless, cold, sleepy, hungry and scared for their lives. Finally, after an age of anticipation, Sergeant White grunted the advance.

"It's pistols, lads, and horses' hoofs," he croaked with a dry throat. "Yell when we're among 'em—but only shoot when you're sure of the target. Now form a loose line and Lieutenant, you take the left wing and Sanchez the right. I'll take the middle and everyone guide on me. It's at the walk— 'til we're spotted. Then it's the gallop. And listen for the recall. I don't want you straggling all over the damn desert— you hear?"

The action started as Sergeant White had said—except the Apaches' night guard was more vigilant than expected. This young Indian, now the proud possessor of a double-barreled shotgun, fired off one barrel in the general direction of the attacking cavalry and scurried off his lookout perch to join his friends, now alerted.

The first rush of the troopers was successful in that several hostiles were downed and the rest held to the small pocket in the ground which was the draw. This fold in the desert was packed with nervous horses and anxious Apaches.

But the troopers, after the surprise of the first rush, were stalled by the natural trench works and the firearms of the Apaches. Both sides were pinned down; the Indians in the draw, the troopers out on the all-too-flat desert floor.

The troopers were recalled and horseholders called out as dismounted skirmishers surrounded the Apaches' draw and began the dangerous business of trying to snipe at a sniper.

Lieutenant Jersie bent low and ran for Sergeant White's sheltering hummock. He found White resting on his back, trying to chew on a piece of Army biscuit. White glanced at the sweating young lieutenant and grimaced at the invulnerable hard tack.

"I need your young, good teeth, Lieutenant. Mine is too old and rotten, and three days from the fort is too far to bust off a molar. If I had a cup with me I could soak this damn biscuit, if I had some water."

"What's next, Sarge?" asked Jersie.

"I'll just try to soften it up with my mouth juices—which ain't too juicy, neither."

"No, I mean about this battle with the Indians."

"I'm sorry to say, sir, after a small first victory on our part—they got us right where they want us."

"What do you mean? We got them bottled up, don't we?"

"We got what? . . . Three-and-a-half days grub left and it's two-and-a-half days to the fort. Them Apaches' could stay in that damn draw for two or three weeks if they wanted, drinking the blood of those horses. The way I see it, our only advantage is that they don't know how hungry we are."

"Then they'll wait us out?"

"Don't think so. They don't know if there's any more soldiers about that will come and help us."

"So—what does that mean?" questioned Jersie.

"They'll try to slip out tonight, most probably."

"Can we stop them?"

"That was what I was trying to figure out, when you busted up my thinking process. Which way are they going to run?"

"I got it," beamed the lieutenant. "It's a modification of one of Caesar's battles, that we learned at West Point."

"I'm all ears—and stomachs."

"What we do is to establish our campfires on one side of the draw. The Indians will think we're all on that side and they go out the other way, except we'll really be over there instead of by the campfires."

The sergeant lay back, toothing his biscuit and pondering on Jersie's plan. "Yup, it'll work. Good plan."

"Why, thank you Sarge," said the lieutenant, smiling.

"Only we'll do it the opposite. We'll make four or five fires, twice as much as necessary. Mr. Apache will figure we're trying to fool him and he will try to sneak out between the fires. That's where we'll nail them. We'll be dug in, waiting for them. Should get three or four—before they go to ground."

"And then what?"

"Beats me—can't think that far ahead anymore."

******

The next morning found the sheriff improved somewhat. Old Hansen came by the Sheriff's Office early to tell Happy Giles that if Deputy Sam would bring the sheriff's horse to his house the sheriff could make the short ride to the office.

Thirty minutes later, after detouring to the bakery, Skinner was sitting in his chair—if not pleasant, at least present. After the coffee was poured and the jelly buns exposed from their grease-streaked newspaper cornucopia, Sam broached the subject of the girl.

"Mrs. Kipp jumped me on the way out this morning. Wants to know what you're going to do about the girl. Did you get a chance to talk to your wife?"

"*I* talked—and talked some more and then some. But I wore her down, I guess. Told her it made no sense keeping Martha's room empty. We shouldn't make it into some kind of a shrine."

"Then what?" Sam asked.

"You're awful nosey, aren't you... about my family's affairs?"

"That's true. A bachelor's inquisitiveness, I reckon. Go on."

"Where was I?"

"You said she'd made the room a shrine."

"Oh yeah. Then she got all misty-eyed and choked-up, going on about Martha and what a wonderful child she was and all. And we were both crying. . . . You know, that was the first time I cried about Martha. I was angry—mad—when she died."

"You drank a lot, too," Sam reminded him. "To get over the hurt."

"Too much for my own good. Lucky I had you to run this place . . . but to get back to the girl, the answer is 'yes'. Gen's going over to Mrs. Kipp's this morning and then taking her to Gompers' for some new clothes. But its not to be permanent; just temporary shelter until we can find relatives or something else. What else have we got today?"

"Marks is burying the girl's father at two o'clock. I told him it wasn't necessary for Doc to look at his body. We know what killed him."

"I can make it, if you help me on my horse. By the way, talking about Marks, what ever happened to Mrs. Ostenhaven's funeral?"

"Not going to be one. Marks is embalming her and sending the body back East in a tin-plated casket. Costing Ostenhaven $150. He said the embalming was very difficult—with all her wounds. Says he sewed for hours, but she still leaked like a sieve—the embalming fluid, that is."

The conversation was broken with the arrival of Charles Van Doormann, publisher, editor and printer of Green Falls' weekly paper.

"I come in my capacity as bearer of good and bad tidings—you can make your own assessments."

"It must be bad—or you would be bothering us for a quote," said Skinner.

"I have a thirty dollar draft for an advertisement and twenty placards celebrating the inauguration of a new stage line to Tucson from Green Falls. Using a Concord coach, no less."

"Does Sweeney know about this?" asked Sam. Sweeney ran the present stage service.

"Got a very bombastic quote from him, only half of which was profanity—have to edit those out. Said nobody is going to run him off, especially some Johnny-come-lately."

"It's bound to hurt him, but he's got the mail and the Mine Association contract," added Skinner.

"Actually, this new service works out good for Green Falls," said Van Doormann. "The new operator, Warner's his name, will be leaving Green Falls on the days that Sweeney's coming to Green Falls. Sweeney leaves Monday, Wednesday and Friday. Warner is going to leave Tuesday, Thursday and Saturday. He's figuring to lay over in Tucson on Sunday and return on Monday. He hopes to get people who would like to visit in Tucson to travel with him on Saturday and . . ."

The editor was cut off by the angry appearance of Gompers, the department store owner.

"Where is it, Skinner? By God, I never thought you fellows would stoop this low!," cried Gompers angrily.

"What *are* you talking about, Gompers?" Skinner sounded angry, also.

"My money—that's what I'm talking about. I want back every damn cent you birds took."

"Wait a minute. What money? The money in the cigar box?" The sheriff *was* angry now.

"Ha—so you know all about it, huh? I want every damn dime of that twenty bucks back, you hear? You've no right to run roughshod with your villainy."

"Wow! Can I quote you on that, Mr. Gompers?" asked Van Doormann.

"Damn right, you can. Make a big headline, 'Sheriff's Office steals honest and fair businessman's savings'."

"Just a moment, Gompers!" The sheriff bounded out of his chair like a coiled spring, grabbing Gompers by the lapels of his tail coat.

"If my memory serves me right—that box was tied up tight with string and only Sam and I have the combination. How did you find out the money was missing?"

"I dropped the box off at the bank yesterday," related Gompers, visible wilting under Skinner's grip. "Told them to return it to my account. This morning I got a message that the money was twenty dollars less than it should have been."

"Twenty dollars—that what you claim I owe you?"

"Well—that's the shortage. I feel you're responsible for it. It was in your safe, theoretically for safekeeping."

The sheriff released Gompers, who staggered back, concerned for his safety. Skinner reached into his vest pocket and took out a small leather purse. He removed a twenty dollar gold piece and grabbing Gompers' right hand, thrust the coin into the businessman's palm.

"There's your twenty, Gompers!" raged the red-faced sheriff. "Take it and get the hell out of here . . . before I do something foolish."

"This is great!" cried Van Doormann, scribbling hurriedly on a sheaf of newsprint. Skinner shot the editor an angry look and pointed to the door. Van Doormann took the hint and fled after Gompers.

"Holy Smokes," said Sam, "and you up for election soon."

"I'm beginning to think Genevieve is right, Sam. This job stinks."

CHAPTER 6

 fter dark, Sgt. White had two troopers lead all the Army horses to the far side of the Apaches' draw.

Trooper Daniels, who was in charge of this ramada, was to circle the draw far enough out of hearing to make it look as if the troop were preparing an ambush. Sgt. White's plan was based on the Apache's acute sense of perception and his natural slyness.

The remaining troopers hid themselves behind bushes and other cover except for old Smith, who had the campfire tending duty.

The moon, but a crescent sliver, set early. Sgt. White, at least on this night, had no fears of sleeping soldiers; they were too concerned with the retention of their scalps to sleep.

Then the Apache came, like a creature from the night. He flitted ghost-like from bush to bush and then slid to his belly, crawling up to the fires. Satisfied as to the innocuousness of the line of fires, he beckoned to those who followed. These others led their own horses and the captured horses, tied tight with booty from the wagons. Soon, these came softly and quietly up to the line of campfires.

"Fire!" shouted Sgt. White, and set action to expression, blasting away with his heavy Colt at the startled figures.

It was over in ten seconds. A handful of hostiles were down and the survivors disappeared back to their lair in the draw. Sgt. White called back the horses and sent out three two-rider patrols to keep the Apaches penned up.

"Do you think they'll try again tonight?" asked Lt. Jersie tiredly.

"God—I hope not. Everybody's exhausted . . . and hungry. Not a good combination." Sgt. White fell silent. Jersie thought the old sergeant had fallen asleep. After a while, though, he did go on. "Whatever happens, Lieutenant, tomorrow at noon we gotta leave. We're at the end of our string and we've got a tough ride back to the post. The men are going on guts alone, right now."

"All right—Write," Jersie tittered giddily as his tongue tripped over White's name. "We leave at noon—positively, absolutely."

******

There were but four mourners: Deputy Sam; the Sheriff; Genevieve, and the ten-year-old Esther. Sam helped Marks to place the shoddy, rough-cut coffin at the bottom of the grave. Skinner, still in pain, sat on his horse, as if cast in bronze.

With the coffin in the hole, Marks took out a hard-used prayer book and read some funeral passages appropriate to a twenty dollar undertaking. When these thin words ran out, Marks offered to give Mrs. Skinner and Esther a ride back to the Skinner home, if they'd wait until he filled in the grave.

"Thank you, no, Mr. Marks," said Gen. "Martha . . . I mean Esther and I need the walk, and besides, we're going to stop at the candy counter at Gompers'. You'd like some candy, wouldn't you, Esther?"

"Guess so," whispered the girl, subdued and shy.

"See, she just loves candy. Good day, Mr. Buller, and thanks again, Mr. Marks. We're having Spanish rice. It's Esther's favorite, she says."

******

The table in the Skinners' kitchen was set for four, with Hansen sitting at his usual place.

"Good," said Gen at the sheriff's entrance. "You're on time for once. I wanted us all together. Would you say grace, Mr. Hansen?"

"Huh, glub," choked the elderly boarder. He had grabbed a hunk of bread at the same instant the sheriff's bruised bottom touched his chair seat. Now he was stuck awkwardly, with his mouth full, under the scrutiny of the ten-year-old. He looked pleadingly to Skinner for help.

"Let me," proposed Skinner, rescuing Hansen from his embarrassment. "Bless this food and drink, 'n' keep us in the pink, amen. Pass the sausages, please."

"That's a strange prayer, Sylvester," chided Gen.

"From the heart, my dear," said the sheriff, handing the sausage platter to Hansen. "Esther, it will be your turn tomorrow to say grace. Do you know a prayer?"

"Not any more," the girl murmured, looking at Gen for guidance.

"I'm sure Mrs. Skinner will help you learn one, won't you, Gen?"

"Yes. We've got a Children's Book of Golden Prayers in the bookcase. We'll look up a nice one for tomorrow, won't we, Esther?"

"Yes'am," said Esther without enthusiasm.

"Oh—talking about golden things, I got this for you, Sylvester; it's from Mr. Gompers." She took a handkerchief-wrapped twenty dollar gold piece out of her apron pocket. "Said it was yours."

"Did he say anything else?" Skinner asked, his voice suddenly harsh.

"Something about his wife borrowing something from a box. Didn't make any sense to me, all the time mumbling and rushing about, like he was."

"Did he say anything about an apology?"

"Not that I heard. Of course Esther was talking about the candy to me. Regular little chatterbox when it comes to candy. Aren't you dear?" She smiled patronizingly at the little girl.

"The gall of that man!" raged Skinner, throwing his napkin at his plate. "I suppose he considers the incident settled—with me getting the money back."

"What incident, Sylvester? What are you talking about?"

"I'm talking about my honor, woman. And my reputation for honesty—that's all." He stormed out of the kitchen.

"My goodness," gasped Gen. "What is that all about, Mr. Hansen? This is strange for Sylvester—acting this way."

It looks like he's mad at Gompers—for something or other."

"Can you talk to him, Mr. Hansen? Calm him down. He's still not himself—from that head wound. Wouldn't want him doing anything foolish."

"Let him stew awhile. I'll go talk to him later—when he cools off a bit. Do you think he's going to finish those sausages there, on his plate? Or his Spanish rice?"

******

The sheriff was on the porch, smoking his pipe and working his jaw muscles—as if chewing a piece of gristle from some strategic part of Gompers' body.

"Mind some company?" asked Hansen. "Manny gave me one of them black Mexican cigars. I saved it for after supper. Like to smoke and watch the evening get dark."

"Suit yourself," muttered Skinner, spitting over the porch rail.

"Looks like something got your goat. Gompers, was it?"

"The man's a complete, pompous jackass."

"What was it this time?" urged the old carpenter.

Skinner stared off in space a moment, jaws twitching. Then suddenly the floodgates burst and the story spilled out in a torrent of turmoil.

The telling finished, he fell silent—exhausted from spewing up the fester of the false allegation.

"You're going to get an apology?" questioned Hansen.

"Tomorrow. When I've cooled down."

"Can I talk with you about something, now that you're not angry?"

"Talk away. I'm fine."

"Gotta go get something first—to show you. Stay right here." Hansen tottered off on his bad knees to return shortly, carrying a piece of woven steel strap.

"What's that?" asked Skinner, interested.

"Didn't know myself—'til I asked around."

"Well—what is it? Looks like wire rope of some kind."

"That's it—a special kind of wire rope. Rectangular-like. One inch by two-and-a-half. You know what this is?"

"I'm waiting, Hansen, dammit, for you to tell me."

"It's the new lift cable that the mines are starting to use on their elevators. Very flexible and real strong."

"That piece doesn't look so strong—it's busted," the sheriff noted.

"That's why I'm showing it to you," Hansen said with a smirk. "I found it under the flooring of Ostenhaven's house."

"What?"

"You heard me. I think it was wrapped around the bomb to contain the explosion. Like a shell casing. If you look real close you can see little wood splinters between the steel strands. I think somebody wrapped that wire cable around a keg or a small cask."

"And the explosive and the shrapnel pieces were in the keg," added Skinner.

"You got it. What do you think of my detective work?"

"Damn fine—for an old carpenter," joked Skinner.

"Ha—I got your case practically solved," the old man chortled. "All you got to do is find out who made the bomb that killed the lady."

"I owe it all to you—the great detective."

"It takes a smart man," agreed Hansen, "to recognize genius."

"Indeed it does," said Skinner, smiling.

******

The day dawned overcast to the desultory firing of both the investing dismounted troopers and the penned-up Apaches in the draw. Both sides were running low on ammunition and saved their shots for sure targets.

The cavalry patrol had left their fort with 60 rounds of .52 caliber metallic cartridges for the Sharps carbine and 30 waxed and twisted paper cartridges for Colt revolvers as their basic issue. Additionally, the pack horses carried a reserve of 500 carbine cartridges and 200 pistol cartridges. By this morning all the basic individual loads of carbine shells had been fired off and the patrol was into its reserve. The revolver powder and ball fared better, but the sidearm was unsuitable for the longer distance sniping now in progress.

If the cavalry's ammunition was a sore point, its rations were worse. The morning grain ration to the mounts finished the feed grain. The water supply was down to three gallons. Only hard biscuit was left; bacon, coffee and flour were gone—but not forgotten. Old Private Smith had pulverized half a dozen biscuits to burn their meal in a frying pan. These burnt crumbs were combined with boiling water to produce what Smith called "poor man's coffee." This brew was, indeed, poor—but it was better than nothing.

At about eleven o'clock a white rag was raised by the defenders in the draw. What firing was going on stopped abruptly and a wizened old warrior rode a paint pony up and out of the draw. He carried the scrap of white rag tied to his war lance. He stopped halfway to where the dismounted cavalry lay in their shallow firing pits and shouted, quite lustily for an elderly man, a string of words.

"Spanish," said Sgt. White. "I'll have to take Sanchez with me."

"Oh, no you don't," exclaimed Lt. Jersie. "What if something happened to you out there? The patrol would never get back to the fort. No—I'm going out with Corporal Sanchez."

"Do you promise not to give away the farm?"

"What do I look like?" answered Jersie.

"A tired, hungry, second lieutenant on his first skirmish," stated Sgt. White. "Don't be afraid to ask Sanchez's advice. He's probably seen more Apaches and other hostile Indians than you've seen pretty girls."

"Now, Sergeant, don't run down my love life—and I'll consult with Professor Sanchez."

It took a while to get Cpl. Sanchez's attention as he was on the other side of the draw, nailing down the back door of the encirclement. But with much shouting and gesturing, he was finally induced to circle around the Indian's hole in the desert floor. All this time the Apache leader sat stoically on his pony's bare back, contemplating the curious ways of the white soldiers.

"He is Slit-Nose," said Cpl. Sanchez under his breath as they approached the Indian, their horses at a slow walk. "He is a war chief of the White Mountain Apache. Given us much trouble in the past."

The Indian dropped his lance tip to the ground in a sign of peace. The soldiers raised their right palms in response. The Apache now spoke a sequence of Spanish in a sing-song cadence.

"He welcomes you as one warrior to another," translated Cpl. Sanchez. "Says your ambush the other night was a masterful piece of trickery."

"Tell him we are not pleased that he attacked the wagons and killed those people." Cpl. Sanchez phrased it in the Indian's type of Spanish.

"He says this is Apache land. The whites had no permission to travel across the land of the Apache."

"Tell him the Great White Father in Washington has said that all the Indian tribes are now his children and that he will feed and protect them. But that they must stay on their ancestral land and not go off on raiding parties."

This speech taxed Cpl. Sanchez's knowledge of the lingua franca of the Western Indian; however he ploughed on, getting the point across with many words, some understood, and a dozen gestures of sign language.

The old war chief gave a hint of a smile at the end of the corporal's speech. Then he rattled off a succession of singsong Spanish. This time, though, the inflections seemed harder.

"He says the White Father has given him nothing," said Sanchez. "He says the land here *is* the ancestral home of the Apache and he would trade the white woman with the copper hair for the freedom of his band."

"What?" cried out Jersie. "What woman?" More talk and gestures were needed.

"He says they have a woman from the wagons. They admired her hair and brought her with them for their sport."

"What do you mean—sport?"

"You know, sir—screwing; poontang—what do they call it at West Point?"

"It's not called at West Point. Officers are . . . well, officers and gentlemen."

"Nobody must have told Capt. Borden, then," grinned Sanchez, "'cause he sure knocked up Mrs. Foyle back at the fort. And him a gentleman, too."

"That's enough, Corporal," answered Jersie. "I'm not here to discuss Army morals. Tell him the Army does not trade for captives. We will attack and kill all the Indians and rescue the woman."

"He says the woman will be killed first—a little at a time," Sanchez translated. "Maybe, Lieutenant, you should go back and talk this over with Sgt. White."

"Think I can't handle this, Sanchez?"

"Well, ah—it don't hurt to have . . ."

"Forget it, Corporal. You're right. I'm going back to the rear. Keep your friend, here, happy 'til I get back."

Sgt. White heard out the lieutenant, putting a patronizing look on his weatherbeaten face. "That's it then, sir; get the woman and the stolen horses and we'll head for home. Remember, 'positively leaving at noon'. And don't feel bad. This sort of thing never ends like the dime thrillers do, with a big victory and a happy ending. We got four or five of them and they didn't get none of us. That's a pretty good patrol report, if you ask me."

The lieutenant trotted back to Slit-Nose. "Sanchez, tell him the Great White Father said they can go in peace if they give up the woman and the stolen horses. If not—we attack. No bargaining."

The Indian agreed—and shouted back to his warriors in the draw. A minute later two braves led out the six draft horses. A red-headed woman was perched on one of the stolen horses. When the braves came up to the truce party, they loosed their charges and with a yell of defiance galloped their ponies back to the draw.

"Sanchez, call off your men," ordered Jersie tiredly. "Tell Mr. Slit-Nose that the Great White Father will watch him to see that he does not kill again."

He turned to the woman, who had slid off the big draft horse. She appeared to be about sixteen or seventeen, with a dirty face full of freckles.

"I gotta walk," she cried almost cheerfully. "Sure can't ride on that nag's backbone after what them damn Injuns did to my private parts."

"I'm very sorry about this Mrs . . . .aah . . . ," said the lieutenant, reddening.

"Boorman and it's Miss. Miss Helen Boorman. And the only reason I'm alive is that they was fascinated by the red bush between my legs. Goodness—they jumped me from dusk 'til dawn. Couldn't hardly sleep at all. And that old man with the funny nose was the worst. He's got a root like your arm and fair pestered me to death. Worsen than the hands on my daddy's farm—and I thought *they* was horny."

"Ah—yes, Miss." The youthful lieutenant's face was scarlet now, in embarrassment. "We're just a small cavalry patrol, but if you need medical attention—or anything else— we'll try to help you out."

"I need a good wash and something to eat. They killed and ate our two dogs. But they didn't last long—only a day or so. One was a little spaniel."

"We buried your family—as best we could. We were in a hurry to get after the hostiles." Jersie had trouble in the role of extending condolence.

"It was Pa's fault," she declared. "Everybody told him it was dangerous. But, oh no, he wouldn't take advice from nobody. I'd be dead, too—if I didn't show them fellows a good time."

"Ahem, yes," answered the young man, kicking his mount to get to Sgt. White more quickly.

******

Charlie Hurst was a paradox. He was a very patient man with a huge contradictory streak of impulsiveness and impatience. He had been patient with the questioning of Tent-Peg Pete, hadn't he? Not beating him—just denying the old prospector food and water. Humane torture, it was. And the old man tricked him and died; without giving up a clue to where his mine was located.

Charlie had then controlled his impatience and had doggedly chased up and down the Santa Catalinas trying to find the old man's mine. He was at it again today.

Suddenly Charlie's plodding reverie was interrupted by a shout from above him. "Hello down there! Have you any water?"

"What, huh?" Charlie yanked on the mule's lead to halt it. "Whatcha want?" he yelled up to the two men leading a donkey.

"We need water—bad. Wait there—we're coming down," the taller man called.

"Damn fools," commented Hurst to himself, "going off in the desert without enough water. Serve 'em right to die of thirst."

The two men rushed down a precipitous animal trail to greet their rescuer. "Oh God—I was never so glad to see anybody in my whole life," gushed the short, chubby one. "Water, please; we're dying."

Hurst handed over a small canteen. "Just a couple of gulps or you'll get sick," he admonished. "What are you fellows doing up here?"

"We're prospectors," said the short one, handing his friend the canteen. "At least we're trying to be. Heard about a gold mine up here somewhere."

"Who told you that crazy story?" asked Hurst. "There's no gold around here." He reached over to recover his canteen.

"Bought a map in Tucson from a man who used to be a partner of Tent-Peg Pete. But when we got the map out here the landmarks look all wrong. Nothing's where it should be."

"Yeah," said the other, "there was supposed to be a spring; a year-round spring. But it wasn't where it was supposed to be. Can you guide us to water? We'd be much obliged."

"Ain't no water here. Closest water is Alkali Wells. That's twenty-five or thirty miles and not much fit to drink."

"What should we do? We got to have water," wailed the chubby one.

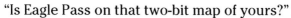

"Is Eagle Pass on that two-bit map of yours?"

"I think so." The taller one pulled a crumpled chart from his pocket and handed it to Hurst.

"There," Hurst pointed out Eagle Pass with a splayed finger. "Follow that pass and you'll come to some ranches. That's the first water. The pass is behind that peak over there that looks like an upside-down chamber pot."

"How long will it take us to get there, mister?" asked the tall one, pocketing his precious map.

"A day and a half, maybe two if you loaf. You got any money? I'll sell you some of my water. Five bucks a quart."

"My God, a man can buy champagne for that."

"Take it or leave it!" Hurst had his hand on his revolver.

"We'll take a gallon, won't we Benny? I got a gold piece left. What are you doing out here, anyway, mister?"

"Running preliminary survey for Western Union. Trying to find a shortcut to Prescott," lied Charlie. "Now let me get your water and get you lined out for Eagle Pass."

******

At nine o'clock Sheriff Skinner went into the office of the Green Falls Gazette. Charles Van Doormann, the editor, looked up at him eagerly, hoping for a cash customer. "Oh, it's only you, Sheriff," he said, letting the smile slide from his face.

"Yeah, it's only me," answered Skinner, "but I got a story for you to cover. Put on your coat and hat and come along with me."

"What kind of a story? Will this take long? Tomorrow's press day and I generally get a lot of last-minute notices to put in."

"I'm going to tree old man Gompers and get back an apology or a strip of his hide—about what he said about our thieving his money. That's why I want you there—to write it up."

"Why didn't you say so earlier?" said Van Doormann gleefully. "Time's awasting—let's go!"

They found Gompers in his cramped office, arguing prices with a ladies shoe drummer. "Black, dammit—they only want black and in the eight-button model and for $2.50. That's retail, not wholesale. So modify your price, or get out."

"I can squeeze out the kid at $1.75 in dozen lots—F.O.B. Springfield, Mass.," offered the salesman.

"F.O.B.? Then it's gotta be $1.50," countered Gompers.

$1.65—I can't go no lower. The partners would turn me out—and then where would you get such good shoes at such wonderful prices?"

"162 $1/2$ and it's a deal." Gompers went for the throat.

"Only if you take six dozen—and I hope I'm here next month." The drummer was wiping make-believe tears from his eyes.

"Now—what are you two birds here for?" queried Gompers, busy scribbling shoe sizes in the salesman's order book.

"I've come for a proper apology, Gompers," said Skinner, flat-voiced. "Not a hand-me-down through my wife. I brought Van along as a witness."

"Well—isn't that cozy? You and the newspaperman. And election's coming up in June. I'll admit my wife made a mistake. That's all you're going to get from me and to tell you the truth, Skinner, I'm getting damn sick of the way you throw your weight around this town. Killing seems to be all you know. You're a dangerous man, Skinner. Too dangerous for a peaceful town. It hurts business. Makes people afraid to settle here."

"Damn you, Gompers!" exploded the sheriff. "I'm still walking with a limp from where your extortionist shot me. And you got every dime of your money back."

"That's your job, Skinner. If you don't like it—quit. I just hope the voters throw you and your toughs out of office. That's why I persuaded Sultan Sanders to come here and oppose you in the election. Now that's a peace officer with class."

"Wow!" cried Van Doormann. "Sultan Sanders who cleaned out Lebanon, Missouri?"

"That's my man. Clean, Christian and courteous—that's our campaign slogan. I'll be seeing you, Van, about some good-sized advertisements and posters," Gompers gloated. "You're washed up, Skinner."

"Better add cunning to that list, Gompers," said the sheriff acidly. "I hear Sultan Sanders is a backshooter."

"He'll be here in a week or so, Skinner. I'm putting him up at Mrs. Kipp's. Come over and shake his hand, if you got the guts."

"What's your reply to all of this, Sheriff?" asked Van. "A new hat in the ring, so to speak."

"I leave it to the voters, Van. When I took over, this place was at the mercy of the Miners' Court bailiffs. I got rid of them and cleaned up the town. They'll remember that."

"And what about his accusations about violence and all the killings?"

"It's a violent place. How many miners are killed down there, doing their job? Twenty last year and that's not counting the maimed and injured. And in the streets and saloons—probably another thirty or so. Look at that fellow Sam killed a few months ago. Was going to blow up the Congress with dynamite. He wasn't peaceful—he was crazy. The West right now is attracting all the bad elements—just like a magnet. Enough said. I'm going for jelly buns."

CHAPTER 7

Jack Sprague, former first sergeant and captain of the guard of the prison hulk "Champlain", was tired and irritable. He had a right to those physical and mental troubles as he had endured five miserable days and nights on the Butterworth Stage Line. Now at Tucson, he had hoped for a four hour layover to bathe, shave and eat a decent meal before boarding the stage to Green Falls.

But his stagecoach from the East was late and the three transferring passengers had time only for a quick walk on their numbed legs to the connecting coach to Green Falls. "Halfa block down 'n' across the street 'n' here's yur bag," said the rushed Butterworth agent.

The coach to Green Falls was almost full. The passengers impatiently waited and chided the grizzled driver Stuart Sweeney, Sr. for the enforced delay.

"Come on, folks!" yelled Sweeney at the straggling newcomers. "We're late."

The new passengers greeted this admonition with evil looks and lewd words. Sprague elbowed his way to the coach's door, threw his bag to the driver and climbed into the coach.

"You're sitting in my seat," he told the miner sitting at the forward facing seat, by the window.

"Who says?" replied the burly miner. "First come, first served, bucko. There's seats in the middle."

"Move quick," snarled Sprague, "while you still can."

"Screw you," said the miner—looking to his fellow passengers for support.

In a flash the spring knife was in Sprague's hand and the slim, pointed blade was an inch and a half into the miner's kneecap.

"Jesus!" screamed the victim, trying to squirm away from the now bloody blade. "Are you crazy?"

"No—just tired. Move while you've still got a good knee left."

"What's going on here?" It was the driver, responding to the noise and the slow entrance of the new passengers.

"Man wants to ride up top," answered Sprague, knife gone as quickly as it had appeared.

"I do not—this crazy man stabbed me in my knee. See the blood?" The miner again looked at his fellow passengers. They offered no help.

Sprague pulled the miner out of the window seat, shoving him at the driver, and took his place. The driver helped the miner up to the roof, while the other newcomers found seats on the uncomfortable middle row that had no back rest.

"Seems there's always an unpleasant person on these coaches," announced Sprague to the gawking passengers. He left it up to them to determine that person.

******

Charlie Hurst began to worry about his water supply. It was the second day after he sold a good portion of his water to the two would-be prospectors. Finally, after a noon halt in which he used another quart and a half between himself and the animals, he was forced to call his exploration quits and head for Tent-Peg Pete's hidden spring.

But this put Charlie squarely on the horns of a dilemma. He was in Furnace Valley, named thus in honor of its summer clime. He had to get into Desperation Canyon for the water. To get there via the valley floor route would take a day and a half. To climb over the spine of the separating ridge would use up less time—if he could find a track across the inhospitable ridge. It was a gamble. If he lost and wasted half a day in the attempt, he could be that much thirstier—if he made the spring at all.

Charlie was confident, though, in his ability as he guided the animals up toward the notch in the stony ridge. Four hours later, after losing time to a blind gully, he was on the top, snaking between the cracks separating huge, cleaved, monolithic stone blocks with only an hour and a half of daylight left. He pressed on towards water, hoping to find a landmark to guide him to the spring.

Suddenly, he was stopped. The narrow watercourse he was following had washed out. He looked angrily at a breach of at least thirty feet of the risky trail that had been his hope.

And to top it all off, the mule started braying and acting up. It gave a jerk of its head and tore the lead out of Charlie's hand. "Dammit!" yelled Charlie. "Come back here, you damn jughead!" The mule kept on and nimbly stepped over the bank, disappearing from view with a switch of its ragged tail.

"What the hell . . . !" exclaimed Charlie, sliding off his horse to look over the edge where the mule had vanished. The mule was there, its ugly head over its shoulder, looking for Charlie to follow. When it saw it was being chased, it trotted down the narrow path to stop by a natural cave.

"Don't tell me," gasped Charlie. "You've been here before. It's another hideout of Pete's." The mule brayed its affirmation, shaking its big head and showing long, yellow teeth.

The cave even had water, although only a slow, sullen drip that would take long hours to fill a canteen. The cave contained two large jute bags, one of which was hung from a chain from the cave's ceiling. Further examination showed this bag to contain whole corn. Evidently this was Pete's food reserve—for himself and the mule. Pete had even fashioned a round rodent collar from a large bucket and hung it halfway up the rusty chain.

"That old man weren't afraid to work," muttered Charlie to himself. "Gotta say that for him. Must have took all day to drill and plant that hook up in that rock. Would have had to build a scaffold to get up there . . . just to hang up the corn bag away from the rats."

If the hanging bag was interesting, the second jute bag was pure fascination. It held ore obviously streaked with gold. This ore was especially rich. Even Charlie Hurst, who knew the gold business, was impressed.

"So you did find it, old man," said Charlie admiringly. "Well, anything you can do—I can do, too." He proceeded to make himself at home, as it was getting dark. He propped a canteen under the drip, gave a good-sized measure of corn to both horse and mule and cracked enough corn to boil up some mush for himself.

All in all, he told himself as he slid between his blankets that night, *not a bad day at all. And one more step to finding old Tent-Peg's mine.*

******

"Sorry I'm late," said the tall, white-haired man, "I been laid up awhile . . . couple of days actually . . . my lungs, you know."

"I know," answered Sam, pulling out a chair for the obviously frail man. "Sheriff, this is Mike Birnby. I left a note at the Belle for him to come in about the bombing."

"I had nothing to do with it—the bombing of Eckhardt's, I mean. I had just gotten to sleep."

"I remember you," smiled Skinner, trying to make the man comfortable, "from when I worked as gun guard at the

New Orleans Belle. You're a dealer, aren't you? I used to watch you from that little balcony up under the roof."

"I was good . . . before the war," Birnby mused. "Used to work the big boats on the Mississippi. Croupier, you know. I was good. Quick, you know. Made good money. That's where I knew Mr. Caudelet. He had the concession on the 'Delta Princess.' When the Yankees took New Orleans, that stopped the riverboats. So I joined up—me and a group of out-of-work riverboat men. We'd hoped to find berths in the Confederate Navy, you know. Instead we ended up as foot soldiers." A coughing fit interrupted his story and he muffled his mouth with a rose-tinged, large handkerchief. The hacking finally subsided but he could only sit, struggling for breath.

"Ah—yes," Skinner temporized. "Not many men returned from the war the same as when they went in. Take Sam here, for instance. Has all kinds of aches and pains."

"He was a tower of strength on the 'Champlain,'" gasped Birnby, wiping his lips.

"Mr. Birnby, the reason we asked you to come here was to shed light on the murder of Mrs. Ostenhaven. Anything . . ."

"That's Mrs. Eckhardt," broke in Sam, nodding apologetically to Skinner.

"Yes—Mrs. Eckhardt," repeated the sheriff. "Her body was riddled with homemade pieces of shrapnel. Like this piece." Skinner took a triangular piece of metal from a cardboard pillbox on his desk.

"Can't help you, I'm afraid."

"Mr. Birnby, did you know Eckhardt was living in Green Falls? Did this knowledge upset you?" Skinner kept the pressure on.

"I knew he was in town. Somebody told me. I dunno, I guess I'm just too sick and too tired to hate Eckhardt—or Finsen for that matter—anymore. Maybe, if I was better, I'd think more about them. But all I want now is peace."

"Was that somebody Otto Floss, Mr. Birnby?"

"Yes—it was Big Otto. But I don't think Otto would make a bomb. Maybe strangle him. But a bomb—no. Otto's all physical, you know. He's had problems—from the hulks, I mean. Terrible dreams, he says. I think that's why he drinks so much. So he can sleep, you know."

"And you had just gotten to sleep, Mr. Birnby, when you were awakened by the bomb?"

"Yes, I generally quit around 2:30. I live with my sister and her family. She leaves something for me in the warmer or else maybe a sandwich. And I bring home some beer from the Belle. Then I read a little, not too long, 'cause Nell complains about the oil—the cost, you know. Then it's bed about 3:30 or so. I sleep with Billy and Bobby—they're her twins."

"But I didn't think it was a bomb, you know. I thought it was just another loud blast from some mine. Happens a lot, you know."

"Indeed I do, Mr. Birnby—don't we, Sam? One last question and you can go. How many other prisoners from the hulks are there in Green Falls, that you know of? You mentioned Otto Floss."

"Well—Sam here and Otto. And Jerry Jones. You remember Jerry, don't you Sam? Lost part of his foot? Oh, probably not. He was transferred from the 'Champlain' to work in the officers mess. That was on shore, Sheriff. Them Union officers had a real fancy place—all built by the prisoners."

"No, didn't know a Jerry Jones," admitted Sam. "Do you know if he works in town?"

"He can't get around so good—from what Otto says. He works with Otto at Busby No. 2. Tell you the truth, I think Otto got him the job—as a bench mechanic—so he can sit down more often. He fixes small machinery. Good man with pumps, Otto says. 'Course, Jerry always seems to be in a lot of pain—the foot, you know. Affected his personality a lot."

The sheriff stood up, signaling that the questioning had come to an end. "Mr. Birnby, we want to thank you for coming here and putting up with our quizzing. I think most of us believe that Mrs. Ostenhaven's death was, if not accidental, then was coincidental—a product of the murder attempt on her husband. But coincidental or not, it was murder. A horrible butchery of an innocent woman. Please remember that and try to help us get to the bottom of this crime. Here," he handed Birnby the piece of rough-cut shrapnel—"Keep this as a memento of our little talk today; we've got a lot more of those that were taken from her bloody body. If you remember anything, even if it doesn't seem very important, please come and let us know about it."

Birnby took the metal piece with reluctance, holding it in his hand as if it were a talisman of death. Then he searched for the correct pocket to store it, finally settling on an empty pocket in his waistcoat. "I'll do that, Sheriff, and, Sam—come over to the Belle some time. I'll buy you a drink and we'll talk about old times on the hulks."

Sam nodded. "I'll come for a drink, Mike—but I won't talk about the hulks; too painful. I'm still trying to figure out how to remember my brother and still try to erase the hulks from my mind."

******

As the sheriff returned from dinner, he approached a large woman coming out of the office. When the woman saw him she gave him a quick curtsy, smiled and then continued down the boardwalk.

"That woman," asked the sheriff of Sam, when inside. "What was her problem?"

"You mean you didn't recognize her? You saved her life last year."

"I did?"

"It's Mrs. Fallon—Dora's washerwoman, remember? That crazy Frenchman shot her in the leg."

"Belgian. Now, I remember her. What does she want?"

"Better hands."

"Better hands?" echoed Skinner. "What kind of hands? Poker hands?"

"No, mon Sheriff, her own, very red, very rough, washer-woman's hands—on the ends of her arms."

"You, Mr. Chief Deputy, have now managed to completely confuse me. Please start at the beginning."

"The poor woman has rough, cracked hands from her work, washing all those towels and sheets at Dora's Sporting House. She was in the habit of treating these red, rough hands with a preparation called 'Dr. Schwabe's Bear Fat Skin Salve.' Our Green Falls pharmacopoeia recently ran out of Dr. Schwabe's salve and Mr. Appleby, the pharmacist, recommended that Mrs. Fallon buy a product called Big Bear Balm. This she . . ."

"Are you serious?" Skinner interrupted.

"Quiet, let me finish," said Sam. "This is an official complaint. Duly lodged with your chief deputy."

"Court jester, more like," added the sheriff.

"I shall proceed with the complaint, if I may."

"Please do, indeed."

"Mrs. Fallon complains that the new salve, to wit, Big Bear Balm, is completely ineffective and—this is the crux of the complaint—contains no bear grease. She says she has used bear grease on her hands for fifteen years and knows its feel, smell and efficacy. She wants Appleby arrested for fraud, misrepresentation and causing her bodily injury."

"Bodily injury?" questioned Skinner, now in his chair.

"Certainly. Her hands suffered—got worse. Want me to rush over there and drag Appleby back to our jail?—The nasty balm crook."

"Thank you—No. *I* will approach Mr. Appleby with politeness and courtesy. I'm sure this is just some type of misunderstanding or . . ."

Skinner was cut-off by the noisy arrival of the stagecoach from Tucson. It stopped abruptly at the Sheriff's Office.

"Hey, Sheriff," came a loud voice from the driver's seat, "get your butt out here! Want you to arrest a passenger."

"Your friend Sweeney calleth—beyond yonder balcony," joked Sam.

"Probably has a drunk who pinched a lady passenger," assessed Skinner.

"Wake up in there!" yelled Sweeney, even louder.

"Come on, Sam, we'll humor him. He's a voter, after all." The sheriff went out on the porch.

"About time—you lawmen could never run a stage line. Don't have a sense of urgency."

"Please—no personalities, Sweeney. What's this about?" snapped the sheriff.

"Got a passenger inside who stabbed that fellow up here." Sweeney pointed his whip at the miner sitting awkwardly on the roof's rear bench.

"Who stabbed you, mister?" Sam asked, his thumb flipping off the restraining loop on his Colt's hammer.

"That fellow in the back by the window—with the three-day beard." The wounded miner tried to point through the stagecoach's roof.

"More like a six-day beard," said Jack Sprague. "And it's Captain Buller, ain't it? A comedown, huh? Just a dirtbag deputy sheriff, now."

"Yeah, it's me, Sergeant Sprague," retorted Sam, "and today I got the authority—not you. Crawl out of that coach."

"Do you know this man, Sam?" asked Skinner, warned by his deputy's unusual belligerency.

"He's Jack Sprague, former Captain of the Guard—of the hulks. Eck . . . I mean, Ostenhaven's pet murderer."

"I was cleared by the Army, Buller," grinned Sprague, climbing out of the stage. "Line of duty. Court even praised my attention to duty."

"Just a Yankee court—whitewashing its dirty work, Sprague."

"You there—the stabbed man; come down here and show me your wound," Skinner called up to the miner on the roof.

"I'll have to have help. My knee's stiffened up on me."

"Help him down, Sweeney," ordered the sheriff.

"Oh sure," griped the driver. "Now I'm an ambulance driver." But he wrapped his reins around the brake lever and crawled back to help the hurt miner down to the boardwalk.

"Are you ready to lodge a charge against this man?" Skinner asked the limping miner.

"Hell yeah. The son-of-a-bitch stabbed me."

"Wrong jurisdiction, Sheriff," gloated Jack Sprague. "If there was a stabbing. I say *if*—it happened in Tucson, not in Green Falls. He'll have to make a complaint in Tucson."

"Well bless my soul," said Skinner. "Sam, your friend seems to be a jail house lawyer."

"He ran a jail house. A big floating one, with a thousand hungry men locked in its bowels," answered the angry deputy.

"Thirteen hundred and fifty-six stinking Rebels at its peak season," grinned Sprague. "Don't sell me so cheap."

"You're right, Mr. Sprague, I'm sorry to say," said Skinner. He turned to Sweeney, the stagecoach driver. "Sweeney, according to common law out here, as a stage driver you've the same authority as a ship's captain. I want you to arrest this man for assault and turn him over to me for investigation and prosecution. Will you do that?"

"What do I have to say?" asked Sweeney, turning around, halfway back to his driver's box.

"Just say, 'I arrest you for assault and turn you over to the civil authorities'."

"I arrest you in the name of Sweeney Stage Lines—how's that?" beamed Sweeney. "Can I go now?—running late."

"Go ahead, Sweeney," agreed the sheriff. "And Sam, take Mr. Sprague up to our jail after you remove all his weapons. I'll even carry his bag in for him."

Sweeney yelled at his team and the coach moved away from the sheriff's porch. But as the stage left, it's space was immediately taken by three riders with a small herd of led horses. The sheriff tossed Sprague's bag into the office and returned to greet the two cavalrymen and the young woman, who rode a dray horse with only an Army blanket for a saddle.

"Are you the sheriff?" asked the Spanish-featured corporal, dismounting stiffly.

"That's what this badge says," replied Skinner.

"I am Corporal Sanchez, from Ft. Lowell. We were sent to escort this lady to the nearest town. She was captured by the Apaches and we got her back in trade for the hostiles' freedom. The lieutenant says to turn her over to you."

"Ah, a present from the Army," said Skinner. "An old adage says beware of Greeks bearing gifts."

"I'm no Greek. I'm a Texan—born in Galveston."

"Hm—yes," muttered the sheriff, at his dying jest. "What's with all the horses?"

"They're hers—at least they was her folks'. All got kilt." This from the tall, skinny trooper.

"Mine now," confirmed the young woman. "You know where I kin sell 'em? Need to buy some clothes."

"This is a mining town; horses are always needed. If these are broke to a team, they'll fetch top dollar."

"You got any coffee, Sheriff?" asked the corporal, succumbing to the weakness of the flesh. "Been three days without any."

"Big pot inside—help yourself." The skinny trooper slid off his mount in a flash to tie the lead ropes of the horses to Skinner's porch rail. The young woman brought up a dirty, bare foot and holding her tattered skirt, jumped down into the dust and droppings of the street.

Luckily, the coffee pot was almost full and Skinner's hospitality remained unblemished. The three riders gulped down the first cup and begged another. "Good coffee," commended the skinny trooper, "Even if it has too many eggshells."

Deputy Sam, coming down the stairs from the upstairs jail, heard the comment and responded, "That's what gives my coffee character, for your information."

"Character?" said the trooper. "Ain't that like them murderers in them playhouse shows?"

"Touchè, Sam," laughed Skinner. "This young soldier knows murderous coffee when he drinks it."

"Bah! Yankee cavalry. What do they know?" countered Sam, pretending to act insulted.

"Knows enough to rescue me," put in the young woman. "And a gentleman, all of them. Ever so kind and helpful."

"Sam, this young lady was taken back from the Apaches. She got a bunch of horses out front she needs to sell. Do you think you could find a dealer that could take them off her hands?"

"If they're any good, I'm sure Ames will help her out," replied Sam. "If you watch the office I'll take them down to him."

"Go ahead—I'm good until supper."

"Just a damn minute, Deputy," objected the woman. "Nobody takes them horses anywheres, less'n I goes. They're my grubstake."

Soon the sheriff was alone in his office. Sam and the young woman, Helen Boorman, had left with her horses, while the cavalrymen went to find something to eat on a chit from Skinner's petty cash account. Skinner went out back and dumped out the eggshells preparatory to building a new pot of coffee. His misgivings about Sam's coffee had been confirmed.

CHAPTER 8

The mule was unhappy about the bag of ore on its back. It had spent too many days under a light load, helping Charlie Hurst sniff out Tent-Peg Pete's hidden camps, to enjoy being a beast of burden again.

But, as testimony to the mule's intelligence, it guided Charlie down an unseen track to link up with the canyon that held Pete's secret spring. Charlie spent the night at the spring, leaving the next morning with full canteens and water bags, headed for Green Falls.

Before noon he was out of the canyon and crossing the flats, bearing hard toward Piss-Pot Peak and Eagle Pass— getting the most from his animals and himself.

Once again though, he was hailed by other wayfarers; this time a party of four dangerous-looking men. Fortunately he had the foresight to obscure the mule's ore bag with his blankets and ground cloth.

"We're chasing after a lost mine supposed to be around here, somewheres," explained the oldest man, a hard-eyed white-beard. "Haven't seen anything like that around here, have you?"

"If I had," replied Charlie, hand on the trigger guard of his Henry, "I'd be working it now—instead of looking for a shortcut for Western Union for $2.50 a day."

"What you got on that mule, mistuh?" asked the negro man wearing a battered silk hat with a snakeskin band.

"Whole corn—for me and the animals. I eat so much corn I cackle like a chicken when the sun comes up."

"Not much of a rooster, then—are you?" taunted Silk Hat.

"I let this Henry do my crowing for me," growled Hurst. "It barks worse than me. And don't be sidling there, trying to get behind me. This here trigger's been honed down to practically nothing."

"Now, now, sir," scolded the whitebeard, "you've misjudged our intentions. We're men of peace. Simple seekers of precious metals. I see you have an abundance of water. I wonder if you could spare some for us—as a Christian gesture?"

"I generally get five bucks a quart."

"Ah, yes, but surely not to friends like us. Friends in dire want of water. There is four of us, you know. You are one lonely soul in the vast desert."

"You're forgetting my fifteen friends in this Henry. I can spare this skin bag of water on my pommel for twenty bucks; should have five or six quarts in it. The bag's worth a couple of bucks alone."

"You're a hard man, my friend," sighed Whitebeard. "Freddy, give the man twenty dollars for his water."

"Why me, Pa?" complained the young son. "You allus got me paying for this or that."

"Do as I say, Frederick. And approach the man with caution—I'm running out of sons."

Young Freddy did as he was told, being smart enough not to screen the other members of his party as he moved his horse towards Hurst.

"And Freddy, my friend," cautioned Hurst, "if you drop that coin you'll follow it with a bullet in the head. Do you hear?"

"I hear," said the youth, both frightened and angry. "Are you going to let him threaten me, Pa?"

"Just give him the money and take the water, Frederick. Leave the bombast until another time."

Once the water and the money were exchanged Hurst called out to the white-bearded leader. "Now, old man, we can part two ways. The first way is that you turn your backs to me and ride off 'til you're little specks in the sand, happy to get the water. The second way is to be angry at our deal and try to circle back to get me and my water; even my whole corn. If you do that, you're dead men. I know every track, every fold in this desert, and I'll be waiting to shoot you. Now you move out, backs to me like the good gentlemen you are. Go on—git."

The four kicked their tired horses into a trot, raising a small dust cloud behind them.

"Ain't we going back after that bastard?" Freddy asked his father once out of Hurst's hearing.

"Never challenge a man in his own front yard, Frederick, especially over only twenty dollars," said the older man. But Freddy noticed that his father turned around for a last look at the man with the rifle and spit toward that direction.

~~~~~~~~~~~~~

Not knowing what to do with Helen Boorman, the sheriff brought her home with him to supper. "I know she's a little dirty, Gen; but I figured you could help her to buy some clothes and get cleaned up. She sold some horses this afternoon. So she's got money to buy some dresses and such."

"There's no doubt about the dirt and the smell, Sylvester. And I feel sorry for her—but I wish you could have warned me."

"Give her part of my portion. I'm not really hungry anyway."

"It's not the food, Sylvester. It's Esther. Oh, you'll never understand. Get her to wash up and bring the straight chair from our room. I'll put her next to Esther."

It was liver day and although liver was not Skinner's favorite food, Gen had today prepared it Italian style, in a brown, spicy sauce, served with homemade flat noodles and sourdough cloverleaf rolls. Mr. Hansen was ecstatic, humming to himself like a cat purring, as he pushed roll petals around his plate to scour every smidgen of sauce.

"You've outdone yourself, Mrs.," complimented the grizzled carpenter, passing his plate to Gen for a second helping. "Isn't she a great cook, child?" he asked Helen Boorman, who was eating in shy silence.

"My mother made good baked items," she replied. "But Abe's wife was the best cook. Could cook anything and make it turn out good." A great glob of a tear rolled wetly down her tanned cheek, to everyone's embarrassment.

"Now, now dear," consoled Gen, leaping quickly into sympathy's breach. "We all know how much it hurts to lose loved ones. I still mourn every day for our little girl. Thankfully, time does heal the wounds to our soul."

"I hope it cures the anger, Mrs. Skinner. It was all my pa's fault. He was a stubborn Dutchman; never listened to advice. Everybody told him it was dangerous to travel alone. But no—he knew it all . . . and look what happened. Everybody killed but me. And I'd be dead too if them Injuns hadn't been fascinated with the red bush."

"And what was this bush, dear?" asked Gen, naively.

"You know, the red hair, 'twixt my legs. Guess they don't have no red-haired ladies in their camps or whatever they call them."

"Ahem, ah . . . I imagine not," said the sheriff, hoping to mask social indiscretion.

But the young woman would not let her anguish slide into oblivion. "They used me, you know, all of them. All the time, too." Another bulbous tear tracked down the wet streak on her cheek.

"Yes, dear," said a reddening Gen, trying to stare the young woman into silence. "But now you're here, safe with us."

"It weren't all that bad," the girl would not stop. "I'd done it before—so I knowed how to please 'em. Them two cavalry fellows, too. The corporal—once a day, took care of him. But, my, that skinny one. He was sure enough eager, if you know what I mean. And built, too—if you get the hang of what I'm saying." She chuckled at her little joke.

"Whoops!" guffawed old Hansen, spitting out a pellet of roll.

"Mr. Hansen, please, we have a young child at the table. Decorum is called for," stated the sheriff, covering his grin with his napkin.

"Sylvester," Gen spoke up suddenly, "I'd like some fresh water. Would you help me with the water barrel?"

"Huh—help you with the water barrel?" echoed Skinner, puzzled by the strange request. Gen's kick to his shins brought him to his feet. "Oh yeah, sure thing—the water barrel." He followed Gen out to the back porch, lifting the lid on the wooden barrel.

"What's this about you needing help?"

"God help me—I've got a loon for a husband. How could you bring that person into my home? She's immoral; a Salome—in my own home."

"I thought Salome was a dancer," replied Skinner lamely.

"And a fornicator. I want that woman out of my house immediately. Do you hear? Right this instant!"

"You mean right now?"

"Oh, wonderful! You *can* hear. Get her out! I'll stay out here until you put her out, understand?"

The sheriff left her glaring at her own scowling reflection in the full water barrel, to go back to the hot, crowded kitchen. "I'm sorry, folks. Mrs. Skinner seems to have one of those hot spells of hers," he related awkwardly. "Probably from being too close to the stove all morning."

"Can I help, Sheriff?" asked Helen Boorman.

"Thanks, no. But she says that Mr. Hansen should take you down to Gompers' for your clothes. And he can point you in the right direction for a room or whatever."

"Me?" said Hansen, suddenly interrupted in his eating.

"Yes, you," reiterated Skinner. "If I go to that S.O.B.'s store, I might punch him and get myself into trouble."

"But we haven't had dessert yet."

"Later on. You can have mine, also."

"It's a deal. Come on, dearie. Let me show you the delights of Gompers Department Store."

"Bah," said the sheriff, watching the pair leave for Main Street.

"Do all ladies have red bushes, Mr. Skinner?" asked Esther, suddenly left alone at the table.

"Good God, young lady!" sputtered Skinner, at a loss for words. "Ask Mrs. Skinner—she's the expert around here. I've got work to do—back at the office."

******

Once out of the house and on his big mare, Gertie, Skinner released his frustration by kicking his horse into an impromptu race down Chestnut Street. But as Chestnut Street ended two and a half blocks away at Elevator Row, it was a short race—although enough to restore the sheriff's spirits.

He turned Gertie at Elevator Row, guiding her through the parked wagons before Busby No. 2 and around the four-story lift building that squatted in slab-sided solidity over the three great maws of its plunging mine shafts.

He had come to question Otto Floss, survivor of the hulks, blacksmith and, if rumor was correct, mean-tempered brute. As Big Otto had not come, as requested, to the Sheriff's Office, he would go to Otto. "Mohammed will go to the mountain," he chuckled at his own wit, thinking of the mountain of Otto.

The one nagging doubt he kept bottled up; ashamed to admit that Sam's partiality to his fellow prisoners on the hulks might influence the deputy's aggressiveness. No—he would question the men from the hulks himself, and to hell with his niggling doubts.

Once at the mine's blacksmith shop, he tied off Gertie to a huge rust-speckled sprocket, canted against the building, that seemed a monument to the steam-powered expansion of the West and Green Falls' mines in particular.

A huge man was at the anvil, slamming at a cherry-red iron bar with a short-handled six-pound sledge in each ham-like hand. At a grunt from the giant, another man would twist the fiery bar to another angle with his straining tongs.

"Nuff," growled the muscled smith. "Heat it up and seat the half-round swage." He stepped back to mop his sweat-shined face with a jute rag.

"Mr. Floss?" Skinner took advantage of the break in the banging.

"Who wants to know?" grumbled the big man, his torso naked behind a sooty leather apron.

"I'm Sheriff Skinner. I asked you to come to my office. I've a few questions."

"Too busy. You want to talk—you come here."

"I'm here now, Floss," Skinner dropped the civility. "And I need some answers about the Ostenhaven murder."

"Don't know no Ostenhaven. Know Eckhardt." He turned to his assistant. "Ease up on the air; don't want to scar that axle."

"This shouldn't take long, Floss," said the sheriff. "You got a better place to talk than this hot box?"

"What's the matter, can't take the heat, lawman? Come on, there's generally a breeze by the back door." He led Skinner to a wagon-sized open door that overlooked a yard bowered with trestles that were festooned with different sized wrought-iron bars.

"That's better," admitted Skinner, "Now tell me about Eckhardt or Ostenhaven."

"What about him? Am I glad his wife died?"

"It's a good place to start."

"I wish it had been him 'stead of her. Never even saw her. That's the God's truth."

"When did you find out Eckhardt was in Green Falls?"

"I dunnno. Somebody told me, I reckon."

"One of your friends from the hulks?"

"Yeah—probably. What difference does it make? I didn't kill him."

"Why?" asked the sheriff. "Not hating him anymore? Getting peaceful in your old age?"

"Me—peaceful? Ask my old lady—or anybody who knows me." The tic by his eye began to tweak faster.

"The bomb that killed Mrs. Ostenhaven was packed in a wooden keg. I saw a similar keg by your front door here. Seems to me it would be handy for you to use."

"Ha, says you. There's hundreds of them kegs here in the mines. All our hardware comes in them. Can't use that to frame me."

"You got me wrong, Otto. I don't want to frame anyone. I want the real killer. Recognize this?" Skinner took the short length of lift cable that bound the bomb from the canvas bag he carried.

"Yeah," answered the big blacksmith, suddenly shocked by the shredded piece of cable. "It's lift cable. I make connectors for it here. Have to use special German steel. But I got no access to the cable. The elevator riggers keep it locked up; costs like hell, they tell me. Something like a buck a foot—maybe more."

"I have something else to show you." This time Skinner came up with a triangular piece of the homemade shrapnel. "There were hundreds of these pieces of iron packed in that keg, along with the dynamite. Then the cable was wrapped around it to concentrate the explosion."

"Oh God." Floss looked pale, under the soot. "Sounds awful. Lemme see that piece." Skinner handed the triangle to Floss, who held it to the light.

"It's cut by a cold chisel," said Floss. "That was too narrow to shear it with one stroke. Took two or three blows. See there—you can count each cut. It's a little bent, too. Don't look like it was cut on a regular anvil. Lots of farmers and such use a piece of railroad rail as a poor man's anvil. The rounded top makes for a poor work surface."

"You think that this wasn't made in a smithy?" asked Skinner.

"Naw, doing this with a cold chisel would be too slow. How many did you say was in that bomb?"

"Several hundred. Maybe three hundred."

"No—I'd use a shear. I could knock out three hundred of them pieces in twenty minutes or so. Quicker even if I had someone working the lever for me."

"The bend in that piece," questioned Skinner, "the bend you think was caused by a rounded surface—could that have been caused by the explosion, instead?"

Floss looked at the triangle again, more carefully. "I dunno. To tell you the truth, Sheriff, I don't know much about the effect of explosives on metal. Once in a while we have to fix something that got damaged by accident in a blast—down there, you know." He pointed to the ground and the labyrinth of mining tunnels. "But I never came to no conclusions—except that explosives are damn powerful.

Naw—all I can say is that it looks like a homemade anvil was used."

"One last question, Mr. Floss. Jerry Jones, does he work with you? I understand that you secured a job here for him."

"Jerry—yeah, I got him the job. Talked to the manager for him. He don't work with me. Works for Pipes and Pumps over in that long shop over there." Floss raised an oak-tree arm to point out the structure.

"Would he have access to metal such as this and elevator cable?"

"I dunno; why don't you ask him? I wouldn't want to get a friend in trouble."

"Was he your friend—in the hulks, Floss?"

"Any prisoner from the hulks is a friend of mine. Sort of a bond, like."

"I know, Mr. Floss," agreed the sheriff. "The war cemented its soldiers together."

"Are you done with me? I promised that axle for nine o'clock and still got a half-hour's work left on it."

"Go ahead, Mr. Floss. And keep that piece of shrapnel as a reminder of Mrs. Ostenhaven's bloody death. I have lots more of them we dug out of her."

"Yeah," said the big smith, sounding not particularly grateful. Skinner left him staring at the vicious piece of metal in his big, grimy palm.

As the sheriff led his horse to where the next potential suspect worked, he suddenly realized he was getting nowhere fast in his investigation.

~~~~~~~~~~~~~~

Charlie Hurst led the mule through the surviving section of Green Falls' Spanishtown to where he rented an upstairs room above a nondescript cantina. The cantina stunk of urine and garlic, but Charlie knew that after a few hours he would overlook the smells and become adapted to town life once more.

Keeping the ore bag covered with the ground cloth, he shouldered the bag and walked through the cantina and up the stairs to his room door. He unlocked the big brass padlock, opened the door and dragged the heavy jute bag into the squalid room.

He went downstairs to wake the dozing proprietor, asking for messages. There was only one—in Finsen's Catholic school hand, stating only, "Report immediately."

"Oh sure. Right away, your majesty," grunted Hurst. "Jose. Paper and pen, pronto." The cantina owner opened one eye, grumbling a string of Spanish about his lost siesta, but quickly produced the necessary writing objects. Hurst was a good patron, free with his money.

Hurst scratched out a note telling Finsen and Ostenhaven to come to the cantina at seven that evening for his report. Then, after giving directions to the proprietor as to where the note should be delivered, he left to care for his animals and his own needs.

CHAPTER 9

In Skinner's absence, and with Deputy Cletus McCoyne present to start his shift at the Sheriff's office, Chief Deputy Sam Buller took it upon himself to investigate the complaint of Mrs. Fallon concerning fraudulent substances in a product called Big Bear Balm. In actuality, Sam was a little miffed at the sheriff for not taking the woman's complaint with necessary seriousness.

It was always dark in Appleby's Pharmacy. The walls of his cramped shop were lined with medicinal storage drawers rather than windows. Sam found Appleby brewing up a concoction on an alcohol flame, stirring it constantly with a stone pestle.

"Good afternoon, Mr. Appleby," said Sam, starting out his investigation with sociable politeness. "Making a miracle cure medication?"

"Sure am, Deputy," grinned the normally somber pharmacist. "This bread soup is about to cure my stomach's hunger pains. Want a cup of it?"

"No thanks, Mr. Appleby, just had dinner at Mrs. Kipp's. I'm here about a complaint—a product of yours."

"A complaint? Someone complained to you? I wish they had come to me first."

"Well, you know, Mr. Appleby," soothed Deputy Sam, "some people don't like confrontations. The complaint alleges that there's no bear grease in your Big Bear Balm."

Appleby stopped stirring the soup and took the small copper pan off the grate. Then he blew out the flame and covered the round wick with a metal sheath. "I got to admit you're right," admitted the pharmacist, finally. "Big Bear Balm contains no bear grease. It does have wool fat, extracts of camphor and balsam and several other efficacious medicinals. But you're right—no bear grease. I'm out of bear grease. Not as many bears around anymore, I guess."

"What happened to something called Dr. Schwabe's Bear Fat Skin Salve? The complainant said that it worked good for her."

"It's Mrs. Fallon, isn't it? You probably can't tell me, can you?" Sam's silence prompted him to continue. "Dr. Schwabe died and took his formulation to the grave with him. I just tried to fill the gap, seeing as I couldn't get anymore of Dr. Schwabe's stuff."

"And you made up the Big Bear Balm here?" questioned Sam.

"Sure. Got Van Doormann to print the labels. Had a pretty good stock of tins. They cost a dime apiece plus shipping. Did you know that? Cost more than the contents."

"No, didn't know that." Sam was beginning to feel sorry for Appleby. "But I think it would be best to get new labels, that have no mention of bears. It confuses the public. And I want you to apologize to Mrs. Fallon and give her back the money she spent on Bear Balm."

"Oh, I can't do that," exclaimed Appleby, pouring the soup into a stone mortar preparatory to eating. "If any of my lady customers saw me going into Dora's establishment my reputation would be ruined."

"Catch her at home. She lives up by the Grand View Saloon on Chinaman's Ridge."

"Yes," agreed Appleby. "I could do that."

"Not could, Mr. Appleby," said Deputy Sam, sternly. "You *must* do that. And tear the bear labels off any tins of the stuff."

"You're a hard man, Deputy. I guess that's from being a prisoner, isn't it?"

"What do you mean?" asked Sam, puzzled by Appleby's statement.

"One of my customers, a Mr. Jones, told me you were on a prison hulk with him. Said your brother was killed there. Says that you were sort of a hero to the other prisoners."

"Everybody was a hero on the hulks, Mr. Appleby."

"Jones was in a lot of pain, what with that amputation to his foot."

"Some men's pain was physical," stated Sam. "Others' were mental. I still get terrible dreams, myself."

"I imagine he's feeling better now—since he can buy all the morphia he needs. He's lucky to have a son that can help him, I guess. Must spend at least five dollars a week on the laudanum lately."

"A son?" replied Sam, doubtfully.

"That's what Jones told me. You know, I'm good at prying people's feelings from them. It's a social talent."

"So I notice. Got me to admitting I have bad dreams."

"See what I mean," gloated the pharmacist. "Now, Mr. Jones had me make up a glass of laudanum, right away, for him. Took hardly no time at all and he was all smiles; no foot pain. That's when he told me about his son helping him with the money."

"Isn't that wonderful," Sam went along with the suddenly interesting conversation. "What'd he say, Mr. Appleby?"

"Said he's in clover now. Can buy all the morphia he needs. 'I got me a fine son, Appleby old boy,' he said. 'Anytime I need money bad—my fine son gives me some. Everybody should have a fine son, like I does.' That's what he told me and to tell you the truth, I think it's grand, a man's boy helping his pa through hard times. Make a body feel good about people, don't it?"

"A fine son, eh? Yes, Mr. Appleby—that really does make me feel glad. I gotta go now; don't forget about Mrs. Fallon, will you?"

"I'll do that, Deputy. Have a good afternoon," the pharmacist called after Sam's retreating figure. He smiled to himself as he dragged a stool up to his stone bowl of soup. "Dogies, but I'm good at making people feel better about themselves, ain't I?" he said out loud, to his empty shop and himself. Then he began on his bread soup.

******

Ostenhaven said he was too excited to eat before their meeting with Hurst. Finsen went along with his boss, agreeing to eat after the meeting. He even suggested eating in the cantina, admitting he liked spicy food, occasionally.

They were early then, for their meeting with Charlie Hurst, as they entered the cantina's gloomy barroom. A scattering of shabby hangers-on turned suspicious faces towards the gringo pair as Ostenhaven questioned the bartender.

"Señor Hurst, por favor."

"Recámara numero dos," said the man, pointing to the stair. "No get wet, señors."

Halfway up the stairs, Finsen called ahead to Ostenhaven. "What did he mean by that remark?"

"Who knows what these Mexicans are thinking? Come on—number two, was it?" Ostenhaven peered at the row of doors lining the corridor, to knock on number two.

"Keep out, dammit!" came Hurst's cry from inside the room.

"That's him. Open the door," said Finsen, puffing from the stairs.

Ostenhaven swung the door open to stare slack-jawed at Charlie Hurst in his bath. The oval wine-cask tub was filled with the straining bodies and dangling legs of Hurst and his landlady conducting soapy coitus within the splashing seas of the dripping tub.

"Be with you in a moment, gents," called Hurst, never breaking the rhythm of his heavings.

"Oh my God!" exclaimed Finsen, pulling Ostenhaven out of the room and slamming the door.

"More likely the devil," gasped Ostenhaven, finally finding his voice. "We shall wait downstairs. Perhaps we can eat while waiting."

"I think I lost my appetite. That woman was naked. Did you see that?"

"How could I miss? Watch that first stair-step."

The man behind the bar grinned at their flight down the staircase. "You no get bath, señors? Next man saves money—fifty cents only."

"No," said Finsen sharply. "We shall eat now. Show us to a clean table—by ourselves."

Finsen and Ostenhaven were tackling tamales when Hurst came down from his bath. A big ceramic platter held a growing pile of corn husks, peeled from the diners' tamales.

"Good, huh?" greeted Hurst. "The dog meat takes the sweet from the horse meat when it's mixed like that."

The contented look on Ostenhaven's face was suddenly replaced by a certain grimness. To his credit though, he expressed his apologies for catching Charlie in an embarrassing encounter.

"That's all right, Mr. Ostenhaven," laughed Charlie, "everything came out all right in the end." He laughed again, coarsely, "Her end, I should say. Jose," he called to the barman. "Bring me some of those doggone good tamales; a big plate and beer; lots of beer."

Then in an aside to his table companions, he whispered, "We got something to celebrate. After we eat I'll take you upstairs and show you."

"Not that woman!" retorted Finsen, making a face.

"Better, gents—gold ain't crabby the next morning."

******

The sheriff found the crippled Jones poking about the insides of a heavy hand pump that was placed on a cribbing of stout timbers.

"I believe you're Jerry Jones. I'm Sheriff Skinner and I've a few questions to ask you."

"Too busy now," came the surly answer. "Gotta have this ready for the midnight shift."

"You can keep on working on it, Jones. Just give me some answers and I'll leave you to your work."

"Go ahead. You can't pin anything on me about Eckhardt's old lady's murder."

"Was it a murder, Jones?" asked Skinner severely.

"That's what everybody says. I hear it was a bomb. You should know—you're the sheriff, not me."

"I have something to show you." Skinner brought out the cable from the canvas bag. "Recognize that, Jones?"

The mechanic gave the sheriff's exhibit a quick glance. "Naw, never seed it before. What is it?"

"Elevator cable. The same kind of cable that is used in the lifts of this mine. And you say you never saw it?"

"Oh, yeah. Didn't recognize it," said Jones, suddenly finding something in the pump that needed his full attention. "Don't fool with the lifts much." This spoken to the insides of the pump.

"How about this, Jones?" the sheriff asked as he pulled out a piece of the shrapnel from the sack. "Can you explain this?" He stepped over to thrust the small metal triangle under the reddened nose of Jones.

"Just a piece of metal, as far as I'm concerned."

"Not just a piece of metal, Jones. It's a piece of home-made shrapnel—that the doctor took from Mrs. Ostenhaven's or Mrs. Eckhardt's body. She was shredded by almost two dozen of these—in the bomb blast. Did you make these pieces for your bomb? The bomb that killed her!"

"Wait a minute." Jones was sweating and his nose was dripping in a greasy smear to the back of his dirty hand as he tried to wipe off the body fluids from his face. "You got no proof against me."

"These triangles were cut on a piece of iron railroad rail by a cold chisel. Do you have a piece of rail you use for an anvil, Jones? Got it at home—nailed to a firewood round?"

"Lots of people got one. That's no crime," whined Jones, starting to shake, nervously. "I ain't gonna answer no more of your questions."

"You will, Jones, by-and-by," promised Skinner. "I'd give you this piece of shrapnel for a memento, Jones, but I've got a good hunch you have a bunch of them already—don't you Jones?"

"I ain't doing no more talking to you. You're just looking for somebody to hang for that killing."

"You're absolutely right, Jones. And I think I've found him. You, Jones. Tell me who put you up to this—and it will go easier on you. Remember that. It could keep you from swinging."

"Get out and leave me work! You can't scare me! I'm innocent! You hear? Innocent!" Jones was screaming at the sheriff.

"I'll be back, Jones," said Skinner, leaving. "Maybe not tomorrow—but I'll be back to arrest you—real soon."

The sheriff came back to his office to find Sam and Cletus relaxing over a checkers game. He stomped past the happy duo to slam his hat on his desk in a show of temper.

"The High Sheriff cometh, Deputy McCoyne," observed Sam.

"And not in a happy mood, I fear, Chief Deputy Buller," assessed the big, buckskin-clad deputy. "Which forebodes unpleasantness for us lowly serfs."

"Fear not, oh great creature of the mountains," Sam went on, "I will brighten his scowling countenance with choice morsels of good tidings. King me, quick, you overstuffed yokel."

"What good news? I could use some good tidings," said Skinner, pouring himself a cup of coffee after scowling at the eggshells inside the pot.

"Item one, mon sheriff—you have one less mouth to feed here at the old calaboose. Mr. Jack Sprague, to my deep dismay, has been bailed out by lawyer David Rose."

"What!" growled Skinner. "I thought you said you had good news."

"He has flown to the bosom of his friends—Ostenhaven and company, where, no doubt, his talents are needed. But fear not—I have better news, which concerns Mr. Jerry Jones."

"I've just come from questioning him and Otto Floss; which is why I'm angry. My investigation is on the rocks—dead-ended."

"Then you'll be doubly glad to hear this. I pursued the investigation, this afternoon, of Mrs. Fallon and the case of the disappearing bear grease."

"Oh great. But I guess it's better than playing checkers and loafing around here," scolded Skinner.

"Not true, mon sheriff. After lecturing Mr. Appleby about fraudulent bear balm and getting his promise to redress the matter, I learned that Mr. Jones had recently come into money to buy large amounts of morphia to relieve his foot pain."

"Money . . . Jones?" Sam had Skinner's attention now.

"Oui, mon sheriff. It seems, according to pharmacist Appleby, that Jones is now receiving money from his son, a rich son. Actually to quote Mr. Jones, he has a *fine son* that sends him money."

"A fine son?" repeated Skinner, puzzled.

"Get it, mon sheriff? A fine son. Fin-sen, Frederick Finsen, assistant to Ostenhaven alias Eckhardt. A play on words. Mr. Jones thought he was being smart."

"Seems like he outsmarted himself. Good work, Sam. You're a good detective. Now . . ." Skinner waited for his pause to take effect ". . . if we could only teach you to make coffee without all those damned eggshells—you'd make a proper deputy."

******

"What! You let the hostiles get away!" fumed the dapper adjutant, Major Poole. He glared at 2nd Lieutenant Jersie and Sgt. White, both of whom had just arrived at Ft. Lowell looking more like the walking dead than the elite of the U.S. Cavalry.

"We was lucky to get the lady back, sir; and we did get five of them with no loss to ourselves." Sgt. White's voice was graveled by dust and lack of water.

"Against the loss of . . . how many homesteaders?"

"Seven or eight, sir," replied Jersie. "Can't remember exactly . . . perhaps after I sleep I can think better, sir."

"After I dismiss you, go to sleep," ordered the major. "But by ten o'clock tomorrow morning I want a patrol report that reflects more accurately the number of hostiles that you killed. With over a thousand rounds expended, our tables show that you probably killed over twenty-five Apaches. No—twenty-five sounds too concise. Make it twenty-seven. And the homesteaders—how many were not adults?"

"Adults, sir?" Jersie was too tired to follow the adjutant's thinking.

"You know, under twenty-one."

"Two kids—and their mother seemed young. Could have been twenty, maybe."

"That's it then, drop the homesteader casualties by three." Major Poole was composing his report to the Department of the West in his mind, trying to figure out how to enhance his own part in the patrol's action. Maybe the reinforcement of the normally small patrol. That coupled with some special instruction to the patrol . . .

"Major Poole, sir?"

"What was that, lieutenant?" Poole's martial message perusings were interrupted.

"Can we go, sir? We're just about dead, sir."

"Weakness, lieutenant. A true cavalryman should never give in to physical weakness. Look at me. Been working since sunup. Probably have at least two more hours with my report to Department of the West. And I'm not the least bit weary. It's clean living. Early to bed and early to rise and abstention from alcohol and the noxious weed. Right, Sergeant?"

"Oh, yes sir. The devil in the bottle, sir," said Sgt. White, winking a bloodshot eye to Jersie.

"Exactly," beamed the polished major. "Now you two get some good rest and don't forget that report. Remember—twenty-seven dead Apaches. Dismissed."

Sgt. White quickly forgot about the twenty-seven figure—but somehow he did recall talk about the devil in the bottle and made sure to rescue that particular spirit from a bottle of the sutler's best.

******

"What was that?" answered Mr. Hansen, stopping his intake at the next day's supper table to come up for air.

"I said," Skinner repeated, "how did the shopping spree of Helen Boorman go? Is she all set for now?"

"I'm sure she should be by now," replied the old carpenter, loading up his spoon with rice and raisins.

"When a person says he's sure, always pays to doubt the cure," rhymed the sheriff, "as my old colonel used to say. Tell me how it went with the young woman. Did she find lodging?"

"Yes." Hansen followed the word with a quick spoonful of rice into his gap-toothed mouth.

"Yes, what?"

"Yes—she's found lodging. Employment, too."

"That was fast." Skinner would not let go.

"Yes—fast."

"Mr. Hansen, something tells me that you are not telling me all you know. Come clean and to the point, if you please."

"Are you sure you want to know?" asked Hansen, pushing his soup plate to Gen for a refill.

"Certainly—why shouldn't I?"

"She's at Dora's," Hansen said in a rush. "And it ain't my fault. It was all her idea—honest."

"Tell me the details—*now!*"

"Now don't get mad. Like I said, it was her idea. As we was going to Gompers', she asked me if there were any sporting houses in Green Falls and I . . ."

"Stop right there!" cried Gen, getting to her feet and pulling Esther from her chair. "Esther honey, go to your room while we have grown-up talk here."

"But I'm not finished eating," pouted the child, her curiosity awakened.

"I'll come as soon as we're finished talking about this. You go read your McGuffey's. Scoot now." Gen gave her a gentle push and waited until she heard the girl's door close. Then she snapped at Mr. Hansen, "Do you mean to say you led that poor girl to that . . . to that . . . brothel?"

"Well, Mrs.—it was more like I was just tagging along. She was hot-footing it towards Dora's. Wouldn't listen to me. Said she'd made up her mind."

"What happened at that . . . that . . . women's house?" Gen had now taken over this investigation. Skinner was only too glad to play second fiddle to his angry wife.

"Well, ah—I introduced her to Miss Dora and . . ."

"You know the woman?" Gen made a grimace at Hansen.

"Just in a professional way, Mrs.," admitted Hansen, hanging his head.

"Yes—and she's a professional, isn't she?" snapped Gen.

"No, no—not that way, Mrs. I did some carpentry for her. Some cabinets and shelves for her linens. She got a whole lot of sheets and towels, you know."

"I can just imagine." Her words dripped with acid.

"Let the poor man talk, Genevieve. You're trying to kill the messenger because of the message." Hansen shot the sheriff a look of gratitude for timely intervention.

"This employment you bragged about. Is Helen now a fallen angel in this—ah, house?" persisted Gen.

"I can't really say, Mrs. After I introduced the girl, Dora took her inside and shut the door in my face."

"Serves you right," stated Gen. "Tomorrow, Sylvester, you must call on that hussy and determine if that child is being held against her will. I've heard about white slavers," (she shot a withering glance at Hansen) "and how they lure innocent girls into those terrible places."

"Pity poor red bush," said the sheriff softly, rolling his eyes at Hansen.

"What did you say, Sylvester?" raged Gen.

"Ah—mighty sure big rush, my dear. But I'll go there tomorrow.

"But not inside, Sylvester. Stay outside. You hear?"

CHAPTER 10

T he inaugural run of Jerome T. Warner's new stage line was not a shining success. Billed to arrive in Green Falls at seven P.M., the wounded Concord stage struggled up to its terminal point at the Marble Palace Hotel almost three hours late. The small gathering of well-wishers and civic officials, who had earlier come to greet the new stage line's first run, had all left in impatient discouragement some time earlier.

No doubt, it was fortunate that a crowd of spectators did not see Mr. Warner's first effort stagger onto Main Street, its off rear wheel bolted together with iron straps holding together the broken felly that caused the delay. The resourceful Warner and his driver had lashed a timber drag under the broken wheel to nurse the coach into the German settlement of Kolbheim, where the wheel was hurriedly fitted with the ugly iron appliance.

After the last disgruntled passenger was helped down with apologies and the too-few items of express unloaded, the coach was led to Ames Livery Yard where the tired team was to be stabled. Then, as the driver and Ames's hired man looked after the team, Warner removed the wheel and rolled it to the wheelwright, where hopefully, that artisan could be bribed to repair it overnight for the return run to Tucson the next day.

******

"To your very good health, gentlemen." Theodore Osten-haven was all smiles as he set the champagne glass down on the mirror-like table at the Congress Hotel Gentleman's Bar. "And now to business," he grinned at his two companions, the sartorially elegant Franklin Finsen and the less ostenta-tiously dressed Charlie Hurst.

"Our first order of business is the assayers report, which is quite astounding. The samples, taken from your bag, Charlie, run $1,375, $1,490 and $1,210 per test—for an average of $1,358.33 per ton."

"Goodness gracious!" gasped Finsen. "That's amazing."

"You're absolutely right, Freddy," giggled Ostenhaven, slipping out of character. "And this latest find of Charlie's has narrowed the search—wouldn't you say that, Charlie?"

Hurst looked at Ostenhaven, giving him the wry smile reserved for poor fools who have no sense or conception of the awful reality of the high desert wilderness. "I reckon you could say that, Mr. Ostenhaven. Before, I was searching an area of roughly 20,000 square miles. Now, like you say, it's narrowed to about 2,500 square miles. But that's still a lot of territory. Iff'n I explored a square mile a day, it would take me eight years to half-ass go over that narrowed-down piece of hell."

"That long?" Finsen exclaimed. "We'd be old men."

"Mr. Finsen," said Charlie. "You might be old by then—but I'll be dried out and no doubt dead. That desert's a damn unkind place. Unforgiving, I mean. This last time I ran out of water and was in a bad way when I stumbled on Pete's hideout. Had to fill my canteen there drop by drop by drop. Took all night to fill one little canteen. No sir—too easy to get in trouble out there." Then he laughed, a short, self-deprecating sort of a laugh.

"What's so funny, Charlie?" asked Ostenhaven, filling up Hurst's glass as if to assure him that for tonight, thirst was no problem.

"See these new duds of mine?" asked Charlie, pulling on the fabric of his new mohair suitcoat.

"Very nice, in a muted way," put in Finsen. "Good material."

"Should be—spent over thirty-five bucks on clothes this morning. Know where I got the money from?"

His companions shrugged their ignorance. "Hopefully not from selling ore," added Ostenhaven. "It would very well give us away."

"Naw, ain't that dumb. I've got my eye on the big money . . . I got it by selling water to all the fools out there in the desert, stumbling around out there looking for Pete's mine. I ask five bucks a quart."

"Explain this to me, Charlie," said Ostenhaven, suddenly grave. "You say there's other prospectors out there—trying to find Pete's mine?"

"I only came across two parties. One of them had a map somebody sold them in Tucson. The map was drawn all wrong—just a cheap gyp. But I guess some people will buy anything—when a gold mine's involved."

"This is a serious complication," stated Ostenhaven. He looked serious. "If too many goldseekers are out there searching, they could possibly find the mine."

"They could," Finsen agreed, nodding his pudgy head.

"So what can we do—scare them off?" asked Hurst. "It would take a regiment of tough cavalry, and they'd still get through."

"Sometimes, rumors work better than regiments," replied Ostenhaven deviously. "You have to play on people's fears. What is feared most out there, Charlie?"

"Injuns, at least by me."

"What else?"

"People over around No Place are worried about a big cat. Say it's got paws big as dinner plates."

"Wait a minute, Charlie," said Ostenhaven. "What is No Place?"

"Oh—it's a little town, like—on the Eagle Pass Trail, back of Ute Point. It's the only water for miles, salty as hell though, but wet. Tastes better if you put a little wine in it or whiskey. Only got a store 'n' saloon and a smithy."

"How do they make a living?" questioned the ever-practical Finsen.

"They run water wagons out to the copper collectors."

"Copper collectors?" asked Ostenhaven. "What do you mean, copper collectors?"

"They're people who pick up the copper nuggets that are all strewn around out there."

"Just laying around?" questioned Ostenhaven. "How big are the ingots?"

"Mostly small, like a hazel nut," said Hurst. "A few are bigger—fist sized. They can pick up fifty or sixty pounds a day if they hustle. It's playing out, though. Not as good as before—from what they say. Some of them are quitting, giving up. What with less ingots and now the mountain lion chewing on people."

"People have been attacked?" It was Ostenhaven, sounding enthusiastic.

"Yeah, guess so. I only saw one fellow, though. Who was jumped, I mean. He's at No Place now. Caulks water tanks now. Scared to go back to copper collecting. Got some nasty scars where the cat bit him. Managed to beat the cat off with his rake. The bites got infected. They opened up the wounds and poured gunpowder down the holes and lit it off. Don't know which was worse—the cure or the bites. But he pulled through, finally. They'd dug his grave already and he just woke up feeling fine and babbling about talking to Jesus. He's still a little off, if you know what I mean. Got any more of that bubble water?"

Ostenhaven signaled to the waiter for more champagne and waited to resume the conversation until after the waiter had served them.

"Charlie," he asked, "if there were more attacks from the mountain lion, would that help to frighten goldseekers away? Severe attacks, I mean. Deadly attacks."

"Should sure help. But it would be hard to find and trap more mountain lions. That's a lot of work."

"Yes," agreed Ostenhaven absently, concentrating on the subject. He toyed with his champagne glass for a moment, making wet circles on the polished table. Suddenly, he stopped. "That's it!"

What's it?" asked Charlie, busy watching his wine's bubbles.

"Claws. Cat claws. If I'm not mistaken, a cat—a big cat, I mean—kills with his claws also, maiming his prey. Then it bites at the base of the neck to kill. If we made an iron set of claws—make it steel claws—that exactly match a real mountain lion's paw, you could kill a few of these prospectors with this steel claw and it would be blamed on the big cat. Then . . ."

"Me?" interrupted Hurst. "I ain't no hired killer. I done a couple of people in, one was a Mexican; but never in cold blood. I'm a prospector, not no killer."

"Oh, Charlie. You disappoint me," chided Ostenhaven. "I had you figured out for a hard man, who wants to be rich and live the good life of wine, women and the song of golden coins in your pockets. I guess I was wrong. I guess this whole project is too big for you. I should have found a big man—for a big job, and big money."

"Wait a minute," objected Hurst. "I didn't say I wouldn't do it. You never gave me a chance to think. How many would I have to . . . to do that to?"

"As many as it takes, Charlie. Maybe two or three will get the rumor rolling. Perhaps more. I can't guarantee a particular number. I can only guarantee one thing, Charlie."

"What's that, Mr. Ostenhaven?"

"That the gold assays out at $1,358.33 a ton and you're in for a third. What say you, Charlie? Are you up to playing the cat?"

"Get that claw made up. Better make it two; one for each hand."

******

The children of the camp saw them first and their youthful shouts of greeting awakened some last reserve of strength in the drooping bodies of the three returning warriors. The running children laughed and shrieked in childish enthusiasm at the sight of the captured horse herd the three warriors drove.

The stolen horses were a gift of the Father Sun and Sky, said old Slit-Nose. A reward for their resolution against the white pony-soldiers. A doubly-sweet reward, for they were stolen from a sleeping band of Arapahos, whose thievery had taken them too far south into Apache domains.

It was good, thought Owl-Who-Kills-At-Night, for without the captured horses, Slit-Nose's survivors would have little to boast about—a short string of scalps and a few of the white man's fire weapons. Horses always made good booty. They were noisy, dust-making plunder—that had immediate worth.

But with all the shouts of praise as the weary braves rode into the village, there now came the shrieks of sorrow and the awful mourning croons of lamentation for the warriors who had been lost on this raid.

Five families would know the heartbreak of their loss. Their women would scar themselves, cutting great gashes about their bodies in futile attempts at balancing bodily pain with their soulful sorrow.

That night Slit-Nose, Beaver Tooth and Owl-Who-Kills-At-Night sat at the place of honor in the tribal circle. Although called as an official tribal hearing into the recent foray, custom called for resolution of minor tribal and inter-clan issues before the principal attraction could be savored. Most of these squabbles involved either ponies or women, or sometimes both. The last was about who had first rights to a large copper pot. This was all grave community business, but it was also entertaining to the assembly who would later fill the day gossiping about the participants and the elders' decisions. All through these minor matters though, a sweet aura of anticipatory suspense was building among the spectators awaiting the first ceremonial telling of the latest Slit-Nose raid.

Finally, everyday petty affairs decided, Slit-Nose was invited by the elders to talk of his raid. This was the moment in the life of the tribe when history and histrionics would fuse into the narrative; told now to be retold a thousand times hence in the oral annals of the tribe.

Perhaps, theatrically, it was better for Slit-Nose to first appear in his normal physical form. Unprepossessing would be an apt description. On the small side; bandy-legged, pot-bellied and with a face made ugly by the wound to his nostril. But that night his silver mane reflected the yellows of the great fire—as did his eyes that glistened, cat-like in the flames' glow.

He rose and walked to a spot opposite the elders, still clutching his scarlet blanket about his thin shoulders. He carried a rifle to his breast; a scarred Sharps cavalry carbine decoratively lined with rows of brass tacks. This rifle was his only theatrical prop—a focus for the crowd's attention.

He began by restating the background of the tribal raids, listing a dozen previous forays and a litany of injustices done to the tribe by the white invaders who had precipitated their problems.

Then he told in expansive detail of the planning and preparation for the raid, padding his speech with the many details his audience appreciated; never using one word when two or more would work in augmentation.

He told of his raiders' long travel and the failing of their ponies; and how the young brave, Small Bear, shared his pony with Beaver Tooth. He gestured to the seated pair with the studded butt of his carbine. And his audience nodded their approval at the two.

Now he spoke of their seeing the white man's wagons, bouncing his gleaming head back and forth, comically, to show his audience how the white man's foolish wagons rocked and lurched as they moved down the trail.

Suddenly Split-Nose jumped forward, almost into the ring of spectators, pointing his carbine at the imaginary rocks as he told of sending young Small Bear to spy on the white men. The scarlet blanket had slipped from his shoulders to the dust of the arena to show his sinewy upper body, oiled and glistening in the fire's light.

"And I told my braves to go into the brush to prepare themselves for battle with the whites, using the power of their courageous ancestors to strengthen them against the fire weapons of their foes."

Then he broke his narrative to show all how he had sat, cross-legged and with his blanket tenting over his head. Then he crooned a plea to Father Earth and Sky from this position in the circle's swept earthen floor; asking for guidance and divine power. The prayer song was of long duration, with many pauses and changes of tempo. Finally at one of the many halts, he slowly rose to his feet—the blanket cast down again as he glided to the ringed spectators and pulled Owl-Who-Kills-At-Night to his feet.

"Mother Moon came to this young brave in answer to his pleas. You know him as Small Bear son of Sees-in-Darkness, killer of Paiutes, a great warrior—celebrated in song and sayings. Now I have given him the name of Owl-Who-Kills-At-Night."

The young brave turned questioningly to Slit-Nose at this. He distinctly remembered naming himself after killing the white guard. He looked to his right forearm, decorated now with a vermilion splotch designating the white's blood that had run down his arm. Slit-Nose sensed the young brave's doubt and pinched the youngster's other arm to restore the youth's respect for the new truth to their saga.

"Tell all now, young warrior—what you saw in the darkness of the sky," intoned Slit-Nose dramatically.

"I saw my . . ." started the young brave.

"He saw a vision in the black roof of the world," interrupted the old warrior, loathe to yield the center of attention. "A falling star, whose tail turned into his knife. A sign from Mother Moon—an omen of success in our attack against the whites." The young warrior nodded his assent to this interpretation, as he realized his place at this public staging.

Slit-Nose went on, telling of the assault and the butchery; somehow leaving unsaid the raping. But he recounted the scalping and displayed the scalps-locks tied together in a cord of horsehair. And then came the battle with the white pony-soldiers and the loss of part of his band to the white's fire-weapons.

Altogether it was a long night, with even the energetic Slit-Nose wearing down towards the close, glad to get to the horse-stealing episode. Several of the elders appeared to be dozing and the children had fallen asleep in their mother's fastness. The huge central fire had fallen to embers. But the drowsy crowd was pleased with Slit-Nose's presentation, satisfied that their tribe's warrior tradition continued.

******

Sheriff Skinner stopped by Madam Dora's on his way to the bakery for the morning's jelly buns. It was a quarter-to-ten and the house-that-was-not-a-home was quiet, lacking the laughter and the tinkling piano music of the later hours. The door was opened by Dora's burly black houseman and bouncer, Horatio.

"No troubles here today," grinned the big Negro, "unless you is here abouts that wife of mine beating on me agains."

"Sadie probably caught you gambling again," laughed Skinner. "Which would serve you right. No, today I have to see Miss Dora about one of her new girls, Helen Boorman. Is Miss Dora up and about yet?"

"I's just took coffee into her, but lemme knocks and tells her you is waiting to sees her." He led Skinner past the ornately-furnished parlor and bar, now abandoned except for the smells of cigars and whiskey—and French perfume. He knocked at the door and stuck his head into the room to announce the sheriff.

Miss Dora came to the door to greet Skinner, her hair upswept, with a pink boa emphasizing her long white neck and the pale cleavage of her still imposing bosom. "Sheriff Skinner," she smiled warily, holding out the fingers of a veined hand in greeting. Dora had poise and most of her good looks, although she was pushing the half-century mark. Skinner gave the proffered fingers an obligatory squeeze as he pulled off his hat.

"What brings you here, Sheriff? Run out of bullets for that little pistol of mine?"

"Almost, Miss Dora. That little pistol has been a big lifesaver for me. But I'm here to see about Miss Boorman. Checking up to see if she is working here of her own accord. I ah . . ." the sheriff stammered in obvious embarrassment, "got sort of a responsibility to the Army, who brought her here, to see that she's not been ah . . ."

"Kidnapped," interrupted the madam, laughing, "and sold to the white slavers to force their licentious will upon this innocent girl."

"Well, not exactly," said the sheriff, reddening. "But something like that. I just need to talk to her and make sure she wishes to stay here."

"In this den of iniquity," added Dora. "Sit down, Sheriff. No, not on that chair—here on the chesterfield—while I rouse your red-headed innocent."

A minute later, Dora reentered her office with a cup and saucer. "She'll be down shortly and we will have coffee together while you wait. Do you take sugar, Sheriff Skinner?" she asked, pouring his coffee from the silver service on the leather drum table.

Skinner was forced to make small talk until a knock on Dora's door relieved him. Helen Boorman entered the room dressed in a green velvet wrapper with white rabbit fur collar and cuffs, that accentuated her copper hair. Her face, although still sleep-puffed, was radiant with good health and humor.

"Good morning, Sheriff, Miss Dora," said the girl. "You looking for me, Sheriff?"

"Well—ah," mumbled Skinner. "Thought I'd . . ."

"He's worried about you," broke in Dora. "Thinks I kidnapped you—to sell your body to sweaty miners."

"No, Sheriff," Helen protested, with a winsome smile. "Don't hardly no miners come here, lessn they're managers or like that. And they ain't *that* sweaty—least when they *get* here."

"I have to ask you, Helen—if I was to escort you out of this house right now, in safety, would you come with me? To leave this type of business?"

"Leave?" questioned Helen, looking at Madam Dora for support. "What for? I just got here. Haven't hardly built up a clientele, yet. Ain't that right, Miss Dora?"

"Will that do for an answer, Sheriff?" smirked the madam.

Skinner refused to be side-tracked. "Just answer—either yes, you'll leave or no—you'll stay in this house. Please—for the record; and I'll respect your wishes."

"I want to stay. I feel to home here. Everybody treats me just fine—'specially Miss Dora. Kin I go now? My gentleman will be wondering what happened to me."

"Go ahead, Miss Boorman, and I hope you'll fare well." The young woman shot a relieved glance at her boss, and fled from the room.

"Satisfied now, Sheriff Skinner?" asked Madam Dora, in a voice full of her own self-achievement.

"Got what I came for, anyway."

"Most men do—who come here. And don't worry about her. Right now she's the new girl, with all the customers lined up to try her out, falling all over themselves like hounds after a bitch in heat. She feels good about pleasuring them—and the attention and the good money." She rose from the chesterfield to go to the window, looking through the delicate lace curtains. She stayed for a long minute, staring out the window towards the tall buildings on Elevator Row—but seeing only herself thirty years before, when her beauty was the talk of the Baltimore bordellos.

"Ahem," expelled Skinner finally, flustered by the usually matter-of-fact madam's retreat to silent retrospection.

"Oh—sorry. This discussion brought back memories for me. Must be getting senile—and soft in my old age."

"We all get older, Miss Dora," said Skinner softly. "The trick is to get smarter at the same time. And in that department—you seem to have no trouble, at least with us minions of the law."

"My goodness, Sheriff, is that a compliment?"

"Consider it more as campaign confidences. I have to run for sheriff in a little while."

"Would it help if I supported you? I could get my girls together and parade to the polling place for you. Maybe carrying a banner of some kind, even if they don't let women actually vote."

"I'd be more happy with fifty posters from Van Doormann. I think they'd be less controversial than a prostitute parade—if you'll pardon my choice of words."

"So be it, Sheriff," Dora said with a smile. "It's posters rather than parades. I'll talk to Charlie next time he comes. Maybe I can work out a trade, if you know what I mean."

"No, ma'am. Don't know—don't want to know. I intend to be a paragon of virtue."

"You won't be able to pull it off, Sheriff. You've made too many bodies here in Green Falls. That's what people remember—always the worst. Take it from an expert. If I could invent a cure for cholera tomorrow, they'd still remember me as the cat-house madam who cured cholera. That's the nature of people—they gotta have something to look down their noses at."

"You're probably right, Dora. But I don't like to think of myself as a killer with a badge."

"Whatever happened to 'if a shoe fits, wear it'? That's what Helen's doing, isn't it?"

"Guess it's easier for her. She's young and single-minded." Then he smiled, saying, "And besides, I don't have a red bush to bring me luck." He got up from the chesterfield, nodded goodbye and left, leaving Madam Dora to guess about the lucky red bush.

CHAPTER 11

An urchin, dirty and street-wary, had brought Finsen's note to Jerry Jones. "Noon," it said, "at my office—F.F." It might be hard to visualize a single-footed man on crutches moving at a sneak; but Jones did and quite swiftly at that—for he smelled money to buy his morphia.

The precise Finsen had a well-executed drawing of a steel cat's claw equipped with a stout wooden handle, crosswise, like a baling hook. He had spent an hour, before attacking the drawing, tormenting a caged alley cat, learning the feline's claw pattern and had come up with a fine representation of a gigantic cat's claw. Our painstaking Frederick was good at tasks such as this.

"Naturally, promptness on this project is most desirable, Jerry my friend," he said. "But the composition and the temper of the claws is very important. Can you find a suitable steel?"

"Got jes' the thing, Mr. Finsen. High carbon drill rod in 1/4-inch. You need two of these things, right?"

"Yes. Two—a pair, just like the drawing. A right and a left. How long will it take, Jerry?"

"For you, Mr. Finsen, I'll work all night. I'll borrow a friend's forge and I'll get them to you tomorrow morning. How's that for quickness?"

"Where, Jerry? I don't want you coming to my hotel—it would raise embarrassing questions."

"How about at Mrs. Purity's place? They got booths there. Make it nine o'clock, at the back of the restaurant. That'll give me time to clean up at home and send my boy to the mine to tell them I'll be out sick. How much will I get for this job, Mr. Finsen? Job like this must be worth a lot to you, huh?"

"Certainly is, Jerry; and I appreciate your talent. How does forty dollars sound; twenty apiece? Now you get out of here, quick—before anybody spots you here. And I'll see you at Mrs. Purity's at nine tomorrow, with the money. Oh—and have those things in a box or a bag. Don't want anybody seeing them."

******

"Dammit—there it is," swore Beau Butler, as he worked the shard pebble out of his horse's hoof with his clasp knife.

"Too late now, Beau," sympathized his younger brother, Robert. "He won't be good for two or three days. Look at all that pus. You'll have to leave him."

"And what—ride double with you to Tucson?" Beau retorted. "No siree, I'll take this nag and trade it, and some boot, for something to ride."

"Whatever you're going to do, you better do it quick. That poster in the post office makes me want to high-tail it from this town as fast as possible."

"That picture could be any of a thousand men in Arizona with full beards. Lousy drawing—if you asks me," pronounced Brother Beau.

"Still makes me nervous. Five hundred bucks reward is big money."

"You're always nervous—ever since Alvin got it."

"Hey," argued Robert. "I got a right to be nervous. They shot Alvin down without a chance. Never hollered 'hands up' or nothing. Just kilt him. We wuz lucky to get away ourselves."

"It don't do no good to cry over spilt milk, little brother, as Ma woulda said. Now, I gonna walk this horse down to that livery stable and do some fancy talking and trading."

Fifteen minutes later found the brothers talking to Mr. Ames, the livery stable owner. Ames had taken the lame horse out into the morning sunlight—poking a rusty awl into the hoof to assess the damage. He dropped the affected hoof to deliver his opinion.

"I'd say it's a lot worse than you let on. Probably be lame a week—easy. And I'll have to clean out that pus and pack it. That all takes time."

"I'm willing to make up the difference—for that paint there. Give you thirty dollars to boot."

"I was thinking more like fifty," bargained Ames.

"For a rough-broke range horse? You can't be serious. Thirty-five—tops."

"It's had some schooling, you know. Fella rode it up from Sonora. I could go down to forty-five."

"More like he hazed it up from Mexico. Thirty-seven fifty."

"You know, this is what I hate about horse trading," said Ames. "The customer always thinks that I should make the grand gesture and come down to split the difference. Well— today I ain't, by damn. If you want that paint it'll cost you $42.50. And that's that. Take it or leave it."

"You're a rotten son of a bitch, ain't you, old man?" bit off Beau.

"Compliments won't get you nowheres," quipped Ames. "But $42.50 will get you a paint horse—that ain't bad lame like this one.

"It's a deal—darn you. You got us over a barrel."

"Strip off that saddle," said Ames. "I'll go write up a bill of sale. Hate to see you get hung for a paint horse."

Once back in his office, Ames motioned for his stableboy. "Listen-up, boy. Walk out of this office natural-like and get over to the Sheriff's Office and tell the sheriff the Butler boys are over here, trading off a lame horse."

"The B-Butler brothers!" the thirteen-year-old stammered, eyeballs big as goose eggs.

"The same, boy. Now walk out of here, nice and sweet, and then run like hell."

******

The four of them were in the back booth of Mrs. Purity's restaurant when Jerry Jones entered. Beside Finsen and Ostenhaven were Jack Sprague and Charlie Hurst, who was unknown to Jones.

Ostenhaven took charge of the conversation as Jones limped up to their table. "Don't bother with a chair, Jones—you'll be leaving in just a minute. You remember First Sergeant Sprague, I imagine?"

"How could I forget him?" replied Jones, tired and in pain from his truncated foot. "Old home week, ain't it; and who's this gent?" he pointed with his chin to Hurst.

"No need for you to know, Jones," answered Ostenhaven. "Does that bag contain the items we require?"

"They're in there. I had to put corks on the tips or they'd have cut their way out of the bag. They're mean as hell and sharp as knives. Watch your step with them. Have you got my money?"

"Freddy," said Ostenhaven, "that's your department. Pay the man."

"Here you are, Mr. Jones." Finsen reached across the jumble of half-eaten breakfasts to hand Jones the money.

Jones moved the bag from his crutch handle to the table with care. "Remember me, folks, whenever you need something special; always quick to oblige."

"You always were, Jones," growled Sprague. "Always were."

"Now Sergeant," said Jones, tucking the gold coins in his shirt pocket, "let's leave bygones stay gone. You treated me rough, but I got through the hulks. That's behind us."

"You lived, Jones, because you're a yellow rat and don't . . ."

"Cut it out Jack," Ostenhaven cut in. "Mr. Jones is a valuable member of our team now. He's correct in saying bygones are bygones. None of us are lily-white about our part in the war. Go ahead now, Mr. Jones; we will be in touch with you in the future. And forget what you made, understand?"

"Yessir, I know what side my bread's buttered on." Jones turned his crutches clumsily and clumped out of the restaurant.

Ostenhaven made sure Jones was gone before continuing his discussion. "So—Mr. Hurst, you now have your implements. Now it's up to you. Terrorize the opposition and find Pete's mine. We're counting on you."

Hurst pushed a half-moon of biscuit around his plate, polishing off the last smears of egg yolk before speaking. "It'll be easier to find a few victims than it will that damn mine. But I reckon it's the only way I'll ever get rich. I've got me some help this time, though."

"Help. What kind of help?" Finsen sounded alarmed.

"A muleskinner and camp-tender. A Mexican. The brother of my landlady. He's named Tino—for Augustino. Good man in the desert—'n' with animals."

Pulling at his long jaw, Ostenhaven asked, "Is this wise, Charlie?"

"It will let me cover more ground," explained Hurst, warming up to his subject. "Along with Tino, I'm getting three pack mules, only they're the smaller, Mexican kind, that Tino favors. This way I won't have to spend half my time coming and going for supplies. Tino will handle that. But I'll need a letter of credit to the store down in Spanishtown that Tino wants to use, plus a couple of months advance for Tino and the animals."

"How much are we talking about, Mr. Hurst?" Finsen asked, in his accountant's voice.

"A hundred a month for Tino and the animals and a credit of another couple of hundred. Oh, yeah—I need an advance, too—make it six hundred, total."

"A considerable sum, Charlie," pointed out Ostenhaven.

"Costs money to make money. Part of that is to pay for that survey equipment that I'm going to start packing; make me look more authentic. I'm supposed to be scouting a telegraph route, but lately I've been looking too much like a prospector. If you think you can get somebody . . ."

Charlie Hurst's bitter remarks were stopped by the sound of gunshots coming from the outside.

"That sounds like gunfire," stated Finsen anxiously.

"Yes. Yes it does—indeed," agreed Ostenhaven, making no move to leave the safety of the booth.

"Want me to check it out?" Jack Sprague's hand touched the reassurance of his hideout pistol, under his coat.

"In a moment, perhaps, Jack. Let's not get involved, except as interested spectators. We'll just follow the crowd. Can you manage the bill, Franklin?"

"My pleasure. Much better than sticking my head into a shooting."

******

The stable boy raced out past Sheriff Skinner, who was negotiating the office steps with the greasy paper cornucopia of jelly buns. Skinner shook his head at the impatience of youth and went into the office to find Sam unchaining the arms rack.

"What's that all about, Sam?" asked Skinner, placing the buns in a safe spot.

"A call to arms, mon sheriff," grinned Sam, shoving cartridges into a Winchester. "The Butler brothers are trading a horse off at Ames' place."

"How many, Sam?" Skinner started filling his pockets with shotgun shells.

"There's only two. Their other brother got killed last month in Lordsburg. That makes one for you and one for me."

"You take the alley, Sam, while I shall stroll down the boardwalk. Figure on killing them quick. I hear they're all fine shots."

"Just hope Ames isn't mistaken," replied Sam and dashed out the back way through the attached stable.

The sheriff stuck two shells into the shotgun and walked outside, heading for the livery stable. He kept the short-barreled shotgun behind his right leg as he strode close to the store fronts.

Sam, running down the alley, arrived at the livery stable first. The alley skirted the livery's rectangular corral in a zig-zag detour. He spotted a man tying a bedroll to the saddle of a paint horse. The man, though, saw Sam as he moved out of the shadows of the alley to stand behind a corral post.

Some sixth sense must have alerted the man behind the horse to Sam's intentions and the man dropped the rawhide thongs to snap a shot off over the saddle at Deputy Sam.

Mr. Ames, to his credit, operated a fairly decent livery business; having a good selection of horse flesh and rolling stock, which had set him back a pretty penny. But when it came to fashioning a corral for his business he had decided to skimp. His corral was more like a barnyard fence than that of a real working corral. No wild or half-broke mustangs would need to be mastered and gentled in this corral. No violently careening broncos would slam against its corral boards. In consequence his corral posts were less expensive four-inch cedar posts. He even saved money by alternating four and six-inch horizontal corral boards.

Suddenly, Sam found himself ducking defensively behind this very thrifty stretch of fencing. The man behind the horse first threw a snap shot at Sam that popped through the top corral board, sending wood splinters at Sam's face. Quickly, Deputy Sam turned sideways to the shooter, trying to make himself a lesser target; but he soon realized that he still stuck out several inches on each side of the skinny post. Cautiously, he brought up the Winchester, hoping for a shot at the man behind the paint horse.

Sam's movement caused the gunman to drop to one knee under the horse and thumb off three quick rounds at the deputy. Two of those slugs hit the post dead center, not quite making it through. The third round, though, slashed across Sam's belly, lacerating his stomach, smashing and snapping the belt and buckle to his trousers.

Fortunately for Deputy Sam, the paint horse had become agitated, especially as the last three gunshots had originated near the paint horse's nether region and brought back a forgotten memory of losing his sexual apparatus at the hands of man. The horse bolted, leaving the gunman exposed. He fired one more quick shot at Sam and ran back to the safety and darkness of the livery barn. Sam recovered enough to snap a shot off at the man just as the gunman passed into the shadows.

Twice a week Susane Maurios, better known as Madam Suzy, bordello proprietress and direct competitor to Madam Dora, chose to take the morning airs of Green Falls aboard Pharaoh, Mr. Ames' best riding horse. She was a fine horsewoman, having been companion to (in order of acquaintanceship) a French marquis, a count of Savoy, a wealthy Austrian landowner, a Russian general, and sadly and lastly, a Virginian plantation owner who lost all to the ravages of war, including his very life.

When the shooting started, she had just finished her morning's ride and was walking Pharaoh through the big double doors of Mr. Ames' combination stable and barn. She was surprised, therefore, to confront a mounted man who was yelling loudly to the rear of the barn, while flourishing a large pistol in a most menacing manner. The man's shoutings spooked Pharaoh and Miss Suzy had to use all of her horsemanship to stay in the saddle. Suddenly, another pistol-toting man ran the length of the barn towards the mounted man.

"Dammit, Robert," yelled Beau Butler, "that son of a bitch winged me."

"Climb on, big brother," called Robert, swinging his horse around and holding out an elbow for Beau to swing up behind him.

"To hell with riding double. I'd soon as get stretched for horse stealing as for mail robbing," cried Beau, pulling Madam Suzy off the skittish Pharaoh. He was halfway in the saddle when he found that it was a lady's sidesaddle with only a left stirrup. But brother Robert was tearing out of the barn, his horse throwing clumps of mud from the small swamp alongside Ames' public water trough. Beau Butler had no choice; he clapped spurs to Pharaoh, following behind his brother—out onto Main Street.

The shots from the livery's corral caught the sheriff by surprise, for he was not yet in position by Ames' front entrance. He began running towards the livery stable, his long legs swooping over the uneven board walks of the fronting businesses. Then he saw Robert Butler—bearded as in the wanted poster—careen onto Main Street, wrenching his mount desperately towards Spanishtown and the river's ford to Tucson.

Skinner slowed to a walk and veered into the dusty street, thumbing back the hammers of the shotgun, still behind his leg. Now he was close to the center of the thoroughfare, still seeming to be just another absent-minded citizen, unconcernedly crossing the busy street.

The sheriff was not the only pedestrian crossing Main Street at that time and place. Jerry Jones had taken his pay from Franklin Finsen and clumped in single-minded pursuit of morphia to the pharmacy of Mr. Appleby. There, the good pharmacist sold him a sizeable quantity of laudanum; even being so kind as to stir up a potion of it for Mr. Jones' immediate relief. After this potion, then, Mr. Jones had exited the pharmacy, full of the euphoria of the painkiller and blissfully unaware of surroundings, shootings or escaping desperados. He swung his crutches down the low steps and into the street, smiling at the sun and it's warmth on his thin, hurt body.

Robert Butler did not immediately recognize Sheriff Skinner for the menace that he was, partly due to having to control his excited horse and partly from having to look behind for his lagging brother, Beau. Then, he saw the tall man in the middle of the street peering back at him over the barrels of a sawed-off shotgun. Robert reacted quickly, pulling his horse away from the man with the shotgun, hoping to force the horse up on the board sidewalk—away from him and the shotgun.

Jerry Jones never saw the horse that killed him, in a clatter of snapping crutches and bones. Skinner held his fire until Robert Butler passed at the distance of thirty feet, loosing both barrels at once into horse and rider. Robert was smashed from the saddle and flung, bloodily, against the wall of the billiard parlor. The horse, hit also, was down in a jumble of boxes and barrels, kicking crazily in its pain.

Beau Butler, following seventy-five yards behind his brother, had seen the tall man in the street smash down his brother. In a rage he tried to bring up his pistol, but the bloody right arm would not cooperate. He grabbed the revolver with his other hand, all the while watching the man in the middle of the street coolly reloading the shotgun. Beau got but one shot off before the man fired again and then threw himself away from Pharaoh's slashing hoofs.

Skinner's buckshot shredded the heads of both horse and rider. But although Pharaoh's brain was dead, his body pounded on another one hundred yards before coming upon a parked freight wagon. Here, blinded and dead, the splendid horse piled its handsome body on the unforgiving end-gate of the heavy wagon, along with the corpse of its rider, Beau Butler.

The sheriff had unconsciously advanced on Beau Butler, while reloading; perhaps it was his infantry training which dictated the advance when under fire. For whatever reason though, Skinner found himself lying on and about the remains of Jerry Jones. Although the neck of Mr. Jones was in complete mis-adjustment, his sallow face was still smiling in testament to either the swiftness of his demise or to death's healing efficacy.

"Mr. Jones, I believe," quipped Skinner, giddy from the excitement of the shooting. "No, don't bother getting up. I'm quite capable," he snickered, getting slowly to his feet. "I guess you realize that this ends your participation in Mrs. Ostenhaven's death, don't you?"

Sam ran up to Skinner, lungs pumping from the exertion. "Who . . . who're you talking to—yourself?" he questioned, blowing hard.

"Not to myself—mon Chief Deputy—but to the late Mr. Jones. A former alumni of yours on the Good Ship Hulks. Say goodbye. He's smiling better in death than he ever did in life."

"I won't miss him," Sam replied bitterly. "He was an informer. We all knew it—too late, though."

"I, for one, will miss him, Samuel; most grievously. For he could have unraveled Mrs. Ostenhaven's death. And now I must start over again."

"There you are, you lousy, badge-toting killer!" It was Ames, having come back from viewing the remains of Pharaoh. "That horse was worth over two hundred dollars, you stupid jackass. And you shot it down like it was a mad dog. Who'll pay me for him? He was worth close to three hundred bucks."

"I thought you just said two hundred," observed Sam with a grin.

"Ain't a damn thing funny about this stupid boss of yours killing my best riding horse, Mister Smart-ass Deputy," raged

Ames. Then he took in Sam's state of dishevelment in the trouser department. "What's with your britches, Deputy?"

Sam glanced down at his trousers, hastily cinched-up with his gun belt. "Beau Butler shot my belt off. A little bit lower and I'd be singing soprano in the ladies choir—but I think I winged him."

Ames turned to Skinner. "I need to salvage the sidesaddle off that horse of mine, if its allowed."

"Well, Mr. Ames," answered the sheriff, scratching his head and looking purposefully dense. "I'd say its your horse, but of course, I'm awful stupid. Probably even too stupid to forward your claim for the $500 reward."

"Who said I said that? You must have heard me wrong. Say, I got a bottle of real Tennessee whiskey in my tackroom. Why don't we celebrate with a little drink?"

When the three got back to the livery stable, Madam Suzy was still there, petite, unsmiling and still a little dusty from her rough handling.

"Mr. Ames," she scolded. "I have remained here, waiting, while you were out, God knows where. I stayed to tell you that Pharaoh seems to favor his right foreleg. I think it should be examined—thoroughly."

"The right foreleg, you say?" asked Ames, caught off guard.

"Certainly. The right foreleg, Mr. Ames. Please see to it. I wouldn't want to see Pharaoh come to grief." She turned from the men and left to return to the sensible seclusion of her sporting house.

Ames looked at the two lawmen and shook his head. "And she don't want Pharaoh to come to grief. It's enough to make a grown man cry, ain't it?"

"Just think of that big fat reward, Ames—and cry all you want," counseled Skinner. "Now, where did you say that Tennessee whiskey was?"

CHAPTER 12

T he late afternoon coach of the Sweeney Stage Lines brought Sultan Sanders to Green Falls. He was met by his sponsor, department store owner Gompers. Mr. Gompers was accompanied by his elderly brother-in-law who, with a teenage stock clerk from the store, held up a professionally painted banner that proclaimed "Welcome Sultan Sanders— Our Next Sheriff." Also with the welcoming group was a three-piece band from Spanishtown, bravely trying to play a military march to honor the occasion.

After greeting the newly-arrived candidate, Mr. Gompers put up his hands and called for quiet in which to make a few choice public remarks. Evidently Sweeney thought the quiet did not pertain to a U.S. mail carrier and continued dropping baggage and express to the boardwalk.

Gompers eyed the stage driver angrily—but afraid of losing the crowd, began anyway. "My dear friends and citizens of Green Falls, it gives me distinct pleasure to introduce you to the next Sheriff of Green Falls, Mr. Sultan Sanders. As many of you already know, Mr. Sanders has had a remarkable career as a lawman. He has cleaned the crooks out of St. Joseph and almost a dozen other towns and cities from the blue Pacific Ocean to the wide Missouri. Please give a hand to Mr. Sultan Sanders."

Gompers paused here to clap his hands as his elderly brother-in-law and the young stock clerk raised a feeble cheer. Sweeney took this moment to yell at his team and the coach drew away from the crowd, which suddenly seemed smaller, without that vehicle.

Hoping to strike while the iron was still hot, Gompers plunged on. "A committee of concerned citizens has banded together, urging Mr. Sanders to come out of retirement—to come to our city, which is now suffering from lawlessness, murder and a complete takeover by forces of rage and ruthlessness. He has promised to run out the brawlers and bandits, the whores and the whiskey sellers—and to make Green Falls a decent and God-fearing city once more. Now, without further to-do, I give you—the candidate for change, our next sheriff—Mr. Sultan Sanders!" He waved at the inadequate musicians to produce a crescendo—which they attempted, heroically, with practiced mediocrity.

Sultan Sanders was a tall man who had evidently aged badly, as his thickening body and florid complexion testified, with high living and hard liquor. The first noticeable feature of this purported living legend, was his walleyes, a condition of the eye that produced a grayish cornea, giving him eyes that resembled those in a long-dead fish.

The second remarkable attraction, besides having a huge tobacco-stained walrus mustache, was the daintiness of his girl-like hands, which were long, slender and pale. He wore several rings on each hand, as if to draw attention to his hands. This call to arms, here at Green Falls, he knew to be his last hurrah. His liver was morbidly engorged and diseased, and now a doctor in St. Louis had found a growing mass in his right lung. But he was determined to go out in style and needed this campaign, with its contributions and congratulations.

He decided to play this first act low-key and humble; time later to turn up the screws and sling mud. "Thank you—good folks of Green Falls," he mumbled, feigning embarrassment and political innocence. "I'm proud to be here—helping you to fight corruption and disorder. I just hope we can beat the crooked politicians and officials. They have a lot of big money on their side. The same old story of the rich against the poor. But I'll leave the campaign finances to Mr. Gompers. He's mighty savvy when it comes to that—'n' honest as the day is long. That's all I'll say for now. Put me in office and I'll let my deeds do my talking."

Van Doormann, the newspaperman, pushed his way through the thin crowd. "And what about your six-guns, Mr. Sanders? I hear that in the past, you've had them doing a lot of speaking."

"When you folks get Sultan Sanders, you get the whole package. My integrity, my reputation for the law, and lastly—my pistols. Hopefully, I can keep their lightning holstered. Every man I've had to kill has caused me sorrow. Please believe that."

"That's all, folks," announced Gompers. "Mr. Sanders has been a long time on the road and can use a clean up and some rest. See us tomorrow night outside the Gompers store and he'll answer all your questions."

The bystanders left, Gompers directing his brother-in-law to furl the banner and return it to the department store. The stock boy was told to gather Sultan Sanders' luggage and follow behind.

"I've arranged accommodations for you at one of our better boarding houses, Mrs. Kipp's, and you'll not have to share your bed," Gompers told Sanders. "We'll help you down there with your bags."

"I'm afraid not, Gompers," said Sanders. "I'm not the boarding house type. Bad for my image. I heard the Congress is the best hotel here. Get me their best room."

"The Governor's Suite?" objected Gompers. "That's quite expensive. Way over our budget. We can't manage that—for sure."

"Just a minute, Gompers," rasped Sultan Sanders, grabbing the department store owner by the wrist. (Those delicate hands were surprisingly strong.) "Let's get this straightened out once and for all. I don't know why you sent for me and I frankly don't care. I'm here to be sheriff. But don't figure that I'm some kind of a puppet on a string. I'm my own man and live my own life—the way I'm accustomed to."

Gompers was frightened, both by the hurting squeeze to his wrist and the unfathomable look in Sanders' eyes. "Well—ah—perhaps we could find something a little more in the heart of the city," he blustered.

"You just do that," retorted Sanders grimly. "Right here at the Congress Hotel." He cast aside Gompers' wrist and led the way into the ornate lobby. "And by the way," he stopped Gompers before getting to the registration desk, "I'm going to need some expense money—and don't try to scrimp there, either."

When Gompers left the Congress Hotel, after seeing his candidate settled in a quite expensive room and shelling out a hundred dollars for pocket money, he was beginning to wonder whether his decision to import Sultan Sanders was really such a wise move.

******

The next morning, when the air was still crisp and the sun was just an orange promise below the mauve mountain rim, a small pack train straggled out of Spanishtown and headed up Main Street for the Holiday Trail. The only attention the men and animals received was from a collection of town curs—more vocal than violent at having their territory trespassed at such an early hour.

This suited the bulky man leading the small train of mules along with his new Mexican mule-skinner. He was going out to do murder, a fact that depressed him; and also leaving to try to find a gold mine in the trackless wastelands, an undertaking that had always awed him. No—the less fuss his leaving generated, the better he liked it. He turned around in the saddle to call to his new employee, "Whip up them lazy mules of yours, Tino. We've got a lot of miles to make today."

"Sí, Señor Charlie," the little Mexican smiled, reaching over to smack his quirt on the last small mule in the string, being most careful to hit the tied-down supplies rather than his mule. "Sí, Señor Charlie, now they go more faster."

******

Milton Marks, proprietor of Green Falls' only funeral service, was unhappy, and he let Skinner know about it.

"It's just not fair—the indigent burial rate, I mean. I end up working for wages. Not a bit of profit. The county doesn't take into consideration that I'm a tax-paying businessman. The rate is just too damn low."

"I entirely agree with you, Marks," soothed the sheriff, diplomatically. "If you wish to protest at the next commissioners' meeting I'll back you up. But let's get back to the Butler brothers. All I need is a certified statement from you that you buried the two men on such and such a date. Sounds simple enough for me."

"Oh sure, simple for you. I'm the one who has to sit down and do all the paperwork. And for what? I'll tell you what—fifteen bucks apiece. That's what. It's just not fair. That Ames, he gets rich on these two and I get poorer. It's just not fair."

"Is that it?" asked Skinner, seeing the light. "You're jealous that Ames is getting the reward, aren't you?"

"No, jealousy has nothing to do with it. It's just the terrible difference between what he makes and what I make."

"Maybe next time *you'll* spot someone who's wanted. Anyway, Ames had a fine horse of his killed during the fracas. He doesn't come out scot-free."

"They had saddles and weapons. I should get a cut of those," Marks persevered.

"They went to the County and Ames tells me he's hiring Rose to sue for damages to his horse."

"There. Exactly. What did I tell you? Ames comes out smelling pretty and I'm screwed at the indigent rate."

"It'll cost Ames; lawyers don't come cheap, even in Green Falls. Now to change the subject—what's with Jones?"

"Thankfully, that's another story. Mr. Jones had a little over thirty dollars on him at the time of his death. That and a hundred dollar Mine Association insurance, less fifty percent because it was not work-related. So with eighty dollars, he's sitting pretty."

Skinner looked at the small bunching of bones that was Jones on the mortician's zinc table. "He don't seem very pretty to me."

"Wait until I'm finished. We are having an open casket ceremony, you know. When I'm done he'll look wonderful."

"And how much is this going to cost his widow?" asked Skinner gruffly.

"A perfectly reasonable amount, Sheriff. Don't get on your high horse with me."

"How much is your idea of reasonable?"

"Sixty-five dollars. It would cost seventy-five in New York or Boston."

"This isn't New York or Boston, Marks, and she's destitute."

"Through no fault of mine, Sheriff."

"He's a veteran—don't you have a veteran's discounting?"

"Ten percent—that would save her six-fifty."

The sheriff looked at Marks, his lips pumping under his mustache. "Then see to it, Mr. Marks—now where's the stuff from his pockets?"

"It's over here, waiting for your inspection, money and all." The undertaker took an enamel wash bowl from a shelf and passed it to the sheriff. "Be careful there, Sheriff. Jones had a large packet of laudanum in his pocket which ruptured when he got run over. That's that white powder—all over everything. I didn't know it was morphia yesterday when I went through his pockets and got it all over my hands. It musta' gone through my skin 'cause I was one happy undertaker yesterday afternoon."

"Have you got something I can poke around with?" asked Skinner. "A stick or something?"

"Got my dentist's forceps," said Marks, opening a drawer in his instrument chest. "Don't ask what I use them for."

"I'd rather not know," replied the sheriff, the chemical smell of the room making him testy. He moved the forceps around through the powder, pulling out interesting objects: a small clasp knife; the burst paper packet; a small brass cylinder sealed with a cork that held five sulphur matches; two gold coins, one twenty dollars and one ten dollars, along with another dollar or so in silver; a triangular piece of wrought iron and half a plug of chewing tobacco, now covered with the morphia powder.

"Ain't that like them iron bits that killed Mrs. Ostenhaven?" asked Marks, pointing to the piece of shrapnel laid out with the other objects from Jones' pocket. "Did you give him one for a souvenir, too?"

"It would seem like I did, Mr. Marks," lied Skinner. "Is this all of his possessions?"

"All the stuff in his pockets. 'Course he had that paper under his shirt. Got a bit bloody, though."

"What paper is that, Mr. Marks?"

"Some kind of drawing. Looks like a sketch of a farm or garden tool. A cultivator, you know. But it would never work. Handle's too short—not enough leverage. And I should know—hacked at enough weeds when I was a young lad— and didn't know no better." He took the folded paper down from the shelf which had held the basin and handed it to the sheriff, who glanced quickly at it and shoved it in his frock coat's inside pocket.

"And that's everything, Mr. Marks?"

"Everything—but don't take the money. Mrs. Jones left it for part of my fee."

"Can you wash off the morphia, Mr. Marks? I wouldn't want to get too happy. It didn't seem to help Mr. Jones."

"Here, I'll get a bucket of water and we can drop the stuff in it. Then I'll drain the water out on my wife's rose bush. Think that will bring on the blooms?"

"Time will tell, Mr. Marks," mused Skinner. "Time seems to have its own way of explaining the past. Just give those roses time."

******

The next day was Sunday, a no work day for most of the miners and a good time to bury Jerry Jones. The two mail robbers had been interred the previous afternoon in a bleak service witnessed only by Marks and a local Mexican who dug holes cheaply. Mr. Jones' burial, in contrast, was mourned by a considerable group of Jones' neighborhood, known either as Hog's Hollow or by Pig's Wallow; it's previous tenants being the former Mexican rancho's pig population. Most of the mourners, it must be said, were attending as the social price to the wake's beer barrel, to be broached immediately after Jerry's last rites.

Skinner attended with Deputy Sam, hoping to glean some obscure clue from among the proceedings. Finsen, if he was really a benefactor of Jones, was absent from the mourners. Jack Sprague, Sam's nemesis aboard the hulks, did make an appearance, driving up to the lonely cemetery in a rented gig. He never left the vehicle, staying behind the clump of onlookers as if counting the crowd. He left as Jerry's casket was being lowered into the ground, as if posted to the funeral only to ascertain, absolutely, Jones' demise.

This trip to the shabby cemetery bothered the sheriff. It was only ten months, or perhaps eleven, since he had buried his daughter, Martha, here. The hurt, he was surprised to find, still lingered, though he had tried to consciously dismiss the loss. He could see the child-sized limestone marker from where he now stood, Gen's pathetically small bouquet of silk flowers from her last visit already faded by the harsh nature that struck down his delightful young daughter.

"That's it then," said Deputy Sam, interrupting Skinner's reverie. "Goodbye, Jerry. You were a sneak and an informer—but you were a part of the hulks."

"And probably Mrs. Ostenhaven's killer," added the sheriff. "See if you can catch Mike Birnby and ask him in a roundabout manner if he still has that piece of homemade shrapnel that I gave him. I need to know if Jones had a piece of it he had kept for a souvenir from his own stock, or did Birnby or Otto Floss give him theirs."

"Are you going to ask Floss about it, too?"

"If I can catch him. He's making tracks for the wake. I bet that fellow can really put away the beer, if he's a mind to." The sheriff hurried off to where he had tied his horse.

Sam was sweeping up the sheriff's office when Skinner returned. A smile was on the generally somber sheriff's face and a distinct odor of beer was on his breath.

"It smells like you went to the wake, mon Sheriff," commented Sam.

"I couldn't corral Floss until he got down to Hog Hollow and that keg of beer. And once there, it being my day off, I quaffed a few with Otto—just to get his confidence, of course."

"Oh, most certainly, mon Sheriff. Just to get his confidence. And what did Big Otto tell you about Jerry and the piece of shrapnel?"

"He still has the piece I gave him. Drilled a hole through it, yet. Uses it for a watch fob. Showed it to me, along with a new five buck watch."

"Same with Birnby. Says he's got his in his stud box—up in his room. I believe him."

"There was one more thing with Otto Floss," continued Skinner. "Does that coffee have ten pounds of eggshell in it?" he asked, interrupting himself.

"Eleven," replied Sam, with an evil grin.

"Forget it. Getting back to Big Otto. He said Jerry came over Thursday, late in the afternoon, around five. Asked Otto if he could borrow the forge for a special rush job that evening. Otto told him to go ahead, just make sure he banked the fire properly when he was finished. I asked Floss whether he knew what Jones was making. He said he didn't, except that whatever Jones was doing, it involved a lot of different curves. Jones had chalked half a dozen curves on the brick casing of the forge."

"That drawing of that cultivator or whatever had a lot of curves in it, didn't it?"

"Sure did," agreed the sheriff. "Whatever it was, he made it there in Otto's forge Thursday night and got paid for it Friday morning in time to buy his morphia and walk in front of Robert Butler's horse."

"Now what?" asked Sam.

"Tomorrow I'll ask around—try to backtrack Jones' movements. A man on crutches—shouldn't be too difficult, hopefully."

Mrs. Skinner was not as blasé about the sheriff's beer quaffing as Sam had been.

"I thought you said you were going to a funeral?" she scolded, upon detecting the odor of beer.

"I did go to a funeral—and also the wake. I had to follow up on a clue."

"Where was this clue—swimming around in a keg of beer? And you're all dirty. Give me that coat. You've been sitting in something."

"Quite possible." Skinner knew when to agree.

"And there's a hole under the sleeve. How did you get that?"

"Don't blame me. It was that Beau Butler. I wondered where that shot went."

"Good God!" fumed Gen. "I have married a lunatic. A crazy man who lets people shoot holes in his clothes. Oh Lord, protect me from fools—especially this sad husband of mine." She stood staring up at her kitchen ceiling, as if it helped to get the Deity's ear.

"It isn't like I gave him permission, Genevieve. He just took it in his head to shoot at me. Besides, it's unkind to talk of the dead like that."

"Oh no it's not. If you're ever killed, I'll cuss you and this awful place until I'm blue in the face! Do you hear that—Mr. Insane Man!"

"Please, Genevieve, not so loud. Don't you realize it's my day off? I'm supposed to be relaxing."

CHAPTER 13

To his dismay, the next morning, Sheriff Skinner found that Jerry Jones must have been possessed of ethereal characteristics even in the morning hours prior to his death. Nobody seemed to glimpse a man traveling about Main Street using crutches. No one at any of the early opening saloons or stores or at the billiard parlor or at the tobacconist saw the ghostly Jerry swinging himself along on his clumping crutches.

The sheriff came to his last hope, Mrs. Purity's restaurant, more for coffee and a piece of pie than in any expectation of discovery. He was greeted there by Rosie, the perennially pregnant counter girl.

"Want yur usual, Sheriff? Coffee 'n' apple pie?"

"With a thick slice of cheese on the side, Rosie," answered Skinner. "How long now, Rosie?"

"Not for another ten weeks, but I'm gonna quit before then. What brings you out in the morning—you're generally here in the afternoon?"

"I'm detecting, Rosie, and doing a poor job of it. I'm afraid Deputy Buller will poke fun at my feeble efforts."

"Whatcha detecting, Sheriff—'bout those Butler brothers?"

"No, that's over and done with. Today I'm trying to find somebody who saw a man on crutches, somewhere on Main Street, on Friday morning."

"Friday," said Rosie, trying to think. "Fridays is creamed codfish day. Kitchen always smells with the fish soaking out the salt—that's how I remember. Like Thursday is corned beef and cabbage day 'n' the place smells of cabbage."

"And does the remembered fragrance of codfish bring anything back to mind?" asked Skinner.

"Sorta thin, with only half of a foot, not very sociable?"

"Sounds like my man."

"He came in here, in the morning. The late breakfast crowd was here. He went right to the back. The rear booth. Never sat down, though—didn't order nothing, not even coffee. Can't make money on people like that, you know. Tips is everything to me."

"Yes—did he talk to anyone here?"

"Not that I know of. I don't like to look like I'm eavesdropping, you know. Some people don't like it—hurts the tips. He just stood there and then set that bag of his on the table. That nice Mr. Finsen paid him some money and he left. He could sure move those crutches when he wanted to."

"Mr. Finsen was alone, was he, at the table?" questioned Skinner.

"Oh no. Mr. Ostenhaven was there; he had ham 'n' eggs and only a half-portion of potatoes. And another man I didn't know—big fellow. And that Jack something—mean-looking man—Mr. Ostenhaven's new assistant at the mine."

"And they stayed on—after the man on crutches left?"

"For awhile—not really sure. But they was like everybody else when the shooting started. Didn't know whether to go out and see or stay in here. Finally—they was last—they paid up and went out."

"This other man, the one you had never seen before, what did he look like?"

"Let's see, he was the sausage 'n' eggs man, with grits and biscuits. Even asked for more biscuits. I remember because I forgot the extra biscuits and Mr. Finsen had to remind me about them—such a nice man—they're three cents extra apiece, you know, if you ask for more. And . . . what was you asking again?"

"What the sausage and eggs man looked like."

Oh yeah. Big man, face 'n' hands like the outsides of a well-cooked pork chop. And he's got something to do with horses."

"How do you know that?" Skinner cut a square of cheese and laid it carefully over the apex of his piece of pie, preparatory to cleaving it with his fork.

"His hat. See, he had new clothes, but stayed with his old hat. A lot of men do. Can't bear to give up the old, comfortable hat—even if it looks terrible. Same with boots—sometimes. Men ain't as particular as women."

"And what about the hat?" Skinner said, mouth full of pie and cheese.

"Watered his horse from it, you can tell—eventually ruins the felt. Baggy-looking and stained. Had an old man for a customer once, who had a mule . . . or was it a burro? Anyway the mule kept eating bites right out of his hat brim. He thought it was funny. I thought it was stupid. But he was a good tipper, so I played along. That's what you have to do in this business to get by, you know."

"Do you play along with me, Rosie?" Skinner was smiling from the pie and the news of Jones' acquaintants.

"Want the truth, Mr. Skinner?"

"The whole truth and nothing but the truth and it shall set us free," said the sheriff—full of good feeling and apple pie and in an expansive mood.

"I'm 'fraid of you, Sheriff. Hope I ain't hurt your feelings. You seem real nice and all, but I keep thinking of all the men you killed—here in town, 'n' I don't look at you like most of my other customers. There—did I hurt your feelings? I'm sorry if I did."

"Don't worry about it, Rosie—I'm used to people being wary in my presence," soothed Skinner. "You should have seen what happened with the ladies when I worked in yard goods last year." He chuckled, remembering the fiasco. "They were buying anything, even the wrong material, just to get away from me. Finally, one . . ."

"There you are," called Charles Van Doormann of the Green Falls Gazette. "Cornered you at last. I need a quick quote. Better yet—a biting rebuttal, full of malicious innuendo."

"You interrupted me at the right time, Van. I was about to spill out my soul to Rosie, here. Sit down and have some pie. I particularly recommend the apple."

"Only if there's no raisin or apricot."

"It's apricot today, Mr. Van Doormann," said Rosie, moving over to the screened pie rack.

"What kind of a quote, Van?" asked Skinner. "About the lack of integrity in the newspaper business?"

"That really hurts, Sheriff," replied Van Doormann with a grin. "Especially as I'm here to report your side of Sultan Sanders' attack."

"I don't even know what the back-shooter said. Please enlighten me."

"Very gladly." Van Doormann pulled a loose fold of foolscap from an inside pocket. "Let me quote the famous lawman. To wit: 'Sheriff Skinner seems determined to prove that he is both a policeman and an executioner here in your lovely city. His wanton killing earlier today of the hapless Butler brothers demonstrates to every good voter that Skinner is a mad dog run amuck among the peaceful flock.

"'Never did he identify himself as an officer. Never did he give warning that failure to surrender would bring reprisal. No, my friends, he just murdered those two misguided young men, with the cruelest of all weapons—a sawed-off scatter-gun.

"'This morning two decent, but deluded, boys were viciously gunned down no more than a block from this department store. And do you want to hear the saddest part, ladies and gentlemen? It's that their murderer walks free upon the streets of this wonderful city. Still wearing the Sheriff's badge—which gives him license, he thinks, to murder again in the name of justice.

"'I ask you—the voters—to strike down this killer with a badge. Elect me Sheriff and the true peace of understanding and brotherhood will again descend on this city like the gentle rain from God's heaven. I thank you all and with God's help we will free this blessed city from violence and favoritism. Good night and God bless you all.'

"Isn't that a stirring speech?" exclaimed Van. "I'm printing it all. It will be in one column and your reaction will be next to it, with a headline that'll say 'Sheriff's Race Off To A Start'. Now—vent your venom, only no swear words."

"I'll make it short, Van. Just say that both Mr. Sanders and myself are shootists. Only I'm a front shooter and Sultan Sanders is a back shooter. The voters will have to choose what they want. End of speech."

"That's all? No appeals to God and country; to Mom and apple pie? How about your war record? Heard you were in a lot of battles."

"Sadly, Van, my record was marching off with a hundred and seven young men from Monroe County and bringing back only four of the original company. Does that show my judgment, or my luck? I know what their mothers would tell you. If you print that, people would think I'm either blood-thirsty or converted to pacifism—both taboo to a politician."

"Ah. You admit to being a politician, now," said Van Doormann, seizing on a crumb. "Last year you wouldn't have admitted that."

"I'm no longer Sir Galahad, Van. The fire of innocence has leaked out of all the bullet holes I've managed to collect since coming here. I've become more practical and try to duck a little quicker."

"I heard you didn't do much ducking with the Butler brothers."

"They were different. Do you want to hear something funny—more like strange, I should say?"

"Go ahead, I'm a good listener, particularly when I'm eating."

"Most bad men, outlaws if you will, are poor shots. They need to get close and do a lot of shooting, and if you aren't looking—so much the better for them. Now, with the Butler boys, it was an entirely different matter. They were both crack shots. Probably much better than me. So I needed an edge—an advantage—to get them. Standing up to them, with a shotgun, I spooked them—even made Beau miss me, though not by much."

"You could have ducked into a building and waylaid them as they rode by. That would have been a lot safer."

"That would be what Mr. Sanders would have done, I'm sure. But, like I said, I'm a front shooter. Now I gotta go; it's Sam's day off and I kept Happy over so I could check up on something."

"Looks to me like you were checking out the apple pie," scoffed Van.

"See, that's what I mean about you reporters, always fitting the action to your story," said the sheriff, putting two dimes on the counter and leaving.

Van turned to Rosie, who was wiping up Skinner's place at the counter. "What's he mean by that, Rosie; fitting the actions to my stories?"

"He means, Mr. Van Doormann, that a lot is going on 'n' he don't care for you to know about it."

"Perhaps, Rosie, my sweet, I could get you to fill me in on what you two were talking about so earnestly when I came in."

"Not on your life, Mr. Van Doormann. They just buried three men that the sheriff was interested in. No way that I'll talk out of turn. Not even for tips."

******

Charlie Hurst and his little Mexican muleteer had paused only in Holiday to water their animals and have a shoe reset on Tino's scruffy horse. By two o'clock they were on the trail again, making the Eagle Pass Trail by the failing light of sunset.

Next morning, at break of day, they were going again, following the trail as far as the cutoff to No Place, on the other side of Piss-Pot Mountain. Tino's small Mexican mules were hardy and were able to graze on brush and scrub that would give a bellyache to a goat.

They made Tent-Peg's hidden spring an hour before noon on the third day; unloading the animals, watering and hobbling them for an extended noon browse. Then the two men busied themselves caching any supplies that were excess to Charlie's first expedition. After a quick dinner of bacon and fried bread, Charlie shooed Tino and his mules back to Green Falls, arranging to meet him again, at this spring, in ten days. As a memory aide, the big man burned ten notches on a stick, telling the small muleteer to cut out a burnt notch every morning to count the days.

Once Tino was gone and Charlie was alone with only his horse and Tent-Peg's mule, he loaded the supplies that were not hidden, plus the mandatory water needed for his first five-day sweep, onto the mule. Then he cleaned the camp, obliterating all traces of man or animal, even to burying the dung. When that was finished he fashioned a brush drag, tying it behind the plodding mule to remove the tracks of his party's presence. Then, he was off to find gold or a victim of the steel claw—and he was hoping for both.

******

The unfortunate death of Jerry Jones presented a problem to Franklin Finsen. Jones was Finsen's only ally, even if he was more of a henchman than friend. Hired assassin would better sum up Jerry's role in their relationship, for it was on Finsen's behalf that Jerry made, placed and detonated the bomb intended to kill Finsen's business partner, Theodore Ostenhaven.

Now Finsen would have to find a new ally. The person that immediately came to mind was former Sergeant Jack Sprague. Certainly, Sprague had the mental and physical abilities to murder. Finsen had seen Sprague in the past. In his post as guard captain, he showed enjoyment in his penchant for cruelty. Yes, Sprague would make an excellent ally, if he could be controlled and trusted.

Happily for Franklin Finsen, his plotter's mind always suspected intrigue. Perhaps Ostenhaven had sent for Sprague to eliminate him. It was quite possible. Ostenhaven was no fool; and slick, too. Witness how he left the scandal of the hulks behind, like a snake slithers out of its old skin.

Yes, mused Finsen. I must be careful. Approach Sprague with care—feel him out. The thought aroused Finsen bringing a flush of blood to his pulse. I'd really like to feel out Sprague, he thought. His hard-muscled body should be exciting. No. Not now—maybe later if things work out. Can't jeopardize my course.

But the thought of Sprague's body would not retire to the hidden lair within his brain. Finally, resigned to the inevitable, he dressed and went out into the noisy night of Green Falls to find a boy willing to clear his mind.

******

They had ganged up on the sheriff—all three of them. They had bided their time, attacking him at his most vulnerable point—the supper table. His faithful wife planted the first dagger.

"I hear you're too good and noble to deign to campaign for office. Going to vacate it by default, inertia, or sheer stupidity," she stated, with the sweet acid of sarcasm, learned, no doubt, at her mother's knee.

"Nice rhyme," came back Skinner, playing for time to formulate a rebuttal. "Maybe I could use it in my non-campaign. I deign not to campaign," he recited pompously, trying out the phrase.

"Keep on treating the campaign as a joke, Skinner, and you'll be out on your ear," lectured Hansen, "with that Sanders fellow ruining everything you've accomplished here."

"I deign not to campaign—or roll around in the mud of political controversy," countered the sheriff, trying to sound pious with a mouth full of pot roast.

"See, you're *not* serious about being sheriff!" seethed Esther, the orphaned waif taken in with all hospitality by the sheriff, plunging her blade into her generous host.

"What, pray tell," asked Skinner, "brought this vituperative discussion about? Who has been telling tales about me? Any more of those carrots left?"

"Me too, please, Mrs.," seconded Hansen, holding out his plate to Gen.

"I was visited by Mrs. Mosely, who heard from her husband, who was told by Mr. Van Doormann, that you refuse to campaign." Gen had her chain of communication ready at hand for her husband's denunciation.

"I never did . . . say that. I did say, to Van, that Sanders was a back shooter, while I was not. Besides, I thought you were less than happy with me being sheriff."

"I'd rather you be sheriff than to be a guard sitting on the roof of some gambling house," Gen countered, starting to lose her patience and temper.

"I sat *under* the roof—not on top of the roof, and it was *Caudelet's* place, not some place," corrected the sheriff, mopping up his gravy with the last pieces of his dumpling.

"We have a mortgage to pay. You need a steady salary." Gen fell back on the practical line of defense, one of many prepared before this battle.

"Shouldn't have any trouble selling this place, if we decided to go back to Rochester and the hardware business," said Skinner smugly.

"What!" Hansen yelled. "And leave me here by myself? I'd slip back into disrepute. Become a drunk again." He sounded outraged by such betrayal and desertion.

"Oh no. You're absolutely right, Hansen old friend," assured the sheriff. "I couldn't leave you to fend for yourself. I will engage a campaign director—in fact, I will engage *two* campaign directors; you and Mrs. Skinner. Mr. Barnum would call you two the bottomless stomach and the perpetual motion mouth. I give you leave to endorse me and publicize me. Just don't ask me to make any speeches longer than thirty seconds. And where the money will come from—only heaven knows."

******

If the sheriff's reference to money from heaven was facetious, at least it was correct in regard to the supernatural. Heaven, though, was not to be responsible for a campaign donation. It came, more precisely, from the devil.

It all started the next morning with a hand-delivered note to Skinner's office that said only, "See me—Caudelet." So the sheriff, with admirable promptness, stopped off at Big Jim's 'New Orleans Belle Saloon and Gaming Hall'. Eight months ago, during the disbandment of the Sheriff's Office, Skinner worked for Big Jim Caudelet as a gun guard. Neither man admired the other. Perhaps their similar take-charge personalities grated on each other. But both had come to respect the other's word, if not his chosen path. Of course, Skinner's jailing of Caudelet's outlaw son a year ago did nothing to promote harmony between the two.

Caudelet was where the sheriff figured him to be, arguing with the bookkeeper over the previous night's profits and losses, at a felt-covered, octagonal card table close to the long, vacant bar.

"Got your message, Caudelet," said Skinner, coming up to the paper-strewn table.

"Want an eye-opener?" asked Caudelet, not looking up. "I got a barman somewhere over there."

"Sun isn't over the foremast, or however the saying goes for telling you that it's too early."

"It wasn't—when you was on the sauce," grunted Big Jim.

"That was then. This is now. What's your problem?"

"I'm trying to get my boy, Thad, out of Yuma prison. That fancy Tucson lawyer of mine says it would help if you wrote a letter stating that the sentencing was too severe for the circumstances, he being so young and all."

"How long's he been in, now?" Skinner sat down on a chair he had reversed, to face Big Jim at eye level.

"Almost a year. It's hard for him. He's a free spirit, you know." Caudelet finally looked up from the ledger book, an almost-pleading look on his jowled face.

"Mr. Caudelet," explained the sheriff, trying to sound sympathetic, but not soft. "If I remember correctly, he got ten years for mail robbery of Sweeney's stagecoach, plus ten years for attempted murder and another ten for lying in wait to commit a crime. And if . . ."

"But he wasn't there for the mail. They wanted the payroll, which was express."

"Don't matter, Caudelet, once they jumped that coach—and you know it. And as far as I'm concerned, your boy got a break when the judge let him serve those three sentences concurrently."

"Does that mean you won't write that letter?"

"Afraid not. It's not fair to the justice system, or your boy, either. He should do time. One of his gang was killed, you know, in that robbery attempt."

"Just a poor half-witted fellow."

"Killed—just the same," argued the sheriff.

"I was going to give you a substantial campaign contribution. Could buy a lot of keg beer and posters for $250.00."

"I imagine I could. Answer is still no."

"You always was too honest for your own good. Cut off your nose to spite your face."

"My nature," conceded Skinner. "You're no sweetheart either, Caudelet."

"Bet if that Sultan Sanders was sheriff, he'd sign that letter so fast your head would swim."

"Quite possibly. Maybe time will tell. I might end up gun-guarding for you again. Is that all you wanted?" Skinner arose and turned the chair around.

Caudelet turned to the bookkeeper. "Give me that envelope, will you?" He took an envelope from the man and handed it to Skinner.

"What's this?" asked Skinner, turning the envelope over in his hands.

A gift to your campaign," scowled Big Jim. "I can't afford to let that crook get to be sheriff. I heard how he works. Knocks a percentage off every place or he finds some kind of an excuse to shut you down. I'm not crazy about you, but at least you're honest."

"I'm not sure that's a compliment, Jim."

"I told you before. Don't call me Jim. Only my friends called me that—and they both died. Now, get out of here and use that money to win your election—I'm not so sure I want you back working here."

CHAPTER 14

As far as Stuart Sweeney, of the Sweeney Stage Lines, was concerned it was purely Warner's fault. And Warner, of the fledgling Warner Stage Company, blamed it on government interference. But before their row was settled both parties were forced to be cellmates in Skinner's calaboose.

It all started on Monday night with a deranged housewife murdering her entire household. Altogether, eleven souls were killed in their beds, whereupon the crazy woman turned the shotgun on herself by hooking the trigger on a bedroom door latch. Neighbors later recalled that she had complained of the wind's moaning, but they never took her seriously.

The next day the massacre was discovered by a local clergyman, who had been attacked by Shoshones on the Sublettes Cutoff as a child. He rode furiously to Fort Lowell in Tucson, sounding the alarm about an Indian invasion.

The Army authorities telegraphed back and forth to their headquarters and were finally told to mount a patrol to reconnoiter the site of the massacre and report, if possible, by heliograph. This area was in the foothills of the Santa Catalinas and, hopefully, was visible to Fort Lowell. In the meantime, the Army shut down all travel from Tucson to points north via the Tucson-Green Falls Trail.

This is where the shoe began to pinch; Warner's Wednesday morning run to Green Falls was canceled for that day and for the immediate future. Warner had express and passengers already ticketed and partially loaded when he was notified by an apologetic second lieutenant that travel north of Tucson was temporarily forbidden due to Indian activity which had claimed over two dozen lives. Warner had to swallow his losses and hope the next day would see the restriction lifted.

Stuart Sweeney left that day *from* Green Falls as usual, southbound, unaware of any restriction on northbound travel. Sweeney, being the cantankerous man that he was, would have left even if he was aware of the northbound restriction.

Wednesday, with the last of the sunlight striking the higher reaches of the foothills, the heliograph winked a message from the patrol leader stating the true cause of the murders and that the area contained no—repeat no—hostile Indians. Thus, both Warner and Sweeney, who had come into Tucson at five p.m., were woken the next morning at 12:10 A.M. and 12:25 A.M. respectively, with the news that their companies could resume operations.

Warner's run to Green Falls, via the Green Falls Trail to the Eagle Pass Cutoff and the German settlement at Kolbheim, thence to Green Falls by the Puzzle River Road, took several hours longer than Sweeney's more direct route. Consequently, Warner's schedule called for a seven A.M. departure. Sweeney left at eight-thirty, so there was no clash between the competitors—at least on Thursday.

This then, put both Sweeney and Warner in Green Falls, ready to leave for Tucson Friday morning, and competing for passengers. Warner delayed his normal, earlier departure time, hoping to entice some of Sweeney's passengers with a slashed fare.

Thus the stage was set for confrontation. Sweeney's very nature was querulous. His single-minded endeavor to bring a passenger service to Green Falls was proof of his drive and determination. When he saw Warner's Concord coach and team parked across the street from the Sweeney departure point, with the usurping coach firm's operator hawking cut-rate tickets to Tucson, Sweeney gave a yell of anguish and rushed the competitor, whip at the ready.

Alerted by his driver, Warner grabbed the whip from the seat of his coach and lashed out at the advancing Sweeney. Suddenly, all caution was thrown to the winds as the two angry rivals were out in the middle of Main Street, striking each other without mercy with their long braided whips.

A good reinsman, as the drivers like to refer to themselves, very seldom used his whip to hurt. The whip was to startle, to get a lagging animal's attention. Now the two were using their whips to hurt, raising cruel welts and cuts with every stroke.

In a flash Warner's whip switched its attack from Sweeney's neck and face to his front leg, wrapping around Sweeney's ankle. Warner pulled quickly on the weighted grip of the whip, sending Sweeney to the dust. At once, the tide of battle turned to favor Warner, who sent a rolling wave of slack up his whip to free its tip from Sweeney's boot.

But Sweeney had twisted to grab Warner's whip, temporarily foiling his opponent's advantage. Then Sweeney, still down in the dusty street, lashed out at Warner with a sidearm stroke that drew blood from Warner's cheek and ear, spinning him to his knees.

Suddenly the sheriff was beside Warner, clubbing him down in the dusty filth of the street. Deputy Sam had Sweeney, who had tried to get to his feet, in a headlock, stripping away his whip. Sam dragged his stooped-over prisoner to where Skinner was roughly hoisting Warner to his feet.

"Let me loose, Deputy!" cried Sweeney hoarsely. "You're choking me!"

"Lay your pistol against his head, Sam, if he gives you any trouble." Skinner had Warner by his shirt collar at arms length, squeezing all the fight out of the smaller stage operator.

"It was self-defense, Sheriff," complained Sweeney. "He hit me first—with that whip."

"He was coming at me with a whip in his hand. I was scared," countered Warner.

"Absolutely disgraceful," pronounced Skinner. "You two are going to jail."

"How long? questioned Sweeney. "I got a stage run to make."

"Long enough to contemplate your behavior. Let him up, Sam, and head him for the calaboose."

Young Stuart Sweeney had to take over for his father and did a creditable job, although his grouchy sire would never admit to it.

It would be a fitting end to this episode to report that Sweeney and Warner became friends because of their forced companionship. Sadly, this was not to be, and their rivalry was now nurtured into hate.

******

Charlie Hurst did not tarry at the hidden spring for long after Tino's departure. There was six hours of light left and he was a man to push his luck, especially when it came to making big money.

The luck hit in mid-afternoon, but it was the bad type of fortune. Charlie turned out to be the unfortunate, when his horse unexpectedly shied out of a sidewinder's path. Charlie grabbed too late for the pommel and sailed off the horse onto a not so convenient clump of rocks. The snap of the ulna bone in his left forearm sounded like the breaking of a dried stick being broken up for kindling; a sound he definitely remembered, even as he struggled to suck in air to his hurting lungs.

It took several minutes for Charlie to recover his breath and rise from the inhospitable pile of stones. His horse was gone, but Tent-Peg Pete's mule had stayed and was now giving him a displeased look for interrupting the afternoon's travel towards his supper.

"Which way did that dumb cayuse of mine go?" Charlie asked peevishly, holding onto his numb arm. The mule answered him by moving off in the horse's tracks.

"Whoa, dammit!" yelled the unfortunate one, grabbing hold of a packsaddle lashing with his good arm and allowing the mule to help propel his aching body in a slow pursuit of the wayward horse.

They found the horse a quarter of a mile away, standing undecided whether to run off to freedom or wait until the man with the water came to claim him. Thirst won out and the horse quite sensibly whinnied an artificial apology at Charlie's and the mule's approach.

The horse recovered, Charlie now had to do something about his arm, which was beginning to hurt rather than just be numb. The first order of business was to hobble the animals in case he passed out while doctoring himself. Next, with difficulty, he cut up his tent poles into four eighteen-inch lengths and slashed the small canvas tent's flaps into two-inch strips. Then he took several large belts from his whiskey jug and placed the cut-down poles and canvas strips next to a nearby barrel-sized rock. He tied off his rope on the rock, wrapping it around the roundness until the rope's loop was close to the rock's side.

Now he kneeled down before the rock as if in prayer, and thrust the loop over his left wrist, tightening it by moving back from the rock.

"It's now or never, Charlie my friend," he spat out and leaned back, his strong body pulling the broken bone back into position. "Holy shit, Miss Agnes!" he cried out as the sweat burst out of his body in a torrent of hurt and exertion. But he kept the tension on the arm as he shoved the sharpened stakes through the material of his shirt sleeve. Then, with the tent-pole splints in position, he wrapped the canvas strips around and around the forearm and the wooden splints, binding the reduced fracture in place.

The doctoring finished, Charlie called it a day and made camp as best he could, hoping the next day would turn out better. But the mule wouldn't let him relax until the animals were unloaded and fed their grain and given water. By nightfall, Charlie was wishing he was back in the big wooden bathtub with his landlady.

******

Dr. Francis A. Parkham, the Episcopal Bishop of Tucson, had taken passage with the Warner Stage Company for the trip to Green Falls via the German settlement at Kolbheim in the Puzzle River Valley. The good bishop had in tow a very earnest young man recently delivered up by an Eastern divinity college. This young man was to be the first pastor of the proposed Green Falls Episcopal Church. The thousand dollars of subscription funds to build said edifice lay in a modest bundle at the bottom of the bishop's religious effects bag—now residing on the bishop's bony knees inside the careening Concord coach.

The coach was careening because that is how vehicles acted when they attempted to make any speedy progress on the Eagle Pass Cutoff, which once was the east fork of the Pernicious Creek. An earthquake, several dozen years back, had united the two creeks' flow into the west fork. Whereupon a misguided gentleman from St. Louis thought the dry east fork's straightness on the U.S. geological map would make it a fine toll road. After squandering five thousand dollars of his good wife's inheritance, attempting to smooth the rocky floor of the former watercourse, he gave up the idea as flawed and fled with her remaining money to the South Seas, leaving her to throw herself off the new railroad bridge at St. Louis.

Fortunately for Mr. Warner and the teamsters who use the cutoff now, Mother Nature almost succeeded where mere mortals failed. Erosion of the disintegrating rotten granite of the creek's walls helped to cover most of the stream bed's boulders—most, but not all, as the bishop was finding out.

Two thirds of the way down from Mesa Grande, the cutoff branches out into a half-acre sized glen. Here the teamsters would overnight, turning their tired stock loose to chew on the willow trees that line a spring whose sulphur content makes it easier to look at than to drink. This is Willow Glen Camp Ground, a place normally unpopulated except at night by tired teamsters and their thirsty animals.

It was one o'clock in the afternoon as the Warner stage slowed and stopped at Willow Glen for its second rest stop of the day. The mustachioed Mexican driver had just set the brake and wrapped his reins around the stout brake lever when suddenly two masked men appeared on horses.

The stockier of the two thrust forward a double-barreled shotgun and demanded the express box. As the express box contained only mail and packages for Kolbheim and no money, the driver was only too happy to oblige.

"See to that box, Gus, whilst I turn out the passenger's purses," yelled the big man to his smaller partner. He then leaned over to open the coach's door. In so leaning, his shotgun wavered from the coach.

Noticing this momentary lapse, the bishop quickly opened the small valise on his lap and secured a very large Colts pistol, which he discharged in the outlaw's face. The outlaw's horse, heretofore quite patient, was startled as much as his former owner, and reared up, throwing down the dead outlaw and running off up the trail in a panic.

Fortunately for the second outlaw, he was behind his horse, throwing open the catches on the unlocked express box. This screening of the second robber allowed the bishop only a shot at the man's rump—which he took, hitting the mark.

This smaller outlaw, even though rump-shot, was evidently a fine horseman, for in a flash he was on his horse and around to the rear of the coach, where the bishop could not see to shoot. Seconds later the man was gone—up the trail on the heels of his dead friend's horse.

"Well—that's that," commented the Episcopal Bishop of Tucson, putting the revolver back in the valise. "Perhaps this would be a good time, my boy," he said to the new priest, "to practice your last rites."

"Ah—right now?" asked the young man, making no move to follow the bishop out of the coach.

"Come on, my boy," chuckled the bishop, examining the inert outlaw. "There's a first time for everything, and you've got to catch his soul before it leaves of its own accord." The young priest did as he was told, and wondered what he had let himself get into on his first assignment.

******

Jack Sprague, Ostenhaven's bodyguard, went to the offices of Franklin Finsen a little after noon. The desks and work stands of the bookkeeping office were empty, with the workers absent at their dinner. Finsen never took the noon meal, believing that the abstinence assisted his waistline, even though he ate twice as much at the evening repast. He looked up from his desk as Sprague closed the door noisily.

"I thought you were supposed to stay close to Theodore," reminded Finsen, not sure this was the time or place to approach the bodyguard with a treacherous proposal.

"Not when he goes underground. That's my only fear; the dark and the closeness, I mean. Ever since I was a kid, helping my pa to dig a well."

"What if someone tries to kill him when he's down there?"

"What if someone tries to kill him when he goes to the out-house? I don't sit there with him in there, neither." Sprague started pulling open the clerks' desk drawers, searching for something only his suspicious mind would recognize.

"Are you looking for something in particular? The clerks think of their drawers as private." Finsen objected to intrusions into his area of responsibility.

"All the more reason for them to be gone over. Here's a fellow interested in big-titted Frenchwomen. Did you know that?"

"No, and I don't want to know," said Finsen defensively.

"Probably better than Frenchmen with big dongs," laughed the bodyguard coarsely. Then he gave Finsen a grinning look. "You got any magazines like that, Frankie?"

"Don't be crude, Sprague. I pay your salary, remember."

"Oh, I remember—and I remember them looks you're always shooting me, and them accidental bumps. You got a yen for me, Frankie?"

"Don't call me Frankie. My mother always called me that. The other children always teased me about that—the way she said 'Frank-eee'."

"Is that why you don't chase the ladies—a childhood thing?"

"Who said I don't chase women? You're putting words in my mouth. I'm just discreet. Something probably completely foreign to you—I imagine."

"Right you are, Frankie," chuckled Sprague, slamming an unprofitable drawer; "I'm indiscreet with everybody—both the ladies and certain gents. At least with the ones who can do me some good—Mr. Finsen—if you get my drift." He gave the short man a knowing look.

"Ahem," gulped Finsen, searching for a thought in his swirling mind.

"Yes," answered Sprague, waiting.

"This is not the time or place to discuss your future, Jack," said Finsen, his glistening eyes betraying his excitement.

"Maybe I could come by your room tonight—after I tuck Theodore in bed. What would be a good time?"

"Any . . . no. Make it towards twelve," Finsen croaked out through a dry throat.

******

It took Charlie Hurst two days to make it to No Place. Two unpleasant, uncomfortable days riding a jolting horse across the hot desert, his arm hurting at every bounce. And then there was the agony of unloading the animals and making camp, only to have to repack everything the next morning.

At No Place he turned his animals over to the combination farrier and wrangler, and collapsed onto a spare pallet in the saloon operator's back room. He stayed there, semiconscious with fever, for three days before his resilient body roused itself. The farrier/wrangler had come over to Hurst's damp and stinking bunk twice daily to pour groats gruel mixed with plum jam down his throat through a rusty funnel that was also used to fill the oil lanterns. No one volunteered to change his soiled bedding, figuring he could do it himself—if he pulled through.

Once out of his sickbed, it took Charlie another three days to get his strength back. The farrier put a more comfortable splint on his arm after pronouncing it 'coming along just fine'.

Charlie made it back to Tent-Peg's hidden spring at midafternoon of the ninth day of his departure from it, to find Tino camping there. Tino had faithfully waited for his employer, although he seemed to have lived quite well, as a serious dent had been made in Charlie's supplies, especially the whiskey stock. Tino, when questioned about this conspicuous consumption, just made an elaborate Hispanic shrug, saying he presumed Charlie was dead. He also added that he thought Charlie was quite ungenerous to question his vigil-tending.

The conclusion of that argument over Tino's living standard was that Tino would have to leave the following day to augment the supply cache. Charlie prepared a note to Osten-haven explaining his mishap and his ability to continue his assignment.

One good thing about Tino's presence in camp, Charlie told himself; he would have someone to cook and pack for him—at least for one day.

CHAPTER 15

War Chief Slit-Nose of the White Mountain Apaches was bored with tribal life. He was tired of hearing his two wives constantly bicker over the trivial items of every-day living. He was jaded by their constant attempts to pull him under their blankets to produce more offspring to bolster their hold on him. "It's all my fault," he told himself miserably, "for having wives that are sisters. They had all their childhood to practice their jealousies."

He got to his feet, adjusting his blanket and tucking the battered rifle under his arm. This rising caused wife number one to call out the fact that the household needed meat. "I'm becoming embarrassed to take meat from our neighbors because *you* never bring game for us to share with them."

"I'm not a hunter," he said. "I'm a warrior, remember?"

"How could I forget; you're always bragging about killing the white men and coupling with their women. Sometimes I think you like white women better than Apache women."

"I took your sister in, didn't I—and her, big with child from that fat fool of her first husband."

"Maybe he was fat, but at least he could hunt."

"Wasn't much good at running from a bear, though, was he?" said Slit-Nose, quickly leaving after getting in the last word. He went to the lodge of Yellow Wolf, the new father-in-law of Owl-Who-Kills-At-Night. Both men were sitting on a blanket before the lodge, passing a tobacco pipe back and forth between them.

"Did you sleep well, Yellow Wolf?" inquired Slit-Nose of the older man, an elder of the sub-tribe, and a man to be kept on good terms with.

"For an old man, with bad wind, I slept well—except when this new son of mine makes noises under the blanket with my daughter, of which I'm sure it happened many times during the night. He has . . ."

"Father Yellow Wolf," interrupted Owl-Who-Kills-At-Night, "were you not ever in love with a young woman who took your breath away?"

"Breath away? Ha!" coughed the white-maned elder. "If making babies with young women is what took away my wind—I have been revenged by my lustful eye. I had three wives, if you do not count that Comanche woman who thankfully ran away, although with my best knife and fastest pony. But it was worth it to be rid of her."

"I remember that," said Slit-Nose. "I was a very anxious young brave who wished to ride with you to hunt the Comanche woman. You told everyone, then, that your other wives were glad to be rid of her; and to let her go back to her tribe."

"I'm afraid I lied," continued the older man. "I was just tired of fighting her when I went to her. She had very sharp teeth and would bite me, you know. Right through a buckskin shirt. It was like mating a bear—the pleasure seldom equals the hurt."

"I never mated a bear," laughed Slit-Nose. "Not even a little bear."

"I should have sold the Comanche woman to you," grinned Yellow Wolf. "Then you would have found out for yourself."

"As I recall—I had only one horse, and I had to bite its ear every time before it would let me ride it. And talking about horses," went on Slit-Nose, "that is why I have come to see you."

"You want to trade for one of my horses?" asked the old man. "I have the six my new son gave me for my daughter. They are still quite wild. Of course I have my four older ones who are showing their age. Which would suit you?"

"None, old warrior. I wish to prepare another raid. I need to leave the squabbles of my squaws. I would rather fight the pony soldier any day than listen to their nagging."

"We move to the high ground soon," said the elder. "It would be safer to have your party to escort us on the journey. How many warriors would you take with you on this raid? We still suffer from the braves you lost on your last raid. We would hope you would use more caution on this next raid. We are not as numerous as before the white man's disease hurt our people."

"All the more reason to attack the whites."

"They are very persistent—the whites. It was easier with the Spanish. They were not as greedy for land. They respected the Apache."

"They should," agreed Slit-Nose, "we fought them for ten generations. We made them keep behind their walls. These new Yanquis come as fast as we can kill them."

"Someday, I'm afraid," nodded Yellow Wolf, "they will come in such numbers that they will bury us with their bodies, and our braves will be made into herders and hoers of corn. . . . But until that time we Apaches will fight. I will speak to the council about your raid." He turned to the young warrior sitting with him. "Do you hear, Owl-Who-Kills-At-Night? You must not be lazy under that blanket with my daughter. Plant your seed in her so that we can have many warriors."

"I hear, my father," laughed the young warrior, getting to his feet. "But now I think I shall go look for some meat. All that work under the blanket will use up my energy."

The word "meat" reminded Slit-Nose of his difficulty. "Ah—if you should happen upon a buck, could you share a little of it with my wives? I'm sure they would be grateful, and perhaps it would spare me some of their nagging noises."

******

The Warner stagecoach that numbered good Dr. Parkham, the Episcopal Bishop of Tucson, among its passengers came late to the German settlement of Kolbheim. The delay was due to the necessity of wrapping the dead outlaw in a tattered piece of canvas normally reserved to shelter passengers who had to ride on the coach's top during rainstorms. Once rolled in this poor shroud, the unlucky highwayman was muscled up to the rear boot and wedged between the larger express boxes and bales.

The smiles of the bishop's welcoming delegation soon vanished as they were drafted to help move the now bloody bundle of the outlaw to get at the express. The bishop was made to relate the events of the man's demise, to his obvious embarrassment as a man of the cloth. He always sincerely regretted, afterwards, his quickness to shoot this type of transgressor. But after killing a score of men, in the war and in the peace that supposedly followed, he realized old habits were hard to break; especially so, when accosted by armed aggressors.

The express and mail delivered, along with the bishop and his neophyte pastor, the stagecoach left Kolbheim for Green Falls, two hours away. The bishop and the young priest were allowed only a quick wash up before the welcoming party ushered them into the newly-built church hall for a fellowship banquet. At the sight of the laden tables of foodstuff, the young priest finally lost his look of doom and muttered a grateful thanks to the Almighty for being alive and in good appetite.

******

Sheriff Skinner was making his way back to his house after his before bedtime trip to the privy when Gen met him at the back stoop with an oil lamp in her hand. The lamp threw light on her ashen features.

"What's wrong, Gen? Who was that at the door?"

"A man from the Watering Hole Saloon," she muttered woodenly. "Said that a deputy had been shot there."

"Oh Lord! Who?" anguished Skinner, taking the lamp from her shaking hand.

"Didn't say. He took off to find Doctor Seevers."

"Damn this stinking job! I was afraid of this. Damn it all!" He kicked off his slippers, shoved bare feet into boots and strapped on his pistol. "Don't wait up for me—go on to bed."

"You think I could sleep—after this? It could have been you."

"Well, it wasn't—was it?" he grunted angrily and left her staring after his black-clad form.

The normally crowded saloon was almost empty; only a few very curious customers staying to watch the killing's aftermath. Happy Giles hung glumly on the bar, fortified by a bottle advanced by the sympathetic barman. Big Cletus McCoyne was crumpled messily in the beer-wetted sawdust, a bloody eruption where his battered beaver hat usually sat.

The sheriff's entrance stilled what whispered conversation there was in the saloon. He squatted next to the downed deputy to place his hand on McCoyne's blood-streaked neck. "Throw me a clean bar rag," he finally commanded the watching barman.

The bartender opened his mouth to protest the use of a clean rag, but decided better and reached under the bar to secure an almost-white rag and tossed it to Skinner, who used it to cover the big deputy's face; fussily arranging it to lay square on the bearded face.

Skinner rose and went over to the bar. Happy guiltily pushed the whiskey bottle away and raised a tear-streaked face to the glum sheriff. "He's dead, ain't he?" It was more of a statement than a question.

"Tell me how it happened, Happy," said Skinner, trying to keep his voice even.

"God, it was so quick," mumbled the normally abrasive jailer and night marshal. "He must have had his hand on that derringer in his pocket all the time. Just whipped it out—'Pop, pop' 'n' Cletus was down. Just like that. Cletus never had a chance."

"How did it start? Did you and Cletus just happen in here on patrol?"

"Yeah—just making our rounds. We walk in and Cletus just nods to Roy—he's the bartender—and this fellow walks up and shoots Cletus. He never said a word—just shot. Twice."

"Where did he go—after the shooting?"

"Out the back," put in the listening bartender. "Like a scared jackrabbit."

"What was his name, do you know?" questioned Skinner. "And what's he look like?"

"Knobby Malone—'count of he's real bald," said Roy, the barman. "Little guy. The kind that walks around with a chip on his shoulder. He's a switchman for that locomotive that hauls the spoils up on the pile."

"Was he drunk?" asked Skinner, trying to make sense out of a senseless act.

"Didn't act drunk. Only had one beer here—and a pickle from the free lunch."

"He ever fight, or anything like that, here—before this? Would you say he's a bad ass?"

"He's the kind, like I said, who's looking for trouble. But he couldn't fight his way out of Sunday school, if you know what I mean. One slap and he folds up. Have you ever heard of a glass chin? Knobby's got a glass body—thin glass, at that. One good push and he quits. He's almost harmless."

"Not tonight—I'm afraid," commented Skinner. "Do you know where he lives?"

"Used to live over at Chinaman's Hill, but about a week ago he moved to Mrs. Kipp's. Bragged about it here. Said he's come up in the world."

"That's a break," said Skinner. "Deputy Sam Buller rooms with her." He turned to Giles, who was eyeing the whiskey bottle. "Stay away from that whiskey, Happy. I don't need another downed deputy. You stay here until the doc comes and arrange for Marks to take care of Cletus. After I wake up Sam and arrest this Malone character, I'll notify Cletus' wife and . . ."

Just then Warner, the stage operator, barged into the hushed saloon, his irritating voice loud. "Finally found you. Do you know your office is locked up? How do you expect to serve the public if you lock your office up? It's disgraceful." He finally noticed the body on the floor and paused in his diatribe.

"Somebody killed?" he asked in a slightly softer voice, looking around the barroom for the first time.

"My deputy, Warner. When he and Mr. Giles, here, the night marshal, make their saloon patrol they have to lock the Sheriff's Office. We have too small a staff to leave it manned."

"Oh shit—another killing, here," marveled Warner. "That's what I needed you for. I got a dead outlaw on my stagecoach. I need him removed. Got a run to make tomorrow morning, early."

"Mr. Warner," stated Skinner acidly, with the anger breaking through, "this is a difficult time for me and my deputies. Deputy McCoyne was a good friend and we have to arrest his murderer. I want you to go back to your place of business; sit down in a comfortable chair; put your feet up and wait for me to come around. I might be an hour. I might be four hours—but you just wait there with your outlaw until I get there. Now I want you, sir, to get the hell out of this saloon and let me do my duty—right damn now, sir. Understand?"

"Gottcha, Sheriff," whispered Warner and left the somber saloon in justifiable haste.

******

Franklin Finsen had set the stage with his usual thoroughness. His large, well-appointed hotel room was clean and neat; the three oil lamps, their chimneys shining and wicks trimmed, were turned cozily low. Room service had brought up a chilled bottle of champagne and a silver tray of canapes, with an abundance of the Russian eggs that Sprague favored. The silver-clad cigar box was open on the table by the wine, its ruby-mirrored lid reflecting burgundy rays from the bedside lamps.

At the cautious knock to the door, Finsen slipped into the thick silk robe, buttoned it tightly around his girth, and let Jack Sprague slip into the room.

"Nice place," commented Sprague, appraising the bedchamber. "Four times bigger than my room."

"Noblesse oblige, Mr. Sprague," answered Finsen. "Perhaps you can enjoy the good life—if things work out right between us."

"That's why I'm here," said Sprague non-committally, trying an egg from the silver platter.

"Do you like champagne, Jack?" Finsen was playing the host.

"Only had it once. When the court-martial acquitted me. Was drinking whiskey with it, though. Maybe that's why I was sick."

"This is good champagne, Jack," explained Finsen. "Comes from the limestone hills of France; you sip it slowly and you can imagine the green vineyards and the blue skies where it was made. Just let a small sip roll around in your mouth to get the delicate flavor." Sprague did as requested, with presumed solemnity.

"Not bad, I guess—for wine. I was always more of a shot and a beer man. Liked to get that glow quick, you know."

"That is something you will have to learn, Jack. A gentleman drinks because he enjoys the taste of liquor, not to become intoxicated. A drunken gentleman is a disgrace to himself and society in general."

"Is that what you wanted me here for—a lesson on how to drink? I thought you had other ideas in your sneaky head."

Finsen ignored the insult, considering it a gambit on Sprague's part. He went over to the open cigar humidor and, taking a cigar, used a silver cigar cutter to nip off the smoothed end. Still ignoring Sprague, he lit the cigar and had it burning nicely before he raised his eyes to the younger man.

"Money, Jack. That's why I wanted to talk to you. Money for you and money for me. I want to dissolve my partnership with Theodore. The bomb that killed Mrs. Ostenhaven was my idea. Made and planted by the now deceased Jerry Jones. It almost worked except that Theodore was on the pot when it exploded."

"And I'm to be Jones' replacement in this partnership dissolvement?" questioned Sprague.

"More than that, Jack, I want to take you in as my new partner, although in the beginning you would be what is called a junior partner."

"What does that mean—moneywise? I don't like the term *junior*."

"A thirty percent cut of the profits, as a start," smiled Finsen, blowing a smoke ring towards the ceiling.

"What about this other fellow, Hurst, the prospector?" asked Sprague, startled by Finsen's treachery.

"A man of limited vision, Jack. He's just a tool to find that mine. He'd never be able to exploit its possibilities once it's in operation. That takes resourceful men, men who can think and act quickly. Men like you and I, Jack. Men who will do anything to be rich and powerful. That's why you're here right now, isn't it, Jack? Money."

"How do I know that you won't have someone do me in later? Like Theodore. Maybe I should just stick to guarding Theodore. Maybe I could tell him about you and the bomb that blew up his Mrs.; might be a few bucks in it for Jack Sprague."

"Just a few dollars, Jack," purred Finsen. "Just enough for some cheap whiskey and a few hangovers. Stick with me, Jack, and you'll be rich. Stick with Theodore and you'll just be Sergeant Sprague—at his service."

"Rich, hah!" laughed Sprague, filling his champagne glass. "I always did want to fart in silk—so what's the first order of business, Mr. Senior Partner?"

"Nothing just yet, Jack. I'm biding my time, waiting for the perfect moment to get rid of Theodore without suspicion. For the time being I will give you a modest advance on your earnings-to-be. But I must caution you not to arouse Theodore's suspicions with your increased wealth. Always remember that Theodore has a very suspicious mind."

Sprague grinned again. "And well he should, Mr. Senior Partner—for you're always trying to kill him."

"It's just business, Jack," reassured Finsen with obvious embarrassment. "I really do admire Theodore, as a man— just not as a partner."

CHAPTER 16

S am Buller answered Skinner's guarded knock on the door with the resentment of one who had been sound asleep. "What now?" he asked, pushing errant hair out of his eyes.

"Cletus got killed," the sheriff grunted grimly.

"Oh no. Not Cletus," Sam groaned. "Come inside."

"Your roommate in there?"

"He's on nights—tends boiler at the Donkey Tail. How did it happen?"

"Not sure of all the details. He was on saloon patrol with Happy. They went into the Watering Hole. This fellow just walked up and shot Cletus under the chin. Twice. Real fast. And then took off out the back way."

"And now we got to chase him?"

"Hopefully not too far. He boards here. A man by the name of Knobby Malone."

"That short piece of shit—he killed Cletus?"

"Everybody said he did, including Happy. Do you know which room he lives in?"

"Either eight or nine—not sure—on the third floor. There's four rooms up there—and the wash room. Eight and nine are on the south side, I think. Never have occasion to go up there much. Hotter up there, under the roof, you know." Sam was dressing as he talked.

"Maybe we should find out from Mrs. Kipp," said Skinner. "Hate to burst into the wrong room."

"Yeah, and she'd have a spare key," replied Sam, buckling on his Colts.

Three minutes later the two lawmen were on the top floor with a very frightened Mrs. Kipp who pointed out Malone's room. "He sleeps with old Mr. Farmer, who's quite deaf. Mr. Farmer has the cot on the right as you walk in." She selected a key on a ring of skeleton keys and handed the ring to Sam.

"Thank you, Mrs. Kipp," whispered Skinner. "Why don't you go back down the stairs for a while." They waited until she had receded down the stairs. "Now Sam—try the door."

Sam gently twisted the white porcelain knob and almost got a bullet in his hand for his trouble. The bullet banged a neat hole only inches from the doorknob and the deputy's hand.

"I do believe the suspect is in there," giggled Sam, shocked by the close call.

"This is Sheriff Skinner! Come out with your hands empty and above your head! Right now, Malone!" Skinner and his deputy moved to positions away from and to each side of the door.

"Come on and get me—if you got the guts!" came the cry from inside the room.

"Then we'll shoot you to pieces," shouted Skinner, and he fired three quick shots through Mrs. Kipp's roof. The noise from the big Colts revolver sounded like a cannon compared to Malone's derringer. The narrow hall suddenly stank of black powder.

"Enough! No more! Don't shoot! I'm coming out . . . don't shoot—I give up!"

The door opened slowly and a smallish, balding man slunk into the hall, hands fluttering over his shiny pate. He was terror-stricken and shaking. "Am I hit? Why are you trying to kill me? I didn't do nothing. You got no right—shooting at me."

"Shut up, Malone!" Sam slammed him against the flimsy wall, which reverberated throughout the top floor, and searched him roughly.

Other doors started opening cautiously; and heads peered around the partly-opened doors. "You people go back to bed. I'm the sheriff, making an arrest for murder."

"M-me—m-murder," stuttered Malone. "I ain't n-no murderer. It was my brother. He's the bad one."

"How come you're sleeping with your boots on, Malone?" asked Sam. "And how come you shot through the door?"

"I thought you was robbers. A man's got a right to defend himself, don't he?"

"You weren't defending yourself when you waylaid Cletus McCoyne," stated Skinner angrily. "Bring that little skunk along to jail, Sam. And don't worry about being too gentle."

Suddenly another man, a white-bearded old man in a faded nightshirt, limped out into the hall from Malone's room. "What do you boys want?" yelled the old Mr. Farmer. "I heard you knocking—jes took me a mite to git up. Rheumatiz, you know."

******

Happy Giles came back to the jail as Sam and the sheriff were locking up Knobby Malone. He was affected by having Cletus gunned down right next to him. The sheriff sent him home to recuperate and asked Deputy Sam to take over Happy's shift. It was midnight of a bad night. Still a long time to daylight and hopefully a clear reason for Cletus' killing.

"I have to go over to Warner, that new stage operator, to his barn, Sam," explained Skinner. "He jumped me in the Watering Hole, with Cletus laying there dead, complaining about a dead outlaw he's got on his coach. Then I'm . . ."

"A dead outlaw? How did that happen?"

"Don't know—was too busy with Cletus. I kicked his butt out of there and promised to catch up with his dead outlaw after we got Malone. But before I see Warner, I've got to see Cletus's old lady. And I dread it. I'm not good at telling people their loved ones are dead."

"You're getting a lot of practice lately. Don't it help?"

"The more I do—the worse it gets, but it's part of the job."

"Maybe you could take Mrs. Skinner with you—to console her, like."

"Cletus's woman is a full-blooded Crow. No white woman would do her any good. I just hope she don't start slicing herself up—at least while I'm around."

"Maybe you can get the daughter to help. She's only half Crow."

"Maybe I should have stayed in the hardware business in Rochester. Worst thing I had to do there was sort out mixed-up bolts and nuts."

The scene at the McCoyne house went better than Skinner had thought it would. The comely daughter translated the terrible tidings to the woman of the former mountain man and Army scout. "She says he was in a hundred battles and had a dozen wounds. He was a great warrior. Was the man who killed him a worthy warrior?"

"He was killed by a sneaky coward who walked up to him and pulled a little pistol from his pocket and shot him under his chin," related the sheriff with a mixture of sadness and anger. "A very unworthy man—who was definitely no warrior." The daughter conversed with the stoic mother, who was stiff as a stone statue except for the tears flowing from her black eyes. Finally the daughter turned back to the sheriff.

"She says that is how the greatest warriors are brought down. The biggest, most noble stag is killed by a little, small worm that chews a hole in his great heart. It is the Great Spirit telling us that all his creatures are equal. The eagle flies in the same sky as the little wren and all must someday die."

"What will you do? There will be a little money coming from the County—for his death in line of duty."

"We will take his body to the mountain and give it to my mother's god. Then we will go back to her people. The money will help me find a husband. Some Crows are now farmers, I hear."

"Please tell your mother how terribly sorry I am about your father's death. He was a fine man and a good friend. I'll have the undertaker release his body to you; and I'll see the money is ready for you by noon. Anything else I can do—a small wagon, maybe?"

"Indians have the horse and travois, Mr. Sheriff. But we should have a letter with the cloth strings to explain how we travel. And we will need his guns. It is a long trip and bad people, both Indians and whites, will try to rob us or kill us."

"I'll see to it," promised the sheriff. "I'll meet you at the undertaker's at noon. And once again, I'm very sorry." The daughter could only nod, trying to hold back her tears.

Warner was busy, changing a brake block on the Concord coach when Skinner entered the stage company's barn. "Thought I told you to lay back and put your feet up," commented the sheriff sociably, trying to make amends for his previous rough talk to the stage operator.

"Don't have the time," replied Warner, banging a bolt through the bracket into the hardwood brake shoe. "There's always something that needs immediate attention. You know, I worked less and made more money when I was a carriage maker. He reached for a wrench to tighten the retaining nut. "You come for the body? It's in the tack room. I'd like the piece of canvas back—need it when it rains."

"I'll have Mr. Marks pick him up. Right now I need to know who he is and how come he's dead."

"Well—I wasn't there," said Warner, walking around to the other rear wheel and attacking the worn brake shoe there.

"All I can tell you is what Jose told me, but he saw the whole thing. Hand me that hammer and punch, will ya?"

"Jose is your driver?"

"Yeah, hell of a good man. Great with horses—tough on his wife and kids, though." Warner pounded out the bolt with the brass drift punch, careful not to injure the bolt's threads.

"So what did Jose see, Warner?"

"They was two of them, masked with their bandannas. One big one and one shorter one. They was hiding at the Willow Glen Campground. Came out after Jose stopped the coach for the usual comfort break. Told Jose to throw down the express box."

"Did they point a weapon at your driver?"

"I dunno—must have. Jose wouldn't have thrown it down without they had the drop on him."

"Then what?" Skinner was anxious to get this interview over and go home to bed.

"The little bandit got off his horse and started opening up the box—which didn't have any cash in it. Just mail order stuff for Kolbheim."

"And . . . ?"

"Well, according to Jose, the other fellow rode over to the window of the coach to rob the passengers."

"How did Jose know that?"

"God, he heard the S.O.B. say it."

"Then what?" asked Skinner tiredly.

"When he reached out to open the door, the preacher blew him apart. Horse took off—toppling him off. Dead as a rotten log. Then . . ."

"Wait a minute! What preacher?" the sheriff suddenly was alert.

"Well he's not really a preacher, 'cording to Jose. Some kind of a high muckety-muck of a bishop. Shoots the first one and then plugs the little man in the ass. But the little one gets away by ducking down behind his horse and riding like he was a Comanche."

"This wouldn't be the Episcopal Bishop of Tucson, would it—by any chance?"

"I dunno. Fellow named Dr. Parkham, says the manifest. Tucson to Kolbheim to Green Falls and return."

"That's him," said Skinner. "Where's he now?"

"Laid over in Kolbheim. Be here in two days."

"What's he doing in Kolbheim?"

"How the hell should I know? You're supposed to be the detective around here." Warner gathered up his tools. "Why don't you go out there and ask him, yourself?"

"That's not a bad idea, Warner. I just might do that. Oh, I forgot—did you happen to recognize the dead outlaw?"

"Frankly Sheriff, he's such a mess, if it was my own brother, I'd have trouble recognizing him. Want to look?"

"I guess I ought to. Maybe I can match him to a wanted poster. Deputy Buller might know; he's better on names and faces than I am."

Skinner followed Warner into the crowded tackroom and they rolled the outlaw from his shroud—to no avail. The man's face was unfamiliar, among other things.

After leaving Warner, the sheriff walked the four blocks down Main Street to the undertaking parlor. Marks was in his small stable, unharnessing a horse from his closed van that he used to retrieve his customers. He had just brought the body of Cletus into his embalming room.

"Looks like I'm a tad late, Mr. Marks," greeted Skinner. "I've got another body for you to pick up."

"I heard you went looking for the man who shot the deputy. Kill him—didja?"

"No, he's alive and in jail. This new body is an outlaw that tried to hold up Warner's stagecoach."

"That new stage line? Didn't waste much time waiting to rob that, did they?"

"Everybody thinks this is the land of opportunity, Mr. Marks—even the stage robbers," quipped Skinner without much enthusiasm.

"I was going to fix my horse up—before I started on Mr. McCoyne—the embalming, I mean. I imagine you'll want a first-class funeral, with the walnut- stained coffin and the solid brass handles."

"For Cletus? Afraid not, Marks. Just clean him up. His woman will be here tomorrow noon to bury him, herself. She's taking him up in the mountains somewhere."

"Bury him herself?" asked Marks, peevishly. "Why'd she want to do that?"

"She's a Crow Indian, Marks. She's going to bury him Indian style, up in a tree or on a trestle of some kind," explained Skinner wearily.

"That's crazy. He's white. Should be put in the ground in a good solid casket."

"Well—she's his wife. How she buries him is up to her."

"What about my fee? Ain't I gonna get something? I've been working the last two hours on him—had to hitch up the van and all."

"Would fifteen dollars ease your resentment? I can get that for you. Did Dr. Seevers look at Cletus before you brought him here?"

"Yeah—the doc checked him out; said he was dead. Head wound. And twenty would be more like my fee."

"Come on, Marks, cut the bullshit. I've had a long, lousy day and I don't need you trying to rob the County." The sheriff was tired and getting angry.

"What about that other fellow—the outlaw? What kind of a service can I expect?" Marks was still trying.

"Doc will have to check him out—make sure how he was killed. After he's done, give the man a pauper's burial—your twenty dollar special."

"No coffin? Just dump him in the cold, damp ground. Ain't Christian—hardly."

"If you're so godly, Marks, buy an old blanket out of your fee. And be sure to have Cletus cleaned up and ready for his wife by twelve o'clock tomorrow."

"It's today, now, Skinner—and I still gotta go get that outlaw yet."

"Then I'll leave you to your work, Marks. Good night," rasped the sheriff, leaving for home.

Gen was still up, sitting at the kitchen table in her dressing gown, drinking coffee and reading from her New Testament. When her husband came in she closed the slim book and went to the stove to pour coffee for him.

"So—who was it?" she asked hoarsely, setting the coffee on the table.

"Cletus—never knew what hit him." Skinner's voice was flat, drained of emotion.

"How old was he?" she asked, not wanting to look at her husband for fear of somehow hexing him and having him killed, also, in his duty.

"I dunno, never asked him. Fifty-five or sixty, maybe. Lived a hell of a life. Did everything. Seen everything. His wife said he was in a hundred battles and was wounded a dozen times."

"And that's supposed to be an epitaph." She sounded angry.

"I guess women look at life different from men," he admitted.

"Thank God for that. At least women have the good sense not to glorify battles and death."

"You left out duty."

"Duty to who—a bunch of ruffians in a hot dusty boom-town that will be gone when the silver runs out? Is that why Cletus died? What about his family—his wife and daughter?"

"They're going back to the Crow nation, wherever that is. Going to plant Cletus in a tree in the mountains on the way, burial Indian style."

"That's awful."

"Cletus would have gone along with it. He probably put a lot of Indians up in trees, himself. Sort of poetic justice, I guess."

"Only a very short-sighted man would think so," she said—finally looking at him.

"You mean like a fellow that left a good hardware business in Rochester to become a sheriff in a dusty town in Arizona?" He said this with a wry grin on his tired face.

"Precisely," she replied, putting her cup into the soapstone sink and heading for the bedroom.

******

Doctor Seevers came down the stairs from the second story jail cell, mopping his shiny face with a red calico handkerchief. "Who in God's name," he complained, "built them damn stairs so damn steep? Have to be half mountain goat to navigate the damn things."

"Blame it on Manny Ortiz, Doc," said the sheriff, finishing up a letter to the Tucson sheriff telling him to be on the lookout for a short man with a bullet in his butt.

"That figures," replied the doctor, trying to find a clean cup in the jumble under the wash stand. "Those Mexicans were only introduced to stairs in the last fifty years. Always used ladders, before that." He found an almost-clean cup only to find the coffee pot empty.

"It's just not my day," he groaned, dropping the cup back in with the dirty crockery.

"Tell us about Mr. Knobby Malone," said Sam, looking up from his chore of running a patch down the Winchesters in an attempt to keep the ever-present dust from blocking the bores.

"He sure ain't normal, whatever that is; but he's not crazy, either." The handkerchief came out again, wiping the drops off the doctor's forehead and eyebrows.

"What is he then, Doc?"

"I'd say, with forty-three years of medical experience behind me, that he's a rotten, perverse, son of a bitch. That's medical talk, my boy."

"So you can report to the prosecutor that he's not insane?" asked Skinner.

"Bet my $7.50 fee on it. I'll put it in writing tomorrow morning. Too hot now. I'm leaving this sweatbox and finding me a nice, cool saloon."

"Aren't you going to stay with us?" asked Sam, putting the last rifle back into the rack. "I was going to make a new pot of coffee—good old 'Rebel Yell' coffee."

"Rebel Yell coffee? What's that? Is it when you take a gulp and yell, 'yikes!—Who put all those damn eggshells in this brew?'" The doctor was still cackling at his joke as he limped out of the Sheriff's Office.

"He just doesn't appreciate a real good cup of coffee," dismissed Sam as he took the empty pot from the stove and added coffee grounds and water from the clay water jar.

"He just doesn't appreciate coffee that tastes like eggshells—same as me."

"I don't see you jumping up to make coffee. You always wait me out. A glaring defect in your character—if you ask me."

"I have to conserve my energy, Sam. This job is making me old. Especially as it's my turn to patrol with Happy tonight."

"You could get Mean Ed to spell you once in a while."

"He's off riding shotgun for Sweeney today; they got a bullion shipment," stated Skinner morosely. "We're gonna have to think about replacing Cletus pretty quick. Got any ideas about candidates?"

"Rome Garrit was looking for a law job. Heard he had words with his captain and quit the Texas Rangers. Something about him having two señoritas that was both his wives. Lutheran ladies wrote the capitol about him. But he got a job as railroad detective in Mississippi."

"Where do you hear all this stuff?"

"Saloons. I'm a good listener. *You* go into saloons to drink. *I* go to listen—and nurse a beer. I'd have made a good spy during the war."

"Then I'd probably have had to hang you—instead of just sending you off on a sightseeing tour of the northern United States."

"How about that kid, Stanley Woods? Every time he sees me in town he asks about a job."

"Never asked me," said Skinner. "Why didn't he ask me?"

"Afraid of you, I think. Works for the D.B., with Hugh Foote. Thinks maybe you're still touchy about that water war. Said you were shooting fellows all around him. Said you scared him silly when you came charging out there all alone, popping shells out of that Spencer like a crazy man."

"He's a cowboy?"

"He likes horses—for some crazy reason. Started out working for the mines as a teamster. Didn't like how they treated their animals and quit. Got a job with the D.B. when that Captain Cabot hired all those extra men to run the settlers out. Been there ever since. Sister lives in Green Falls; husband works for a mine. Want me to ask him to come in to see you?"

"What's your impression of him, Sam?"

"Pretty good man—if you ask me. Slow to anger. Got a sense of humor. Good sized and strong. Knows how to ride and shoot. He can . . ."

"Missed me," interrupted Skinner.

"Probably didn't want to shoot old folks," countered Sam.

"We'll give him a try. Tell him a sixty-day appointment at sixty dollars plus five for his horse. He's to supply his own pistol. Shells on us. We'll see how he works out. Don't promise too much, you hear? Sometimes you're too damn generous."

"Like when I put the eggshells in the coffee?"

"Exactly."

Chapter 17

In a long, gruelling meeting, the Tribal Council approved Slit-Nose's request for a new raid. All the elders had known it would be approved, but here was a good forum for expounding on one's philosophies and prejudices. So one by one the great old warriors recounted their adventures and offered their generally unwanted advice. The moon had long set and the early morning sky was overhead when finally Slit-Nose was allowed to accept the council's assignment. That, too, called for a wordy speech.

On the second evening after the great council meeting the members of the raiding party; eighteen braves and would-be braves began, their ritual purification. First, for many hours in the sweat house, body cleansing, and then later by narcotic soul purging under the shaman's ministrations.

The following noon the raiding party left the village, most still giddy from the effects of the night before, although their determination was evident and their ponies fat and rested. Slit-Nose rode at the van with Beaver Tooth, while Owl-Who-Kills-At-Night rode far ahead as the scout. He was sad to leave his new wife, but he was proud to be an Apache warrior, honored by his tribe for his prowess in battle with the hated whites. Already the young braves looked to him as a warrior recognized in songs and stories. He recognized his responsibility to those young braves and vowed never to show weakness or indetermination. Had not his destiny been revealed in the heavens?

******

Charlie Hurst spotted the smoke at twilight, when the sun had dropped far enough behind the purple-hued chain of mountains so that its light was concentrated high above the shadowy convolutions of what passed for land in the high desert. It was just a thin plume of light gray smoke, but it stood out like a barber's pole in the contrast of the twilight.

"Two miles, maybe less," Charlie said to the mule. "Think we should mosey down there and see who's our neighbors?" The mule only twitched its left ear, as it figured Charlie had already made up his mind.

"Cat got your tongue, huh?" chuckled Charlie, hoping that his streak of bad luck was coming to an end.

The smoke was coming from a small canyon whose major attraction was the dead skeleton of a gnarled and spiral-grained pine. Husbanded properly, this fallen tree could fuel a hundred stingy campfires.

Charlie helloed the camp as etiquette and prudence demanded, and was invited to come into camp. "Just come in empty-handed, mister," was the proscription added by the resident campfire builder. The person turned out to be a youngish man, pointing an old but evidently serviceable Enfield.

"This is great," gushed the young man. "I'm dying for company. Haven't seen a soul for two weeks. Are you a prospector, too?"

"Naw, I'm with Western Union," said Charlie. "Trying to find a short way to Phoenix. That's why the tripod and transit."

"Gee. I just always thought the telegraph just took the easy way. I got some tea—coffee gave out a couple of days ago. Would you like some?"

"Sounds good. No, it costs close to five hundred bucks a mile to run the telegraph line. Every mile I save is money in the bank for them. Can't take it over too rough country or the pole wagons couldn't get through. Sort of a compromise, you could say. Are you chasing gold, or silver?"

"Both, I guess," grimaced the young prospector. "Without much luck with either. Did you ever hear of Tent-Peg Pete's big strike? It was supposed to be around here, somewheres. I got a map. Bought it in Tucson from a fellow who was a former partner of this Pete. But I can't seem to be able to orient the map to the terrain."

"Might have been the earthquake couple of years back? Broke up the big ridge, looks like," said Charlie, lying with a straight face.

"Gee—you think so?"

"Wait 'til morning, kid. I'll take you out and set you straight."

"I'd sure appreciate that, mister. My name's Andy. Andy Forrest, with two r's. Say—I gotta little bit of whiskey left. Would you like a drink? Sorta celebrate you setting my map straight."

"Thanks, Andy—but let's wait until I take care of my animals. Then we'll have your whiskey and I'll share my bacon with you."

Charlie had the whiskey. But by that time Andy Forrest was dead; hit quickly from behind with the steel claw. The young man had managed to turn around and stare, wide-eyed, at Charlie. Charlie hacked at his neck, ripping the side of his head and slashing the great blood vessels of the throat.

"I guess you was right, kid," laughed Hurst. "You really was dying for company—or was it from company?"

The next morning Charlie Hurst loaded the dead man on the man's horse and headed back to No Place to show off the rogue lion's latest victim.

******

Mr. Hansen came in for breakfast with a wicked grin on his wizened face that belied trouble for the sheriff.

"Told him yet, Mrs.?" chuckled the boarder, reaching for the coffee pot to fill his cup.

"Not yet, Mr. Hansen," replied Gen. "I knew you would want to be here and see Sylvester sputter."

"Sputtering Sylvester, the Sheriff," said Hansen. "I like the ring of that. Yes sir."

"I take it this has something to do with your going to my opponent's election rally last night," rasped Sheriff Skinner, pushing a small lake of extra gravy over an almost bare biscuit. "No doubt you two have some moronic phrase from Mr. Sanders' slimy mouth that will cause me to lose my temper—thus beginning your day with pleasure. Please, do not keep me in suspense. Shoot me with your deadliest dart."

"How about selling Helen Boorman into white slavery?" announced Hansen, working the pepper grinder over his biscuits and gravy. "How's that for a deadly dart?"

"It's not true," snorted Skinner. "Absolute rubbish. I provided a bed for her, here, in my own house."

"Sanders told the crowd that you used your position as sheriff to force this poor child into a life as a prostitute. 'This tragedy-wracked, sweet young lady, her family cruelly murdered by the savage Apaches, was sold into despicable slavery by the sinister sheriff who promised to protect her.' That's what Mr. Sultan Sanders said about you."

"Did they believe him? The crowd, I mean."

"They sure booed you. 'String him up! Put him in his nice new jail and throw away the key!' That's what the crowd said."

"They know not where they speak. I refuse to sling mud. I will campaign cleanly."

"Are you going to answer his charges?" raged Hansen, his anger causing him to gulp his food even faster than usual.

"At the proper time and place. I will not precipitously plunge into the mire of senseless invective."

"Whatever happened to 'He who hesitates is lost'," brought up Hansen. The argument was lighting a flame in his normally vapid eyes. "This is politics, dammit, not a ladies' social."

"I appreciate your concern—both of you," answered Skinner. "But it is completely out of character for me to get up on a soapbox and trade accusations and insults with Sanders. Perhaps you two think different, but I consider myself a gentleman. Maybe I don't have the money or the fancy clothes or a university education, but the Congress of the United States gave me a commission as an officer and a gentleman and I have tried to live up to that honor. 'Nuff said."

"You *are* a gentleman, Sylvester," Gen reached over to affectionately push straight an out of place lock of hair on her husband's greying head. "And you were before you became an officer."

She turned to Hansen, who looked to her with the expectation of more biscuits and gravy. "Frankly, Mr. Hansen, now that I think about it, I don't want Sylvester cheapening himself by exchanging verbal abuse with Mr. Sanders. As head of his campaign I will see Mr. Van Doormann and have an answer to those charges placed in the Gazette."

"You, my dear, are at liberty to quote me as saying that Mr. Sultan Sanders is a back shooter. That is a true statement." The sheriff allowed himself a smile for the first time that morning.

******

UNITED STATES ARMY SIGNAL CORPS
TELEGRAPHIC MESSAGE

TO: *CG US ARMY* DEPT OF THE WEST
FR: *CO FT APACHE* ARIZ TERR
SUBJ: *HOSTILE INDIAN ACTION REPORT*

RETURNING SALT RIVER PATROL REPORTS ATTEMPTED
AMBUSH FIVE FREIGHT WAGONS BOUND FLORENCE ARIZ
STOP ATTACK OCCURRED APPROX 25 MILES SW OF JUNC-
TION CANYON CREEK AND BLACK RIVER FOUR DAYS AGO
STOP REPORT 2 WHITES KILLED 3 WOUNDED WITH 4 WM
APACHE DOWNED STOP THIRTY HOSTILES BELIEVED HEADED
DUE SOUTH FROM AMBUSH SITE STOP REQUEST INSTRUC-
TIONS STOP

******

UNITED STATES ARMY SIGNAL CORPS
TELEGRAPHIC MESSAGE

TO: *CO FT APACHE ARIZ TERR*
FR: *CG US ARMY DEPT OF THE WEST*
SUBJ: *INTERCEPTION ORDER*

UPON RECEIPT THIS ORDER CO FT APACHE WILL IMMEDI-
ATELY ESTABLISH SCOUTING LINE ACROSS PRESUMED WM
APACHE RETURN ROUTE WITH MINIMUM FORCE STOP CO
ABOVE WILL HAVE ONE TROOP INTERCEPTION FORCE ON
THIRTY MINUTES READY AT FT APACHE STOP CUT THE
BEJESUS OUT OF THEM ON THEIR WAY HOME STOP P.
SHERIDAN CG STOP PERMISSION TO DISBAND ABOVE FORCE
AFTER THREE WEEKS IF NO RESULTS STOP.

******

UNITED STATES ARMY SIGNAL CORPS
TELEGRAPHIC MESSAGE

TO: *CO FT LOWELL TUCSON ARIZ TERR*
FR: *CG US DEPT OF THE WEST*
SUBJ: *HOSTILE INTERCEPTION ORDER*

UPON RECEIPT THIS ORDER CO FT LOWELL WILL WITH ALL
POSSIBLE SPEED MOUNT A REINFORCED CAVALRY TROOP
PATROL IN AREA BOUNDED BY MORMON TRAIL GILA RIVER
LINE 20 MILES EAST OF SAN PEDRO RIVER AND SOUTH
BOUNDARY GREEN FALLS COUNTY STOP REPORTED 30 WM
APACHES ATTACKED WAGON TRAIN 4 DAYS AGO VICINITY 25
MILES SW OF CONFLUENCE CANYON CREEK AND BLACK
RIVER STOP DURATION OF PATROL IS TO BE 3 WEEKS IN
ASSIGNED AREA STOP PERMISSION TO RESUPPLY WITH
CIVILIAN SOURCES IS GIVEN QM VOUCHER DW 533 DASH 71
STOP

******

Second Lieutenant Jersie stomped into the shabby headquarters at Fort Lowell. The Regimental Sergeant Major
raised his balding, lizard-skinned head to glower at the
unnecessary noise to his sanctum. Seeing the red-eyed lieutenant before his desk, he pointed his bullet head towards
the adjutant's open door. His face set in the hard lines of
tiredness, Jersie strode heavily into Major Poole's presence.

"Oh. There you are, finally, Jersie," commented the prissy
Adjutant. "Sorry to have to rouse you from your slumber," he
said almost happily, as if Second Lieutenants should not be
allowed to rest.

"Yessir," replied Jersie, stifling a yawn.

"Razor trouble, lieutenant?" Poole snickered evilly.

"Runner said you wanted me immediately—sir."

"Ah . . . yes. This came in from Department of the West."
He handed the telegraph flimsy to the lieutenant. "It's a reaction to a patrol report from Fort Apache. Rather extreme, I
might add."

The young lieutenant read the message, blinking his over-
taxed eyes several times to focus them. "How does this effect
me sir? Our troop just got in last night from a fifteen day

patrol. We're supposed to be on stand down today, except for a stable call at ten."

"Exigencies of the service, Mr. Jersie. The troop is needed. You read the order from General Sheridan."

"Yessir, but the . . ."

"No buts, lieutenant. Go get Captain Stebbin. He'll have to lead the patrol." Major Poole prided himself on his firmness; no wishy-washy talk from him.

"Sir, Captain Stebbin will be un . . ."

"Enough, Jersie!" Poole practically screamed. "Bring in that whiskey-soaked, bloated captain of yours for my orders—and alert your troop sergeant. Immediately."

"Yes, sir," said Jersie, now stone-faced with rage.

Jersie left the headquarters cursing the stupidity of an organization that placed men such as Poole in positions of authority. He was still fuming when he knocked at Captain Stebbin's quarters door. After several progressively louder thumps, Jersie let himself into the poorly-lit room.

Captain Stebbin lay on his back, the rumpled bedclothes covering only his heavy-set, underwear-clad body. He reminded Jersie of a basking walrus pictured in a childhood book. The storybook walrus held a parasol, though, in its flipper, while Stebbin's fat fingers clutched an empty whiskey bottle.

The room stank. A symphony of stenches. From discarded sweat-grimed clothing, spilled whiskey, dead cigars, and the worse smell of all, his raw and rotten toes and feet. The scum, pus and serum from his fungus-ruined feet had drained onto the captain's bedclothes, staining them with a disgusting yellowish puddle of gore.

"Sir! Captain Stebbin, sir! Wake up!" Jersie pushed at the captain's inert form. "You're wanted at headquarters, sir. A patrol."

"Go away—and don't come back another damned day." Stebbin's eyes were still closed.

"Can you walk, sir?" Jersie pleaded. "Just a little bit? To see Major Poole, sir? Please."

"Hell no, I can't walk, you shavetail S.O.B. I had to cut my damn boots—to get them off my stinking feet. Ten-dollar boots, too—in St. Louis. That's what happens if you don't take your boots off for twelve days, m'lad. Remember that. Hear? Pour some whiskey on them toes, will ya?"

"The bottle is empty, sir. Why didn't you take them off every night, sir?"

"Wouldn't you like to know? I'll tell you, mister. The third night out, I tried. They wouldn't come. Feet all swollen up. If I ever got them off I'd never get them back on. And what kind of a cavalry man would I be with just my stocking feet in the stirrups?"

"The Indians don't wear boots, sir."

"And they don't have stirrups, either. That's why they can't fight worth a damn from the back of their ponies—got no purchase, you see. Takes stirrups to get your weight behind a blow."

"Sir, what are we going to do? Major Poole wants to see you. He got a patrol order from General Sheridan, himself."

"Tell you what, Jersie, my boy," said Stebbin, swinging his pitiful feet to the side of the bed and sitting up. "Go get Sergeant White and bring him here, and I'll show you how Emperor Darius the Great fought his battles."

Thirty minutes later the sergeant major and Major Poole were both surprised to see Lieutenant Jersie and Sergeant White carry in a heavy oak armchair which held the even heavier Captain Stebbin. For the occasion, the overweight captain had consented to be dressed in his uniform blouse (the spare clean one, it should be noted). The chair-borne warrior balked at breeches, though; and his now sixteen-day-old long underwear had to suffice as knightly hose.

"Good God!" exclaimed Major Poole, who hardly ever used invective on duty. "What is this all about?" The reptilian-faced Sergeant Major stood gap-jawed, staring at such blasphemy in his holy place.

"You sent for me, did you not?" stated Stebbin with poor grace and absolutely no military etiquette. "I am here." He managed a salute which caused the lieutenant to duck and lose his grip on the chair's arm. The sedan chair of Darius the Great banged down heavily on the plank floor of Poole's office.

"As you can no doubt see, and most certainly smell, my dear major," continued Stebbin, "I am hors de combat—a victim of my cursed boots and circulatory ills."

"You'll have to see the surgeon. Do you think you could ride by tomorrow?" The major showed tender concern—for mounting the ordered patrol.

"Most certainly. I can ride a wagon—or preferably an ambulance with its better springing."

"No, I meant a horse. I need a troop commander for an interception patrol." Poole was worried.

"Give me a chariot and I shall lead as Caesar led his legions—and don't forget a good chariot driver." Stebbin was grinning at Poole's predicament.

"Oh, my God," murmured Major Poole.

"What was that, sir?" asked Jersie tiredly.

"Nothing," said Poole. He drew himself erect, his uniform tailored perfectly to his thin body. His face suddenly shone with a glow of inner strength and determination.

"I shall lead the patrol," announced Poole, visualizing himself as Charlemagne taking up the sword to fight the Moors—or was it the Goths?

"You?" answered the surprised trio of Sergeant White, Jersie and Stebbin, aghast at the idea.

"Certainly, me. Just because I, personally, have been too busy as an administrator to get out in the field much, I am certainly capable. I was at Bull Run, you know. Lieutenant Jersie, you and Sergeant White take Captain Stebbin to the surgeon and then prepare your troop."

"But, Major . . ." interrupted Sergeant White.

"We march tomorrow, Sergeant," ordered Poole, cutting off objections. "First light tomorrow—we march to death or glory." The Sergeant Major saw a strange light in Poole's normally placid eyes, and fled to the security of his desk.

******

"Are you ready, Mr. Van Doormann?" asked Genevieve Skinner. "I don't want you to miss a word of this."

"Oh—I'm ready, Mrs. Skinner."

"This is going to be a paid advertisement. I don't want you rewording and editing it like you do, just to fit it in somewhere, Mr. Van Doormann."

"I guarantee it will be complete, even to any grammatical mistakes, Mrs. Skinner."

"I will not make grammatical mistakes. Now take this down.

"My name is Mrs. Genevieve Skinner. I am the wife of your sheriff, Sylvester Skinner. I am also his campaign manager because I work for nothing and know more about him than anybody else.

"I know he is very honest as we have to live on his salary, which is less than most mine mechanics bring home. Twice my husband had to clean up this town to make it safe for honest people. The first time was when he was first appointed. Then it was the Miner Court Bailiffs who saw their positions as a way to coerce tribute from the merchants and saloon owners.

"The second time he had to run off the riffraff was when the crooked Federal officials dissolved the Sheriff's Office and put the court constables in charge of the law. Again, kickbacks and extortion flourished. Finally, when they murdered the mine police chief, President Johnson sent my husband back to Green Falls as a special temporary Federal Marshal to make Green Falls safe once more.

"Now Mr. Gompers, who owns the department store, is angry at my husband, and has brought in a so-called famous lawman to run against him in this campaign. I asked my husband 'Why is Mr. Sultan Sanders famous?' He told me that when Mr. Sanders is the marshal or the sheriff he becomes a tyrant—those who do not cooperate with him politically and financially end up dead—shot in the back by Mr. Sanders . . ."

"Whoa—wait a minute," interrupted Van Doormann, "I can't print that. That's libel. He could sue me to pieces."

"Not you, Mr. Van Doormann—me," stated Gen smugly. "Remember, this is a paid advertisement. I am responsible for the content. You have only accepted my notice on good faith, just as you would for a notice of a horse for sale. You would not question the advertiser whether or not the animal was blind or had the heaves."

"Maybe he could say that I'm your agent; get me that way," said the publisher, thinking up excuses.

"There is no third party, Mr. Van Doormann. I am not in a business relationship with your readers, nor do you represent me to them. Only you and I have a contractual relationship. I promise to pay you for printing my notice. You promise to print it in your next edition. I alone am responsible to Mr. Sanders. Now here's the honest truth about Mr. Sanders' allegations about my husband and Miss Boorman. Are you ready?"

"Wait a minute. How come you know about the law and all that agency stuff?"

"Mr. Van Doormann, Sylvester and I were partners in his ironmongery business in Rochester, New York. I insisted upon this, for it was my money that provided the firm. Well, I should say it was my aunt's legacy to me. So, as a full partner, I was able to represent the business, myself, in court on suits to recover debts, etc. Now can we continue?"

"Yes, ma'am; and let the chips fall where they may. I don't want any contractual troubles with you, for sure."

"Very good, Mr. Van Doormann. Now to continue . . ."

CHAPTER 18

C harlie Hurst spent two days in No Place. Two days and whiskey-blurred nights, telling and retelling of his finding of the lion's kill. Charlie was a natural at pot-stirring to milk confusion and trouble from the situation. Those nights he would sit, half-drunk and all smiles, to drop choice morsels of discouragement and despair into talk about the lion. Soon the lion was inflated to a huge, ghostly spirit, stalking the puny desert dwellers in retribution for killings of his or her: 1. mate; 2. offspring; or 3. parents.

No Place, without regular delivery of newspapers, was always lacking in argumentative inspiration. The killer lion was just what the local debaters needed—a new topic, and a target at that. No one who had seen the young victim's bloody body could dismiss the lion as fakery or rumor. It was real and could be outside in the dark right now, thought the No Placesonians. "Something's making the horses nervous. Maybe *you* ought to take a look. Take a gun with you." And Charlie fueled the fires of fear—with a straight face at all times when being watched.

On the third morning Charlie left No Place, with food and water aplenty, animals reshod and with a clean shirt on his back. He felt the sirens' sweet call to find another victim for the notorious lion. Charlie was enjoying himself—and the tumult he caused.

******

Love had come to the House of Countless Loves, Dora's Sporting House. The house of assignation had suddenly become a place of amorousness to Henry Stultz. Henry had fallen head-over-heels in love with Dora's new acquisition to her staff, the laughing, lithesome Helen Boorman.

Fortunately for this course of true love, Henry was a very rich man, the sole owner of a middling-sized mine sited smack astride the richest part of the silver-bearing reef. Henry had bought out his two partners when the three had dug to forty feet with results that paid less than wages. Then, working alone, except for an old Mexican to work the bucket's windlass, Henry dug deeper. At sixty feet he hit pay dirt and never had to muck out a shaft again. Now, he had ninety-seven men working Henry's Hope. He lived in the Congress Hotel and had sizable sums in three different banks and brokerage houses.

But for all his money, Henry Stultz still remained a Hoosier farmer. He dressed frugally, drank on occasion only and wagered never. Some thought Henry a plodder, albeit a wealthy plodder, who stolidly tramped down life's path, dumb to the beauty and the flowers lining the route. In two words you could sum up Henry's life; dull and dollars. Which was just fine with Henry—for he had his mine and his bank accounts. If he was dull and drab—so be it.

That all changed the afternoon he saw the shining, copper-colored head of Helen Boorman. Henry, as they say in the ladies' romantic novels, was smitten, good and truly. He had stopped, staring at the winsome Helen who, with a sister from Dora's establishment, had exited from Gompers' store with a string bag of purchases.

Helen and her friend turned the corner and Henry felt panic at the thought he had lost his ideal. He chased after the two, politeness to pedestrians forgotten in the haste of the heart. At the corner he saw their withdrawing figures, laughing and talking as they walked the dusty side street. He made to follow then, taking a step in their direction, but stopped when he noticed several of the dislodged foot-travelers staring at him, speculating on his antics.

Henry turned about, tipped his hat in societal acknowledgement, smiled an apology to the disturbed and beat a hasty retreat to the store from which the two ladies had come.

"Pardon me," Henry said to the first clerk he came upon, a dour-faced matron dressed in an old-fashioned black, bustled frock.

"Yes? May I help you?" answered the woman, with little grace.

"Those two young ladies—who uh, just left here—would you happen to know who they are?" Henry was talking too fast—blurting out words in hectic confusion.

"My Lord, no!" She looked at Henry with distaste. "I certainly do not know them—but I know *what* they are."

"They are?" Henry did not understand her statement.

"Some refer to them as fallen angels. I think of them in biblical terms—whores."

"They're . . . ah . . . that?"

"Definitely. They ply their so-called profession at Dora's house of ill repute. Couldn't you tell? No honest woman can dress like that—so expensively, you know. They probably make more in two nights than I make all month." She paused to do the multiplication in her head. "And I have to stand on my feet ten hours a day."

"You said Dora's?"

"It's on First Street, back of the Chinese place. Across the alley, I mean. I thought every male over fourteen knew where Dora's and Suzy's sporting houses were." She gave him a searching look, as if probing his masculinity.

"I guess I've been busy with other things," Henry admitted, unsure whether this was the correct explanation. "I have a mine, you know. Keeps me on the jump," he added, trying to bolster his image.

"Then you can afford to chase after them . . ." she hunted for a name . . . "vixens. My late husband would sneak out on me to try out them women—and me working to put bread on the table. Good Lord knew what He was doing when he struck down that deceitful man."

"Oh, I'm very sorry." Henry did not know what else to say to this bitter woman.

"I'm not, except if the winter is too chilly. Even then, a warm brick from the oven is better and easier than putting up with a worthless man."

"First Street, you say?"

"Can't miss it. Big, expensive place, painted gray. But you best take a box of bonbons with you; helps to get their attention."

"Well if you think . . ."

"They're in confectioneries, two aisles over. Let me call Mrs. Sherwood. She's up on her tarts."

Upon the advice of the saleslady, Henry selected several elaborately expensive boxes of sweets. Then he walked slowly back to his hotel room, rehearsing, over and over, what he would say at Dora's.

At eight o'clock, Henry presented himself at the large gray house on First Street. He was wearing his best suit, the black mohair with the pin stripe and the vest with the silver silk piping. A new silk hat sat on his head at a slightly rakish angle to compliment his solid silver-headed walking stick. Henry had tried to look elegant and had succeeded.

A very large Negro man greeted him at the door. "Good ev'nens, suh. I is Horatio, the houseman. Youal a littles early for the ladies. Would youal likes to waits in the bar?" His huge hand reached out for the topper and the stick; Henry held on to the bonbons.

"I would like to see the proprietress," stated Henry, reciting from his planned address.

"Please, suh, waits right here." The houseman gestured to a pair of brocaded chairs that flanked a marble-topped credenza and disappeared down the hall with the hat and walking stick.

A few minutes later, Henry was ushered into a velvet-walled salon, where a graying, but attractive, lady rose from a gilded writing table to welcome him.

"Good evening," said the woman. As she smiled the age lines around her mouth disappeared, making her face softer. "You wanted to see me? I'm Dora, the prioress of this place."

"Ahem." Henry had to dredge up some moisture for his suddenly-dry throat. "This afternoon I had the good fortune to see a very attractive lady with beautiful copper-colored hair. I was able, upon inquiry, to find out that she is a resident of your . . . er . . . ah . . . house. I wish to make this young lady's acquaintance. Frankly, madam—oh, sorry, I mean Miss Dora—I am quite smitten with this lady."

"You and a hundred other men of our fair city, Mr. . . . ah . . . ?"

"Stultz. Henry Stultz."

"Of the Henry's Hope mine?"

"Yes. I was lucky," said Henry modestly. "I'm hoping my luck is now turning in the direction of love. Can I see her? Talk to her? I know what happens here—and it doesn't matter, really."

"Love conquers all. Is that it, Mr. Stultz?"

"Hopefully, yes. Could you tell me her name?"

"Her name is Helen Boorman. She is eight . . ."

"Not the girl in the paper? The one who was captured by the Indians?"

"That's her, a very game young lady. Still interested—or has cupid's arrow suddenly fallen out of your heart?"

"Oh no. That experience just shows her character. When can I see her—tonight?"

"She's not scheduled for tonight. Indisposed, you could say. But, I imagine if you'd be content with just talking, she might be available. I'll have to ask her. Why don't you stay here while I find out if she's up to chitchat? I'll have Horatio bring you in a drink. What'll it be—rye?"

"Oh no. Wouldn't want whiskey on my breath. Could I have tea, instead? With lemon, if you got any, please."

"One teapot coming up," confirmed Dora, leaving the room and making sure to close her door on a million-dollar catch.

******

Sheriff Skinner was waiting for the Warner stage as it came jangling and squeaking to a stop. The sweating six-horse team was tired and numb to the hustle and bustle of the busy street. The sheriff helped the two female passengers to exit the coach and then greeted the bishop as he came down.

"Why Sheriff, how kind of you to meet us," replied Bishop Parkham. "I'd like to introduce you to Reverend Thorpe. He is to be the pastor here in Green Falls."

"Glad to meet you, Pastor." Skinner was surprised at the firmness of the young priest's handshake. "You've got your work cut out for you here. Green Falls is still pretty rough on the outside."

"And on the inside, also," added the bishop. "But something tells me that you're not on a courtesy call, Sheriff. Does the welcoming have anything to do with my dispatching of the highwayman?"

"Good guess, Your Excellency. I need to get a statement from you . . . and one from your new pastor, here. He's a witness—is he not?"

"Afraid I was, Sheriff. But I was scared silly. Paralyzed with fear is the expression, I think. Divinity school doesn't prepare one for repelling robbers."

"I was telling the young vicar," observed the bishop, "that sometimes a minister out here needs a cross in one hand and a Colts in the other. In fact, I'm sorry to say that I keep the pistol at the top of my ministerial case, above the altar cross."

"I'd say," chuckled Skinner, "that would be called rendering unto Col. Colt what is due him; but that's not helping me to clear up this shooting. Frankly, Bishop Parkham, I'm wondering if you've got an itchy trigger finger. People seem to be always getting shot in your vicinity. Right now, I'm asking myself, is this coincidence or are you one of those fellows that seems to be always in the eye of the whirlwind? Which is it, Your Excellency?"

"Have you ever heard the saying that the Lord works in mysterious ways His wonders to achieve?" asked the bishop, his gray eyes staring down this backwater sheriff.

"And you are God's instrument. That's how you account for your adventures?"

"Aren't we all?" countered the bishop. "Aren't you in the eye of the maelstrom, here—Sheriff, though you be?"

"My job is to chase those whirlwinds and to pacify them," said Skinner evenly. "That's what I'm paid for."

"And you do your duty, I'm sure, and enjoy it, I'm equally certain. I recognize you as one who wears the robe of authority, and wears it comfortably. I know—for I wear the garments of God's kingdom, myself."

"Where does your revolver come in, Bishop? What happened to turning the other cheek?"

"Alas, Sheriff, you have found me out; I suffer from a weakness of the faith and flesh. I believe a live cleric is more useful to the church than a dead martyr, especially here in the West, and also if it's I who keeps on being the live cleric."

"Well thank you, Bishop. It is refreshing to hear a preacher admit to being human," commented Skinner. "I'll let you go now. I know you're anxious to wash up. Just make sure you drop those statements off at my office in a day or two; and Pastor, it was good making your acquaintance." Skinner left the two clerics, walking to where his horse was tied.

"I always pictured Western lawmen as being rough and tough," observed Pastor Thorpe. "This sheriff seems to be almost gentlemanly and soft spoken. Is he an anomaly or am I missing something?"

"From what I've heard," answered the bishop, "your gentlemanly sheriff gunned down half a dozen of the gang of bully boys that formerly held this town as their own fief. That was a year or so ago. Since then he's doubled or tripled that. They say, once he's in a fight, he's the original definition of berserk."

"And he was chiding you for killing that robber?"

"Well, that and another small incident when I had to dispatch a cook in a restaurant here. It was ruled justifiable homicide, though."

"Kill a cook! Here—and you an Episcopal bishop?" The young cleric was stunned.

"He broke my tooth—the cook, that is—or was. A threat to any diner. But I admit now, upon retrospection, I probably was somewhat precipitous. Wouldn't do it today, probably."

"My bishop shoots people," thought young Pastor Thorpe. "Dear God, what have you led me into? Please see that I never get him angry at me."

******

Trooper Daniels slowed his loping mount and turned it alongside the head of the cavalry column. "The spring's still running, Sergeant. Ain't no river, but it'll be good enough for us."

"That's the best news I've had all day," rasped Sergeant White. "How about asking Corporal Sanchez to take a set of fours and go back there with you and run a little scout around it. I feel better bedding down in a place where I know the neighbors are friendly." The young trooper nodded his understanding and pulled up his horse to let Corporal Sanchez come up in the plodding column.

"There you go again, Sergeant White," scolded Major Poole, "making command decisions. Don't you understand that I'm the commander of this column; not you or Lieutenant Jersie—me."

"Sorry, Major," replied Sergeant White flatly. "I figured this was just a little housekeeping chore. Didn't know that you wanted to go with Sanchez."

"I didn't want to go with Corporal Sanchez. I just want to issue the orders. That is why I am wasting my time having to command this ragtag bunch of misfits. It takes a seasoned officer to lead a patrol like this." As he said this, Corporal Sanchez and Trooper Daniels galloped off from the column followed by the four other troopers who made up the scouting patrol.

A moment later, Lieutenant Jersie spurred forward to inquire about the mission of Corporal Sanchez. Major Poole had the young lieutenant riding at the rear of the column to keep an eye on the superannuated private who led the pack animals, one of which carried Major Poole's commodious wall tent and tent furniture.

"Where is Sanchez off to, sir?" inquired the bored lieutenant. "Is it a patrol? I could have led it, you know."

"Lieutenant Jersie, you are absent from your post at the trail of the column!" fumed the major. "If and when I need your advice on a simple housekeeping matter, I will summon you. Until that time, Lieutenant, I wish you to follow my orders. I want you back there making sure that fool Simmons doesn't lose my tent and supplies."

"They're all right, sir. I make Private Gillies check the ropes every time we stop, sir."

"You just keep doing that, Lieutenant, and leave the commanding to me. Now—take your post, *sir*."

Lieutenant Jersie slapped his campaign hat with a gauntleted hand in a rough salute, loosing a small cloud of dust, and kicked his horse out of the column and back to the dusty tail end of the troop.

"They don't turn out officers at West Point like they used to," commented the major to Sergeant White.

"Don't make nothing the way they used to, sir," grumbled Sergeant White. "Especially majors," he thought to himself, "who go off in the damned desert with more baggage than the Queen of Sheba would take along."

It was the troop's fourth day on patrol, and they had made only three normal days' travel. This was due to the abbreviated marching day by Major Poole's direction. A late start and an early camp at night, along with a too-long midday halt, all added up to lost miles.

"A flying column?" sneered Sergeant White, inwardly. "More like the damn infantry, taking forever to get somewhere too late. Oh, well—at least we'll never catch up with any hostiles this trip."

******

When Skinner sat down to his dinner, his eye was caught by the letter laid out above his plate. "What's this?" he asked Gen. "Not another epistle from your jug-eared brother, bragging about how much money he's making lately. That fellow never lets go."

"He just wants what's best for me, Sylvester. And no, it's not from my rich brother—it's from some attorney's firm in Cincinnati, Ohio. It's about Esther. They were contacted by that lawyer in Tucson that you asked to try to trace Esther's relatives."

"Did they come up with something?"

"An uncle in Cincinnati that owns a brewery. Quite an affluent gentleman, according to the letter. They're sending a draft to pay for Esther's trip to Cincinnati. The lawyer in Tucson has found a woman in Tucson who would like to visit her mother in Columbus and will escort Esther to Cincinnati for her own expenses."

"And when will Esther be leaving? Have you told her yet?" asked the sheriff, ladling more of the cream gravy over the uneaten portions of his pork chops and homemade noodles.

"I will, when she comes home from school," said Gen, pouring herself coffee. "She's adventurous. She will like the idea of the trip. I've a hunch she will be glad to leave us. Too much discipline with us. Her father spoiled her, I'm afraid."

"She's a bright little girl. Whenever I talk to her I think I can see gears turning around inside her head. Like a fancy music box. What's happened to Hansen? Not like him to miss a meal."

"I fed him earlier. He's off, handing out flyers on Main Street. Said he wanted to catch the noon crowd in the eating places."

"More like the saloons," quipped the sheriff.

"Don't say that, Sylvester. He's been very good and very sober."

"Just making sure that he doesn't have to go through my cure again, tied up in Sweeney's stable for a week."

"You are a cruel man sometimes, Sylvester."

"It's a cruel world out there, my dear, for a falling-down drunk or an out-of-work sheriff. Let me tell you."

"You're not out of work, Sylvester. Not again and not if I can help it. That is why the flyers."

"Does Sultan Sanders hand out flyers?"

"No, he does not."

"Wonderful. I've got a chance, huh?"

"Well, I'm not all that sure. Mr. Sanders gives out cigars, that Gompers gives him to hand out, from his store."

"I hope they're cheap cigars—and knowing Gompers, I imagine they are."

CHAPTER 19

A white man could teach an Indian a few things. For instance, he could teach the red man how to quick-load a musket by spilling powder down the barrel, dropping the ball down the barrel on top of the wadded cartridge paper and then rapping the butt plate, hard, against the ground. That saves fooling with the ramrod while facing a charging foe. Or an Indian could be taught how to set a fire with a magnifier glass, catching the sun's rays on a handful of dry tinder.

But if there was one subject where the Indian "wrote the book," it was on how to lay an ambush. It was something he was born knowing, like when a duck knows it's time to say adios to cold weather and head for warmer waters.

Old Slit-Nose had been a part of half a hundred ambushes, either as the ambusher or as the ambushed—on the receiving end. This wagon train ambush, though, presented an elementary problem. The terrain was almost entirely devoid of cover. The trail lazily followed a dry wash which had sloping, almost nonexistent banks. To make matters worse, this particular freight convoy was guarded by outriders, five tough-looking Mexicans who seemed the type who collected Apache ears as a hobby.

So the freight wagons lumbered across the barren landscape at an economical pace that favored their mules, as Slit-Nose circled around them, cautious to remain unseen; a fox surveying a henhouse that was patrolled by a very mean mastiff.

Finally, after long hours of dogging his quarry, the solution to the lack of cover came to the war chief; spider holes. They would dig small pits into the flat desert to conceal themselves. Then, at close range, throwing off their pit's natural-looking coverings, they would fire on the protecting guards and gobble up the wagons.

Leaving Owl-Who-Kills-At-Night to monitor the wagon train, Slit-Nose drew off the warriors to a spot several hours up the trail, a site hidden from the outriders' observations by a knoll that pushed the wash out of its mostly-straight course, to curve in a half-moon path around the obstruction.

The ambushers used their knives and their hands to dig out the spider holes, piling the displaced soil in their blankets to carry it beyond their holes, and scattering it naturally among the rocks and sparse vegetation beyond the wash. It was from this poor brush that they wove flimsy frames that would support their sand-covered blankets that made the lids for their spider holes.

An hour's fast and sweaty work saw their work completed. Slit-Nose ordered the eight best riflemen into the holes as the horse holders took charge of their ponies. Slit-Nose and Beaver Tooth moved between the spider holes, inspecting and correcting any deficiencies in their disguises. Then the area was carefully brushed to remove all signs of Apache involvement, and Slit-Nose led his remaining riders to join the horses hidden in a gully which lay a considerable distance from the teamsters' track.

After a short wait Slit-Nose's group was joined by Owl-Who-Kills-At-Night, who announced the wagons' immediate arrival, a closer meeting than had been anticipated due to the difficulty in digging the spider pits.

Slit-Nose slid off his pony to draw a diagram of their attack in the sand of the gully's floor. "Once the white men see their Mexicans killed," he told his braves, "they will bunch their wagons together for mutual protection. But as they have few wagons, it will be difficult for them to build a wall of wagons to fight behind; there will be many gaps that a brave warrior can penetrate.

"The whites are a worthy foe. They are brave and well armed with the guns-that-shoot-many-times. They will wait to shoot until we are very close—for they want to kill with every bullet. My plan is to attack them as the wild cow attacks its foe. The cow knows that its great horns reach far to the front of its head and uses its horns to hook around an enemy's defenses. We shall do the same as the wild cow. When we ride out to meet the whites I will command the left of our line of attackers. Owl-Who-Kills-At-Night will lead on the right—the right horn of our wild cow, and Beaver Tooth will direct the center, making sure always that the head of our wild cow is well behind the horns."

Slit-Nose knelt and smoothed a square of sand. Then he drew the horns of his cow in the sands, using two gnarled fingers, sketching a flattened U-shaped line of attack. "This is us, the horns," he continued, "and this is the wagons of the whites." He drew a circle in the center of his U.

"As you see, the tips of the horns are beyond the whites, while the head has still not closed with the enemy." Then, reaching out to his sketch, he slashed lines from the horns' tips into the rear flanks of the enemy. "As the wild cow hooks its foe from the side, so shall we—wounding the whites—as they watch the head of our wild cow."

"And my braves and I must play the role of the possum—not killing the whites?" questioned Beaver Tooth, with displeasure.

"You must endure their fire, my son. It is by your courage that we on the horns' tips can get into position. Yours is the most dangerous position." Beaver Tooth brightened at this and the war chief went on. "When the two tips of our horns rip into the sides of the whites, the men who face you, Beaver Tooth, will turn to fire on those horn tips. Then, brave Beaver Tooth, will you charge into the front of the whites and kill them."

"It is a very good plan," affirmed Beaver Tooth, "and I and my braves will endure the fire."

"I never doubted you, Beaver Tooth. I have never doubted any of you—or you would not be with me now. There are only a few moments now. Each of you should use them to ready yourself for death here—and life with the Great Spirit." He stood up and led his pony away from the group to commune with his maker.

******

"Deputy Buller," called Skinner, seeing Aaron Rose enter the Sheriff's Office, "we've got company—prime up the coffee pot."

"Don't bother—please," greeted the prosecutor. "I've tasted his Rebel coffee before—and my stomach duly rebelled. Once is all I can take. But I did bring some jelly buns along—to soften the bad news that I bring."

"I hope it's not that you're going to stay here as prosecutor. I was hoping your smarter brother would take your job and we'd have a good prosecutor for a change," quipped Sam.

"Just for that—I'll stay and prosecute you for cruelty to coffee beans. The jury would never leave the box to convict you." Rose deliberately walked past Sam to hand the newspaper-wrapped buns to the Sheriff, who opened up the cornucopia-shaped package.

"Now that I have the buns," said Skinner, "you can go ahead with the bad news."

"Ready? The Chief Judge granted a change of venue for Mr. Malone. Ruled that killing a popular lawman like Cletus

McCoyne would prejudice a jury of local citizens. And I'm afraid I agree with His Honor, myself."

"That's just great," snapped the Sheriff. "Where is this exalted jurist having him tried?"

"Don't know as yet. The Judge's clerk pinned a little note to the order saying they're looking for a peaceful town to conduct the trial in."

"A peaceful place—in Arizona Territory," scoffed Skinner. "If you find one—let my dear spouse know. She's convinced the Wild West is named Arizona."

"Aren't I gonna get a bun," griped Sam, "or are Confederate heroes soon forgotten?"

"Who said you were a hero?" questioned Rose.

"A very pretty lady did—last summer. When I told her about my wartime adventure with an amorous fat lady wearing a hoop skirt. Almost impaled my eager manhood on my own sword."

"And that classifies you as a hero?" asked Skinner.

"Most certainly. That and having to hide from her angry brother in a rose bush with my trousers at half-mast. Talk about war wounds. Now do I get a bun—or two?"

"How can anyone deny a real live hero?" said Skinner, tossing him a bun.

"I can't stand all the talk of combat and war," announced the young prosecutor. "I won't be able to take my afternoon nap, for fear of terrible dreams." He turned to leave.

"Go ahead, jeer me," Sam yelled after him. "You didn't see those huge barbs on that rose bush."

With Aaron Rose gone, it was quiet in the Sheriff's Office; quiet if one discounted the heavy wagon traffic on noisy Main Street, or the clump-clump of a pacing prisoner in the upstairs cell. The sheriff and Sam chewed, thoughtfully, on the jelly buns, washing down their sweetness with Sam's Rebel coffee.

"So—how do you feel about Malone's change of venue?" asked Sam, waiting for the right moment.

"At first I was disappointed. Sort of angry that we weren't allowed to clean up our own mess. Avenge his death with a Green Falls jury and a stout rope. But then I thought, it's not going to make any difference to Cletus. He's up in some tree, or whatever, moldering in his shroud. So why stir up all the hate by having the trial here? I don't need any more dyspeptic problems in my stomach; getting old, I guess. But I'm afraid that means that you and Happy will have to go off to wherever the trial will be held."

"Why me?" Sam shot back. "I wasn't a witness. Happy was there. He's the witness, not me."

"We'll have to transfer Malone. That will be your job."

"Why couldn't Happy do it—if he has to be a witness?" argued Sam.

"Because I don't trust Happy to deliver the prisoner, if you must know. He'll be out of his element—outside Green Falls, I mean."

"For that assignment I should have the last jelly bun," said Sam, petulantly.

"Too late, Deputy," gloated Skinner. "I just polished it off."

"See—that's what always happens to us minions. We are taken advantage of by our so-called leaders. There's no justice in the law and order business. Just for that I'm gonna make the next batch of coffee with even more eggshells."

******

Sheriff Skinner was alone at the Sheriff's Office. Sam Buller had left, his shift finished. The new deputy, Stan Woods, had gone to his home at his sister's house for an early supper before the second half of his tour, which included the saloon patrol with Happy Giles. This was the quiet hour in the office that Skinner enjoyed, finishing up any pending paperwork and writing up the day's happenings in the day book. The quiet this evening, though, was broken by the noisy entrance of Captain Mosely, the Chairman of the County Commissioners and Skinner's boss.

"Trouble, Skinner," announced the perspiring banker, raising the tails of his swallow-cut coat to plop tiredly into Sam's vacant chair.

"I'd be surprised if it wasn't," commented the sheriff, putting the steel nib pen into the tarnished brass holder and blotting the journal page with a half-moon-shaped blotter. "Almost everyone coming through that door has got trouble that only we can solve. Why should you be different? What's the problem, Captain?"

"A freighter just dropped off a message from No Place."

"What place?"

"No Place. Don't feel bad if you never heard of it before. Our county and Graham County has been feuding over who had jurisdiction—for tax purposes. Now Pinal County is trying to horn in. Until the lines are surveyed properly No Place is up for grabs. I figure if we answer their call for help it will help our case with the Territorial Legislature. There are considerable copper deposits around No Place."

"I should have known," observed Skinner. "Never figured you for an altruist."

"I'm not," replied Mosely, proudly. "Leastwise when it comes to county affairs. Generous governments go broke. Name me one generous government that's still around."

"Can't. Especially yours," grinned Skinner.

"I take that as a compliment."

"You would. What is wrong at No Place?"

"A killer mountain lion, terrorizing the community. Supposed to be huge; has killed two men at least, and savaged several others. The last killing was two or three days ago."

"Where does the Sheriff's Office come in, Captain? Want us to arrest this lion?"

"Sarcasm has no place in public service, Sheriff. I want you to hire a hunter and fund it through this office."

"Why my office? Think we need the work?"

"It's public safety, isn't it?" answered Mosely. "And besides I've got too many county accounts already. I'll advance your account. Don't worry about the money."

"But I do. I have to—with a parsimonious supervisor such as you. But I'll try to find a hunter for you—first thing tomorrow."

"No great big expedition, Skinner. Just a man and a couple of dogs. Keep it cheap. Those folks don't pay any taxes, yet."

"I can't promise anything. I'll have to talk to the man."

"What man is that?"

"Poke Blaney," answered Skinner quickly.

"Isn't he the fellow that had his dogs killed that time you were shot? As I remember, we had to pay out damages to him—a costly affair."

"Everything costs, Captain. At least it seems to in this business—either in lives or money. Aaron Rose told me earlier this afternoon that Malone will be tried elsewhere for killing Cletus."

"Sorry to hear that," said Mosely. "The hotels and saloons were hoping for quite a few visitors to watch the trial. They will be disappointed."

"Yeah," answered Skinner flatly. "What a shame."

******

Poke Blaney's ranch, if a hut set on an acre of hilly rock and brush could be called a ranch, was back of Chinaman's Ridge and could be reached by a roundabout trace that led from the Holiday Trail. It was eleven o'clock and hot, but Gertie seemed to enjoy the exercise and the sheriff gave his horse her head and she pounded up the ankle-deep, dusty trace.

Blaney had a seven foot high paling fence around the shack and its immediate yard to pen up his yelping canine population. The dogs must have been barking extra loudly to announce the sheriff, for Blaney came out of the small back-house pulling up his pants. He came up to the gate in a veritable sea of dogs, of every size and shape, all howling for his attention.

"Git down, dern ya. Don'tcha see it's the sheriff?" He slapped at the swirling pack with his shapeless hat. One dog grabbed the hat from his hand and dashed around to the back of the run-down shack, followed by the whole, noisy bunch.

"Heh! Works every time," grinned Poke, revealing gums where his teeth once lodged.

"Good morning, Mr. Blaney," greeted Skinner. "I think you just lost your hat."

"Naw," corrected the dog man, "they jes run around with it to see if I'll fuss at them. They're like children, you know—'cept smarter. What are ya here for? Come to buy a doag?"

"I need to hire your expertise. A lion is on the loose up by No Place, if you know where that is."

"Sure do. What do you take me for? But frankly, Sheriff—if you don't mind me stating the obvious—you've got a hell of a dang nerve trying to hire me after what happened last time. I don't know if you remember, but I sure does. Ten of my best doags shot down dead by that Captain Cabot fellow and his darkie. And now . . ."

"I'm truly sorry about that, Mr. Blaney. I got hit, too—if you remember," said Skinner, trying contrition.

"Served you right. It was your idear. And what about me having to give a dern lawyer twenty-five dollars to get me a sixty dollar settlement from the dern county?"

"I'm sorry about that, too, Mr. . . ."

"Weren't right; that's only six bucks a doag. They was worth twenty apiece, at least." A tear slid down Poke's grimy cheek, triggered by the sad memory of his murdered dogs. "Wasn't right, nohow."

"You're our only hope, Mr. Blaney, to stop the lion from killing more people." Skinner poured on the soft soap.

"I don't hardly have the right doags, anyhow," stated Poke, twisting around to see what mischief his errant pack was doing.

"And people's pets," said Skinner quickly—afraid of losing Poke's services. "Their dogs. Snatched right off their doorsteps."

"Their doags! The lion got their doags!" Poke was indignant at the thought. "That's terrible."

"It surely is, Mr. Blaney. That's why your expert knowledge is needed to get rid of this scourge that's killing all their dogs."

"I don't work cheap."

"An expert never does, Mr. Blaney." The sheriff spotted light at the end of the tunnel. "We'll pay top dollar."

"It'll take eight doags," mused Blaney, planning his hunt. "Five dollars a day for me 'n' the doags for a thirty day minimum. Plus a sixty dollar bonus for killin' the lion. After forty days I'll work for free until I'm out two months. If I can't git it in two months, I ain't gonna. And fifteen bucks for each of my doags kilt. How's that sound?"

"Expensive," said Skinner. "But I agree."

"I'll need some grub money. When ya want me to leave?"

"How about tomorrow? Come by the Sheriff's Office; I'll have a voucher ready for twenty dollars."

"I'll need forty; gotta rent a special rifle, plus all the doag food, you know."

"Forty it is. And bring back the skin if you want the bonus."

"You'll get it . . . dern lion—killing doags, anyways. Deserves gett'n' kilt."

******

Very few ambuscades are completely successful, trapping all those ambushed in the vise of the ambush. A determined, pre-planned defense can blunt the terrible surprise of the ambush. And, as in any battle, luck and the action of heroic individuals can turn tragedy into triumph—or at least, survival.

So it was with Slit-Nose's trap. The planning and execution was good. The enemy just did not cooperate fully. The leader of the spider hole snipers was to shout to bring his braves out of their holes and fire on the outriders. This first volley was ragged—more like a scattering of shots. But two of the Mexicans were downed and the others forced to retire to the safety of the wagons, which had closed ranks with admirable swiftness.

Now came the attack of the wild cow horns. Slit-Nose's group and Owl-Who-Kills-At-Night's attackers charged to the sides of the stalled wagons, facing a fusillade of the defenders' fire. Slit-Nose's pony was hit, spilling the old warrior mere yards from the forted wagons. His braves abandoned their attack to concentrate on rescuing their leader.

On the other flank, Owl-Who-Kills-At-Night ignored the heavy firing to kick his pony through a gap in the wagons into the center of the white's defenses. He fired both barrels of his shotgun at the defenders, seeing hits each shot, but then with his weapon empty, he was forced to flee before the determined pistol fire of the enraged whites.

The Apaches' frontal attack was broken by the remaining Mexican guards, who burst out of the wagon fort to meet the braves knee-to-knee with superior firepower. Beaver Tooth was killed almost immediately and his younger braves, unnerved at their leader's death, turned tail at the Mexican's onslaught.

Slit-Nose, re-mounted finally on a loose pony, signaled a retirement and the Apaches drew off to lick their wounds and plan their next attack. The horse holders were sent to recover the spider hole braves, who had slipped from their holes during the confrontation. Slit-Nose would rather have had them remain in their holes, adding their fire to the attack, but such a static position was unthinkable to the individual Apache, used to his personal freedom in the slash-and-run tactics.

Suddenly, the wagons took the advantage that the Apache withdrawal had provided by moving out southwestward on the trail, their original direction. This time, rather than forming a loose string of wagons, they were in a tight diamond-shaped mass to provide group protection. The wagons were moving fast, the teamsters whipping their teams into a lope in an effort to put distance between themselves and the Apaches. And worse, the remaining Mexican outriders had formed a thin screen behind the wagons, evidently determined to harass pursuit with their repeating rifles.

The Apaches looked to Slit-Nose for the order to follow and attack. He sat on his newly-claimed pony, staring stonily at the departing wagons, lost in thought. The younger braves belatedly looked to Owl-Who-Kills-At-Night for a spokesman. He accepted their challenge and guided his pony to the old warrior's pony.

"Do we follow, my chief?" the younger man asked, eyes averted for this insolence in questioning the old warrior's leadership. "Our ponies are still strong, as are we."

"Send two braves to retrieve Beaver Tooth. He must be cared for properly," ordered Slit-Nose.

"And the whites, my chief? Do we follow?"

"No," stated Slit-Nose, flatly—almost sorrowfully. "We have lost the surprise. It is not the Apache way. To continue, I mean, unless we had overpowering strength, which we do not have. No. We must find a weaker prey. Those Mexicans were very good; experienced and not afraid. Tell the young braves to learn by those Mexicans' bravery. We must always learn from our enemies—and respect them and what they can do to us."

"Where does the trail take us now, my chief?" asked Owl-Who-Kills-At-Night, sad for this disappointment to the old warrior.

"We will leave the trail and seek the ranchos to the north of where the white men dig in the earth for the bright metal. They must be taught to fear the Apache and not trespass on our hunting grounds. But first we must see to Beaver Tooth."

"And Small Hawk, also, my chief. His thigh was shattered by the white's fire."

"He shows no fault?" questioned the old man, turning to study the wounded brave.

"He is an Apache brave, my chief," answered Owl-Who-Kills-At-Night simply.

"See to him, also. But he must ride on with us. There is no other way."

And so Beaver Tooth was bound tightly in his blanket and carried up to the nearby knoll where his remains were wedged fast to a rocky outcropping that overlooked the barren desert trail on which he was killed. Small Hawk's leg was bound, also, with a poultice of muddy vegetation. He died, though, as the sun left the land, drained grey by the loss of blood—much as the desert looked as it lost its living light.

CHAPTER 20

The next morning when Sheriff Skinner was at the bakery buying buns, the baker's wife demanded news of the "huge, man-killing lion," before she counted out the buns. It was the same all over Green Falls; people stopping him in the street, perfect strangers running up to question the effort to track "the killer." Skinner was angry and upset by all the hoopla and hullabaloo, and said so to Deputy Sam when he returned from the bakery run.

"Somebody blabbed, dammit!" he exploded to the hapless Sam. "And I'll bet a dollar his first name is Captain Mosely. Damn loose-lipped politicians, anyhow!"

"Rumors travel fast in small towns," stated Sam primly. "Smaller the town—bigger the rumor. My mother used to love a good rumor. Said that all the time. Started most of them herself—bless her nasty little mind."

"This ain't funny," Skinner retorted, opening the buns. "Mrs. Seevers collared me to ask was it true 'that Sultan Sanders is outfitting a bunch to capture and cage the lion.' Had to tell her that I didn't know. Great words from a man who's supposed to be in the know."

"Sure wouldn't want to vote for an ignoramus like you," Sam chortled. "So what are you going to do?"

"Tell Poke Blaney to hurry up and shoot that lion, when he comes through to pick up his money. Maybe that will take the wind out of Sanders' sails, when he sees our man on the go."

Poke Blaney came—and went—with a noisy congregation of dogs that managed to agitate every horse and mule all the way through town. Blaney was gone, but the rumor had turned into a cause cèlèbre, with Sanders promoting the idea that the present sheriff was lackadaisically-minded when it came to citizens' safety.

Playing to the crowd of loafers and freeloaders that formed his entourage, Sanders proclaimed a citizens' crusade to capture the lion and make the streets of No Place, and hopefully Green Falls as well, safe for women and children. With department store magnate Gompers putting up the cash, Sultan Sanders, as sheriff-candidate, would form an expedition to capture what was being called "the great cat."

Sultan Sanders thought of himself as a romantic, which was no doubt true, and as such, viewed this expedition as larger-than-life. He went all-out (on Gompers' money) to field an impressive force. Fortunately for the department store owner, there were no elephants to hire in Green Falls, or even half a thousand spear-carrying Nubian warriors for use as beaters to corner "the great cat." But he did find J. Malloy-Fitzpatrick to head the crusade. Mr. Malloy-Fitzpatrick was a derelict, left floating about Green Falls with the demise of the circus that formerly provided him with a position as animal trainer. The circus owner had sold the big-top tent several years earlier to an enterprising gentleman who turned the huge tent into a hotel for miners, making himself wealthy and providing the first-ever profit to the circus owner, who quickly decamped with his money, stranding performers and menagerie alike.

For a short time, Fitzpatrick survived by helping the animal-hungry miners convert the zebras and camels into beasts of burden, but the circus animals quickly succumbed to the killing conditions in the mines and Fitzpatrick was soon without work. A cleverly crafted Certificate of Veterinary Medicine gave him hope for a while, but ineptitude and an inordinate taste for whiskey soon reduced Fitzpatrick to trading horse-doctoring for drinks.

Now resurrected from poverty by the chance of fate, Malloy-Fitzpatrick basked in his new position as expedition leader. Six hangers-on were hired. Pack animals were procured, as were supplies, equipage and saddle horses. A frantic Gompers, eyeing the spiraling expenses, was coerced into funding a folding cage made of a steel framework and wire-rope sides. This contraption was to pen The Great Cat.

Four days after Poke Blaney's departure Sultan Sanders conducted a departure ceremony before the Gompers Department Store. Fortunately for the occasion, it was Sunday and the Mine Association Band, brave in their blue and gray uniforms, were able to stir the throng with their rousing rendition of the 'Old Gray Mare.'

An itinerant preacher, who generally augmented the take from his gatherings by selling a pamphlet luridly titled "Lust in the Scriptures—Evil Unveiled," was hurriedly pressed into service to pronounce a fiery invocation over the humbly-bowed heads of Fitzpatrick's clumsy chasers. This solemn occasion was spoiled, though, when the preacher was forced to yield to a coughing fit. The hardy lion- hunters, thinking the prayer had ended, began to lead their animals off down Main Street. Only Sultan Sanders' keen sense of the ceremonious and his angry exhortations were able to re-form the expedition for the last of the good shepherd's gasped blessing.

Then, with blaring band and cheering crowd, Fitzpatrick was given his marching signal and the crusade moved out to the yells of Fitzpatrick's crusaders. The ungainly lion cage brought up the rear, its sections strapped onto a pair of patient mules. Sultan Sanders remained on Gompers' broad sidewalk, accepting the good wishes of the thinning crowd as he watched his expedition slowly lose itself amid the heavy traffic of Main Street. He was still gazing down the busy thoroughfare when his friends finally prevailed upon him to come into a nearby saloon and buy them drinks.

******

The knocking on his hotel room door roused Theodore Ostenhaven. He had dozed off at his desk while burning the proverbial midnight oil, reading a new book on hydraulic applications. Shaking off his tiredness, he arose from the desk, extracted a derringer from the middle desk drawer and slipped it into the pocket of his dressing robe.

A careful opening of the door disclosed the elderly night bellman. Ostenhaven relaxed his grip on his pocket pistol and opened the door full way.

"Sorry to bother you gov'ner," began the brass-buttoned bellman, "but there's a gent at the desk who's wanting to see you. The night clerk said I should asks you first."

"What kind of a gent?" asked Ostenhaven grumpily. "Does he have a name?"

"'e's not really a gentleman, sor. 'e's a Mexican. Says he owns some cantina like—wheres you 'ave a friend that 'as a room. Name of Erbst, 'e says."

"Herbst? Could that be Hurst?"

"That's it Gov'. 'urst, it was. Should I show 'im up? 'e seems in a 'eat to see you."

"Bring him up, but if he has any weapons, have him leave them at the desk, will you?"

A few minutes later the bellman escorted the visitor to Ostenhaven's door. The man was Charlie Hurst's landlord, the grinning husband of Charlie's bathing companion. The swarthy-faced innkeeper came through the door, peering around at the appointments of Ostenhaven's luxurious room.

"Muy grande," conceded the visitor. "How much zees room it costs?"

"A lot. What is your business? Something to do with Charlie Hurst?"

"Sí. I am Jose Merino. Señor Charlie, he has zee room weez me."

"I know. I was there. Go on," said Ostenhaven, trying to speed up the meeting.

"Señor Charlie, he is out in zee mountain now. Weez heez beezness."

"Yes." Ostenhaven did not want to reveal anything about Hurst's business.

"Charlie, he geev my wife's cousin money to bring him zee food and zings on zee mules. Tino eez zeez man's name."

"I'm familiar with this. Mr. Hurst has told me about this man. Go on. I want to go to bed."

"When I tell you what happens—maybe you don't feel like no sleeping."

"Indeed—then don't keep me in suspense."

"I am a poor man, señor. My cantina eez how you say, zee sheetz. No good. Now you, señor, are a man weez mucho dinero—very rich. For what I tell you—I must have money. Maybe wan onnerts of dollars. Wan onnerts dollars to make many, many thousand for you, señor. What do you say? Weel you geev me money?"

"How do I know that what you will say will be worth anything?" bargained Ostenhaven.

"I tell you one leetle word and you see zat Jose Merino he tells zee truth."

"Go ahead. Tell me the word. I promise nothing, though." Ostenhaven was tired and wanted to end this charade.

"Zee word eez 'gold mine,' señor."

"What about a gold mine?"

"Zee money, señor. You will geev it to me?"

Fifty dollars for sure. For openers. A lot more if your information is any good. Go ahead."

"I zink Tino he finds zee gold zat Señor Charlie, he looks for."

"How do you know this?" Ostenhaven suddenly felt his stomach roll sickly.

"Tino he come back weez zee mules loaded weez zee gold rocks. He takes zem to a Mexican man and quick he got money to geev to heez wife. Much money. Zee woman, she buy nice zeengs. My wife, she tells me."

"How much money, Mr. Merino?"

"Maybe three onnerts dollars, maybe more. Now Tino goes back to zee mountain. He takes two more mules. Pays dollars for zee mules. Beeg mules. Mor' beeg zan hees old mule. Now he got many mules."

"And no message for me?" asked Ostenhaven. "From Charlie?"

"No, señor. Now you geev me money—yes?"

"I must see my friend, here in the hotel, to get it for you. Stay here. You've earned your hundred dollars. Better yet, why don't you wait in the bar? Tell the barman I said to give you a drink."

"Señor, ah . . . I zink zey don't like a Mexican man like me . . . in zair saloon." Merino made a gesture towards his nondescript clothing.

"Just tell the barman that Mr. Ostenhaven desires that you be seated and served. I'll be down there quickly. Now, go ahead—go down there." He shooed Merino from his room and quickly changed into a proper coat.

Finsen's room was just two doors down the hall. Ostenhaven tapped on the door. After several tries he switched to loud knocks. Finally Finsen angrily stuck his head around the door.

"Oh—it's you, Theodore. What's the matter? Trouble at the mine?"

"Worse," answered Ostenhaven. "Trouble with the Hurst operation. Can I come in? Don't like talking in the hall. The walls have ears, you know."

"Oh . . . ah . . . room's a mess," parried Finsen. "Let me throw something on and I'll join you in your room. Won't take a second."

"Bring a hundred dollars with you. I've got to pay off an informer. He's down at the bar now."

"I'll bring the money. Won't be long." Finsen drew back into his room, closing the door.

"What's that all about?" questioned Sprague from the bed, reaching out a muscular arm to grab the half-empty bottle on the night stand.

"Theodore's all upset about something connected with Hurst's mission. I have to go over and get the details. Something about an informer telling him something. I have to get out a hundred dollars for this fellow." He went to the night stand and took a leather-bound Bible from the drawer and unlocked a leather-strap clasp with a key from a gold chain around his neck.

"So that's what that key is for," observed Sprague, setting back the bottle.

"A secret between us, baby," whispered Finsen, blowing a kiss to the naked Sprague.

"Baby! Does this look like it belongs to a baby?" laughed Sprague, lifting up his genitals.

"Now," scolded Finsen, "don't talk dirty, especially as I have to leave for a while. And don't drink too much while I'm gone. You get too rough when you drink."

"I thought that's the way you liked it, fat man. Rough and ready—always ready." He released his manhood to reach for the bottle again, with a wicked grin on his sharp face.

******

Charlie Hurst's second lion victim was an old prospector who greeted the supposed surveyor of the telegraph wire with open arms.

"Hot damn!" exclaimed the fuzzy-whiskered miner. "Now I got somebody to celebrate with besides this stupid burro of mine. I still got a half-bottle of devil's dew left. You got any more whiskey with you?"

"Depends on what we're celebrating," replied Charlie, eyeing his prey.

"My good luck. That's what."

"You hit a big strike?" asked Charlie, immediately interested.

"Well—nothing that'll make me a millionaire, but it'll pay back some grubstakes and still leave me enough for a fling in Tucson."

"What did you find—gold or silver?" said Charlie, trying to act disinterested.

"Neither. Found some turquoise nuggets in a wash. Got a good-sized sack of them. Should be worth three hundred or so."

"That much. Maybe I should quit surveying and start looking for turquoise."

"It's a matter of luck," said the old man, passing a brown-glass bottle of whiskey to Charlie. "The color, I mean. This stuff is the valuable sky-blue type. You don't get so much for the green kind, and even less for the yellow-green stuff."

"Well," said Charlie, "here's to the sky-blue kind." He took a big swig and then back-handed the old man with the bottle. With his new victim unconscious, Charlie freed the steel lion's claw from his baggage and finished the job.

Backtracking to a point near No Place, Charlie left the old man's body close to the trail the copper collectors used in their travels. The burro was a bigger problem. It had to disappear completely, which meant burying it under enough sand and rocks to discourage predators, both four-footed and feathered. Charlie was hot and tired after the burial of the burro, but the bag of turquoise helped to make up for the perspiration. It was only just, Charlie thought to himself. A proper wage for a proper burial—even if it was only a burro.

******

The idea had been dreamed up by Van Doormann to sell the expensive placards that his printing shop would produce. The debate between officeholder Sylvester Skinner and office seeker Sultan Sanders would rival the Lincoln-Douglas debate and mark the final fortnight of the campaign.

It was to be a torchlight meeting, utilizing the imposing second floor porch of the Congress Hotel. Van Doormann sold two hundred large placards to the Sanders camp at sixty cents each, complete with a picture of the smiling Sanders, with his name in sixty-four point type. Gompers cleverly donated one hundred brand-new straw brooms to the cause and the handsome placards were tacked onto the broomsticks, two to a broom for a double-faced effect. "The emphasis is on sweeping Skinner out of office," chortled Gompers, pleased with his ingenuity.

Genevieve Skinner, her campaign funds dwindling, had to be content with a smaller, no-picture placard; twenty-five of them at thirty-five cents. The sticks came from Manny Ortiz' used lumber yard and were salvage plaster lath sticks, rough cut, with splinters. These were allocated one-to-a-placard, single-faced for economy.

The night of the great debate fell ingloriously, due to a late spring drizzle caused by an unexpected cold spell. Sultan Sanders shone resplendently in a new white linen suit and white silk vest, courtesy of Gompers' menswear department. Encircling his thickened waist was a splendid double holster crafted in white morocco leather, which held two nickel-plated Colt revolvers with their mother-of-pearl grips out-thrust to the front of the silver-conchoed holsters, as if to signify to all that Sanders' pistols would be used quickly in the public behalf.

Skinner seemed drab in comparison, wearing his black mohair suit, the one he bought six months before for daughter Martha's funeral. His gun belt was black, also; used, but serviceable, thanks to elbow grease and saddle soap. His Colt was the same pistol he carried through the war, and as a field grade officer, was allowed to purchase at a good price upon deactivation and discharge. Its bluing was worn and the checkering of the walnut grips was no longer sharp. But it, too, was adequate and serviceable. That's how Skinner compared himself to the vision in white that would soon debate him; he felt adequate—not gaudy. He was almost proud of his Spartan image; Sylvester Skinner—just plain folks, only with a gun.

The great debate opened with Van Doormann introducing himself to the crowd as the debate's moderator and warning the crowd to mind where they held their lamp-oil fueled torches. He got a laugh from the crowd by asking those who held the brooms if they would please sweep the Congress Hotel's boardwalk after the debate because the hotel's management was very fussy about their premises.

After the laughter and hoots from the crowd died, he introduced the principals, having them shake hands, boxer-style, before they faced off. Sanders, as the challenger, was to argue his candidacy first. But in contravention of the ground rules, he took the podium to introduce his campaign manager, Mr. Gompers, who proceeded to laud his political nominee. Skinner threw a scowl at the moderator, who seemed suddenly busy, looking in an opposite direction.

Gompers, contrary to expectations, made a fine speech from a prepared sheaf of papers. He quoted from Shakespeare, Benjamin Franklin and the Bible. All later agreed, at least the Sanders supporters did, that it was a terrible shame that Gompers fumbled his papers too close to the row of stubby hurricane lamps that lined the front of the podium. The papers suddenly burst into flames, forcing Gompers to jettison the burning mass into the street below. Fortunately, this area had only a scattering of audience, being too close to the hotel for proper viewing. Mr. Gompers had parked his open buggy there, filled with campaign literature.

The burning mass fell directly into his buggy, and the handbills, placards and posters promptly caught fire. Gompers' buggy-horse, noticing this large blaze close to its hindquarters, became excited enough to break its bonds and gallop away in the direction of Spanishtown, pulling the flaming buggy behind it.

The fleet-of-foot rescuers caught up with the fiery vehicle and soon extinguished the flames. The horse had managed to trap itself amid the empty cages of the live chicken market and its only real damage was a scorched tail.

The interruption to the debate proved to be fatal. By the time the crowd returned to the Congress Hotel, the slight drizzle had turned to real rain. Sanders, soggy in his soaked white suit, tried to rally his supporters, but they decamped, taking their brooms with them. Skinner did not even bother to go upstairs to the porch, preferring to shake an occasional hand down in the muddy street. At last, with the rain now strong enough to chase off even the most ardent partisan, Skinner walked home. He was wet, yet pleased with the direction the 'great debate' had taken. He had never wanted to toot his own horn and was relieved that he was spared that ordeal.

Gen had left the Congress when the heavy rain began to fall. She was standing before the range in her nightgown, arranging her dripping frock on a kitchen chair before the heat.

She turned to her husband as he came through the rear door, dripping water on her bleached floor. "How did it end up?" she asked.

"Just fine," said Skinner. "Best debate I was ever in . . . got any coffee left?"

CHAPTER 21

The Apache raiders fared better the following week. They had paralleled the old Mormon Trail, hoping to snatch up any lightly defended freight outfits that used the old track. They found none of these but did manage a sunrise swoop on an isolated ranch a few miles off the old trail. A family of six and their two ranch hands died quickly by Apache standards; the woman last, after she was used.

The ranch's small horse herd was hazed out with the Indians when they left the burning ranch, as were the milk cow and her calf. They headed southeast, now following the foothills of the Tortilla Mountains.

That night they ate the calf and the young braves milked the mother, shouting and laughing as they collected the milk in pots stolen from the ranch.

Slit-Nose made a short speech, emphasizing that the spirits were helping his band now and that further success was assured. Owl-Who-Kills-At-Night listened to the old warrior drone on about past and coming victories and wondered at the young and boisterous braves' naivete. Then he questioned his own thoughts, almost wishing to be home with his bride. He could still feel the smoothness of her skin, the eager fullness of her breasts; he still had the smell of her, the musky, woman smell she made when he laid with her. He could feel the roughness of the goat-hair blanket on his bare back when she was under him and the grip of her legs. But he was an Apache warrior. His heart should not be with her. But it was.

******

The partnership—the private arrangement between Ostenhaven and Finsen—was sent spinning into turmoil with the news that Hurst's mule packer, Tino, had quite possibly found Tent-Peg Pete's mine.

"We've got to make contact with Hurst immediately," stated Ostenhaven, in his calm, deliberate way. "And it would not hurt to intercept this Tino fellow, either."

"I could get the mine's location out of him in no time at all," volunteered Sprague, cracking his knuckles in an approximation of what he would do to the mule packer.

"I told that landlord to notify me if he comes back to Green Falls," continued Ostenhaven. "Worse come to worse, we might have to extend some type of partnership to him— at least for awhile."

"That's crazy!" snorted Sprague. "He stole that mine from us. Right from under our noses, probably."

"It would be just a short-term solution," added Finsen, who had been quiet with his thoughts. "But I believe some of us have to journey out and find Charlie Hurst and get to the bottom of this."

"I could go," said Sprague. "But I'd need a map or some-thing . . . to find my way."

"I dislike putting this idea forward," continued Finsen, ignoring Sprague's offer. "But, Theodore, one of us, you or I, has to go out there and straighten this matter out."

"You can't go, Franklin," replied Ostenhaven, pulling on his ear to help himself think. "You have to finish that ten-year projection the home office wants."

"I could turn it over to Mercer. He's a capable clerk."

"More like culpable, when you're not breathing down his neck, if I remember right. He would make a complete ruin of it and risk that extra capitalization we're counting on for those lower levels . . . No, I'll have to go. I've got nothing on the fire that MacBurney can't handle. He's got a head on his shoulders and will be pleased for an opportunity to show it. But I'll have to take Jack, here, with me. I'm not much of an outdoorsman." Sprague and Finsen locked glances at that statement.

"Certainly. After all, he's your bodyguard, is he not?" agreed Finsen. "When would you go, Theodore?"

"Not really sure. Soon as possible. How long will it take to get prepared, Jack?"

"Just you and me and one pack horse," said Sprague, thinking fast. "Let's see . . . ten o'clock now. How about two o'clock? That would give us five hours, at least, on the trail today. I'll have to talk to somebody who knows the way. Where, by the way, would we be heading?"

"No Place," said Ostenhaven, smiling at the name. "We're in a hurry—to go to No Place."

******

The heavy rain continued the next day in Green Falls. Skinner inspected the ford across the Little Fish River, aptly named for its lack of swimming creatures, when he went for the jelly buns. The poles that marked the crossing showed a rise in the river of almost a foot above the normal late May mark.

When the sheriff returned to the office Sam traded him a letter for the package of buns. "Postmaster sent this over special; came in on the Warner stage last night. It's from the Army in Tucson, warning us that a bunch of Apaches are loose and have attacked a freight outfit southwest of the Black River."

"What's the Army doing about it?" asked Skinner, hanging his hat and slicker near the stove.

"The usual, according to the letter. Sent out—quote, strong patrols, unquote. They want us to notify all the northern outlying settlements. But we're not supposed to spread panic or disrupt commerce."

"That's easy for them to say," commented the sheriff. "Why don't you take that Army letter over to Van Doormann and have him make up a couple of hundred copies to put in the Post Office? They can pass them out to the folks who come in to pick up their mail.

"It's raining outside," observed Sam. "I'll get very wet. It would be better if you, who are wet already, make the trip to Van's. Makes a lot more sense, don't you agree?"

"Now that you mention it, I'm afraid I don't. Your reticence, though, reminds me of Army rain training."

"Rain training?" questioned Sam, skeptically.

"Ah yes, with Little Mac. General George B. McClellan, the great training master of the Army of the Potomac. 'We fight little, but train rigorously' was our motto."

"Really?"

"No, but it should have been. One rainy day, when our division was supposed to have had sidestepping maneuvers . . . you know, moving laterally on the battlefield as if you were reinforcing a flank . . ."

"Us Rebels didn't do much of that," interrupted Sam. "Mostly just charged up hills . . . which was funny; never did charge down hills. You'd think it would be fifty-fifty—half up and half down—but it weren't."

"If I may be allowed to continue with my original exposition. The sidestepping training was canceled due to difficulty in communicating in the rain. Fine, we all said. Stir up the fire and roast some more coffee beans in the frying pan, we said."

"Sounds too good to be true," said Sam, reaching for the coffee pot.

"'Twas, for surely. Down came the order from the Army commander, Little Mac. All infantry units not in actual contact with the enemy would practice route marching in the rain to accustom said units to poor weather marching conditions."

"So—you learned to march in the rain."

"Sam, it was hilarious, if not wet and muddy. Whole divisions were marching to and fro, all trying to make a march in different directions and return to their bivouacs. The Rebels, across the river, thought we were preparing to attack and rushed their batteries down to the fords and commenced a barrage, which knocked down a lot of trees. All this Rebel counter-activity scared Little Mac and he quick-ordered everyone to quit marching and get back to their original positions. We all would have laughed—if we weren't so damn wet and muddy."

"And that is training to march in the rain," said Sam, sneaking another bun while his boss was lost down memory's lane.

"And that is what you'll be doing, you bun-naper; learning to walk in the rain. Get going."

******

Trooper Daniels was seen galloping back to the slower-moving formation. He was waving his hat, trying to get the troop's attention, an unnecessary effort, as the Apache-anxious troopers were extremely conscious of their surroundings. As he usually did, when all eyes were on him, Daniels slid his sweating horse to a Pony Express stop and saluted Major Poole with an exaggerated motion.

"Smoke up ahead, sir," gasped the young cavalryman. "Big smoke. Like a house burning."

"Indeed," replied the prim major, trying to show coolness in the face of fire. "Is that a reason for taxing your mount?"

"Sorry, sir," said the unabashed trooper. "Thought you'd want to know."

"I do want to know, trooper," scolded the major, "But not at the cost of your mount. You must cultivate the appearance of military decorum. Calmness and sureness mark the experienced soldier. Now—you say the fire seems large?"

"Big fire, sir. Lots of smoke."

"I think that would call for a reconnaissance. Don't you agree, Sergeant White?"

"Whatever the major wishes," said the sergeant patiently, concealing his exasperation at the slow pace of this patrol.

"Good. I wish for Lieutenant Jersie to take a set of fours and determine if the fire is of suspicious origin."

"Very well, sir." Sergeant White pulled his horse out of formation and trotted back down the line of troopers. Lieutenant Jersie was almost at the end of the column, just before the pack horses. Jersie brightened upon seeing the old sergeant coming back to him.

"Something for me—at last?" Jersie asked, impatiently.

"He who waits finally gets it—in the neck," Sergeant White stated. "Our illustrious commander desires that you take a set of fours and scout out some smoke Daniels found. Take Daniel with you, also—to guide you . . . and on second thought, take Corporal Sanchez with you. I'd feel better if he's along to give you advice. And listen to him. He's seen more Apaches than you've seen pretty girls."

"Which men should I take?" Jersie asked, suddenly dry-mouthed at the thought of a hostile engagement.

"Hmm," thought Sergeant White, spitting to aid his mental process. "Take Bronson's set. They're all bachelors and none of them rookies. And remember to keep in touch with the column. Don't let us blunder into anything."

"Can I go now, teacher?" kidded the lieutenant.

"Go on . . . and remember to pay attention to Sanchez."

"Why do I get the feeling that Corporal Sanchez is in charge of my detail?" grinned Jersie, kicking his mount forward toward the stopped column.

"Because he's the smart Mexican and you are the dumb lieutenant—sir," yelled White at the young officer's quickly-moving form.

In half a minute, Sergeant White was back at his place alongside Major Poole at the head of the again-moving column. The little major greeted his return with anger.

"Can no one in this troop understand an order, Sergeant White? I thought I was very clear and distinct. I said Lieutenant Jersie and a set of fours. Instead of five people leaving this column I suddenly see seven riders detach themselves. Are you hard of hearing or just plain insubordinate?"

"Neither, sir," answered Sergeant White, expectorating grandly at a trail-side target. "Just extra cautious when it comes to Apaches. I figured that you really wanted Corporal Sanchez to go with Mr. Jersie as an Indian advisor . . . and Daniels knowed the way to the smoke. That's the two extra riders, begging your pardon, sir."

"Er, yes. I see your point, Sergeant," replied the major, with little grace. "But next time—consult me first. Remember, I command here."

"Oh, yes sir. I won't forget," fibbed Sergeant White, wishing for the thousandth time that Captain Stebbin was there, rather than Major Poole.

******

Helen Boorman, for all her experience with masculine ardor, had never known the warmth of true male love. Raised by an overworked mother and a demanding father, she was part of a family team that struggled for a living. Love or affection had no time or place in the Boorman family. Her attempts at romance, sneaked behind the barn with the lonely ranch hands, were only frenzied seconds of carnal heavings, made all the more frantic with the fear of discovery by the forbidding father.

Now Helen was treated to a new kind of love—a caring romance with a man in love, not lust. Suddenly Helen was overwhelmed with the many evidences of Henry's romantic feelings and wealth. Green Falls had few flowers, the only outlet being a small stall adjacent to the live chicken market in Spanishtown. Henry delighted in emptying this flower stall, sending its entire contents to Dora's place. Other love-gifts arrived hourly at Dora's, overflowing from Helen's room. There were flowers and potted plants everywhere about Dora's establishment; even the barroom smelled of them. Dora, when questioned by members of her clientele about the lavish display, would just smile and say something about the foolish whims of the lovesick. She could very well smile, for Henry's largess had extended to her. She had relinquished any financial claim to Miss Boorman.

Soon, Henry had moved Helen from Dora's house to a suite of rooms in the new Marble Palace Hotel, run on the European style by an emigré well versed as a hotelier.

A lady's maid was hired to serve Helen, and hopefully, to smooth the young beauty's rough edges. This woman, an immigrant from London, had opened a millinery shop in an effort to support herself when her husband was killed in a mine accident. Henry purchased her struggling shop at a princely price to persuade her to assume the boudoir duties.

The love affair between the millionaire mine owner and the beautiful courtesan was the talk of Green Falls. A fairy tale come true for every overworked woman to dream about as she sweat over her scrub board, and a reminder to every man who dreamed of riches that indeed there was a pot of gold at the end of the rainbow; a red-headed siren waiting for only him.

At first, Helen wondered about her knight-errant. She wondered if he was normal in treating her as a romantic object, rather than a sex object. Then, as she grew to know and understand Henry she basked in his love and affection and she came to love Henry.

She had always been a talker, even as a child. Her mother had called her Miss Jabber, slurring the words to "Mis'-Jabber," because Helen had always thought that however bad a situation was, talking made it better. Perhaps she thought it gave her a small measure of control. Her brusque father had learned to preface each command to her with, "now shut up and listen to this."

Heretofore, her amorous experiences caused her to talk non-stop, dredging up all manner of subjects which proved uninteresting to cowhand and customer alike. Even the Apaches, used to screams and sobbings, were startled, favorably, by her torrent of talk. Now, in the safety of Henry's gentle presence, Helen felt secure enough to stay silent. Their eyes did their talking for them, or perhaps their smiles, communicating in the ageless language of lovers.

This evening was special. After the waiter had cleared the meal from the room, Henry had knelt before her to plight his troth, pledging his undying affection. She smiled, rising to her feet and pulling Henry upright and into her embrace. "Forever and ever, Henry dear," she whispered, kissing him gently.

Then, taking his hand, she led him to the long French window that looked down on the rain-swept Main Street below. They stayed there, hand in hand, sufficient unto themselves and sure in their love, watching the storm chase the stalwart few of the night's revelers to shelter.

******

The rain stopped sometime during the early morning. By dawn the wispy clouds were fleeing before the sun. Skinner rode down to the ford to watch Sweeney's coach navigate the flooded Little Fish. Sweeney had his older son, Stuart, and his wrangler, Jesse Salinas, positioned upstream on two big wheel horses. These horses were connected to the side-shackles of the coach by ropes, helping to support the coach against the push of the current. This morning, also, Sweeney had a six-horse team, adding two of his semi-retired horses as swingers.

Fortunately, the crossing never became dangerous. The water was still below the floorboards of the coach and the river, although fairly swift, had not begun to capture large boulders in its grasp as had happened in the previous flood.

The fording successful, the support lines were cast off and Sweeney shook out the reins over his team as Mean Ed yelled and threw rocks at their rumps.

The sheriff turned his horse away from the river and towards the bakery. It was his day to buy the buns.

******

The troop came up to the smoldering, stinking ruins of the ranch at dusk. It had started raining and the cavalrymen were in their ponchos, plodding through the sticky mud. They were at the 'walk and lead your mount.' Evidently their superiors had determined that they would camp at this sad place for the night.

Lieutenant Jersie was waiting with Trooper Daniels, upwind of the ranch house. Major Poole wearily raised his arm for the halt. "Report, Lieutenant," he rasped, wrinkling his nose at the smell of the charred bodies.

"Everyone's dead, from what we can tell. Four or five of them. Burnt up. No hostiles. No horses, either."

"When did this happen?" asked Poole. "Got any idea?"

"Corporal Sanchez thinks it happened early this morning. A surprise-like. Probably caught them in bed."

"Form a burial detail, Sergeant White," ordered the Major. "What kind of scouts have we out, Jersie?"

"Corporal Sanchez posted two men on that first ridge, sir. And another man in that draw—over to the left. He took one man to follow the hostiles' tracks. Saw him heading south—sort of."

"Damn!" exploded Poole, petulantly. "I didn't want the command split up!"

"It seemed logical, sir," said the young lieutenant. "Determining the hostiles' direction, sir."

"Yes," Poole replied sourly. "Call up Simmons, Lieutenant, and have him set up my tent. Upwind . . . over there by the well. Daniels, I want you to see to my horse. Make sure you got the mud off those hocks. What kind of a guard were you going to set, Jersie?"

"Not too many, sir. Figure the Apaches are long gone. Four men and a corporal on two-hour tours, I guess."

"I don't believe in guessing, Lieutenant. Make it eight men and put one near my tent. Got that?"

"Yes sir. I'll pass it on to Sergeant White. Now I'll see about your tent, sir." Jersie saluted and walked off tiredly to see to the major's comforts.

CHAPTER 22

The rain had slowed them down. Theodore Ostenhaven was not much of a horseman and was over-cautious when the trail was slick. Jack Sprague was about to give up on any hope of getting to No Place, when they stumbled onto Charlie Hurst.

"I say," stated Ostenhaven, glad for a break from the torturous saddle, "this is a stroke of luck."

"It's a small world, Mr. Ostenhaven, even in the desert," greeted Charlie, happy for the company.

"What's this about your friend Tino finding the mine?" asked Sprague, skipping the social niceties.

"Who? What? Tino found the mine?" Hurst was shocked.

"He evidently found *some* mine," said Ostenhaven, rubbing his rump. "Whether it's Tent-Peg's mine is another question. That is why we're here—trying to find out why he is suddenly wealthy."

"Why that sneaky little . . . ah . . . sneak!" exploded Hurst. "After all I done for him!"

"Gold has a way of doing that, Charlie," Ostenhaven said piously. "When was the last time you saw him—and where?"

"Eight—no. Nine days ago. He was supposed to meet me at the hidden spring three days ago. That's why I was headed out. I'm getting real short on grub . . . and he found the mine. A gold mine?" Charlie couldn't get over Tino's discovery.

"He brought a pack train of high grade ore into Spanish-town," Ostenhaven continued. "Sold it to some fellow there and went on a spending spree. Should we camp here, Jack? I don't feel like going on."

"Why not? We found Charlie," said Sprague.

"I can't believe it," moaned Hurst. "That must be Morales . . . the man buying the ore. He's a slippery character. Tino better watch him close."

"Tino better watch *us* close," noted Jack Sprague. "We need to give him a chance to save a life, his own, maybe."

"Franklin thinks its best to offer him a partnership, Charlie. At least for the present. But we have to find him first. Do you have any idea where he can be?" Ostenhaven's usual optimism seemed to have deserted him.

"Let's talk it over after supper," proposed Hurst. "I'm starved. And we'll have to camp higher up. The snakes are too thick here for some reason."

"Snakes!" exclaimed Ostenhaven, heaving himself up into the saddle. "Why didn't you tell me that sooner?"

"I guess the news about Tino drove the snakes right out of my mind," grinned Hurst, winking at Sprague.

Later that night, under the guise of checking for hostiles, Charlie handed over to Sprague one of the steel lion-claw weapons. Sprague was evasive about its intended use and Charlie did not push him. Sprague was not a man to push.

******

At noon of the same day Sweeney angrily drove his coach back to the far bank of the Little Fish. A passing rider brought terse orders to his stage station to again bring out the old wheelers to anchor the fragile coach against the swift water.

Skinner spotted Jesse Salinas and young Stuart trotting down Main Street on the ancient horses encumbered with coils of rope, and knew something was wrong. The fording again went smoothly, although the water had risen several inches and a hot breeze tried to turn the coach into a boat, pushing against the flat side of the stage coach.

Once up on the near bank, Sweeney halted his coach alongside Skinner's horse to lay angry words on the wondering lawman, who had inquired of the problem.

"The damn road's out—that's what. Thirty-five . . . maybe forty feet, slipped out—just before you get to Dead Man's Curve. Damn dirt's all down in the bottom of the damn canyon. Need a damn bridge to get across it now."

"Sounds bad," agreed the sheriff, trying to be sympathetic.

"Sounds bad? . . . It's a goddamn catastrophe. I'm out of business. Until its fixed. And there's a couple dozen freighters backed up there."

"Guess they'll have to use the Eagle Pass cutoff, won't they?" replied Skinner.

"Oh, sure," said the old man bitterly. "Won't hurt those freighters too much—'nother half a day, probably. But me—I can't use the damn cutoff. That's that SOB Warner's route now. I'm stuck with this no-good, damn road."

"It's been blocked before, Sweeney. And repaired. Always gets repaired—eventually. I'll stop by and let Captain Mosely know about this. Maybe he can send Manny Ortiz out for a look-see."

"Won't do no damn good, too big a job for Ortiz. I'm gonna apply to use the Eagle Pass cutoff. I carry a lot of bullion out; maybe I can get the Mine Association behind me."

"Won't hurt to try, Sweeney. Meantime I'll let the powers-that-be know about the road."

The sheriff found Captain Mosely at Mrs. Purity's, eating apple pie and drinking coffee. Mosely tried to squirm down in his chair when Skinner entered the restaurant, hoping to avoid him.

"There you are; Mr. Smith said you were here."

"Remind me to fire that blabbermouth. It's getting so I can't get a free minute to myself. Want some pie? It's French apple—with raisins. I'm having it with cheese, trying out your suggestion. You bringing bad news? If you are, I'm not buying. Well? What is it?"

"I reckon I'm buying," said Skinner. "The Tucson road's washed out—bad, according to Sweeney. Thirty or forty feet slipped out; just north of Dead Man's Curve."

"In our county?" queried Mosely glumly.

"I'm afraid so. It's our responsibility. The freighters can use the Eagle Pass cutoff. It will add at least a half-day to their haul, though."

"What do you suggest, Skinner?"

"Get an estimate on repairing the break, and work from there. There's all kinds of fancy engineers here in Green Falls."

"That's what's got me scared, Sheriff. Fancy engineers with expensive ideas on how to build things. Go find Manny Ortiz and tell him to take a look at it and let me know tonight what it'll take to fix it—the cheap way. Sorry you won't have time for your pie. But duty calls, don't it?"

"How come I thought this was your problem, Captain?" asked Skinner, shaking his head at his boss's logic.

"It is, Sheriff. I'm just delegating it to you for the time being. That'll give me time for another piece of pie.

******

Poke Blaney made it to No Place on the third day. He had added another man to his outfit, unbeknownst to his superiors in Green Falls. The man was an Indian by the name of Ute Joe, who was actually a Navajo. Ute Joe had two passions in his small, clouded world. The first was a love of whiskey that was the ruination of his life. The second, more minor love of his life, was hunting. If the white man had not come upon the Indian nations with his cheap rot-gut whiskey, seducing everything of value from the native inhabitants, Ute Joe would, no doubt, be known around the campfires of the hogans as a great hunter of animals.

As a young brave he was a fine hunter, always able to bring home a stag, no matter how poor the hunting. But that was before the bottles started coming. Now Ute Joe eked out a pitiful existence, cleaning out the privies of white people who laughed at him and called him a "stinking Injun drunk," and cheated him of his wages by giving him the whiskey that made him forget how much he was owed and by whom.

The first two days on the trail with Poke Blaney were pure hell for Ute Joe, the Navajo. Days of walking in the hot sun and the cold rain; days when his body cried out for alcohol; days when he would puke up the meals that Blaney forced upon him, and nights when he would lay shaking and sweating and seeing terrible things in his troubled dreams.

Now on the third day, Blaney noticed the difference in the Indian. He ate smaller portions of Blaney's plain food and managed to keep them down. His eyes lost the bloody glaze and his gait turned from shambling to steady; and most remarkable of all—he could smell again. This was a mixed blessing because he could smell the putrid odor he presented—even the dogs considered him disgusting—interesting, but somehow unworthy to be a man.

"Why you bring me with you, old man?" finally asked Ute Joe, at last able to think clearly. "What you do with this drunk, no-good Indian?"

"You're the only man in the whole world who smells worse than me."

"I don't believe. You speak shit." The Indian spit to emphasize his statement.

"*You* smell like shit," countered Poke Blaney. "When are you gonna clean up? You're making my dogs throw up."

"Got no water. No clean clothes."

"Got no damn pride, either. Thought you was a hunter. Can't you smell the water down in No Place? If you're such a great hunter, crawl down that mountain and find enough water to wash your stinking ass. Don't bring back no whiskey, though, or I'll break your legs and leave you here for the coyotes to chew on."

"You'd do that? I thought you my friend!"

"That's why I'd do it. Put you out of your misery." Poke threw a rock at one of his dogs who was getting too aggressive with another dog.

"Let me take that black bitch with me," said the Indian. "I tie her up on the upwind side."

"Just so's you bring her back. And don't forget about the whiskey. I've put up too much with you to have you get drunk on me—now that we're close to the lion."

"Big lion, huh?"

"Yep, killed two men and tore up several others. That's why I need you. Ain't never killed no lion yet."

"I kill three lions," bragged Ute Joe. "One I kill with arrows. Two arrows. One in front leg and I track two days to find it."

"I know," said Poke, "that's why I brung ya."

"Two lion I shoots—with trade musket. I got real close—maybe fifteen paces. Only got one shot; big bullet. I shoots in eyes. Both lions. Eyes good because man puts glass eye in lion head, after scrape out brains. Bring good money. Wife buy copper pot. She like shiny stuff. I go now. Come back no stink. I promise."

Just before dawn Ute Joe, the hunter, returned to Poke's camp. He was clean and sober; clear of eyes and steady of hand. He brought two chickens with him, their necks wrung. He had with him the bitch dog, also.

******

The next few days brought both good news and bad tidings. The County Commissioners, meeting in extraordinary proceedings, approved Sweeney's plea to use the Eagle Pass cutoff until such time as the Green Falls-Tucson Road was repaired. In deference to the Warner Stage Line, Sweeney could not carry passengers; only express and mail destined for Green Falls or Tucson. Additionally, the Sweeney line was prohibited from stopping at the German settlement. This dispensation allowed the Sweeney line to at least survive and retain its mail and express contracts.

Manny Ortiz returned from the slipout site with fairly good news. The landslide, he claimed, happened due to the interaction of a slippage between a rock slope and an alluvial deposit that had become saturated with runoff water, allowing the soil to slide down the mountain.

Manny's solution was to construct a half bridge, fastening it to the solid rock and bracing it with four wooden piles anchored in the sloping surface of the rock face. Manny estimated it would take about three weeks and would cost a thousand dollars for a wooden structure or twice that for an iron-beamed affair with a wooden deck. The Commissioners immediately opted for the wooden bridge and ordered its accelerated construction. The financing of this structure was turned over to a committee headed by Captain Mosely.

The closing of Sweeney's passenger runs, however temporary, posed a problem to Sheriff Skinner. He had planned to send prisoner Knobby Malone, the murderer of Cletus, via the Sweeney line to Tucson. Accompanying the killer would be Deputy Sam and Jailer Giles, the necessary witness.

Skinner had hoped to send Esther on the same coach to Tucson with Deputy Sam to meet up with her lady escort for the trip to Cincinnati. The sheriff was hoping that Sam's good sense would sniff out any unsavory situation as to the escorting lady's purpose in the assignment. Now Skinner's hopes were dashed on the rocks of reality—much like the Tucson Road was slid into the canyon.

He felt comfortable sending prisoners on Sweeney's coach. Sweeney, while being rude and ill-tempered, was very dependable. His coaches got through. Warner's new line, using the rougher Eagle Pass cutoff, evoked no such assurances in the sheriff's mind.

This problem called for a family council, which was convened at the supper table that evening. Skinner led off by stating that the switch of stage lines caused him apprehension, especially with Esther's proposed presence.

"It's just too much to ask of Sam," explained the sheriff. "It's one thing to transport a prisoner on a strange coach, but it's another added responsibility for Sam to shepherd Esther. I just want everything to run smoothly."

"I thought Mr. Giles had to go, being a witness in the trial of that terrible man," Gen countered.

"He does. We can shackle Malone to Happy. They'll make a pretty pair." No one laughed at this—so he had to chuckle, himself.

"Why can't you just put a tag on my jacket, with where I'm supposed to go?" complained Esther, trying to assert her independence. "I read a story about a girl who traveled all the way to San Francisco like that. She even won money in a poker game."

"That's out of the question, young lady," objected Gen. "I think I should go," she continued, "to assure myself about this woman. Sometimes a woman can pull the wool over men's eyes."

"They do all the time," commented Skinner.

"What does that mean?" answered Gen, heating up.

"Nothing, absolutely nothing," Skinner backed out of that trap quickly.

"What about me?" asked Hansen. "I mean if you go, where would I eat?"

"I'd leave a bunch of corn dodgers for you, and you can fry bacon—can't you?" said Gen crankily.

"Dodgers don't help my dyspeptic stomach," complained the old man. "Too greasy."

"I would buy you a meal ticket from Mrs. Purity," announced Skinner. "A three dollar one."

"Sounds fair," said Hansen, mollified.

"And I would take Deputy Buller's place," stated Skinner. "Could even make the trip into a little holiday. Maybe a second honeymoon."

"Would be the first, Sylvester," reminded Gen. "And a stagecoach ride can never be thought of as pleasurable."

"If the meal ticket was for five, I could have dessert with every meal," spoke up Mr. Hansen. "That would make it more pleasurable to me, your running out on me like this, I mean."

"I'll pay the difference if you water my flowers while I'm gone—twice a day, mind you."

"Done," agreed the old man. "Always did like holidays."

******

The troop got a late start the next morning. Corporal Sanchez had returned after dark the evening before with information about the Apaches' route. Sergeant White wanted to get a jump on the raiders with a three A.M. start. Major Poole, though, was worried about "chasing about in the dark" and set the march for daybreak, thus protecting the Indian's ten-mile lead.

Generally speaking, the two sides were evenly matched when it came to a chase such as this. The cavalry mounts were larger and better fed than the Apaches' ponies, and had the advantage in endurance, what riders called "bottom" in their horses. The Indian advantage, the leavening agent in the chase, was their determination not to put horseflesh before their own flesh. They would run their ponies to death to keep out of the troopers' swathe. This was absolutely opposite to what cavalrymen were taught. A cavalryman who allowed his mount to founder risked court martial. A trooper's mount was his partner and his pet. An Apache's pony was just horse meat; only an animal to serve until its death.

The Apaches had by now veered completely away from the Mormon Trail, cutting southeastward through the Tortilla Mountains. Corporal Sanchez thought they were heading for a crossing on the San Pedro. Sergeant White declared it was too early to tell, while Major Poole was very content just to trail the raiders. What the major lacked in aggressive patrolling procedures, he more than compensated with his creative patrol reports to higher authorities. He was quite content to continue to reduce his supplies, peacefully, day by day, until it was time to return to the scheduled boredom of garrison life. Promotion in the Army, he was sure, rested more on time in grade than in merit. He would stay safe—and wait his promotion out.

******

Mr. J. Malloy-Fitzpatrick might not have been a renowned wild animal hunter, but thirty years in the circus trade had made him a superb camp manager. One man of the entourage, a one-handed packer named Clamp Rafferty, in deference to a swiveled device that took the place of his missing hand, had some experience hauling out copper ingots from No Place and managed to find the party a decent campsite in the mountains fifteen miles south of that hamlet.

The camp had ample firewood and an oozing spring of red-tinted liquid that Clamp Rafferty claimed was water. The animals at first disagreed with this assessment, but eventually their thirst overcame their prejudice. Unfortunately, the human members of Fitzpatrick's party had more sensitive digestive systems and the camp cook had to filter the sienna-colored sludge into something that could possibly be used to boil coffee or simmer frijoles.

Mr. Fitzpatrick, drawing heavily on his circus training, had brought a number of tents with the expedition. The placement of these tents and other amenities consumed their first day, so it was not until their second morning that Fitzpatrick could dispatch three pairs of hunters to search for sign of the lion. Several men were left in camp to assemble the lion cage. This proved to be quite difficult because none of the party had ever seen the cage erected. On the second attempt the crew found they had it assembled upside down and thus, were able on the third attempt to set it up properly.

With the cage finally erected, Mr. Fitzpatrick had the three immature goats turned into its confines. These goats were to be bait for catching the killer lion, and had been brought, trussed up in jute sacks, on the pack animals. Whether these goats would work as lion lures was uncertain. But they did seem to draw coyotes, much to the chagrin of the night guards, who felt compelled to drive these slinking creatures off with gunfire. This episode intruded on the men's sleep and all hands were very eager to find lion sign and tie the bleating kids to their waiting bait stakes.

Fitzpatrick's party, up in the mountains before No Place, never noticed Poke Blaney and Ute Joe, who plodded past them, far down in the flats. The lions, though, in the first low rise of the foothills, smelled Blaney's dogs on the first puffs of the gentle breezes that started to flow from the warmer valley floor.

The female, with the protective instinct of her gender, rose to her feet for a better sniff. The great bulging bag of her belly, showing the advanced state of her gravidity, swung clumsily under her as she advanced, muzzle upraised to the scent. She stopped and, turning to the male, growled a low warning. The grizzled old male opened one eye, looking at her lazily. Then he snuggled back against his rocky nook, scratching himself. He was old and wise and arrogant—for he considered himself the king of the hills.

CHAPTER 23

"B"ut that's the day before the election, Sylvester. Surely you would want to be here for the voting!" Gen was shocked at the timing of their departure.

"I don't see how my presence would influence a rational man's vote," said the sheriff, moving the butter crock to within better reach on the kitchen table. "I've shook a thousand hands and slapped almost that many backs. Besides, I thought I was running on my record. What happened to that campaign idea?"

"People got dim memories," noted Hansen, talking with his mouth full. "They need to be constantly reminded, all the time."

"Well Mr. Co-campaign Manager, you will have to do the reminding. I have a writ to produce Knobby Malone at Tucson day after tomorrow, election day notwithstanding. And that means I take Esther at the same time, on Warner's stagecoach, and it's going to be crowded, seeing as Sweeney is temporarily out of the passenger business."

"You might get back here to find out that you're not sheriff no more," retorted Hansen. "Any more of that fresh bread, Mrs.?" he asked Gen.

"For you, yes," replied Gen, getting up to slice several more hunks from the warm bread. "None for you, Sylvester. Your stomach won't accept it."

"Who made you the boss of my stomach?"

"Twenty-six years of hearing you complain about your stomach troubles," said Gen, stonily. "It's called self-preservation—*my* self-preservation. Certainly not yours—the way you gorge yourself on fresh bread . . . and then whimper all night about stomach pain."

"I do not whimper," stated Skinner. "Maybe a feeble fret, occasionally—at the most."

"Ha," grunted Hansen through a mouthful of bread. "I can hear you moaning from the woodshed."

"Caesar received more sympathy from the Roman senators than I get from my own household. Would it be too much to ask if this meal includes dessert?"

"Cottage pudding and maple syrup sauce," said Gen, "but you have to wait. Mr. Hansen is not through his dinner yet. Will we be staying long in Tucson? I need to know what to pack."

"One night only. Have to quickly return to the eternal appetite, here."

"Don't forget the meal ticket for Mrs. Purity's," reminded Hansen, reaching for another piece of bread.

******

On the second day of their hunt Poke Blaney's pack of hounds picked up the lion scent. Rosie, the lead bitch, could hardly contain herself with the joy of the airborne odor and seemed to squat every few feet to relieve herself, all the while trying to convince her master of the importance of the smell.

"Something's got them stirred up," agreed Ute Joe, wading through the pack. "You going to turn them loose?"

"Damn," swore Poke Blaney, who seldom used profanity. "It'll be dark in two hours 'n' we'll lose the doags. "Think we can pick up the scent first thing tomorrow? Or will the lion skedaddle?"

"Lions are sorta lazy," Ute Joe yelled, above the noise of the pack. "They generally pick out a place about four square leagues to hunt in, maybe more or less—depending on the game. But once they find a good hunting ground, with water, they won't leave. You maybe think they left, but they probably just circled around behind you. That's their weakness— they think they own the place. Don't scare easy."

"Then we'll camp for the night," declared Blaney, "and head out at daylight. We've got two days' water left. Lord willing, that'll be enough."

This time Ute Joe was wrong about the ways of mountain lions. Of course he did not know there was a pair of lions, and that the female was heading for a safe place to give birth. By the next morning the lions had gone, leaving only a fragile scent to mark their spoor.

~~~~~~~~~~~~

Discouragement was alien to Charlie Hurst. Perseverance and persistence to a set plan was his strength. By this means he had slowly worked his way out of the mines. He had started in the mines at ten, a spindle-legged, scrawny kid who earned forty cents a day leading a pony that pulled a coal cart through the pitch-dark tunnels under Pennsylvania. Then he was a drill grinder at fifty cents and finally a miner making close to a full dollar a day, based on his coal tonnage.

He left the mines, taking a wealthy man's place in the Federal Conscription of February 1863 for the sum of two hundred dollars, soon spent in debauchery. He was assigned to a pontoon and bridging train in General Meade's army and by war's end was a sergeant. Discharged, with twenty-two dollars in his issue trousers, he headed to the booming gold and silver fields.

He first went to Colorado, where he quickly traded his headlamp and shovel in on a more lucrative career as a fixer, an assistant to small-time speculators, the craft sharks who circulated among the mining towns, nosing about to do deals on supplies and equipment or procuring immigrant men for the meat grinder of the mines.

Charlie became known as a good man to see about converting pilfered highgrade or getting a quick, high interest loan. Even the rich mine owners and managers looked to Charlie when they needed an overly-loud complainer quieted.

But now Charlie was beginning to believe that he was laboring in a futile vineyard, condemned to a constant search for a gold mine never to be found. He had moodily made an early camp; determined to fry up the last of his bacon to salute his return trip to Green Falls on the following day. While the bacon was sizzling and snapping on the tiny fire he finished off the last of his whiskey to smooth the gall of frustration. Finished with the bottle, he flung it underhanded across the nearby dry wash in an arc, watching it curve, waiting for its smash.

And then he saw the flash—not the bottle at its apex, but a twinkle high up on the mountain, miles away. Again the gleam. The sun, still shining brightly just over the shoulder of the opposing range, was striking something shiny. Charlie rushed to the telescope in his saddlebag, rescuing the blackening bacon on the way.

The telescope showed a tiny, flea-sized procession winding down an invisible trail, moving slowly down a precarious path. Charlie yelled in exuberance.

"Hot damn! Tino, you little son of a bitch, I got you now!" He slammed the telescope closed and went back to his meal a happy man.

******

The sheriff, using the weight of his office, arranged for Warner to bring his coach first to the jail, ostensibly to load the prisoner, Knobby Malone. He also utilized this stop to bring Gen and Esther aboard the coach, settling them in the most comfortable, front-facing, seats. Their party numbered five with Happy Giles, to whom Knobby was shackled, and Skinner. At the regular starting place Warner loaded five additional passengers: two miners; the Episcopal Bishop, Dr. Parkham and Mr. and Mrs. Henry Stultz, newlyweds off to San Francisco. The two miners, seeing themselves outranked by officialdom, millionaires and the ecclesiastic, grumbled but obliged by taking seats on the coach roof. Warner climbed up to the guard's seat and gave his reinsman the word to move out to Kolbheim, the German settlement and first scheduled stop.

Kolbheim was two and a half hours by coach from Green Falls. There, a woman was added to the coach's inside passengers, forcing Gen and Esther to squeeze together alongside the Bishop and the dumplingish new acquisition. Skinner sat on the backward-facing seat while Malone and Jailer Giles made do on the floor, leaning against the doors. The newlyweds had joined Skinner on the front seat.

It was uphill from Kolbheim on the Eagle Pass cutoff, steeper than the now-closed Tucson Road. The six-horse team was a must, what with the alluvial soil and sandy traps of the ancient watercourse that begot the wagon trail. Occasionally the horses could be coaxed into a trot on a short downhill section, but always the agony of the next grade quickly awaited them. At one steep ascent the male passengers were ordered out to walk by the reinsman yelling, "Out and foot it, all and every mother's son, or my nags is surely done and soon forgot."

"The rhyme is apropos," complained the bishop, trying to watch his steps in the gravel to spare his low-cut boots. "But the meter and grammar could use some work."

"His skill, Your Excellency," grunted Sheriff Skinner, "lies in his hands, not in his verse. I surely wish we could trade this coach for an Erie Canal boat. Now *that* is stylish travel.

Maybe not as fast as a steam train, but smooth, stylish travel, and without the soot of a locomotive."

"You are familiar with the Erie Canal, Sheriff?" asked the bishop, now red-faced from the climb.

"As a boy I lived only a few miles from it. Sometimes I would accompany my father to Albany with our cheeses on the packet boat. Four miles an hour, night and day, if it was a fast packet. All done with two horses, and so smooth.

"One time when I was thirteen or fourteen I went with my father in the middle of a terrible stormy night to repair a break in the canal. Must have been two or three hundred men and women working waist-deep in the water to plug the hole. Took all night and most of the next day. I remember I got fifty cents. My first big money. My father got two-fifty, what with his team. I'll never forget the torches and the cold water—and the spirit of the people, determined to save their canal. And they were just farm people—working for a few coins."

"Shows what people can do, when they want to work together," commented the bishop, puffing badly.

"That's what made the war so awful, Reverend. I heard a politician who was making a speech when they opened one of the new double locks on the canal. You know, so the barges could go both directions at the same time. He said that the canal was a bigger project than all the Egyptian pyramids put together. Just imagine if all the millions of men and money wasted in the war had been used to advance our society. We could have a canal clear across the country or maybe ten railroads or whatever. Something to be proud of— not sorry for, like the war. I lost a son in the war . . . did I ever tell you?"

"No. I'm sorry. I was a chaplain in a Massachusetts regiment. I saw so much horror—yes, and bravery. I still have awful dreams. I've prayed a thousand times to God to have Him heal my mind. But I guess He wants me to remember the frailty of man. Perhaps to emphasize the spiritual side of His children . . . praise the Lord, Sheriff. The coach is stopping and our poet beckons." The men piled back in (Knobby was pushed in) and the door latched, and they were off again.

******

They talked about it later, the sheriff and those who lived through it, trying to figure out how they just drove into an Indian raid. The consensus was that the wind was wrong and the noise from the coach and the team was just too loud to hear the firing until it was too late. Happy Giles also believed the reinsman was nearsighted and didn't see the Apaches until it was too late.

The long and the short of the episode was that the stage-coach drove right up to the Mesa Grande Saloon and Store when that establishment was under considerable attack by a good-sized group of angry Apaches. The stagecoach and the passengers paid the price.

A lot of credit should go to Jerome T. Warner, the stage-line operator, who was acting as shotgun guard. He held the Apaches at bay while the passengers scrambled to safety within the saloon and store. The reinsman died fast and first, whether caused by his myopia was uncertain. The same quick fate caught the fatter of the two miners—dead from an Indian lance while his less fleshy partner scurried to shelter. Warner almost made it, but fumbled his second reload, to chase an errant cartridge when he should have been shooting. He went down with a young brave's shotgun blast that took off the back of his head.

Two horses were shot and down in their chains, the off leader and the off swinger. The near wheeler was panicked and tangled in his chains. But by then the remaining passengers were within the stout adobe walls of the Swanson's store. Skinner was the last to enter, firing off his loads to hold off the attackers.

"Hot damn!" yelled Mrs. Swanson, the volunteer Deputy Sheriff of Mesa Grande. "I knowed the sheriff would rescue us! Where's the rest of the posse?"

"Posse, hell!" exploded the Sheriff of Green Falls, laying out paper cartridges for reloading on the bar. "I'm supposed to be a passenger—a paying passenger."

"Well," rationalized Mrs. Swanson, "we're glad you could stop by. Those savages seem quite determined."

"Should I put the beam back on the door now?" asked Mr. Swanson, seemingly dazed by the commotion.

"Go ahead, pa," said Mrs. Swanson, evidently in charge of the defense. "And then go behind the bar with Emma. You can reload when our guns go dry."

"Who else is here?" asked Skinner, pointing out a shuttered window to Happy Giles to use for firing at the Indians.

"Mr. Jessup and his Mexican is in the back bedroom and hall. But Jessup ain't much of a shot. The Mexican makes up for him, though. Could use somebody in the upstairs guest room. It's got a window to the side towards the freighter's corral."

"Reverend, could you . . ."

The bishop waved his acceptance and ran up the stairs, pistol in one hand and ecclesiastical bag in the other.

"Can I help? I've got a derringer here." Henry Stultz produced a short-barreled pistol.

"Here—take the Springfield," said Mrs. Swanson. "Pa don't want to shoot it, anyway. Shoots a mite low and to the right. So aim at the right shoulder and you'll get 'em in the gizzard. Here's a bag of cartridges and there's a little tin of caps in the bag, too."

"Henry, you be careful," called Helen. "I'm too young to be a widow."

Gen took Esther around behind the bar and turned the Swanson baby, Emma, over to her control. The baby smelled and Esther stated the obvious. "Aunt Gen, I think the baby needs changing."

"That's nice, dear," replied Gen. "Use that dry bar rag there and see to it."

"Oh no, not my clean bar rag!" wailed Mr. Swanson. "It'll never get clean."

"Doesn't look very clean now, mister. Go ahead, Esther. Do as I say."

Mrs. Swanson went into the store and brought out several used weapons, evidently part of her sales stock. Skinner handed the Enfield to the skinny, surviving miner and appropriated the Henry for himself.

"How long has this been going on?" he asked Mrs. Swanson.

"'Bout half an hour before you rescued us," giggled the female deputy. "They rode up and demanded food and guns. I said, 'sure thing' and slammed the door and set the bar across it. Jessup and his man was having lunch in his office next door and they came running in the back door. That Jessup can run pretty good for a fat man. He just . . ."

Happy Giles interrupted from the front window. "Hey, Sheriff. Don't look now, but them redskins is burning the coach. Might catch the porch on fire once it gets going."

"How's the water situation, Mrs. Swanson?" asked Skinner, finished loading his Colts.

"Good. Got two pipes from the big water line the freighters put in. Got water in the kitchen and there at the bar. It's from the spring up by the quarry. Cost the freighters fifty dollars—what with the cedar piping. Goes over to their corral. Runs all the time."

"Well, I think you'd better get everything that can hold water in case that porch goes."

"Won't burn too much. Put a tin roof on last year. Just the supports will burn. I hope. But I'll get some pails and buckets. We got three hundred and thirty gallons of beer in the cool cellar . . . if the water ain't enough."

Happy heard that. "The water should do it, Mrs.. Gotta save the beer for drinking. Ain't that right, Sheriff?"

"Mr. Giles, if we live through this, I'll buy all you can drink at one sitting."

"Hallelujah!" cried Happy. "I heard that. Look out, you red devils! I got an interest in this here war." Setting action to words, he fired twice, quickly, through the shutter's loop-hole. "Think I got one already."

"Just great," muttered Mr. Swanson as he levered down a ball in a spare Remington. "Only a hundred more to go."

******

The big sign proclaimed "We're Painting the Town Red. Have a red beer on Sultan Sanders for a pre-election celebration."

The candidate was standing on small, bunting-draped dais, handing out long strings of tickets, each of which was redeemable at any saloon for a schooner of red-tinted beer.

"You gonna vote for me tomorrow, my friend?" Sanders asked every supplicant for brew, eliciting a promise for every string of tickets. The beer tickets were Gompers' idea; a move designed to allay the saloon keepers' resentment with the free, widespread distribution of their profitable product. Every saloon had been issued a large jar of reddish dye (secretly made of pickled beets) and an eyedropper for administering the coloring into the beer. Gompers promised repayment of each ticket at six cents, giving the saloon an extra cent reward for the red dye trouble. Everyone was pleased. Ten thousand tickets had been bought from Van Doormann. A large part of the Green Falls population would go to bed inebriated this night and awake to wonder at their red tongues and lips the next morning.

All in all it was a grand party, especially for a pre-celebration. Mr. Gompers went to sleep that night happy with the thought that his candidate was a shoo-in and that the autocratic Skinner was to be tossed out on his ear. That image was enjoyable to Gompers; Skinner lying in the dust of Main Street, badgeless and rejected. "Serves him right, fooling with me," smiled the merchant king as he dozed off, happy with the dream.

******

The Apaches waited until the saloon and store defenders were busy with the fiery porch to mount their first concentrated attack. This assault came at the rear of the building where Jessup, the quarry operator and his Mexican assistant, Miguel, were posted.

Skinner had anticipated an assault, somewhat, and had Gen and Helen doing most of the firefighting with Henry Stultz helping when his duties at the store's front window permitted. Luckily the surviving miner was a veteran and efficient under fire. Skinner gave him the spare Remington pistol as a supplementary weapon to the single-shot percussion Enfield.

With the miner, Mrs. Swanson and her repeating rifle, and himself, the sheriff had a three man (or two man and a quick-shooting woman) force to repel any assault that would gain a foothold in their sanctuary. Mr. Swanson, armed with his under-the-bar shotgun, hopefully, could protect the firefighters in case of a second assault upon the charred, but still strong, front door.

The counterattack trio, hurriedly named and briefed, were soon committed into the breach. The perspiring Jessup, his old fowling piece emptied, had fled the Swanson's bedchamber three jumps ahead of several determined Apaches, one of whom was carrying a sledge hammer belonging to the quarry.

Miguel, armed with a huge dragoon revolver, stayed at his back door post longer, making the Apaches pay, but finally, concerned with being cut off by the attackers, retreated back up the hall, firing when he had a target.

The Apaches, then, were in the rear hallway, forcing the now wounded Miguel back into the store. Skinner's trio arrived as Miguel, whose ammunition was exhausted, tried to use the big pistol's butt as a weapon and got a lance in his ribs in the unequal combat.

Miguel reeled and fell, snapping the lance in two. With Miguel down, the hallway held only Indians and the counter-attackers filled the tight space with bullets, stopping the assault in a gory tangle of half-naked Apaches and blood.

The plucky Miguel was pulled out of the pile, badly wounded but swearing strongly. Mrs. Swanson put a shot into each Indian's brain to assure their confidence (the defenders'—not the Apaches'). Skinner posted the miner at the back door and browbeat the frightened Jessup into returning to the bedroom, where they piled the corn husk mattress against the shattered window and reinforced it with a heavy bird's-eye maple chest of drawers. The sheriff stayed with Jessup as the heavy man nervously loaded his fowling piece and set the caps. Skinner cautioned him to fire only one barrel at a time, keeping the other barrel always ready for emergencies.

When he returned to the saloon, Skinner found Miguel stretched out across two tables, being worked on by the former firefighters: Gen, Helen and the German woman. Gen had lost part of her hair and was scorched about the face and eyebrows, while the hem of Helen's velvet skirt was burned almost to her knees. Mr. Swanson was loading his wife's weapon, as that good woman was busy nursing her infant.

Happy, seeing the sheriff's return, called to report that he had finished off the coach horses as the fire had trapped them in their traces. He had also manacled Knobby Malone to the wrought-iron section of ore-track rail that served as the bar's footrest.

"Gimme a gun to defend myself," argued the murderer. "I don't want them Injuns getting what little hair I got."

"No way, Malone," barked Skinner, stopping at the bar to reload his half-spent Henry. "But I got a slug here for you if they get too close. Just like you got Cletus. How's that for fair?"

"Thanks a lot—for nothing," growled Malone.

"No thanks necessary—it's my pleasure."

The incongruity of Mrs. Swanson sitting calmly on the littered floor behind the bar nursing her babe, when only minutes before she had callously given the downed Apaches their coup de grace, was too much for Skinner. He started laughing, unable to control himself.

Miguel, on the tabletops, turned to glare at the mirthful lawman, inappreciative of levity while he was in pain.

"What's so funny, you stupid Gringo?" the blood-soaked Mexican croaked. "You never saw no Mexican blue blood? I am from the line of the conquistadors, I want you to know."

"You sure showed it back in that hallway, my Mexican friend," replied the abruptly sobered sheriff. "You were a regular one-man army."

"Sí. That is true," smiled Miguel—and straightaway died.

CHAPTER 24

C harlie Hurst had gotten the jump on his prey, Tino the muleteer, by leaving camp at the near-midnight moon rise. He picked his way carefully across the valley floor to where he thought the mountain trail started. It was Tent-Peg's mule who nosed out the narrow, indistinct trail. It was soon verified by mule droppings and Charlie felt the flush of excitement dampened in the chill of the desert night.

Tino was still sleeping when Charlie found the little muleteer's camp in the early gray of the false dawn. Cautiously, Tino's rifle was removed from his reach and then he was aroused with a strong kick to his ribs. Tino sat up, startled by the sudden wakening. Then, as comprehension came around, so did his toothy smile.

"Señor Charlie, I look all over zee beeg mountain for you. I have zee beeg luck to share wiz you." He tried to get up but Charlie pushed him back with his rifle barrel.

"What kind of luck?" growled Charlie.

"Zee bes kind, Señor Charlie. You an' me ees going to be reech." Tino was on his knees now, the smile even broader. He was talking for his life, and they both knew it.

"What'd you find, Tino—and where?" Charlie cocked the Winchester's hammer, ominously.

"Up zere, Señor Charlie. Good ore, lots of bright gold, señor. Half for you, señor, and half for Tino who finds eet. Zat's fair, ees not, Señor Charlie?"

"That what's in those sacks, Tino?"

"Sí, Señor Charlie. I bring eet to zee assay man in Green Falls. I zink eet bring mucho dollars."

"How about you showing me where this gold mine is, Tino my friend. Then we'll talk about your split. I hope you remember that you were working for me when you found it. Maybe even give you a third interest."

"You good man, Señor Charlie. I tell my wife, Conchita, an' my leetle childrens. You good man."

"Sure I am, Tino. Now give them mules of yours some water and check their hobbles. We'll pick them up on the way down, after you show me our mine."

"Sí, sí, Señor Charlie. Tino ees good, ees he not—for finzing zee mine?"

"That's right, Tino; you got the luck working for you," said Charlie convincingly. "I got the patience and you got the luck."

******

On the evening of the day Ostenhaven and Sprague separated from Charlie Hurst for the long ride back to Green Falls they came across J. Malloy-Fitzpatrick's main camp. Actually, their path was lower, but they saw the camp's smoke and, like a lonely ship in the ocean, veered their course to talk up a strange sail. Fitzpatrick's camp was deserted, though, except for a camp guard who evidently had a cache of whiskey at his disposal. Although half-drunk, the man was affable, inviting Ostenhaven and Sprague to supper with him.

"Damn glad for company, I can tell you. Got some still-fresh bacon and I'm gonna make up a mess of frying pan biscuits with the bacon fat. We'll have a real feast."

"That's kind of you," replied Ostenhaven, ever polite and the gentleman, even when he hurt from the saddle. "Would it be too much to ask if we could camp here?"

"No trouble at all. There's water over there, only it's awful strong. That's why I cut it with whiskey. To tell you the truth,

I'm glad for the company. Gets sorta spooky at night with all those damn coyotes yapping and wailing all night 'count of them damn goats. Wasn't happy when ole Fitzy left me here, I can tell you."

"Where is he now? Do you know?" asked Sprague.

"Not real certain. South, in the hills—somewhere. Looking for that lion. And I'm stuck here watching that damn cageful of goats."

"What are the goats for—food?"

"Yeah—food. Food for a hungry lion. But why they left them here with me, I dunno. Sure would be quieter at night without 'em to rile up the coyotes."

"We thank you for the hospitality," replied Ostenhaven, not really sure about the presence of a large population of coyotes. "Jack, could you take care of my horse and I'll have a go at putting up the tent. Would it be all right to place it close to the fire?" he asked of the camp guard.

"Fine with me. I generally bundles up next to it, myself. Somebody tole me that them coyotes is afraid of fire. So I stays close to it in the dark."

"What about the goats? Ain't you afraid for them—what with the coyotes?" asked Sprague, trying to seem convivial.

"Naw—they're bolted in the cage. At least the damn thing is good for that. Weighs six hundred pounds if it weighs an ounce. Like to kilt the damn mules—galled them bad, both of them. Hard to get a purchase on all that iron. Crazy, I say. A cage what's good for nuthin', if you asks me."

But the camp guard was to be proved wrong. The imposing cage was useful to Jack Sprague. He slaughtered the goats the next morning and then conveyed the unconscious forms of the guard and Ostenhaven on one of the horses to the cage. There, he dragged them in with the slaughtered goats and used the steel lion's claw to mutilate both men and goats, reducing all to an oozing, fly-infested scattering of carrion.

When Jack Sprague was finished with the gory job he stood back from his work as an artist would assess his representation. He smiled at the bloody mess he had created. Then, leaving the cage door open wide to the ever-present scavengers, he saddled his horse and loaded the pack animal and set off to bring the news to Green Falls of the lion's latest trespass.

******

The young vaquero was pleased. One moment he had the unenviable task of breaking the new horses to halter and the next moment the English lord had picked him, Felipe, a fairly new ranch hand, away from the snubbing post to ride to the Mesa Grande store to collect the mail. The store had a supply of candy: peppermint sticks, rum balls and his favorite, the tooth-breaking horehound drops, bitter and minty and so delicious. He had brought money, two half-dimes, and would buy a large package of the candies.

The day was hot but the trail was flat and his horse eager for decent exercise, the two-mile ride a romp with candy at its end. And yes, don't forget the mail for the Charleton Rancho. But suddenly, almost to the store, Felipe heard the firing. He slowed his horse to a trot, immediately wary, for he had heard the stories told about the Indians. He crossed the Tucson Road to get into the low foothills around the quarry which gave him protection against casual observance.

From the quarry he could look down at the store and saw the gunsmoke spilling from the store and the Indians firing and flitting about the store like angry hornets. He tried counting the attackers and gave up after twelve, unsure if he was counting the same Indian twice.

An Indian kicked his pony away from the firing, heading to a small enclosure that held two mules still chained to their singletrees. Felipe left hurriedly to avoid detection. He had seen enough to warn the English lord of danger to the rancho.

******

"We got powder and ball aplenty. But the metal cartridges is getting short," reported Mrs. Swanson to the sheriff, who was sitting on the bar's footrail, his long legs sprawled out before him.

"Then we'll have to save the repeaters for emergencies and use the older rifles for this damned sniping," said Skinner.

Henry Stultz left his front window position to get in on the conversation. (Evidently, millionaire mine owners take poorly to the role of private soldier.)

"Be dark soon," observed Stultz. "They should leave us alone then."

"Who said that?" Skinner was testy with the millionaire.

"I'm told that Indians don't fight during darkness. Something about their religion or their spirit being lost in the dark."

"Well don't bet on it. They're a terror day or night, and they can see better at night than a white man."

"I didn't know that. How come they can see so good at night?" The thought had subdued the younger man.

"I figured something to do with their history and upbringing. They don't have oil lamps and candles to light up their lodges. And their diet. At least that's what Cletus used to say. If they think the dark gives them an edge—they'll take it."

"Can we stop them in the dark? I'm worried about Helen, you know." It sounded like he was also worried about Henry Stultz.

"That was, Mr. Stultz, what Mrs. Swanson and I were trying to figure out before you came looking for a good word. Go back to your post; there is no good words. Go shoot an Apache— while you can still see them." Henry left, like a spanked puppy.

"Sorta hard on him, ain't you?" objected Mrs. Swanson. "He's out of his world here, shooting at Injuns."

"Maybe I can scare him into trying harder. At least, maybe, keep him awake. God, I hate amateurs. Lost half a thousand of them in the war."

"So what does the veteran colonel suggest for tonight?"

"We need to take the wind out of their sails. Cut the Apaches' confidence; besides, I was only a major."

"Good enough for this dump. This ain't exactly Gettysburg."

"If it was a big battle," mused Skinner, "some Jack-a-dandy staff officer would send down to brigade for a sortie in force to annoy the enemy. Maybe even provoke him into doing something rash."

"Is that what we need?" she asked quietly.

"Perhaps. I'm just thinking out loud. We don't really have enough people to sally out, effectively."

"Our repeaters give us an advantage. You, me and that miner. We could break into their beauty sleep. But you got the miner holding down Miguel's old post at the back door. How about your prisoner? Would you trust him to hold that post?"

"I could talk to him, I guess," said Skinner. "Appeal to his good side, if he's got one."

"That would free up the miner. And I got two more Enfields you could arm the women with."

"What about Mr. Swanson—will he fight?"

"For Emma, the baby, he will or I'll throttle his skinny neck. I'll go scare him now."

"And I'll talk to Knobby. Maybe we'll make it. At least we'll die trying, anyway."

Skinner duck-walked down to his prisoner's end of the footrest. Malone turned sullen eyes on the sheriff's interruption of his misery. "Come back to mock me some more?" he rasped.

"I've come with a proposition, Knobby."

"You need me to fight, huh?"

"That's right—in one respect. We need you to take Miguel's place."

"That back door is a one-way ticket to hell. You know that. And you're asking me to sacrifice myself?"

"Knobby, face facts. You killed a deputy—just on a whim—and you'll swing for sure. I'm giving you a chance to redeem yourself."

"Is this the Jesus argument?"

"Don't you believe in the hereafter, Knobby?"

"Never thought much about it. Death, I mean. Never figgered on dying. The booze had me. Know what I mean?"

"I was there once, myself. After my daughter died. What I'm asking—we're asking—is that you have the courage to fight to save us all."

"And after—if I live thought this all—I swing for murder? Don't sound quite fair. Kill a loud-mouthed deputy and it's called murder; kill an Apache or two and it's public service. Strange, huh?"

"The world is a strange place, Knobby. Nobody said it was perfect."

"But heaven is, huh? Will you guarantee I get to heaven if I die by that back door?"

"Sure, Knobby. I guarantee it—for what that's worth."

"Skinner, you're a liar, but I respect you for being a straight lawman. I'll do it. I'll take the back door.

"One little detail that I omitted, Knobby."

"What's that?"

"You're to be manacled to your post. I don't want you changing your mind and sneaking off."

"What the hell, why not? Only chain me by an ankle so I can reload better."

"Your ankle it is, Knobby." The sheriff stood up to call to Mr. Swanson to take Happy's place as Giles would have to unlock Malone from the footrest. Mrs. Swanson came with one of the spare Enfields and a supply of paper-wrapped cartridges and a pill case of percussion caps; and then Knobby was escorted to his post.

******

Felipe had just brought the news of the Indian attack at Mesa Grande. Luckily for George Charleton, Fourteenth Earl of Ruddhampton, now trying to regain his fortune in the cattle business in America, his foreman was at the main ranch arguing about moving a herd further into the summer range. The foreman, Two Finger Tommy Bates, was part wrangler, part cattleman, and all Indian fighter.

"First off, we gotta send for the soldiers," stated the grizzled old-timer. "Next we gotta get El Teniente back here quick with his gunslingers." El Teniente Valdez, an expatriate Mexican lancer lieutenant from Emperor Maximilian's Mexican adventure, was the Charleton enforcer. The private policeman of George Charleton's huge ranch was concerning himself and his half-dozen rough men with rustlers and nesters, always a problem in the unfenced great tracts.

"We should notify Captain Butler, also," put in His Lordship, unwilling to forfeit all generalship to his more experienced foreman. The Butler spread was the Charleton neighbor to the south, towards Tucson.

"Yeah," agreed Tommy, "the galloper we send to Tucson can ride by Captain Butler, but I dunno about sending help to Mesa Grande. We don't have enough men around here to protect ourselves."

"I hadn't thought of sending help, I must admit," said His Lordship. "How many men, all told, have we here?"

"'Bout ten, including the cook. I'll have to send Felipe, here, to Tucson and I'll probably send Whitey off to find Teniente and his bunch."

"What can I do?" asked Charleton.

"Get Jorge the cook to move his supplies into the stone house. And water, too. I'll get the gallopers going. And then I'm gonna go on a scout—toward Mesa Grande. You'll have to make the stone house ready. Can you do that?" The old foreman gave the Englishman a hard look.

"Most certainly. I come from a military line, you know. My father fought with Wellington."

"Good. Now you maybe get to fight with the Apaches. Come on, Felipe, I'll tell you what to tell Butler and the Army." Two Finger Tommy pulled the young vaquero off to the stable.

******

The following passage was part of a conversation with Chief Slit-Nose, recorded in 1887 by an Indian Bureau employee:

The whites were behind their thick walls and well-armed. My braves, now down to eleven, were forced to fight from behind whatever poor cover they could find. I think of myself as a great warrior with much experience in war, having received my name, Slit-Nose, after my wounding by the Arapaho when a young brave of only fourteen summers. I am not a magician or a shaman and I am not able to produce victories out of a campfire's smoke.

I realized, especially after the disastrous attack on the whites of that afternoon when four braves were trapped and killed by the whites, that we must have a great plan to root them from their lair.

I sent my nephew, Swift Arrow, to bring in a mule of the whites for a feast. That night we would eat the mule and dance a dance to refresh our enthusiasm for battle. I picked two braves who would watch the whites, firing occasionally as needed to frighten them into staying behind their walls.

In this choice of braves, I made a mistake—an old man's error. I must admit to the fault of vanity. All during this long raid, for the many suns on our quest, I had noticed the young brave, Owl-Who-Kills-At-Night, becoming, more and more, the natural leader of our war party. I am ashamed to reveal that this was partly my fault. The long travel had tired me as never before, and my bones hurt, causing me to withdraw and my influence on my braves to wane. I found myself speaking complaints rather than the necessary assurances. Slowly the braves turned to Owl-Who-Kills-At-Night for advice and the small instructions needed for the march or the attack. I allowed this gradual minor assumption of command, for I thought it easier having a strong second commander; much as the white soldiers have lesser leaders with slashes on their shirt arms.

I was wrong. Perhaps the white soldiers can split their loyalty between big chiefs and little chiefs. The Apaches cannot. Always, a strong man is sought for instruction. Many times when a war chief is killed, the braves will flee, unable to continue fighting until a new leader is found.

Thus was I jealous of Owl-Who-Kills-At-Night. In an effort to regain my authority, I began assigning him tasks that took him away from the band. Scouting was good to this end. It kept him away and also provided us with excellent information. The young brave was good. Perhaps too good to suit his master.

This night of the feast and the dance, I posted him at the front of the white's storehouse. I also placed my nephew, Swift Arrow, to secure the rear of the whites, hoping to raise his stature in the band as a rival to Owl-Who-Kills-At-Night, diminishing his power over my braves.

Swift Arrow, though of my family, would never be a great warrior. He always had a silly smile, even in war-paint, and a stupid jest about serious matters. Also, sadly, he was a glutton, even measured among the Apache, famed for periods of starvation and intense eating. Yes, fat, lazy and a clown. And I was given the task of making him an Apache warrior by my sister, who had given up on the job as hopeless.

Now we know that it was Swift Arrow who found the white men's whiskey in the small home alongside the storehouse, for after the whites had inflicted their revenge, striking our camp in the darkness and retiring quickly, we found Swift Arrow unconscious and likely near death. Immediately I thought of my sister's grief; the cutting she would make on herself and the wailing. But the stupor of my nephew was due to whiskey, not wounds, and I was disgraced. Two more dead braves, several more wounded, and any war-like thoughts of my surviving braves were lost in their worry of the whites' abilities.

At the first glow of the sun we left, our only prizes an obstinate mule and an overly-large riding horse. We crossed the wagon road, heading for a ranch that was said to have many horses. We could not return to our tribe without some fruit for our efforts—and losses. I had failed to embarrass Owl-Who-Kills-At-Night, shaming only myself and my family.

(End of excerpt)

CHAPTER 25

T he election polls in Green Falls opened at nine A.M. and would close at nine P.M. The voting place was a tent erected before the Post Office, a position normally occupied by horses tethered to the hitchrack. No provision was made for voters in Holiday, Kolbheim or any other far parts of Green Falls County. This became a sore point in future elections, that outer electorate claiming lack of representation, and this policy was changed four years later with the introduction of an at-large commissioner and polling places in Holiday and Kolbheim.

Election day was a brisk business day for the saloons. Gompers hustled through the crowded polling lines, handing out his red-beer tickets. Sultan Sanders took his stance just outside the polling tent, shaking hands with each of the voters as they passed in line. He was not alone, as most of the commissioner candidates were also there, jostling the harassed electorate.

Van Doormann, the newspaper publisher, voted at eleven for all the incumbents and then rushed back to his print shop to set up type for an election special edition that proclaimed Sultan Sanders the new sheriff. Van Doormann was a trained reporter and knew a landslide when he saw it.

******

The incumbent Sheriff of Green Falls was, at the time of the poll opening, in pain. He had been wounded during the sally, while making a quick retirement. He was shot above his left boot in the calf muscle. The ball missed the bone, but bruised it, passing out of his leg cleanly. At first the wound had numbed the leg, allowing Mrs. Swanson and Gen to clean it out and sew it up. By near sunrise, though, the pain had come and with it, the sweats.

Mrs. Swanson offered some pain drops, to be mixed with water. Skinner declined, fearing it would compromise his alertness, as he feared an attack at full light.

Thankfully though, the day brought peace. Mrs. Swanson and the miner reconnoitered outside the store and reported the Apaches gone, along with Jessup's mules and horse. Later that morning, Miguel and the charred lumps that were Warner, the near-sighted driver and the fat miner were buried beneath the pepper tree at the rear of Jessup's small stone house. The Episcopal Bishop officiated.

The congregation was ragged and tired, especially Jessup and the miner, who had dug the graves. Happy Giles wore a turban-like bandage on his head that covered a sutured wound to his right eyebrow and forehead; the result of a splinter rent from the window shutter during the early morning's desultory sniping. Knobby Malone wore a splint on his left elbow to protect a smashed elbow; only strong spirits and Mrs. Swanson's laudanum drops keeping him from excruciating pain.

The Reverend Bishop was also wounded, a slashed right cheek now cross-hatched with the German woman's stitchery and smeared with cobwebs from the cool cellar. Sheriff Skinner watched the proceedings from a chair by a window of the saloon, unwilling to limp out on his sore leg.

No sooner was the ceremony finished and the mourners returned to the saloon, with the exception of the miner who volunteered to backfill the graves, than Sweeney's stagecoach came roaring up to Mesa Grande.

The older Sweeney had stopped the coach as far from the fire-blackened front of the store as the road would allow and did not set the brake, in anticipation of a fast departure.

"Hello, the saloon!" shouted young Stuart, with the better lungs. "Show yourself if you're alive."

The defenders, to a man (and woman), yelled to establish their presence, the miner running over, waving his shovel like a battle flag. Assured of the Apache withdrawal, Sweeney set the brake and climbed down to take in the scene of battle.

"Lordy, folks! You was lucky," Sweeney exclaimed, when the front door of the store and saloon was hurriedly forced open on its warped and blackened stiles.

"It were shooting—not luck, I'll have you to know," corrected Mrs. Swanson. "We just plain out-shot them Apaches."

"Would ya say the bar's open?" ventured Sweeney. "I could use a cool beer."

"Don't see why not," agreed Mrs. Swanson. "Pa, bring up a couple pitchers of beer."

"We got enough damage here without giving out free beer," argued Mr. Swanson, rising Lazarus-like from his safe spot behind the bar.

"Just get the beer and be glad you've still got hair on your head. Let me worry about the damages," scolded his wife.

"Sweeney," called Skinner, rising awkwardly from his chair. "Have you room for ten people to Tucson?"

"Got room but no license to carry passengers—only mail and valuable express."

"That was yesterday, Sweeney. We buried your competition just before you got here."

"He was on that coach?" Sweeney seemed surprised at his adversary's death. "He didn't work it every day . . . same as me."

"He died holding off the Apaches—so we could get out . . . and into the saloon. Saved most of us, I reckon." Skinner's bad leg suddenly gave way and only Sweeney's quick help averted a fall.

"You better get off that leg," advised young Stuart, who had tied off the brake and climbed down to see the damages.

"I got a chair inside," grunted Skinner, mouth wide with the pain.

"And you should be in it instead of dancing around there on the wreckage of that porch," railed Gen, taking charge of her husband.

"Dammit, woman!" fumed Skinner, trying unsuccessfully to free himself; "I am trying to arrange passage for us with this man."

"He'll give us passage, Sylvester, or Helen and I will use those rifles on him. Won't we, Helen?"

"Mine's loaded and ready," said Helen, retrieving her Enfield.

"Don't shoot, ladies," Sweeney called out, laughing. "I know an emergency situation when I see one." He turned to his son. "Boy, give them horses a bit of a drink while I figure out where to stow all these new passengers."

"You won't have to worry about our baggage," Helen observed. "It's all burned up . . . just ashes."

"Don't worry, dear." Henry came over to console her. "There's plenty more where they came from."

"Speak for yourself, Mr. Millionaire," snapped Gen, suddenly worried more about appearances than Apaches. "This scorched rag I'm wearing used to be my best frock."

******

The half-dozen defenders of Charleton had worked feverishly to prepare the headquarters house for the Apache attack. The gallopers had hazed out the dozen horses in the stable on their way for help. Hopefully those horses could be retrieved after the hostilities. Charleton had Felipe ride his blooded stallion to Tucson to protect the horse from the Indians. The cook shack had been stripped and the provisions stacked in the stone house that was Lord Charleton's office and living quarters.

This house was twenty feet square and built for just these circumstances. The eight windows of the house were more like firing slits than windows and were protected by heavy, loop-holed shutters. The only door was four inches thick, reinforced with iron strapping and plated on the outside with eighth-inch sheet iron for fire protection. The roof was of Spanish tile. The cellar held two forty-four gallon water casks, along with powder, shot and metallic cartridges for five thousand rounds of fire.

The last barrel had just been filled from the well next to the cook shack when the lookout called out that Two Finger Tommy was coming in at reckless gallop.

"They're acoming! 'Bout a dozen of them, slow-like, favoring their ponies," Tommy shouted, swinging down from his lathered horse. He stripped saddle and bit from his mount and banged a leathery hand on its rump to chase it off.

"How long before . . ." started Charleton.

"Five . . . ten minutes, maybe," interrupted Tommy. "But they'll nose around a bit before they try us. Maybe tonight—who knows?"

"I thought you were the Apache expert," said Charleton.

"Ain't no sech thing," said Tommy, carrying his saddle into the stone house. "Even an Apache don't know what another's gonna do."

"And that's all you can tell me?" scoffed the English lord, following his foreman into the gloom of the shuttered house.

"I can tell you one thing, Mr. Charleton."

"What's that?"

"They ain't crazy. If they think we're too tough they'll vamoose. The only time they make a suicide charge is when they're trying to protect their women 'n' kids. Just relax and wait for them to start something."

Tommy was right. The Apaches encircled the headquarters buildings, moving like swift shadows, to loot whatever they thought of value and could carry off. They burnt the cookhouse first and then the stables and smithy. They saved the bunkhouse, using it as cover to picket their ponies.

Then, an hour before dark, they probed the strength of the stone house, sniping from the west side where the setting sun blinded the defenders. Charleton had a family photograph, taken in kinder times, which graced his mantlepiece. The picture's frame was glazed to protect the fading ferrotype from the elements. The glass was removed, scored and broken into two parts which were smoked over a candle.

It took one man to hold the smoked glass and another man to align and fire his rifle, using the smoked glass. The Apaches, this time, were held from the house. When the sun finally fell behind the distant mountain, the defenders were relieved—until they realized that the darkness would again favor the Indians.

The cook had salvaged his day's bread, although cooked too fast to half-risen loaves. He cut sandwiches made from the soggy bread and pickled beef. The defenders had little appetite; fear and apprehension fueling their bodies at this first clash. Hunger would come later, along with fatigue and the reckless disregard of the damned.

******

The mine was rich—fabulously so. Way beyond Charlie's most optimistic dreams. He could see that within the first few feet of the mine's concealed portal.

Tino had seen the madness in Charlie's face and had tried to bargain for his life. Something about "secret things you should know, Señor Charlie," but the blood lust of the gold had taken over Charlie's mind and body. Suddenly the revolver was in Charlie's hand, firing of its own volition, and Tino was dead—underneath his little mule, feet in the air, still tied together; his bloody head on the rocky trail.

Charlie's hands were shaking as he freed Tino's body from the bounds, for he needed the rope whole to fashion another load of ore for Tino's mule. Tino was sent flying over the trail's edge and Charlie spread his slicker out by the portal and filled it from the rich clumps of ore on the tunnel's floor.

Then it was back down the trail to the waiting pack train and back to Green Falls, committing every natural feature to his memory—too jealous of his secret to draw a map. In the past he had been solicitous and saving of his animals—not this trip. The excitement of the find had overtaken him. Far into the darkness and then extra-early on the next day he drove the animals, cursing every stop, every delay. He skipped the noon off-loading and grazing, further weakening the little mules. One mule balked, refusing to go on, and Charlie beat it to death, transferring its cargo to his riding horse, which he then had to lead.

This crazed determination made for a faster trip—at the expense of the animals, which were in poor condition when finally they tottered into Green Falls. Avoiding the mules' normal stabling spot in Spanishtown, Charlie led them via back alleys to Ames' stable and arranged for their care and for the secure storage of their cargo, a premium price being paid for Ames' silence. It was almost six in the evening, giving Charlie time for a bath and the requisite ministrations of the landlord's wife.

The bath had calmed Charlie, or perhaps it was the land-lord's wife's soothing service. He felt wonderful as he crossed the ornate lobby of the Congress Hotel. He was relaxed; he was clean and well dressed—and he was rich, very rich. He knocked at Ostenhaven's door. No one answered and he tried again, louder.

A door down the hall opened, quietly, stealthily. It was Sprague's head that emerged, eyes questioning the noise at Ostenhaven's door. Hurst turned toward the inquirer.

"I'm looking for Ostenhaven," said Hurst, uneasy at Sprague's presence. "Do you know where he is?"

"Ostenhaven?" repeated Sprague, as if surprised that someone pounding on Ostenhaven's door might be interested in that man's whereabouts. "Oh, yeah," replied Sprague, recovering his aplomb, "he's out of town . . . won't be back for awhile."

A muted voice called from within the room behind Sprague and he withdrew his head from the door to answer. Hurst heard him say, "It's Charlie Hurst. Looking for Ostenhaven." More talk came from within and Sprague pulled open the door. "Mr. Finsen says to come in," relayed Sprague brusquely.

Franklin Finsen was seated behind the desk in his shirt-sleeves with a brocade silk vest tight across his prominent paunch. The room was hot, even with the window open to a breeze that sucked the curtains out past the windowsill. Finsen was processing a cigar, coating it with saliva from his small, pink tongue.

"Welcome back home, Charlie," greeted the little round man. "Want a cigar?" He nodded to a silver-topped humidor on the desk, and struck a match to light his cigar. The little, piggy eyes surveyed Hurst behind the match's flame.

"Later, maybe," said Hurst, trying to get a feel for the link between Sprague and Finsen. "I was hoping to see Mr. Ostenhaven—something special."

"Good news, Charlie—I hope." Finsen said it with a cherub's smile.

"I found the mine. It's all we hoped for—and more.

"Excellent, Charlie. Most excellent. And Tino. What of him?"

"He had an accident. Fell off the trail. I brought his pack train in with me. The ore and the mules is at Ames' place. On the hush—for extra money."

"How much ore, Charlie?" The piggy eyes were bright.

"Around half a ton, maybe seven or eight hundred bucks worth."

"It's that good?" broke in Sprague.

"Best I ever seen," said Hurst. "Where's Mr. Ostenhaven? He'll be glad."

"Yes, he will. Unfortunately he is out playing lion hunter. Jack, here, dropped him off at Mr. Fitzpatrick's hunting camp. Seems he had an insatiable urge to shoot a lion."

"I tried to argue him out of it," confirmed Sprague. "Wouldn't listen to me. Told me to go on in and he'd follow later. When I get urges they ain't about shooting no mountain lions."

"Yes, but be that as it may, I'm sure that if Theodore were here he would have us move ahead on the mine. Get it producing as soon as possible. What about access to the mine, Charlie?"

"A narrow trail, hung on the side of a mountain. But I got an idea for a chute—only its about five hundred feet down to a dry wash that could maybe be made into a wagon road. But it would cost money."

"Would it be possible to start small, using pack trains while we explored other alternatives?" asked Finsen, scribbling figures on a sheet of paper.

"Don't see why not. But first we got to record this mine, legal-like."

"You are so right, but this calls for a celebration. Jack, can you get them to send up some champagne? It's just too bad Theodore isn't here to enjoy it, isn't it?"

******

A rifle shot, booming across the shallow ravine, jerked the weary troopers erect in their saddles. Every man turned his eyes to where the shot had originated.

"Here comes trouble," rasped Sergeant White, recognizing the two oncoming riders as Army scouts Pecos Bob Portland and his Comanche partner Spotted Dog.

"True—oop halt!" yelled Major Poole, raising a tired arm. "Officers forward, you too, Sergeant White. I believe this should be a message."

"I'm afraid you're right, Major," grunted the old sergeant. Lieutenant Jersie loped up from his position at the column's trail, excitement fairly bursting out of his dust-covered face.

The two scouts came up at the trot, their horses sweating hard from the chase. Portland gave Major Poole an offhand, civilian's salute. "Afternoon, Major. Got any chaw, White?"

"Forget about the tobacco," hissed Poole. "Do you have a message for me? How did you find us?"

"A blind digger Injun could have found you. I seen less trail left by a buffler herd. A big un."

"The message, please, Mr. Portland. If you haven't lost it during your travels."

"Got it in my head, Major. Had to use the paper for my sanitary duties, you might say."

"I am rapidly losing my patience, Portland." Poole's face reddened, exacerbating his new sunburn. "Tell me the damn message!"

"Why, shore thing, Major. The's what we come fur. It was from Gen'l Sheridan hisself. Said to get yore butt to Mesa Grande 'n' Charleton Ranch. They's under attack by yore Apaches."

"My Apaches . . . General Sheridan said that?"

"Waal, maybes not exact, but tha's the drift of it. He's dead set on yore fellers catchin' them Injuns. To tell ya the truth,

Major, I think he thinks them Apaches is makin' fools out of you—'n' the whole damn Army, if you know what I means."

"Mesa Grande?" asked Lieutenant Jersie. "This troop went through there last winter, on our way to that fight between the ranchers and the German settlers. It's on the other side of that mountain ridge. But I don't know if there's a decent trail through that ridge."

"Son," replied Portland, with a handful of Sergeant White's tobacco about to go into his mouth, "that's what me 'n' Spotted Doag is here fur. We'll get ya across 'n' then ya kin kill all them Apaches 'n' get a pile of medals."

"How far, Portland? How many hours?" Poole took charge of the conversation.

"Waal—whatcha think, Spotted Doag?"

The Indian had figured it out ten minutes ago, but realized that a quick reply would not seem as profound as a delayed answer. He turned his head slowly until his gaze locked on the mountain barrier. He stared long seconds at the mountain, trying to look very Indian, a son of nature—privy to all the secrets of this land. He milked the silence a little longer and then spoke.

"Much rock, much hill to climb. High, like eagle flies. Bad trail. Fall down, you die. No water."

"How far—how long, damn it?" snarled the major.

"Maybe twenty-five white man mile. Ten hours—maybe." He held up ten grimy fingers as proof of his exceptional accuracy and acumen.

"Sergeant White, Lieutenant Jersie!" Poole lowered his normally tenor voice to that of a gruff warrior king. Suddenly he was Hannibal urging his Carthaginians to climb the snow-capped Alps to engage the enemy and secure his empire.

"We will cross that ridge with all possible speed. The Apaches must be met. Tighten all girths, warn your troopers. Now is the time this troop will show its mettle. Mr. Portland!

You and your assistant will take the point. At the trot, if you please."

The general wanted blood, did he? Then he, Major Hiram Poole, would give him the savages on a silver platter . . . or was it draped dead on their own shields? Doesn't matter anyway. "At the trot, by twos—forward ho!" Hannibal . . . er ah, Hiram Poole was off to death or glory.

CHAPTER 26

Sylvester Skinner opened his eyes, slowly—one at a time. He saw Gen's figure slumped into a wicker chair next to his bed. The room was whitewashed adobe, with a low ceiling that accentuated the stifling heat. "Is this hell?" he croaked hoarsely, mouth bricky dry.

Genevieve heard him and roused herself, sweat shining on her haggard face. "Almost," she muttered. "It's Tucson . . . and you're laid up in a hospital again. Second time within the last six months."

"What's a matta with me? Got any water?"

"You're running a fever. The doctor had to go in and clean out your leg better. He said he saved it from being amputated."

"Hah, they all say that. Please . . . some water." She took a tin cup and filled it from a clay water pot hanging in the corner of the room.

"Here, let me help you." She pulled him up with a damp hand. "Mr. Malone lost his arm. The doctor had to take it off."

"Where is he? Malone, I mean. Did Happy deliver him all right to the sheriff here?"

"They signed that paper for him, but had Mr. Sweeney take him and you to the doctor here."

"I don't remember that," said Skinner, reaching for more water.

"You were passed out. The both of you, from drinking all that whiskey after we left Mesa Grande."

"God bless Mrs. Swanson and her jug of booze. I remember that and sitting on the floor of Sweeney's coach. God, my leg hurt. Don't feel too bad right now. How long have I been here?"

"Tonight will be the third night; it's Wednesday night."

"Oh my God—Esther. What happened to Esther?"

"She's gone, with the woman, heading back East. I envy them."

"What about the woman? Did she seem . . . ah, genuine?"

"Yes. Met her husband and two older children of theirs. They weren't happy about her going—even for a few months."

"And Esther's gone."

"Yesterday, on the Butterworth Stage. God help them. I'm beginning to loathe traveling." She took the empty cup and got some water for herself.

"And we made it through the Indians—to Tucson."

"No help from you and your drunken crony, Mr. Malone. They saw one Indian, according to Mr. Sweeney. They said he just rode the other way. Other fish to fry, Mr. Sweeney said."

"Sweeney," repeated the sheriff, trying to sit up in bed. He got his good leg on the floor, at least.

"What about Mr. Sweeney?" asked Gen, keeping him from attempting to get up.

"If today is Wednesday, then Sweeney leaves tomorrow for Green Falls. Get us a ticket on that coach."

"The doctor would not let you travel. Perhaps in a week."

"Mrs. Skinner . . . Genevieve . . . do you think I'm a reasonable patient?"

"A terrible patient. Obstinate, obdurate . . ."

"Then you know that I'm leaving. Tell Sweeney to pick me up first, here at this sweatbox. I will sit on the floor, tell him.

And find me a crutch or a cane—something to support myself. Also a clean shirt. Buy me a clean shirt. Who's got my Colts?"

"Mr. Giles took it."

"Then tell him to clean it and load it. Might be Indians on the way back."

"And you're going to fight them—on one leg?"

"One leg—no legs—what does it matter? Go on. Get out and do what I told you. We're going to go home."

"Green Falls? Home? What an awful thought. But I'll go get the tickets and the shirt—if only to go out of here and find a breeze."

"And my pistol!" yelled Skinner to her departing figure. "Don't forget my pistol!"

"Sylvester Skinner," she shot back, "the scourge of the Sahara, or whatever they call this terrible place."

"You got it. That's me," he retorted. He twisted around in the bed, hurting his bad leg. "At least when I'm in better shape," he said to himself, biting his lip with the pain. "Sometimes."

******

The lion's skin gave Poke Blaney's pack animal a fit. The roughly cleaned skin exuded lion odor, especially the flesh side, as the heat soured the tissues. The Indian blindfolded the frantic animal, which helped somewhat; at least it halted her frantic attempts to see from where the strong scent was originating.

"I give up," declared Blaney as he chased his dogs away from the miserable pack animal for the hundredth time. "We've got to go down to No Place and get enough salt to clean this skin right, or we ain't gonna ever get any peace. Which way's quickest?"

"Go to that smoke," replied Ute Joe. "That No Place. Stupid white man name. Indian had better name."

"I can't see no smoke," complained Blaney.

"You white man. Got no good eyes. Smoke is there, all right. I see it good."

"Well, good for you, eagle eye. Lead off . . . Hey! What did the Injuns call No Place?"

Ute Joe looked over his shoulder at Blaney and grinned, "City of the Rats. The white man poison most of the rats. Now maybe only ten thousand."

"I hope the doags like rats; I sure don't. Go ahead, you lazy Injun, set a decent pace."

******

They arrived at No Place in the purple haze of sunset's last minutes. Poke left the Indian to tether the dogs and set up camp on the outskirts of the ragged hamlet while he rode over to the saloon to inquire about salt and supplies. For a small community, the saloon held a surprising number of customers, all seemingly in a contest to see who could drink the most beer, the fastest. Poke elbowed a place at the bar and was quickly rewarded with a mug of beer from the hustling barkeep.

"Business always like this?" Poke asked as he came up with the requested dime.

"It's beer day. It's like this for two days—until the beer's drunk up. Then it's back to whiskey until the wagon comes back in a week. Six forty gallon barrels—generally 'bout a day and a half."

"Why so fast?" asked Poke, draining his mug.

"I dunno, thirst I guess—and the water's awful. Salty as piss."

"Hey, that's what I'm lookin' fur. I needs salt to rough cure a lion skin. At least five pounds."

"You might take a little from those bodies. That animal trainer fellow bought all the store had—to salt them down until he got that lion he was . . ." The bartender stopped, the question still taking form in his head.

Poke answered the query for him. "Guess I got it first, huh. A big, old male."

"Hallelujah!" the barkeep shouted. "Hear that, boys? This here feller done killed that killer lion. Mister, you is a real hero to us folks here. The beer's on the house for you. All you can drink. This is sure a wunnerful day. Thank God—no more lion worries."

Poke Blaney was later to blame his offer on all the free beer that he had consumed. He became unusually verbose about midnight, after convincing the bartender to send someone with the salt to Ute Joe to properly clean the skin. This man was also to verify the kill for all those unable to leave the saloon because of the beer day activities. Then, in a fit of soused generosity and civic goodwill, Poke Blaney offered to carry back the bodies of the lion's kill if the returning beer wagon carried the lion skin—at a distance from his dogs, of course.

And so, unknowingly, Blaney brought the mutilated remains of Theodore Ostenhaven and Fitzpatrick's camp cook to Green Falls. Poke Blaney's beer-y condition the next day precluded any deep thought or perhaps he would have noticed the discrepancy in the distance between the dead in Fitzpatrick's camp and where his dogs cornered the male lion for the kill. But he did not. Ute Joe did, but Indian-like he kept it to himself.

******

Charlie Hurst was angry and let his bad temper show. In his mind the absence of Ostenhaven was altering the business arrangement, for the worse. Finsen and Sprague seemed to have a secret design of their own. This particular argument was about Sprague going with him to map the trail and stake out the boundaries of the mine prior to registering it.

"It *does* make sense, Charlie," soothed Finsen. "Two men can get the job done faster. You practically said it yourself, about building the monuments. Each one will take time—and effort."

"Nothing I can't do by myself. If Mr. Ostenhaven were here, he'd back me up, I'm sure of it."

"Charlie, look at it my way. Theodore left me in charge when he went away. I wouldn't be surprised if he came in any minute, with all kinds of questions on why we're not pushing forward. We need to get the mine into production right now, while the gold market is high. The longer it takes, the more we have to lose. There's all kinds of talk in Congress about a bi-metal monetary base. It's absolutely essential that we go into production quickly. And here you are, being stubborn and uncooperative."

"All right! All right!" Charlie capitulated. "But he's got to follow my orders. I'm the boss on this. You tell him."

"You're the boss, Charlie. Is that understood, Jack? You two have to work together." Finsen attempted to put his stubby arms around their shoulders and failed, grabbing their elbows instead.

"Six o'clock tomorrow morning, Sprague," barked Charlie, coarsely. "I'll be outside with the pack mule, waiting for you. Think you can make it?"

"I'll be there," returned Sprague icily. "You look to yourself."

"Yeah—I will. One eye on the trail and one on you." Hurst left the two, shutting the door loudly.

Finsen scowled at the closed door and was about to comment when Sprague waved him quiet. Sprague waited ten seconds and then cracked the door to peer into the hallway. Satisfied, he closed the door softly.

"He's gone," reported Sprague.

"He suspects something. You'll have to watch him, he's wary—and experienced."

"So am I," answered Sprague, sounding dangerous.

"Just be careful. Don't give him a chance to hurt you. After you get to the mine, will no doubt, be the most treacherous time."

"Don't worry, Franklin. He won't make it back. I promise. We've got too much to lose to screw it up."

"Please be careful," said Finsen, gripping Sprague's hand. "I don't want to lose you."

******

Sweeney had brought a short wooden board to support the sheriff's leg. The thin board was laid across the seats, holding the wounded leg at the upright. Fortunately, this run was not crowded with passengers and allowed this improvisation.

"To what do we owe this consideration, Mr. Sweeney?" asked Gen, surprised by the gruff stage operator's sympathetic action.

"Figured I better butter up our newly-elected sheriff. I might need a favor in the future."

"You mean Sylvester *won*?" Gen was shocked, as she thought Sanders would win easily. "I don't know whether to be glad or sad. There goes any chance of going back to Rochester, at least for now."

Skinner, immobilized in the coach, had heard. "How much did I squeak by with, Sweeney?"

"Real close," laughed the grizzled stage operator. "His three hundred to your sixteen hundred. Shows you how dumb the voters are."

"I'd say it shows how dumb you have to be to want to be sheriff," countered Gen. "He's been shot four times in the last two years, for your information."

"Only once bad, Gen," corrected Skinner from inside the coach. "That time with the Germans when I got it in the head."

"Oh, I'm so glad to hear it. Those other wounds—and this one don't really count. Just remember that, Sylvester Skinner, when you start hurting on this trip. *This wound isn't so bad.*" She said the last sarcastically, lowering her voice, trying to imitate her husband's disparagements.

To counter Gen's gibes, Skinner tried to be stoic and silently endure the trip's jolting agony, but the ride was pure anguish on his leg. By the time the coach arrived at Mesa Grande the sheriff was wordlessly cursing every bump and bounce on the road.

When the coach stopped for the dinner break the sheriff would have been content to stay resting in the coach except that he desperately needed to relieve himself. The trip to the privy seemed to use up what little strength he had accumulated in the few days of his convalescence, and he dropped into a chair in the barroom, obviously spent. Gen pulled Mrs. Swanson from her serving duties to get her assistance.

Soon the two came back from the kitchen with a plate of buttered bread and a small glass containing a potion of opiate.

"Now eat the bread and butter," commanded Mrs. Swanson sternly. "It'll settle your stomach. And then the draft. It'll help you relax."

"Can't," groaned Skinner. "Got to be ready for the Injuns."

"My goodness, ain't you heard?" The Cavalry chased them off—probably in their own territory by now."

"Are you sure?" asked Skinner, relief flooding his drawn features.

"That's what the rider from Charleton said. According to him, they was holed up in the ranch house until the Cavalry come up smoking. Was a pretty sharp fight and only a few Apaches got away. They burnt down a bunch of buildings, though, and killed one ranch hand and wounded the cook. But I guess the Cavalry evened that up. So you can take that laudanum with no worries."

"The Apaches are gone?" Skinner could not believe it.

"Gone—but not forgotten." She said it as a matter of fact. "We was hurt, but nowhere as bad as Jessup. He lost Miguel, two mules and his riding horse."

"We had Indian trouble in New York," broke in Gen. "The Mohawks. But that was a hundred years ago. It's peaceful there now."

"It will be peaceful here, too," replied Skinner. "The Indians are outnumbered. This was sort of a last gasp." He drank down the potion. "Is this guaranteed to give me a good trip?"

"It'll numb you up so's you wouldn't mind the bumps," replied Mrs. Swanson. "We'd better get you in that coach while you can still move a little."

"Hand me my stick, Gen," said the sheriff, "and I'll show you ladies some fancy stepping. That bread's got me going again." But the gallant grin came off his face when he put his weight on his hurt leg.

******

Spotted Dog's estimate was slightly optimistic. He did not take into account the night's utter blackness and the weariness of the troopers and their mounts. It was going on four A.M. when the troop trailed down the worst of the ridge to where the rolling foothills lay. Portland found them a reasonably flat space and Major Poole called for an hour's halt. No fires, no tents, double sentries and sleep by your mount.

The hour went too fast, as attested by the groans of the awakened. But they were troopers and familiar with the hardships of the field. They saddled their horses, formed their troop front, were counted and were led off within three minutes of their first call. Major Poole was at the van, a more weary Hannibal, his face the color of the dark gray of the predawn murk.

They halted at the Tucson Road for a quick pull on their canteens and a hard biscuit. Spotted Dog came galloping back from the point and growled something in Comanche to Bob Portland.

"Firing up ahead!" exclaimed the scout. "From the Charleton ranch!"

"We'll give you a four-minute start!" shouted Major Poole. "That will put you a mile ahead, Portland. I don't want to ride into any ambush. Understand?"

"Me neither, Major! That's how come I still got my hair." He motioned to the Indian scout and they galloped off across the road.

"Bugler!" summoned Major Poole.

"Yessir!" The bugler tucked a half-eaten biscuit into his blouse and kicked his horse forward to the small major.

"Have Lieutenant Jersie report to me and tell Private Simmons to lay back with the pack animals. Tell him to be especially careful that my gear doesn't get damaged. Got that?"

"Yessir." The bugler trotted his horse to the rear of the column. Soon Lieutenant Jersie came forward.

"You want me, sir?"

"It looks like the Apaches are at the Charleton ranch. I want to go in with troop front for maximum flexibility. You can wheel right or left as the situation requires. Don't commit to the charge unless the Indians are in the open. Then . . ."

"You want me to lead, sir?" Jersie interrupted.

"Of course. I'll stay to the rear to stabilize the wings if you have to wheel. Portland should be about a mile ahead— looking for ambushes. Just play it safe. Don't storm into anything you can't handle. I'll take the last set of fours with me to reinforce any problem you might run into. Any questions?"

"Well, er—I . . ."

"Good," said Poole, cutting him off. "Take your post. Bugler, stay with the Lieutenant. And take the guidon, also." The Major yanked his horse around and quickly trotted off to the rear. There, he detached the last four troopers, moving them, and himself, further to the trail of the column.

"Welcome to the joys of command, Lieutenant, sir," teased Sergeant White. His face was deformed with a huge cheekful of tobacco.

"By the look of that chaw, Sergeant, we must be going to a fight."

"That we are, Lieutenant. A civilian once told me, before I smashed his snotty nose, that is what us soldiers gets paid for. And all the time I was thinking it was for stable call and wood-cutting detail."

"Think we'll get Slit-Nose this time?"

"I'd be surprised. But even the smartest fox gets caught sometimes."

"Bet you a bottle of whiskey we catch him. How say you, Sergeant White?"

"Only one bottle? Oh, I understand. You're a poor second lieutenant. I accept the bet. No cheap whiskey, now."

"I am an officer—and a gentleman. We officers do not deem it proper to use rotgut whiskey. Something you rankers should consider."

"Listen to this, will you, McMurty," said White to the guidon, who was eavesdropping. "Fuzz on the lieutenant's cheeks and whiskey on his brain. What has West Point sent us?"

"It's society in general, Sergeant. The youth of the republic reflects its loss of values."

"Very true, McMurty. That is how Rome started going downhill. And now, my young lieutenant, I suggest getting this column in troop front and moving out at the trot."

Lieutenant Jersie grinned and gave the commands. The troop spread out in line abreast and went forward at the trot, the guidon pennant hung against its staff, almost limp in the morning sun. The juices of battle had begun to flow in the men's blood. Suddenly they were no longer tired and aching. Some looked to the battle with outward bravado; some with fear and dry throats, and some with thoughts of home and loved ones. But they moved out willingly, in the unity and brotherhood of their troop front—for they were the Army's best. They were U.S. Cavalrymen.

CHAPTER 27

The following is an excerpt from an interview with Chief Slit-Nose, conducted by an assistant to the Commissioner of the Indian Bureau in 1887:

The whites had fled to a lodge made of stone. It was a good place to fight from, almost like one of the fortresses the Spanish used to hide in when my father and his father would raid the hated Spanish. My band was now of only nine warriors, with myself. We had lost half of the fine braves we had begun with. We had captured only sixteen horses and one mule, having eaten the other mule in a celebration which was not strictly justified.

This stone lodge battle was a poor fight for Apaches. We are best when we surprise an enemy, running or riding through or over their weak defenses. We burned the shelter where the whites kept their horses and the place where they make the iron shoes that the whites like to fasten to the horses' feet. Also, their cooking place was burned. We did not burn their long sleeping lodge, using it instead as protection for our horses and our braves who fired at the stone lodge.

Behind this stone lodge was a dry creek with banks as high as a warrior's head. To this ravine I had assigned Owl-Who-Kills-At-Night and another brave, to fire on the whites. But I was troubled with the thought of rushing the stone lodge because it would kill more of my braves. We were more or less at a standstill in this battle and I was thinking of leaving, even though it would cause us shame to again leave a battle.

As I sat behind the whites' sleeping lodge, trying to decide what to do, Falling Hawk came up riding very fast and recklessly in the manner of excited young braves on their first raid. As Falling Hawk was inexperienced, I had set him to watch the white man's wagon road. I had reasoned that if trouble would come, it would come by way of that wagon road.

I was proved right, as Falling Hawk reported, making me feel better because of my previous mistakes with Swift Arrow at the last battle. The message that Falling Hawk brought was bad; the pony soldiers were at the wagon road—between twenty and thirty of them. A Comanche scout was following our trail that the band had made coming to the rancho of the stone lodge.

My first thought was for the safety of my warriors. Our ponies were rested, while the soldiers' ponies had probably been ridden hard. That meant that in a chase we could get away from this band of pony soldiers. Also, we had many captured ponies we could ride, making our escape assured, if I wished to leave the battle.

But we needed a victory; something to brag about at the campfires of our home, and I began to think. When an Apache thinks of battle, he first thinks of ambush—how to surprise the enemy. To the south of the stone lodge was a small, low knoll. Only the height of two or perhaps three warriors and about a hundred paces in length. If I could lure the pony soldiers close to this hill, then a quick charge from behind the hill would shatter their lines. We would ride through them and then away, showing the pony soldiers our fighting prowess.

I ordered Falling Hawk to take the extra horses away, on our line of retreat. We would catch up to him at nightfall, under the a big mountain to the east. Then I sent word to Owl-Who-Kills-At-Night that when the pony soldiers came, he alone should stay in the ravine, firing fast, as if he were five or six warriors, to lure the pony soldiers into our ambush. In this way I hoped, also, to rid myself of Owl-Who-Kills-At-Night and the division of my authority.

There would be only seven of us to slash into the pony soldiers. We would not kill them all, but we would certainly kill and injure many of them. The ones of our tribe, who follow us, would tell stories of this day—about Slit-Nose and his charge through the pony soldiers.
(End of excerpt.)

******

Charlie Hurst met Sprague early that morning for the long ride to the mine. Hurst had Pete's old mule in tow, loaded down with supplies and digging equipment to erect the claim monuments.

Jack Sprague was smiling, obviously making an attempt at affability. He had a leather-covered case tied to his saddle, in addition to a set of saddlebags.

"What's in that case, Sprague?" questioned Hurst.

"It's a violin. A fiddle, Charlie my friend. I bought it last night. I'm going to entertain you tonight—by the light of the moon."

"Can you play it, or am I gonna be listening to you try to learn?"

"Charlie. Charlie. Have some faith in me. I used to play the fiddle when I was a kid. Of course it was my old man's and too big, but I done pretty good. My old man used to play at all the local affairs. Singing Dan Sprague, he called hisself. And he'd come home drunk almost every night and punch my mother in a fit of remorse. A proper son of a bitch, he was. A sweet man, though, if you could catch him sober, which wasn't often."

"If you was good with the fiddle, how cum you got into this bodyguard business?" asked Charlie, leading the way through the early morning traffic on Main Street.

"It was the Army's fault. There I was, training for the priesthood, practically, when the dirty draft snatched me away from the sweet bosom of my dear family. I had trouble with my sergeant and he invited me behind the cook tent. I beat him so bad the captain made me a sergeant, so I would fight on the regimental team. That's where Theodore found me and made me his captain of the guard—and I became a proper bully boy. And do you believe me, when I say I got to enjoy it?"

"I believe it, Sprague," replied Charlie. "Now let's cut the palaver and put some trail behind us."

******

Spotted Dog had come racing back to report the sound of firing to the east. "They mights be fighting," advised Pecos Bob Portland. "Then again, they mights be foolin' us inter thinkin' that. That's the hell o' trying to figger out the Apache."

"I'm sure not going to let them get away if I can help it. Dammit! Blow gallop, bugler," swore Jersie.

"Make it canter, Lieutenant," advised Sergeant White. "That's fast enough on these nags."

"Go ahead, bugler, make it canter," corrected the lieutenant.

"Keep an eye on the wings, McMurty," called out White. "Let 'em catch up."

"Burnt building ahead, Lieutenant, 'n' shooting!" yelled Portland.

"Pistols, present!" shouted Jersie to the bugler, who blew a quick tootle. The troop was not armed with sabers.

"Guide right, McMurty!" yelled Sergeant White. "Around that stone house."

"Injuns firing from behind that house!" screamed Jersie. "Blow left wheel as we get to that house and we'll roll 'em up." The bugler nervously eyed the diminishing distance to the besieged house.

"Now!" screamed Jersie to the bugler, who brought his bugle to his lips and blew "wheel to the right."

Jersie's head swung to stare in utter horror at the bugler, as Sergeant White's knee suddenly banged against the young lieutenant's leg as the old soldier followed the command to wheel right, knowing that it was wrong, but following orders regardless of consequence.

Major Poole and his four-man section were two hundred yards behind the troop's line abreast. Private Simmons, a boozy perennial professional private, was leading the three-animal pack train, staying close behind Major Poole's section for protection. All at once, the second-in-line of his pack horses stumbled in a varmint hole, causing Private Simmons to lose the leads to all the pack animals.

That loss of control, aggravated by the downed animal and the shooting, combined to panic the two other horses. Without any warning, they bolted away from the firing, running towards a low hill to the left of the stone house.

"Major!" yelled Private Simmons, torn between concern for the downed horse and his escaping charges.

Major Poole looked back to see the horse with his tent and gear dashing obliquely off the field to the left. At the same time he noticed the troop wheeling strangely to the right, away from the stone house and the battle.

"Corporal Tyrone!" shouted Major Poole to the section's corporal, "Catch that pack horse! It's got my tent! After it, you men, or I'll have your stripes!"

Corporal Tyrone, with fifteen years service and six always-hungry kids, knew a threat when he heard it. "After them horses, lads!," he cried, setting action to words as he swerved his mount, drubbing it with his revolver barrel to get it up to a gallop. It took only a few seconds before Major Poole and the set of four were in pursuit of the escaping pack horses, now part way up the little knoll.

******

Charlie Hurst and Jack Sprague were making good time. At noon they were ten miles up the Eagle Pass Trail and they stopped for a quick meal of beef and bread and to give their animals a little time to graze on the sparse vegetation.

After forty-five minutes of this relaxation, they tightened girths and swung up again in their saddles. A mile more on the Eagle Pass Trail and they left it to use a poor track that Charlie had found as a shortcut toward Piss-Pot Mountain.

While the two were on this shortcut they missed Poke Blaney, Ute Joe and the wagon with the empty beer kegs and the salted lion's skin on the Eagle Pass Trail. The bodies of Ostenhaven and the camp cook, although salted also, were traveling poorly and stunk to high heaven. Poke Blaney was sorry he had ever thought of packing them out. Even the dogs were offended by the stench. But Ute Joe, leading the pack horse, thought it rather funny. White men, for all their superior attitudes, smelled just as bad when dead as rotting red men did. He wondered if that held any significance.

******

Headquarters
Second United States Cavalry Regiment
Ft. Lowell, Tucson, Arizona Territory

Hostile Action Report

1. Having been ordered to intercept and engage a band of raiding hostiles from the White Mountain Apache tribe by the Commanding General of Western Department of the U.S.

Army, Troop C of the 2nd U.S. Cavalry Regiment was detached from Ft. Lowell. This troop was commanded by the undersigned, Major Hiram C. Poole. Second Lieutenant Jersie was second in command of the troop which numbered only thirty-five enlisted men due to reduced tables and the rigors of the service.

2. Approximately the first six days of this patrol were spent in marching northward to the interception area west of the Tortilla Mountains. On the seventh day of the patrol a burning ranch was seen. Upon reaching this ranch, it was found that it was a scene of massacre. Eight bodies were found there and properly buried. It was estimated that the hostiles had preceded the patrol by some five of six hours. Scouts were sent out that evening to locate the Indians' trail.

3. The next morning, having found the hostiles' trail, the troop took vigorous means to close with the raiders. But the hostiles with their fresh, captured horses managed to slip away into the Tortilla Mountains.

4. While continuing the search for the hostiles, the patrol was joined on the twelfth day by Army Scout Portland who brought new orders directing the troop to Mesa Grande and the Charleton holdings, which were to the east across the ridge of the mountains.

5. With admirable skill and fortitude Troop C executed a night forced march across this ridge to arrive at the Tucson-Green Falls wagon road at dawn. Normal provisions having been exhausted, the last of the hardtack was issued and the tired troop rested while Mr. Portland's Indian scout ascertained the hostiles' direction.

6. This scout quickly returned with the report that firing was observed from the Charleton ranch. The undersigned directed 2nd Lt. Jersie to form the troop in line abreast and move to the aid of the ranch. The undersigned led a four-man section of the main troop to follow closely and support any necessary actions of the main troop.

7. The Troop, approaching the ranch buildings, saw some of which were smoldering and noticed a stone ranch building being fired upon by a number of hostiles entrenched in a nearby ravine. The line abreast took immediate action to assault this hostile firing position.

8. At this time, the undersigned suddenly noticed activity on a slight rise to the left of the stone house. Aware of the propensity of the Apache to use ambuscade tactics, the undersigned led his four-man section immediately at the suspected hostile force, determined to blunt the Apaches' ambush.

9. The Apaches, over a dozen well-mounted braves, came charging down the rise, aiming to strike at the line-abreast troop's flank. The small section met them at the foot of the gentle slope, discharging their pistols at the hostiles at short range.

10. The Apaches reeled in hurt and confusion, although several braves had the presence of mind to fire on the section. It was at this time that Corporal Tyrone received his fatal wound, as did the undersigned receive a ball to his left upper arm.

11. With pistols empty, the undersigned rallied the survivors of the section, leading them to a place where they could dismount and provide carbine fire.

12. With unusual perception, for an inexperienced officer, 2nd Lt. Jersie wheeled right the troop, whose left flank was threatened by the remaining Apaches. Then reversing their direction quickly, the troop charged the hostiles, inflicting severe casualties.

13. It was at this time that the Apaches' leader, Chief Slit-Nose, was unhorsed and sustained a fractured ankle. Seeing this, most of the hostiles who were still uninjured surrendered. Two hostiles were seen to flee the field. A section was detached to secure their capture, but the hostiles, mounted on fresh horses, evaded this capture.

14. An English gentleman, Lord Charleton, was extremely pleased by the expeditious arrival of the Troop. The defenders suffered one death and the wounding of their cook, which they took most sorely—his incapacitation, that is.

15. After resting the balance of the day and the following night, the undersigned led the Troop back to Ft. Lowell. The Troop's dead and wounded were returned with the Troop, along with the Apache prisoners.

Respectfully,
Hiram C. Poole, Maj. U.S. Cav.

Addendum To Report
Troop Casualties:
Killed—Corporal Peter Tyrone
   Pvt. William James
Wounded—Major Hiram C. Poole
    Pvt. Henry Klaus
    Pvt. Hugo Franz

Apache Casualties:
Killed—Six
Wounded & Captured—Three

******

Deputy Sam Buller learned from young Stuart Sweeney that the evening stagecoach had brought the sheriff home.

"And how's that for service?" bragged the young coachman. "We took him right down Chestnut Street, right to his house. And Pa and I carried him right into the house and laid him down on the chesterfield."

"How's he look?" asked Sam, concerned.

"Sorta old and hurting, if you knows what I mean. Trip was tough on him."

"Thanks, Stu—appreciate the information." Sam drained his stein of beer, gave the younger man a friendly squeeze on the shoulder and left for the sheriff's house. He found Skinner eating cornmeal mush at the kitchen table. His game leg was resting on a low stool with an embroidered seat cover.

"You can't be too bad off, eating like that," greeted Sam.

"Cornmeal was the only food left in the house," growled the sheriff. "Our trusty boarder, here," he nodded in Hansen's direction, "ate everything else. It's a good thing we have wainscoting on the walls; he would have eaten the wallpaper."

"Would not," answered Hansen, handing his bowl to Gen for a refill. "Besides, it was your fault, getting shot like that. The meal ticket from Mrs. Purity got used up and I coulda starved."

"When do you plan on coming back to the Sheriff's Office?" asked Sam, offhandedly.

Skinner looked up at Sam, the tone of the question alerting him. "Why? Something important?"

"Maybe yes—maybe no. It's about your erstwhile opponent."

"Who? . . . Sanders?"

"Himself," confirmed Sam. "Can I smoke here, ma'am?" he asked Gen. She nodded acquiescence and he dug out a battered, stubby pipe and tobacco from a breast pocket.

"What about?" Skinner was tired, trip-worn and needed no more problems.

"He's taking his defeat badly. Sorta gone crazy-like."

"In what way?"

"Drunk most of the time. Mean drunk. Scaring sensible people. He's going to rub some young gunhand the wrong way and somebody will end up dead."

"Why don't you warn him off?" asked Skinner.

"Had him in jail, one night, for drunkenness," admitted Sam. "But it didn't seem right, me preaching to him, I mean. I figured it would be better for you to do it. Someone with equal rank, if you know what I mean."

"I'm not up to it tonight, Sam. Maybe in a few days, when I feel kinder and more humane. What else has gone to hell since I left?"

"Besides Sanders, it's been quiet. Oh, Poke Blaney brought a couple of bodies back from No Place earlier this evening, along with the skin of a lion. He said they was killed by the lion. All ripped up, he claims. I told him to take the bodies to Marks. They was real ripe. Stunk to high heaven, even though they was salted down."

"Who were the men? Blaney know?"

"Said he didn't know. Said they had told him at No Place that Fitzpatrick brought them in, bought enough salt to salt them down and said he'd be back later. Blaney said the folks in No Place asked him to bring them here, 'count of being the county seat."

"Get Doc to try to make sure of the cause of death. Maybe somebody will recognize them."

"If they can get close enough, maybe."

"I'll try to get to the office tomorrow, Sam. A good night's sleep will . . ."

"Not on your life, Sylvester Skinner," interrupted Gen. "Doctor said to stay off that leg at least a week. And I'm going to make you stick to that."

"Maybe in a day or so, Sam; gotta keep the little woman happy."

"Hah!" said Gen—loudly.

******

Sam left the sheriff's office fifteen minutes late for his meeting with Doc Seevers at Marks' undertaking establishment. He purposely dawdled, hoping to stay away from the stench of the bodies as much as would be possible. Luckily, he had timed his arrival almost perfectly. The doctor was just finishing up his examination.

"Sorry I'm late, Doc," Sam whispered lamely. "Got held up. You're sure fast today."

"Riper the cadaver, the faster the exam," answered the crusty old surgeon, breathing through his mouth to lessen the smell. "I should charge extra for the decomposition odor. But seeing as there is two bodies here, I'll skip it."

"I recognized one of the deceased, Deputy," boasted Marks. "I embalmed his wife a few months back. Got a good fee for that. He was a generous man. Had a big space between his front teeth. That, and his height, cinched it."

"Wedding band helped, too," scoffed the doctor.

"So who is . . . or who was it?" asked Sam, holding his bandanna to his nose.

"Theodore Ostenhaven," said Marks. "Wedding band reads 'Theo and Anna May 4, 1862.' Anna was the wife's name. You remember, the one with all them pieces of shrapnel in her."

"I remember," replied Sam, "and now her husband is here, killed by a lion."

"In a pig's eye!" snorted Doc Seevers. "Didn't fool this old doctor. See this lump on the scalp? Fractured the skull. Then whoever did it scraped up the head and shoulders with some kind of sharp tool to make it look like claw marks. A clumsy attempt to make the killing look like a lion's work."

"Would have fooled me," said Sam. "'Course, I'm no doctor."

"That's why I'm here, Deputy—to ride herd on your ignorance. I'll tell you what alerted me. Won't charge extra for the lesson, either."

"I'm all ears," replied Sam, trying to sound humble when his stomach was threatening to erupt from the stench of the bloated bodies.

"The hands and arms gave it away. Almost every person I ever saw who had a fight with a large animal, like a bear or a cougar or even a big dog, ends up with wounds on their hands and arms. Fighting the animal off, that is. One fellow had teeth marks almost to his elbow, trying to stuff his arm down the bear's throat."

"I see."

"'Nother thing. Most big animals eventually sink their teeth in their quarry's throat or neck. These bodies had no teeth marks, at least killing teeth marks. They did show signs of being mauled and ripped by predators, most probably coyotes or foxes—something like that, with canine type jaws."

"So it's murder. Both of them?" asked Sam.

"Both had their heads busted, under that superficial scalp damage. Looks something like what a rifle butt would do. Now—lesson's over and I'm off to wash away this smell in rye whiskey. I'll have my written report to you by tomorrow and would appreciate prompt payment."

"Thanks, Doc. I believe I'll join you for a quick one."

"What about me?" asked Marks. "What kind of funeral should I make? I don't even know who that other man is. Who'll pay me?"

"Lets see," said Sam, thinking aloud. "Ostenhaven worked as the manager of the Stella's Stake Mine. His friend, a Mr. Finsen, is an assistant manager. He's the closest to next of kin you'll find. The other man, I don't know. Write down a good description of the man. Maybe that will help identify him. Then figure on a pauper's burial. How much is that now?"

"Twenty dollars," replied Marks quickly—too quickly.

"Thought it was fifteen.

"Coffin wood went up."

"Go ahead. I'll get Captain Mosely to argue with you about the charges."

"He thinks an old blanket's good enough. Hell of a Christian, he is. 'Specially for a public official."

"And you are, Marks?" commented Sam, as he fled the stink.

CHAPTER 28

"Plam!" a heavy slug ricochetted off the stone of the half-finished claim monument. Moments later the sound of the shot cracked across the rocky slope of the mine's boundaries.

"Damn! How'd he get up there?" swore Charlie Hurst, instantly regretting his decision to establish the monuments before settling with Jack Sprague. "Well, two can play at that game," he said to himself, diving into a waist-high dry wash with his quickly-grabbed Winchester.

He scooted twenty-five feet up the wash before cautiously raising his head for a quick look. "Wham!" A round kicked gravel into his face, half-blinding him. "Shit, that SOB's good! I gotta get out of here before he nails me." Bending double, he scurried down the wash towards the animals and the hasty camp at the mine-head. Sprague must have changed his position after his first shots because he fired again just as Hurst jumped down and out of the wash to the cover of the mine-head.

But Sprague held the advantage of the high ground. Charlie had only time to grab a canteen from the mule's packsaddle and duck into the safety of the mine tunnel. "I can wait him out here. Might even sneak out in the dark," thought Charlie. "If he tries to come in the mine, he's dead meat. Just relax, Charlie old boy, and wait him out."

******

Charlie Hurst lay against a mine support timber which afforded a view of the mine entrance. The mine had dangerously few supports. God only knew how Tent-Peg had managed to get the beams into this mine. It was a long way to any trees.

"Old man had determination. Gotta say that for him," mused Charlie. He thought again about his cigar. It had been in his shirt pocket when he piled into the dry wash. The fall had broken it; it was crooked, like a dog's leg, with a rent in the middle. With deliberate care, exaggerated by the situation, he separated the two halves, sealing their tattered wrappings with generous amounts of saliva.

Now came the match problem. Charlie was down to six matches. "Well, you can't smoke if you don't have a light," he reasoned, lighting the best-looking half of his twin cigar stubs. Suddenly his reverie was interrupted by a shout.

"You in there, Hurst?"

"Why?—Gonna say you're sorry?" Charlie shouted out towards the daylight at the mine's mouth.

"Hell no. I just got a present to deliver, with Finsen's and my compliments." As Charlie watched, an arm threw a bundle of dynamite sticks into the tunnel, its short fuse sparking in the dimness of the mine.

It took Charlie a couple of seconds to recognize the danger and another few seconds to react. He was erect and running when the blast brought down the tunnel's opening.

******

"So what did he say, sir?" questioned Sergeant White. The troop was on an easy duty day. Earlier they had cleaned their weapons and gear. Now they had stable call and when that was accomplished they had the rest of the day to themselves. Second Lieutenant Jersie had come from the regiment's headquarters directly to the stable area, ostensibly to check on the troop's mounts.

The young lieutenant looked about the stable before answering. An officer caught disparaging another officer senior to him could face collapse of his career. Sadly, the U.S. Army, like every body of men since history was recorded, fostered toadies and self-servers eager to gain advantage by tattling on their fellows. Satisfied they would not be heard, Jersie spoke, albeit softly.

"The report stands. Unless I want to face court martial for ordering a retreat before the enemy."

"It was no retreat!" fumed White. "That shit-ass bugler blew the wrong call. We wheeled right instead of left."

"You don't have to tell me, Sergeant. I was there, supposedly in command."

"But, you rectified the situation. You ordered wheel about and we ran over them Apaches."

"That was later. The damage to my credibility was done already. Anyway, that's what Poole said. So the report stands."

"And he becomes a hero, the dirty sod. And all for chasing after his damned great tent."

"Count your blessings, Sergeant, at least you lived through the scrap."

"Better than Tyrone and James did, I allow that. Never really got to know James. Too new. Just came from Jefferson Barracks."

"How about Mrs. Tyrone?" Jersie asked. "How's she taking it?"

"She don't realize it yet, but she's better off without him. He beat her and the kids. He was a bully. But it'll be awhile until she figures that out. Are the funerals still set for tomorrow?"

"Ten o'clock. Colonel's supposed to be back tonight. Coming in with the paymaster, I hear."

"Will wonders never cease. It's been less than three months. They'll be some drunken soldiers tomorrow night."

"Don't forget that whiskey you owe me," reminded Jersie. "No rotgut, either."

"Do you mean you'd hold me to a silly bet?"

"Indeed I would—and will," grinned the young lieutenant. His first smile since the bugler blew that wrong call.

******

When Owl-Who-Kills-At-Night saw the pony soldiers charging towards him, he knew he would soon be killed, and he began to sing his death song. He was alone in the small ravine, having no pony on which to escape the pony soldiers. He sang his song and continued firing at the whites as he was instructed.

But just when it seemed that the pony soldiers would ride to the edge of the ravine and shoot down at him, the Great Spirit saw he was soon to be killed and saved him from death by turning aside the pony soldiers, sending them towards the Spirit of the North. But the pony soldiers resisted the Spirit of the North and turned back to fight with Chief Slit-Nose and his small band of braves.

Owl-Who-Kills-At-Night then worried how he could escape the many pony soldiers and the Great Spirit saw this worry and sent him a horse on which to ride away from the battle. The pony was a fine pony with a blanket of blue and edged in the color of the sun.

Then Owl-Who-Kills-At-Night got up on the fine pony's back and spoke to himself, saying, "I am an Apache warrior and must go to the side of my chief who is now beset by the pony soldiers."

The Great Spirit heard Owl-Who-Kills-At-Night and spoke to him thus: "You shall be the hope for your tribe. I shall grant you great power and you will lead your people for many years." Owl-Who-Kills-At-Night heard the Great Spirit, but his soul argued against leaving the battle. The Great Spirit then told Owl-Who-Kills-At-Night, "I am the one who says when to go away and when to come in return. I ordered the rain to fall and the sun to shine and the nuts to grow upon the tree. My power is very great."

Then the Great Spirit said to the fine pony he had provided to Owl-Who-Kills-At-Night, "You will take this warrior in safety to his tribe and he shall be powerless to stop this journey." And so it was, although Owl-Who-Kills-At-Night tried to control the fine pony, he could not; not the leather strips that are fastened to the iron piece in the pony's mouth and not the beating that Owl-Who-Kills-At-Night inflicted on the fine pony with his gun barrel had any effect on the course of the fine pony. Owl-Who-Kills-At-Night was led by the fine pony to his friends with their captured pony herd and thence to his village where he was received with much honor as a great warrior and a true successor to Chief Slit-Nose.

From "A Tribal Chronicle," by Francis Red Hawk, written September 1896 (courtesy of Arizona Archives Association).

******

The sheriff held off going back to duty until the third day back from Tucson. It was mainly Gen's intransigence concerning his recovery that kept him home the extra day. He went into the office by way of the stable, checking on his horse after his prolonged absence. Sam heard him come in and stuck his head around the connecting door.

"Oh, it's you," Sam grunted, face still puffy from sleep.

"No brass band," asked Skinner, "to welcome me back?"

"You're lucky that you caught me awake. Stan and I are on sixteen-hour days, what with both you and Happy gone. We do a lot of dozing lately. Come on in—Stan left fresh coffee."

Skinner negotiated the three steps up to the office from the stable with care and was surprised to find a blanket-wrapped form sleeping against the wall, under the rifle rack. The man was using a saddle for his pillow.

"Who's that fellow, Sam? You're not renting out sleeping space here, are you?"

"Wish I were—could use the money. No—it's a U.S. Marshal. Brought in a prisoner. I guess they had to hoof it halfway back from Holiday. The marshal made the prisoner tote his saddle."

"Anybody we know? The prisoner, I mean."

"Herbert J. Early. Claims to be a relative of Jubal Early."

"One-Legged General Early? Or was it his arm?"

"That what he claims."

"What's the charges?" asked Skinner.

"Mail robbery and malicious wounding. Town Marshal Zack recognized him and arrested him. This marshal was supposed to take him to Santa Fe, only some woman tried to rescue him. Both of their horses were shot and the woman got away. Now he's waiting to get authorization to take the stage. Probably be here three or four days."

"And he's going to sleep here on our floor?"

"No. I'll find him a bed somewhere, later on when I got time."

"I could talk to Gen, I guess. We've got a spare room now that Esther's gone."

"She leave all right, with that lady from Tucson?" asked Sam.

"Guess so. Gen saw her off. I was sweltering in that hot box of a sanitarium. Windows were so small the flies had to slide in sideways. Never drank so much water in my life."

"How long before you can put a boot on that foot?"

"The foot's all right. It's the boot top, rubs the wound. Just at the wrong place. Besides, it sweats too much in a boot. At least it did on the way back in the coach. And the salt from the sweat irritates the wound."

"You'd look funny chasing a bank robber, wearing a carpet slipper," said Sam, with a laugh.

"I don't figure on chasing any bank robbers. At least until my leg heals," stated Skinner. "If I paid, would you go after the jelly buns?"

"If you pay every day, I'll go fetch 'em every day and twice on Sundays."

"Just today will be fine. Gives me a chance to clean and reload my Colts while you're gone." Skinner put an old newspaper on his desk and laid his pistol gently on it. Sam finished his last gulp of coffee and left, slamming the new screen door.

"Damn," groused Skinner, "just one more thing to go bang around here. I must be getting old." He started prying the caps from the pistol cylinder. Once the caps were off, he started drawing out the charges, separating ball, wad and powder. The screw had scrapped the balls, affecting their accuracy and he relegated these to the remelt jar. The chamois wads were inspected and those unhurt by the screw were saved. The black powder was tapped out into an old soup bowl for disposal. It could have been salvaged, but the savings were not worth the risk of a misfire, especially true for a lawman's pistol. Suddenly the new screen door slammed shut again, causing Skinner to swivel angrily around toward the door.

"Dammit Sa . . ." the oath evaporated on the sheriff's lips. A comely woman was standing inside the door, a napkin-covered basket in her gloved hands.

"Excuse me, sir," she said hesitatingly. "I wish to visit a Mr. Early. I believe he was brought here last evening." She smiled shyly, bringing out the dimples on her tanned, pleasant face.

"Sorry, miss," replied Skinner. "My deputy is out for a few minutes and I had a run in with an Apache bullet last week and won't be able to make those stairs for a while."

"Could I go up there by myself?"

"I'm afraid not, miss. Actually, visitors' hours are three to four, but I'll bend the rules for a pretty girl. My deputy can take you up, Miss . . . ah . . . what was your name?"

"Dean. Priscilla Dean, but I'm afraid I won't be able to wait." She drew a small nickel-plated pistol from the covered basket, pointing it with a very steady hand at the surprised sheriff.

"I guess you must be the woman that shot the marshal's horse yesterday."

"And he shot Herbie's horse, or we would have gotten away." The smile was gone from her face now. "Where is the jail key?"

Skinner nodded to the ring of keys on the wall.

"I think you took the wrong time to clean your pistol, Sheriff."

"Looks that way, Miss Dean."

"Now, what do I do with you? I guess I could lay you out with that stove poker."

"I'd rather you wouldn't, miss. You might end up braining me and face the rope for killing a lawman. I suggest manacling me with my hands behind the chair. The manacles are on the other wall, above your sleeping friend, the marshal."

"Does he have a pistol?"

"I think that's his, hanging on that chair."

She moved sidewards, her pistol never wavering, to take the marshal's pistol from the holster. She had slid the handle of the basket down her forearm to grasp the heavy revolver.

"Now," she said, "get that manacle on yourself." Skinner obeyed, limping over to take the manacles off their peg.

"Can I fire up my pipe again first, miss? It'll keep me happy in my captivity."

"Make it quick."

Skinner looked at her while lighting his pipe. She had, somehow, lost a great share of her attractiveness, he thought. The pipe lit, he chained himself to the chair, Miss Dean obliging on the last manacle.

"Now understand this, Sheriff," she said coldly. "Herbie is my man, and I will kill to get him out. If you try shouting or banging, or whatever, my first bullet is for you, right in your privates. If I can't have any loving—you won't either. Got that?" She had gotten positively ugly now. The more so with her threat to his masculinity.

Skinner nodded his head while drawing on his pipe. She made a quick check of the snoozing marshal and dashed up the stairs, the ring of keys jingling.

The sheriff turned his chair towards his desk where the unloaded Colts there mocked his capture. Then he heard Sam outside on the porch, talking to someone. "This is not the time for social pleasantries, Sam, dammit!" he shouted silently to himself. Then he heard the two love birds coming down the steep stairs, feeling carefully for each narrow tread in the shadowy stairwell.

"Now," said Skinner soundlessly. He leaned over the soup bowl and dropped his red-ashed pipe into the small pile of black powder.

"Whoom!" exploded the powder, singeing Skinner's face in a blast of flame and smoke. Blindly he kicked the rolling chair backwards, hoping to find the door. He banged against the door frame, half in, half out. Then a strong hand pulled him out—to careen and crash over the porch's edge and into the dust under the hitching rail, landing on his bad leg in a spasm of pain. He heard firing through the haze of his pain and his face felt like it was on fire. Suddenly, one of the horses that were tied to the rail became crazed with the shots and stomped him, turning the pinkish haze to carbon black.

******

Charlie Hurst lay on his belly in the choking air of the mine tunnel, glad to be alive. He had been hit and pounded by several flying rocks and was bruised but evidently unbroken, as all his extremities still responded to his brain's frenzied prodding.

"Oh shit! Now what?" he shouted. But he could not hear his words—he was deafened by the blast. He felt blood running from his ears and nose. He could barely breathe in the dust-laden air.

"Gotta find good air," he croaked, deaf to his words. He stood up and tried walking on the blast-littered floor, stumbling again and again until he was stopped by a rock wall.

"I need a torch," he reasoned and feverishly ripped off his neckerchief and lit an end of it with one of his few matches. The cloth was damp with sweat, smoldering more than burning, but it helped to find a candle stub stuck to a timber by an L-shaped spike.

"Good old Tent-Peg," gloated Charlie, "I knew I could count on you." He held the now-lit candle out at arm's length, attempting to see further, and noticed the candle's flame tipping gently away from him, and the thin smoke drifting off down the tunnel.

"A draft," thought Charlie. "And a draft means a hole and a way out of here." Buoyed by the discovery,he walked carefully, eyes always coming back to the candle's flame. He found another candle; this one more of a glob of melted wax layered to an outcropping of rock, but it could be used and he stuck it in his pocket. The air was better now and he could breath more easily.

"I'll find that opening and get out of here. I know where the water is," he told himself, confidence flooding through his body. "They'll learn they can't count Charlie Hurst out. I'll make it back and make them bastards pay. So help me, I will."

******

Skinner groaned and reached up to test his aching head. There was a thin bandage wrapped around his head. The arm movement triggered a stabbing pain in his side. "Oh damn," thought Skinner, "it's a dream and I'm back in the Germans' hospital, slurping down all that damn broth."

"Our patient is coming around," Doc Seevers told Gen. "How do you feel, Sheriff?" he shouted into Skinner's ear, causing Skinner to grimace.

"Oh, God, I'm in Green Falls—in the care of a quack!" Skinner groaned. "I was hoping for a better doctor."

"Sylvester! Stop that. You're embarrassing the good doctor!" Gen exclaimed.

"Good. What happened to my head and my side? I remember about the black powder scorching my face."

"Near as we can tell, Sam's horse stepped on you," grinned Doc. "Busted a couple of ribs and put a fine lump on your head."

"Fine for you—hurts for me," complained Skinner. "What about that woman and her lover boy? Did they get away?"

"Sam killed Mr. Early," said Gen grimly. "The marshal jumped up and grabbed Miss Dean and she was wounded in the scuffle, in the stomach. She's here—on the other side of the curtain."

"She's not good." Doc shook his head to emphasize his diagnosis.

"A shame," grunted Skinner. "Why would a woman get into something like that?"

"Love, maybe—or maybe habit," said Gen. "Like in my case with a fool of a husband who gets brained or burnt or shot, regular as clockwork. I don't know. If I had any sense I'd go back to Rochester and live alone. My brother would put me up, you know. I could teach school or something."

"And you'd have to stare at those big ears on your brother at every meal," teased Skinner. "It would serve you right for deserting me. Genevieve, in the land of the elephants."

"It's that knock on your head, Sylvester. It's made you crazier than ever."

"Don't knock it if you haven't tried it," murmured Skinner, "said the farmer as he kissed the cow." Then his eyes closed and he drifted off under Doc's potion.

"He's crude and rude," commented Gen.

"He is surely. Especially about me being a quack. But he's one hell of a sheriff."

"Who wants a sheriff? I wanted a stay-at-home husband. But all I got is a human target."

CHAPTER 29

Charlie felt better now that he sensed a way out of the mine and the chance of retribution to those who had tried to kill him. The tunnel floor was fairly smooth now that he moved further from the blast's rubble. The draft seemed ever stronger, the candle flickering to an invisible, minute breeze.

The candle's light showed a rough bridge before him. The floor planks seemed to have been laid to conserve material. The six-inch wide planks were spaced about three inches apart, making the flooring look like the end gate of a wagon when laid on the ground. Below the short bridge was a dark hole, sinister in appearance. "A black shaft to hell," thought Charlie.

But the candle flame pointed towards the continuing tunnel and Charlie took the challenge, stepping forward with caution, fueled by desperation and the basic will to live.

Perhaps it was Charlie's ears, now deafened by burst drums; or possibly no person could have heard the slight, the insignificant click of the trigger-latch arming itself, preparing to open the oiled lock that joined the two halves of the bridge together to make a solid-looking floor.

Charlie advanced slowly, taking small, tentative steps, then, as his full weight was at the center of the slatted bridge, without warning it suddenly collapsed downwards, both hinged halves parting at their mutual joint, opening like a set of double doors to dump their prey, in this case Charlie Hurst, down nature's bottomless pit.

The trap almost worked. No doubt for most men it would have meant their death, dashed to pulp at the foot of the black pit. But Charlie was quicker than most men and he had the instant presence of mind to grab for the slatted floor before him as it was falling to the vertical. He got his right hand through a space as the other hand struck solid plank. For one terrible, long moment his whole body was hanging by the outside bulge of his thumb joint while he slid his other hand down the plank, frantically groping for a hold. His thumb joint, cut to the tendons by the rough edge of the board, slipped, but Charlie suddenly had two fingers on the plank's edge. Two strong, work-toughened fingers. Then it was four fingers supporting his dangling body and his left hand found a purchase.

Now he had time to breathe and a few seconds grace to call down a curse on the builder of this trap. "Damn you, Tent- Peg! You tried to kill me. You old sonabitch!" At this hectic moment, Charlie could be forgiven for not remembering that *he* had killed Tent-Peg Pete in hopes of finding this mine. Ironically, Charlie had also forgotten Tino's warning "of secret things you should know." But now he had been taught that Tent-Peg had been unfriendly to intruders.

Charlie pulled himself up the ladder-like bridge floor, drawing on the untapped store of strength in his powerful frame. When he had heaved himself up on the rocky floor of the pitch-dark mine tunnel and off the dropped bridge section, he was amazed to sense the bridge halves swing up to the horizontal again, setting the trap once more.

"Tent-Peg, you old rascal," shouted Charlie to the angry buzzing of his deafened ears, "what else do you have in store for me?" Then, true to his character, Charlie found the candle glob in his pocket and managed to light it. Once again he started down the tunnel, eyeing both the flickering flame and anything of a suspicious nature in the tunnel; once again he was walking into trouble, but this time not of Tent-Peg Pete's creation.

******

Something woke the sheriff. It was an unusually warm night in Green Falls. Doc Seever's adobe, with its thick walls, generally was close to comfortable, but this night, Skinner's night shirt was damp with sweat. "That's what woke me," reasoned the sheriff. "It's the heat. Wish I could just lay here naked." He pulled up his night shirt to just short of indecency, hurting his ribs in the process. He lay still, courting sleep and its oblivion to the heat.

Then he heard the sound. A scraping noise, as if something was being dragged across the rough tiles of the floor. Again the noise—this time longer and a little louder. Closer, maybe. The sheriff was wide awake now, his head turned toward the unknown fear.

Skinner slowly swung his legs over the floor, stifling the urge to scream with pain. He grabbed the handle of the heavy earthen water jug. It would do for a weapon. "I'll sure look funny if this just turns out to be an armadillo or some other critter," he told himself. The noise continued, at intervals, coming closer to the white canvas curtain that partitioned the sickroom.

The room was lit dimly by a sconce-mounted oil lamp, its wick turned down to a faint flame. Mrs. Seevers would come in every few hours to check on her patients and needed the illumination.

Again the noise, very close. The curtain was being drawn slowly back. "Ain't no critter," thought Skinner, readying the heavy pitcher. "God, I sure hope I don't have to wrestle. My side's not up to it."

Suddenly the curtain was ripped back and the intruder was in Skinner's room. It was Priscilla Dean, dragging her bed behind her by the manacle fastened to her ankle. She had a pair of scissors—more like shears—gripped between her teeth, as if some pirate bent on pillage. Her face was a mask of hate—and pain, no doubt, from a hemorrhaging stomach wound.

"You rotten bastard!" she gasped when she saw Skinner's eyes peering at her through the mask of his bandages. She tugged at the heavy bed, trying to move it closer to the sheriff. Her strength, though, had failed. Her bloody gown was witness to her dying state. Frustrated by her inability to move closer, she took the shears from her teeth and tried to hurl them at Skinner. This, too, failed. The shears flew under Skinner's bed, banging against the tiles.

"Doc!" called Skinner loudly. The effort hurt his face, pulling at the burns.

Mrs. Seevers came first, a professional nurse, clothed in her dressing gown. "Oh my goodness, what's happened?" she asked, shocked by the bloody scene.

"She tried to kill me," replied Skinner quietly, trying to favor his facial muscles. "Don't like me, I guess. Do you, miss?"

"Why didn't you just sit there? You and your damned pipe! Now Herbie's dead."

"And I think you'll be, too, Miss Dean; looks like you busted something inside you," Skinner said objectively.

"Here, honey, let me help you to lay down. Then I'll get the doctor." Mrs. Seevers pushed the hurt woman back on her bed. But by the time the doc was roused from his alcohol-induced sleep and stumbled in to help, it was too late.

"She's dead," grunted the half-awake doctor, closing the dead woman's eyelids and putting the lamp down on Skinner's night stand.

"Good riddance," stated the sheriff, replacing the water pitcher.

"You're terrible," retorted Mrs. Seevers. "She was such a pretty girl. How could you say such a thing?"

"It's easy. I say it about everybody who tries to kill me."

"I'm going back to sleep, mother," said the doc. "Can you handle things here?"

"Help me push the bed back where it belongs and we'll leave her until morning. I feel a breeze and I don't want to waste it with working."

"A breeze?" spoke up Skinner. "Leave that curtain open, will you, Doc? I've been waiting all night for a little cool."

"The body won't bother you?"

"Not a bit, Doc. Unless she's got a ghost and I'll worry about that when I see it."

******

Just past the bridge that doubled as a trap, Charlie found a wide spot in the mine tunnel which accommodated a wooden turntable. The turntable was fitted with curbs, evidently to position and turn a small ore cart so that tailings could be dumped down the natural shaft to hell.

Further on, Charlie found the cart. One stubby wheel was off and laid to the side. It looked as if Tent-Peg Pete had been interrupted while repairing an axle. Charlie could almost feel the grizzled miner's presence hovering over him.

"I ain't afraid of you, Pete! You're dead and I'm glad! You were bad, Pete—trying to kill me, but I got you first!" This outburst made Charlie feel better, even if he could not hear his shouts.

Another fifty feet down the mine the tunnel suddenly split into twin tunnels at a "Y," with each arm splitting off at angles. Charlie was puzzled until he noticed the candle flame leaning towards the right hand tunnel. The draft seemed stronger.

All at once the chosen tunnel became a cave with a lowered ceiling that forced Charlie to duck his head. The cave twisted to the right abruptly, showing a glimpse of daylight at its end. The candle flame flickered crazily now and Charlie felt the draft on his sweating face.

The excitement of the daylight must have overpowered Charlie's senses for he did not immediately smell the fetid odor of the cave. Then the feline feral stink came through his bloodied nose even as the mother lion gave a warning growl, rising and dislodging her pair of nursing cubs.

Too late, the puny candle reflected the yellow eyes. The first lunge of the lioness swept away the light and took Charlie to the rocky floor. In an instant her powerful jaws had clamped on Charlie's neck, as she sank her deadly fangs deep into his throat. She shook him as if he were a child, cracking his vertebrae. In only seconds Charlie was dead. But, unlike his bogus victims, Charlie Hurst's killing would not add to the lion's legend, for only a few of his gnawed bones would be left from the lion's dinner.

******

The sheriff was sent home by a determined Mrs. Seevers, made testy by Skinner's persistence in being a poor patient. The bandages had been removed and his visage was newly buttered with a greasy coating that ran onto his shirt collar as the temperature climbed. Gen had trimmed his singed mustache into a stubble that matched the grey whiskers now sprouting on his cheeks through the fatty smear of the noxious medicament.

That same day Jack Sprague returned to Green Falls, reporting to Franklin Finsen on his entombment of Charlie Hurst. Because of this latest murder, they decided to delay the registering of the mine, reasoning that a few weeks, or perhaps a month, would allow any memory of Charlie Hurst to fade.

The death of Ostenhaven, though, was now a matter of public record, and the newly-formed partnership of Finsen and Sprague could not avoid questions concerning Theodore

Ostenhaven's demise. Apprised of Sprague's arrival by those who would curry favor with the law, Deputy Sam Buller paid a visit to the offices of the Stella's Stake Mine.

Ostenhaven's former assistant engineer, a young Cornish emigrè, was now nervously holding down the mine's operations. He ushered Sam into Franklin Finsen's accounting domain, where languished Jack Sprague, former bodyguard, now reduced to certifying time cards to justify his salary.

Sam dived into the inquiry, resolved to maintain professional objectivity with the man who had killed his brother. "I heard you were back, Sprague. I imagine you've heard that we identified a body as being that of Theodore Ostenhaven."

"Yeah. I heard," said Sprague, laying aside his work and turning his lean body around on the cane chair. "Damn shame. But I warned him about trying to hunt that lion."

"Why did you have to warn him, Sprague?"

"'Cause he was no hunter. That's why. As an outdoorsman, he was hopeless. That's why he had me."

"And you weren't there when he needed you."

"I see what you're driving at, Buller, and you're wrong. Theodore wanted to do it alone. That's why he sent me away. He was like a little kid—playing the big hunter. That cook didn't help none, either."

"What cook was that, Sprague?" Sam eased himself down on the edge of Finsen's desk. Finsen pretended to be busying himself with his accounts, but actually was following the conversation with baited breath.

"That camp cook at Fitzpatrick's camp. He was the only one there. He egged Theodore on. If it wasn't for him, I don't think Theodore would have tried it—the lion hunt, I mean. But that cook kept telling him what a big hero he'd be if he bagged that lion. Theodore wanted to prove that he was heroic—to himself, if nobody else. To disprove what that Army investigation tried to frame him with."

"So when did you leave him?"

"Let's see . . . Was it ten days ago? Maybe not that long. I think it was a Wednesday."

"And he was alive—in good shape?"

"As good as ever. Theodore was never really healthy. He said he had breathing troubles when he was a child. He stayed indoors a lot. He caught a bad cough, there in Brooklyn, the last winter of the war. All that coal smoke was bad for him, he used to say."

"We didn't have enough coal to let that bother us, Sprague," commented Sam bitterly.

"Is this getting personal, Buller? Can't you let bygones be bygones? The war's over."

"It's hard for me, I admit. But I'm not bringing it up now. There's always later."

"Anytime, Buller. You just say the word and I'll shoot you into dog meat. Are you done your questioning? I've got work to do."

"I reckon I've learned as much as you want to tell me, Sprague. I'll leave it for today."

Finsen roused himself from his figures, sensing something in the deputy's last statement. "Is there any incongruity involved in Theodore's death, Deputy? I thought it was definite that he died at the hands of the lion. Oh, I guess hands is the wrong word for an animal, isn't it?"

"Yeah, I guess you could say that there's a little problem," answered Sam, picking his words with care. "The doctor claims that animals go for the windpipe, leaving terrible wounds to the throat."

"And that's the problem—in Theodore's death?" asked Finsen, trying for an inquiry of his own.

"That's the biggest," said Sam, tersely.

"Just an opinion, if you ask me. Not real evidence, is it?" Finsen smiled for the first time during Sam's visit.

"You're right. Just an opinion of an old doctor. But I'd appreciate it if Mr. Sprague, here, would stay in Green Falls.

At least until the sheriff's back to duty and has his say on Mr. Ostenhaven's death."

"Wasn't planning on leaving—to go anywhere, Buller," put in Sprague, roughly.

"Fine. And I'll remember that get-together, Sprague," replied Sam, getting off of Finsen's desk and leaving the office.

The two watched the deputy's departure in silence, allowing the lawman to get out of earshot. Then Finsen finally exhaled noisily through his lips. "He knows something, Jack. We've got to watch our step."

"Maybe. Maybe not," answered Sprague, going to the window to assure himself of the deputy's leaving. Satisfied, he swung around to Finsen. "It could be just an attempt to rattle us. An opening move, maybe, to see if we do something stupid. But I'm sure that someone must have seen Hurst leave town with me. We have to come up with a good alibi about good old Charlie."

"What about his horse? Did you bring it back with you?"

"No. It's dead and over the side of the trail to the mine. I did bring that mule back, though. Charlie said it was lucky. Didn't help him much, though, did it?"

"Better get rid of it. Surreptitiously," advised Finsen, wiping his suddenly sweaty face with a large, yellowed handkerchief.

"I'll bring it down to the mine animal herd. It won't last long underground."

"Do that—and come up with a story to cover Hurst's demise."

"Too bad the mine ain't missing any money. We could say he went south with it."

"I could arrange that . . . no. He didn't work for Stella's Stake. How about Indians?"

"How about that cantina owner? Wasn't it you who said Charlie was fooling with his wife?"

"That's it, Jack, cherchez la femme. Blame the woman. Find somebody to spread a rumor to that effect, in Spanish-town. Know anybody who could do that?"

"Several. But it'll cost."

"How much?"

"Don't be cheap, Franklin. We got too much to lose. A hundred. Fifty apiece to the men I got in mind."

"You got it," said Finsen, getting up to go to the safe in the corner. He felt much better now. The situation was under control.

******

This article appeared in the *Green Falls Gazette-Fidelity*, dated Friday, 18 June, 1870.

T. J. FOLEY WINS THE LION'S SHARE

Yesterday evening a rapidly healing Sheriff S. Skinner, a hero in last week's abortive jail rescue attempt, drew the lucky raffle ticket belonging to T. J. Foley, winning for the popular bartender the pelt of the reputed killer lion of No Place. The sponsors of the raffle, the Christian Ladies Guild of Green Falls, prevailed upon the county supervisors to grant them the lion pelt, taken by Mr. P. Blaney and his assistant Ute Joe.

Mrs. Mosely, C.L.G. president, stated that the monies raised would be used for decorating the Episcopal church, now under construction. Reverend Thorpe, the newly appointed rector, was on hand to congratulate the winner, who stated that he was Roman Catholic.

******

Before reporting for his return to duty, the sheriff had a few personal errands to accomplish. Visit number one was to the barbershop where he instructed the barber to soak the accumulated gum of ointments off his face with steaming towels. Then the barber brushed a lather of soap on his stubbly face and whisked away the whiskers with his keen razor, outlining his now abbreviated mustache in the process.

"Your face is still sorta blotchy, Sheriff," said the barber. "Perhaps I could dust it with talcum to hide them white parts, where you lost the skin."

"Forget the powder, Gus," replied Skinner, "I'll let the sun fry up what's left of my face. I'm not trying out for a job as a stage actor."

"Anything you say, Sheriff," answered the barber, whipping off the protecting towel and dabbing on some stinging bay rum. Skinner grimaced as he descended from the chair. His ribs were still pained and were wrapped in bindings, which Gen always seemed to pull too tightly for comfort.

The next stop was the bakery, where Skinner bought a dozen jelly buns to improve his reception at the office. He was in luck with the buns; this day the filling was blackberry jelly, which generally was reserved for Sunday. The sheriff took the blackberry filling as an omen.

"The old Romans might foretell their fortune from the entrails of a goose," he told himself, with a smile, "but I'll take the insides of a jelly bun any day—tastes better, too. I've got a feeling that I'm due for a good spell of luck. Blackberry—and it's not even Sunday. Imagine that!"

CHAPTER 30

"Deputy Buller is out talking to somebody about that eaten-up body," greeted the new deputy, Stan Woods. "Is them buns for us? I can make fresh coffee. Happy made what's in the pot now."

"Happy's back, is he?" asked Skinner, easing himself in his chair.

"Came on the stage last evening. Came over and took his shift. Said he missed this place. Can you imagine that?"

"Yes, son, indeed I can. What did he say about Knobby Malone?"

"They hanged him day before yesterday, Happy said. Had a big crowd. Hanged two other men, too, Do we ever get to hang anybody here?"

"Hope not. How are you coming along as a lawman? Any problems I could help with?"

"The more I learn—the more I see I need to learn, if you know what I mean. But Mr. Buller is a good teacher."

"He is a fine deputy. It's his horse I don't enjoy. Stupid nag stepped all over me. My ribs still aren't right yet."

"Should I make new coffee then, Sheriff?" asked Stan.

"Good idea. Make it before Sam gets back and tries to make his evil concoction."

"You mean his Rebel coffee, with the eggshells?"

"That's it. The same coffee that poisoned Robert E. Lee."

Sam appeared in the doorway, letting the screen door slam on its counterweight. "Did I hear my coffee being maligned by a Yankee carpetbagger?"

"I only told this young lad the truth. To save him from terrible constrictions of the bowels," countered the sheriff.

"Don't believe a word of it, Stanley. That recipe is what gave the South its fighting spirit. Something them Yankees never had."

"Talking about the spirit world, what did you find out about Ostenhaven?" asked Skinner.

"Not too much, which is probably my fault. I have trouble being objective with those two."

"Which two?"

"Sprague and Finsen. Sprague claims that Ostenhaven told him to leave, so that he, Ostenhaven, could go after the lion by his lonesome. Which is a damn lie. Said there was a camp cook, holding down the camp, that egged Ostenhaven into chasing the lion."

"And you didn't believe Sprague?" asked Skinner, holding his ribs with one hand to reach with the other for a jelly bun.

"No way. Ostenhaven wasn't a man of action. He was a planner. A behind the scenes man. I'm not sure he could even shoot. Say, are those blackberry?"

"Sorry you noticed. Could that cook be that other, unidentified body?"

"Most probably is. Remember that drawing that Jerry Jones chalked on Otto Floss' forge?" asked Sam, reaching for a jelly bun. "At the time we thought it was a garden tool—right? Now, I'm thinking it was some kind of instrument to make it look like a lion was killing people. You know, making those slashes."

"Do you think Sprague has such a tool?"

"I could ask the manager over to the Congress to check out his room."

"If there is such a tool, leave it in place and we'll arrest him in his room. Then we'll find the tool and connect it to Sprague."

"That leaves Finsen in the clear," said Sam. "Sprague wouldn't implicate him."

"Maybe Finsen will get frightened and spill the beans on Sprague," countered the sheriff. "But finding that tool would help."

"Soon as I finish another bun and some coffee, I'll mosey over to the Congress and have a little talk with the manager."

"Just don't let Sprague catch him rifling through his belongings. He's a dangerous man."

"So am I, Sheriff. Just look what I do to these buns."

"That's the trouble with you small town deputies—you do more eating than shooting." Skinner said it with a broad grin, even if it stretched his new facial skin; he was happy to be back.

******

Sam was waiting in the office when Skinner returned from his dinner. "I sent Stan home until five," he told the sheriff. "I figured now that you and Happy are back, we can more or less get back on the old routine."

"How's Stanley on the saloon patrol? Is he nervous?"

"Doesn't show it, if he is. Seems pretty steady to me. He had to cold-cock a drunk miner last week. He just smiled at the fellow and stepped in and tapped him with his pistol barrel, sweet as you please."

"Just so he don't start enjoying it."

"I don't think he does. It's just part of the job. Want to hear what happened at the Congress?"

"Oh yeah. Gen's pot roast made me forget my responsibilities. What happened?"

"Nothing. A big zero. The manager stayed up in Sprague's room so long I was getting nervous. Finally came down and said he couldn't find anything that looked like a garden cultivator. That's what I told him to look for."

"So there goes your theory about . . ."

"Hold on, I'm not through," said Sam, interrupting the sheriff's verbosity. "The manager said Sprague has some gear stored at the livery stable. Said he had to send a bellboy over there yesterday to fetch a sack of rocks Sprague had forgotten to bring . . ."

"And you went over there?" Now it was Skinner's turn to do the interrupting.

"I surely did. Ames said Sprague had just been there and led away a mule he had brought back with him from the desert. Ames says that he recognized the mule as belonging to an old prospector named Tent-Peg Pete. This Pete used to stable the mule with Ames whenever he came to Green Falls. According to Ames, Tent-Peg Pete disappeared a while ago under circumstances *very peculiar*, as they say in French."

"Why peculiar?" asked Skinner, loading his pipe.

"Because it was bandied about town that Pete had found a rich strike. At least that's what Ames says. I never heard anything like that, personally."

"His disappearance was never reported—at least to us. And you say Sprague took the mule away this morning?"

"Must have been right after I questioned him," replied Sam thoughtfully.

"Think you could have spooked those two?"

"Could be. But a mule . . . ?"

"That belonged to a disappeared prospector. Is the plot thickening?"

"If it is—I'm having trouble seeing through it. But wait. I'm not finished about the livery stable."

"Don't let me stop you—go on," Skinner said, firing up his pipe.

"There was a packsaddle Ames was keeping for Sprague. Ames said it was really Pete's. A good stout canvas one, tarred to make it waterproof, with double cinches."

"A fine packsaddle, I'm sure," commented Skinner impatiently.

"Yeah. Well, in the packsaddle, among other things, was the claw tool."

"What did you do with the tool?"

"I left it there, in the packsaddle."

"Good," said Skinner. "I think I see a way out of this pea soup. Go tell Rose what you told me and see if he will draw up a statement saying that Ames identifies the packsaddle as belonging to this Pete. Then supposedly all the contents of the packsaddle could be reasonably construed as belonging to Pete. As a disappeared person, that would put his belongings legally under our control pending settlement of his estate."

"Then I can bring the tool back with me?"

"Get another statement from Ames to the effect that the tool was found in the packsaddle, which was kept under his care. Was the packsaddle locked up somehow?"

"It was in the tack room, which they keep their eye on."

"That will have to do. Now all we got to do is match up the tool with the wounds."

"You mean we have to dig up those bodies?" asked Sam.

"Maybe we can confront our villains first and see if they'll spill the beans. It will save digging. And bring the whole packsaddle back here. It might have more interesting things in it besides the steel claw."

******

After supper that evening Skinner arranged to meet Sam at the Congress Hotel. The plan was to confront Sprague with the steel claw and demand an explanation. County Attorney Rose had warned Sam that the tool presented very circumstantial evidence, although it would be sufficient for an arrest on suspicion until the tool could be matched with the wounds to Ostenhaven and the cook.

The two lawmen found Sprague together with Finsen in the gentleman's bar. Finsen came to his feet, behind the small, round table which held their drinks, pulling at his vest with his pudgy, white fingers. "I hear congratulations are in order," he smiled, "for your part in the apprehension of the lady jailbreaker, Sheriff."

"Thanks, Finsen," replied Skinner. "But we're here tonight on other business."

"More questions, Skinner?" asked Sprague acidly. "I thought your man, here, did all that this morning."

"Something has come up, Mr. Sprague, in connection with the deaths of Theodore Ostenhaven and a cook named Bertram Wells." Skinner turned to Sam. "Show him the tool, Sam." Sam obliged, drawing the steel claw from a cloth coffee bean sack.

"I believe this tool was used," continued Skinner, "to create the impression that Ostenhaven and Wells were killed by a lion, thereby attempting to cover up the fact that they were actually clubbed to death. Mr. Sprague, I am arresting you on suspicion of murder. Will you come peacefully, sir?"

"You're crazy. That's not mine. I threw . . . I mean, I never saw that before."

"It came from a packsaddle that you brought out of the desert and left in the livery's care. Your pistol, Sprague."

"Sure, sure. I don't want no trouble," offered Sprague, removing his pistol, butt-first. Suddenly, in a fast, practiced spin, the revolver was upside down and fired at Sam, who was knocked backwards, sprawling on an adjacent table that collapsed under him. The sheriff dived to the floor, hoping to be shielded by Finsen, who had returned to his seat. The fall, on his unhealed ribs, almost caused the sheriff to lose consciousness, but he groped to his knees, pistol in hand, to find Sprague gone.

"Sam—is he dead?" shouted the sheriff to Finsen, whose face had turned chalk-white. All Finsen could do was stare, open-mouthed, at Sam's body on the floor.

"Sam, are you all right?" Skinner had crawled over to the inert form of his deputy.

"Not quite," groaned Sam. He tried to get up and quickly gave up the effort, to lie amid the littered pieces of the broken table. "Table's broke and I'm busted up, too. It's my ribs, I think," he croaked.

"Just lay still, we'll get the doc over here," commanded Skinner. He got to his feet, shakily,as Stan Woods and Happy Giles stormed into the barroom, pistols drawn and looking for trouble.

"Heard the shot," gasped Happy, short of breath. "We was up the street on saloon patrol."

"Jack Sprague shot Sam," Skinner explained, holstering his pistol to clutch his sore ribs.

"Not me," gasped Sam. "Hit this claw thing and it whacked me in the side. I think my rib is broke."

"*You* got a broken rib?" Skinner tried to laugh but quit because of the pain. "Welcome to the club. Now you know how I hurt from the drubbing of your half-witted horse."

"Is that supposed to make me feel better?" complained Sam. "It's a wonder that I'm alive. Where is that claw thing anyway?"

"It's over here," replied the sheriff, bending his knees to retrieve the bullet-damaged claw tool. "You'll probably have to explain to the jury how it became battered, if this case goes to trial."

Skinner sent the two remaining whole deputies out to look for Sprague, knowing though that it would most likely be fruitless in the dark. Doc Seevers came and took charge of

Deputy Sam, having him placed in a stout armchair to be carried to his little hospital.

Next, Skinner had to determine what to do with Franklin Finsen. Although he was sure the former sergeant-major was involved in some type of conspiracy, there was no direct evidence to support this theory. Reluctantly, Skinner told the pallid fat man that he was free to leave the scene, but not the city of Green Falls. "I'm not through with you yet," the sheriff warned him.

The saloon's swamper came to remove the debris from the broken table, mopping up the spilled drinks and the sludge from the overturned spittoon. "Come on folks, party's over," called the barman. "Forget this business and have one on the house." Skinner went and claimed his drink; then he left the bar, discouraged by the course of the night's events, to take over Happy's night tour at the Sheriff's Office until that worthy returned from the hunt for the elusive Sprague.

******

The new seven-day clock on the sheriff's wall, a gift from the Mine Association to expunge their collective guilt from the nitroglycerine explosion at the main ford on the Little Fish the previous year, bonged a solitary note. This caused the half-asleep sheriff to raise one eyelid to verify the time. Satisfied that one bong still signified one o'clock, he tried to find a more comfortable chair position to ease the pain on his tender ribs.

A knock at the door made Skinner open both eyes. "That you, Happy?" he called, taking his feet from the desk top in anticipation of a trip to unlock the door.

"No, it's Hansen, Skinner! You got trouble."

"That's my middle name," yawned the sheriff, crossing to the door and unlocking it. "What kind of trouble would get you out of bed, Hansen? You're not hungry, are you?"

"Not right now," replied Hansen, slipping in the door. "But I'll probably be at breakfast time—when your wife won't be there to cook nothing."

"Excuse me, Mr. Hansen. It's late and I'm tired. Could you please explain what the hell that means?" Skinner was almost shouting by the time he got to the end of his question.

"It means your wife has been abducted from your house."

"When was this? Who took her?" Skinner was suddenly wide awake.

"'Bout twenty er thirty minutes ago. I been looking all over town for ya."

"From the beginning, Hansen. How'd this start?"

"I was sleeping. Then I got woke up by a big argument in your house. When the windows is all open I can hear everything that goes on in your house—from my room in the shed."

"That's pleasing to know. Don't stop."

"Well, I've heard you and your Mrs. doing a lot of arguing since I been boarding with you, but it didn't sound like you—arguing with her, I mean. Somebody else. So I goes and peeps in the parlor window. Guess what I saw?"

"I'm in no mood for games, Hansen. Out with it."

"It's Sultan Sanders and he'd been drinking and he's pulling on your Mrs. and she's slapping at him. And then he backhands her and she's quiet. Knocked out, like. Then he throws her over his shoulder. Then I get brave, er foolish, er both and raise up in the window and yells at him to put her down."

"Good man, Hansen."

"Yeah. Almost got me killed. He pulls out his pistol and points it right at my head. I said to myself, 'you is dead, Olaf, old man.' But he didn't shoot. Changed his mind, I guess. Then he talks to me. Can you believe that?"

"I believe it—go on. What did he say?"

"Said to tell you that if you wanted your wife that you should come to Gompers' store and get her. Sounds like a trap to me. He sure didn't seem very friendly."

"How drunk was he?" asked Skinner, checking his Colts.

"Not falling down drunk. Mean drunk, like. Are you going?"

"Certainly." Skinner took the spare pistol from Sam's bottom desk drawer, checked its loads and shoved it under his trouser belt. "I got a job for you Hansen," he said.

"Want me to back your play? You'll have to lend me a gun."

"No gun. Try to find Happy and the new deputy, Stan. They're in town somewhere—hunting a fugitive named Jack Sprague—who hurt Deputy Buller."

"Hurt bad?"

"Just a rib or two—like me."

"Want me to go now? Looking for the deputies, I mean. What should I tell them, by the way?"

"To go to Gompers'. To help me with Sanders. Go on— git!"

"I'm going—and you take care—and your Mrs., too. Good cooks are hard to find, you know. And I'll bet she'll be mad when this is all over."

"I'll settle for that, Hansen," agreed Skinner. "I'll settle for that just fine."

******

The object of the deputies' manhunt had gone to ground; his own home ground. Jack Sprague had dashed out of the Congress to duck into the first saloon he came upon. Then, it was through that busy watering hole as if he were in dire need of relief in the smelly latrine at the building's rear. Instead of turning into the facility, though, he went up the alley and back to the rear service entrance to the Congress Hotel, climbing the service stairs to his floor and room.

As he waited for the arrival of Finsen, he utilized the time to load the expended cylinder of his revolver. It took Finsen another forty-five minutes to leave the shooting scene and return to his room. Sprague met him at Finsen's door as the sagging little fat man was working the lock.

"Oh, it's you!" exclaimed Finsen nervously. "You scared me—sneaking up like that."

"Open the damn door, Franklin. I don't want to be seen," rasped Sprague. He pushed Finsen inside as the door was unlocked and closed it quickly as soon as he was in the room.

"They're looking for you, you know," said Finsen, trying to stay calm.

"I imagine so. I've got to leave town, Franklin. I'm finished here. If they catch me—I'll hang. And the worst part is, that claw wasn't the one I used on Theodore. It was Hurst's."

"They won't believe that, Jack. Here, I have almost a hundred dollars in my wallet. That will get you a long way from here."

"A measly hundred bucks? And I leave the mine to you? You must be joking."

"It's not a joke. You're done, Jack. Outlived your usefulness. Send me your whereabouts in a month or two and I'll try to send you some more."

"I want more right now, Finsen!" raged Sprague, "You're not getting rid of me for just a hundred bucks."

"You got rid of yourself, Jack. But I'll send you money later on, when the mine is producing. Just trust . . ."

"Like hell I will!" snarled Sprague, crashing his pistol barrel against Finsen's temple. "Damn you rich bastards with your lily-white hands! Well, you hired yourself a killer—only you're the one getting killed this time." He pounded Finsen twice more, feeling his skull crack with the beating.

"Now, I believe it's Scripture time," grinned Sprague, holstering his pistol. He went to Finsen's Bible and shook the bank notes from the gilt-edged pages. "Seek and ye shall find, Franklin, and this will take me a long way south."

******

Gompers Department Store was dark when the sheriff arrived. The only outside light came from the pair of feeble-flamed oil lamps that flanked the double front doors. The tin-roofed awning, that stretched over the boardwalk, closed out any ambient light from those nearby saloons and gaming places still open.

"If I was he," Skinner murmured to himself, "I'd figure that anybody would try to sneak in through the back way. That being the case, I'll come in the front." Setting action to words, he hoisted a convenient barrel sited near the entrance to display rakes and shovels and heaved it through the glass panes of one of the doors. Gasping with the pain from the throwing effort, he quickly slipped through the shattered door and moved away from it.

At first the darkened store was silent. "Ominously quiet," thought Skinner. "Like those little creeks that led into the Potomac that we had to sneak across to nab a Reb . . . grab a Reb and you can go back to bed," he giggled to himself, nervous with the anticipation of trouble.

As he knelt behind a counter, his night sight gradually returned. Little by little he could discern objects about the store. The new skylight, built into the roof after the first Congress Hotel's disastrous fire burned the rear wall of Gompers' store, provided some light. Skinner could see now that he was behind a display of cast-iron cook pots. Suddenly he had an idea and stuck his pistol back into its holster to free his hands.

Then, using extra care to be silent, he lifted the lid from an extra-large Dutch oven and tried to stuff it under the back of his frock coat. He had hoped to be able to wedge the heavy lid under his trouser braces. Finding this impractical, he laid the lid gently on the floor and unbuckled his pistol belt to bring it outside his coat. Rebuckling his pistol belt tightly over the coat made a pouch that would now hold the lid, which he jammed past his sore ribs until it protected most of his back. "Now Mr. Back-Shooter, I'm ready for you," he panted, drawing his pistol and cocking the hammer.

All at once the silence of the store was broken by a banging sound. Skinner was familiar with the layout of the store, having worked there for half a day the previous year when the sheriff's staff was abolished by political connivance. The drumming was coming from the office. It sounded as if someone was banging his heels against a wall or the floor. "Possibly Gen," he thought to himself.

"What are you waiting for, Skinner?" called Sultan Sanders. "I always thought that reputation of yours was built on bullshit. Now I know for sure."

"Where's my wife, Sanders?" cried the sheriff, moving towards Sanders' voice.

"Choking on her gag—last time I seen her. Might be dead by now, for all I know."

"Are you man enough for a face-off, Sanders? Or do you like crawling around on your belly like a snake?"

"Face-off suits me just fine, Skinner. How about a truce while we light a couple of lamps?"

"Go ahead. Light your lamp, Sanders. One lamp should be enough, even with your bad eyesight."

CHAPTER 31

"Damn you, stop that banging on this damn door!" shouted an aggravated Ames, opening the small side door of his livery stable and sticking a tousled head through the opening.

"We're closed," he griped. "Go away. Come back another day, dammit."

"I need a horse, Ames," snapped Jack Sprague. "I'd like that one I had last time."

"I don't rent no horses in the middle of the damn night. Never get them back. You wear out your welcome here tonight?"

"Don't sass me, old man. I'm not in the mood for it. I'll buy that horse—and the rig."

"Four hundred bucks—to you, Sprague," replied Ames.

"That's highway robbery, you stinking crook."

"Compliments wouldn't help the price none. Go somewhere else, if you can."

"Four hundred, then. Go get him ready."

"Lemme see the money first. Somehow I lost my faith in humanity, especially when it's dark."

"Strike a light and I'll show you my money," argued Sprague.

"Come on in and I'll get the nag. But I'm not giving you that same saddle. That would be another fifty, if you want that newer one."

"Get it, old man; I'll have the money for you when you're finished."

"Humpf—better have," said Ames, lighting a lantern and taking it away with him to the stalls.

******

"That's strange," said the new deputy, Stan Woods, to himself. He and Happy Giles had separated, hoping to cover more territory in their search for Jack Sprague. He had come through the alley that paralleled Main Street. The alley made a jog around the livery stable's small corral, giving Stan a good view of stable's big double doors. One of these doors was ajar, opened three feet or so, allowing a shaft of lantern light to weakly paint a yellow patch partway into the dun of the dusty corral.

Stan had been a deputy sufficiently long to sense the unusual from the ordinary. The livery's door being open was not the usual, nor was it extraordinary, but it was certainly worth a quick look.

Stan's quick look found the unconscious Ames, bleeding from a hit to his head. A bucket of water brought him around and he told his tale of woe to deputy Stan, bemoaning the loss of the horse and saddle.

"Have you an idea of which direction Sprague figured on going? Tucson maybe?" asked Stan.

"Beats me. Oh God, shouldn't had said that. But I think he wanted to see Sam Buller, though. Asked me how to find Mrs. Kipp's boarding house. Said he owed Sam something—before he left."

"And you told him where Sam lives?"

"Yeah, I guess so," confessed Ames, holding a dirty handkerchief to his bleeding head. "Seemed all right at the time."

"You better go find the doc and get your head sewed up," said Stan. "I'll go and try to head Sprague off."

"Don't hurt that roan of mine. It ain't paid for. It's a hell of a good horse. Too good for a livery horse." He had to shout out that last part because Stan had left at the run.

******

Sultan Sanders fired up a match, using its light to find an overhead lamp. He got the lamp burning with the same match and lowered the glass chimney to quickly blow out the shortening match. He turned around, facing the sheriff.

"How are we going to do this? On a count?" he asked, pulling his white coat free of his pistol butt.

"Tell me one thing, Sanders," questioned Skinner. "Why are you doing this? Taking my wife and this gunfight?"

"Just say you thwarted my plans, Skinner. 'The will of the people,' said that jackass Gompers. I don't give a damn about the people. I care about me. I lived big and I wanted to die big. Remembered, I mean. The doctors say I only have a couple of months—if that long—before my liver shuts down completely. Under this powder my face is as yellow as a Chinaman. I wanted your job so I could die a hero in some shootout."

"You can't count on a shooting happening just to please yourself. Lawbreakers don't work to a schedule, you know."

"I know that. I was a sheriff when you was slopping hogs, or whatever you did. I figured on manufacturing a shootout. I'm good at that."

"So I heard. I think we've jabbered enough, Sanders. Go for your iron and I'll take your lead."

"You got craw, Skinner. I'll give you that . . ."

Skinner closed his mind to Sanders' talk, concentrating only upon the white-clad man's hands. The fingers of those hands; long, white, strong fingers, a pianist's fingers, were gently flexing alongside the white trouser seams. Suddenly Sanders' left hand seemed to drift out towards Skinner, as Sanders' left shoulder shrugged.

"Damn," said Skinner to himself, "a lousy palm gun;" but he was reaching for his own pistol even as the thought was growing to a warning.

The sheriff saw the small two-shot pistol slap into Sanders' waiting fingers; saw the tightening knuckle compressing through the open trigger guard as the blued, dual-barrels swung towards him.

Skinner heard the noise of the two shots, coming almost together. Behind the veil of gunsmoke, Sanders' bulky form was still standing. Then Sanders grimaced and looked down at the growing crimson stain on the white silk of his vest.

"I didn't think you could beat me—not with my palm gun," he sighed sadly.

"There's always somebody faster than you," said Skinner. "I try to remember that."

"I think I should sit down. Would you help me?"

"Fire off that other barrel into the roof and I might."

"You're not a trusting man, Skinner, but I'll oblige you." Sanders had to awkwardly point and fire the palm pistol at the ceiling because the mechanism inside his sleeve would not allow his wrist to turn.

"It's too late, Skinner, I'm . . ." Sanders staggered forward, falling on his face with a resounding crash.

"Sheriff! Is that you doing all that shootin'?" came a yell from the direction of the smashed front door.

"It is I, Happy. Or maybe I should say, it's me," tittered Skinner, giddy with the flood of relief. "Come on forward. The show's over."

"That ain't the way I heard it," said Happy excitedly. "Ames has been pistol-whipped by that Sprague fellow. He says Sprague has gone looking for Sam, over to his boarding house. Ames says Stan took off at a run to try to head Sprague off. My God—what's that lump on your back? Are you broke up?"

"No worse than usual. I gotta see if Genevieve is all right. I think she's tied up in Gompers' office."

Not only was Gen trussed up in the office, but she was accompanied in her captivity by Mr. Gompers, hog-tied and purple-faced with rage and lack of breath.

"Are you all right?" asked Skinner of his wife.

"She's fine. I'm the one about to expire. Did you catch that madman?" gasped Gompers.

"He caught something," replied Skinner. "You'll need another candidate come next election."

"No more politics, Skinner. And I have to apologize. I don't know what got in me. False pride, maybe."

"Knowing you, Gompers, you'll get over it quick enough. I have to leave now. Sam Buller's in trouble. Happy, see to these two and have somebody notify Marks to come and get Sanders. Tell him the doc doesn't need to examine him. I know what ailed him. Got that?

"I'd feel better going with you. That Sprague is slippery."

"You just do what I tell you. Now I got to run, if my ribs will let me."

******

After Doc Seevers had bound up his ribs, Deputy Sam took baby steps back to the sanctity and the hospitality of his room at Mrs. Kipp's. Most nights, Sam would have the room alone, his roommate working the late shift at a mine. This evening, though, must have been an off day, for the roommate was asleep on his half of the bed and snoring a beery sonata. Sam struggled out of his boots and gun belt to ease his hurt body down on the bed. But pain and the nocturnal nostril noises of his roommate were too much for Sam's sleep. After ten minutes of listening to the snoring, plus the nagging discomfort of his ribs, he gave up on the bed, heaved his hurt body to its feet and crept down the stairs to the hopeful solace of the padded rocking chair in Mrs. Kipp's parlor. There, exhausted by the long day and the pain to his ribs, he soon fell asleep.

Mrs. Kipp occupied a room off the kitchen, sharing the bed with her fourteen-year-old daughter, Gloria. Mr. Kipp was now only a memory and a fading image on a tintype, having been killed by runaway team, years previously.

Jack Sprague would have been a good cat burglar, if he had chosen that line of endeavor. Of course, it was helpful that Mrs. Kipp's front and rear doors were never locked. Surmising that a boarding house keeper would sleep near her kitchen, he found her door, verifying it with a quick flash of a match: Private, Mrs. Kipp, Manager.

The two ladies were roused from their sleep by the cold steel of Sprague's boot knife against their cheeks. Mrs. Kipp tried to resist to protect Gloria, only to be knocked unconscious by Sprague's fist.

"Sam Buller's room number?" Sprague snarled. "Tell me quick and I won't kill you." He relaxed the hand over Gloria's mouth.

"N . . . n . . . no numbers any more," stammered the frightened girl. "Since the trouble with Mr. Malone."

"I'll kill you, so help me. What's the room number?"

"It's the robin room," the girl tried to explain. "Mama don't like room numbers anymore. Our rooms are named after birds now. Like blue jay and thrush. He's in the robin room, at the head of the stairs."

"The robin room. Ain't that sweet? Girlie, you stay right there until I . . . no. Tell you what; put on a robe or a dress real quick. I think I'll take you along with me in case the law gets too close. Just remember one thing—if you so much as makes a peep—I'll slit your little throat from ear to ear. Now get ready. I'll be back for you in two shakes. And don't light no lamps, hear?"

He left without getting her answer, finding the stairs to the upper floors. Another quick match showed the proud portrait of a male robin, head raised as he devoured a worm. "Very fitting," commented Sprague silently. "The death of a worm."

Quietly he tiptoed into the room. One man was in the bed, snoring under a sheet. Six swift stabs ended the snoring. Sprague wiped off the bloody knife with the foot of the sheet and went back downstairs.

The girl was sitting on the bed, facing away from him, still in her nightgown.

"Not ready, girlie? Too late now. We gotta go." He leaned over the bed to grab the girl, but she shrank away from him, but then she turned towards him to fire a huge Colt dragoon pistol. The revolver sounded like a cannon in the small room. Sprague, off-balance from his lunge, was flung against the washstand, smashing the crockery and ending up against the closed door.

"Are you dead?" cried the girl, struggling to recock the hammer.

Sprague tried to push himself off the floor but the bones of his right arm were useless, held only by the muscles of the upper arm.

"Oh God, girlie, don't shoot me again, please," groaned Sprague, finally getting his feet under him and half-rising to his feet.

Gloria later told Sam that she would not have fired again if the intruder had not tried to regain his feet. Her second shot took him in the chest, killing him instantly. She then sat on the bed, holding the big, ugly pistol in her lap, and cried.

Sam Buller was the first to reach the room and had trouble, what with his bad ribs, in pushing open the Kipps' door. A hastily-lighted lamp showed the sordid scene. The shots had roused mother Kipp who, though battered herself, rushed to console her daughter.

Deputy Stan arrived in time for the awful news from the robin room, brought downstairs by a gaggle of bewildered boarders.

Skinner heard the shots while still two blocks away, but he could not speed his pace because of his painful ribs.

When he finally arrived at the boarding house he found Sam directing two boarders, who had loaded Sprague's body onto a window shutter and were attempting to carry it outside through the crowd of onlookers.

"I'm sorry, Sheriff," apologized Sam. "But Mrs. Kipp insisted that Sprague be removed from her bedroom. I saw the corpse before it was moved, though."

"And that little girl killed him?" asked the sheriff, incredulously. "Sure it wasn't you, Sam?"

"Wish it were, Sheriff. But it was a little girl with a great big pistol. Supposed to have been her daddy's. The other body is still upstairs, by the way."

"What other body? What kind of a crazy night is this, anyway?"

"My roommate, Cecil Franks. I guess Sprague thought it was me. He forced the girl to tell him which was my room, only I wasn't there."

"Where were you?"

"Sleeping on the rocker in the parlor. My ribs wouldn't let me sleep in the bed—that and Cecil's snoring."

"The rocker help any?"

"Guess so. I was sleeping until the shooting woke me up."

"Think a rocker would help me?"

"I dunno. Try it. You got that rocker on your porch. But put a pillow down on the seat—and maybe one on the back."

"I had to kill Sanders—did you hear?" asked the sheriff. "He grabbed Gen and took her to Gompers' store. Had Gompers tied up there, too. Wanted to draw me out—or in. Wanted a showdown. He got it."

"Three killings tonight," commented Sam. "Busy night for a Thursday."

"Can you and Stan handle things here? I'd like to go home and check on Gen."

"Go ahead. But I'll be late tomorrow morning. I walk real slow lately."

"So do I, Mister Chief Deputy," answered Skinner. "So do I."

******

Gen was still up when the sheriff came home. "What's the matter, Genevieve, too excited to sleep?"

"That, and worried about you and Mr. Buller. I made fresh coffee and I have a few of those raisin cakes left. Won't you sit down . . . what is wrong with your back, it's all lumpy?"

"That's a souvenir from Mr. Sultan Sanders," laughed Skinner. "I put a pot lid in my coat in case he'd back-shoot me. But he fooled me and tried to use a palm gun."

"What kind of a gun is that? Is it made from a palm tree?"

"No it's a little pistol that fits up your sleeve and . . . aw, forget it. It didn't work, anyway."

"Take that pot from your coat, Sylvester. It makes you look like my great-aunt Sarah from Troy. The one with the humpback."

"Wasn't she the one with the mustache who gave us a barrel of apples for our wedding present?"

"No, that was Aunt Philippa, on my father's side. Aunt Sarah gave us the chamber pot with the gilt angels for handles."

Mr. Hansen came through the open back doorway just as Skinner released his gunbelt, allowing the cast-iron lid to crash down upon the kitchen floor. Hansen jumped back at the clatter, shielding his skinny chest with his blue-veined arms.

"Excuse me, folks," he said after recovering his self-possession, "did I hear someone mention raisin cakes and fresh coffee?"

"Indeed you did, my friend," Skinner told him. "Anyone who could face down Sultan Sanders without a gun can claim my share of the raisin cakes."

"How many would that be, would you think? These nighttime adventures sure make me hungry."

Epilogue

T he finding of Franklin Finsen's body by the hotel's chambermaid on Friday morning wrote an end to the criminal file of the Ostenhaven bunch. The Green Falls survivors of the federal prison hulks, their numbers now down to three with the death of Jerry Jones, attended the joint funerals of former First Sergeant Jack Sprague and Sergeant-Major Frederick Finsen, who were buried side by side at the old cemetery. These survivors attended the sparse ceremony, they all agreed later, not to honor their enemy but to lay to rest their sad memories of those terrible times on New York's East River.

In February 1900, all Union and Confederate veterans' remains were removed from the disreputable old cemetery and interred in the new cemetery's Garden of Valor, established with the advent of the Spanish-American War's dead. Sprague's and Finsen's well-tended graves are there, graced by a War Department marker stating their rank, name and military organization and are regularly decorated by the Boy Scouts. Theodore Ostenhaven, due to his name change, succeeded in his anonymity and his remains still lie lost in the ruins of the old cemetery.

The rumors of Tent-Peg Pete's golden bonanza have proved a modest gold mine for the town of No Place, providing work for outfitters, guides and wranglers to those adventurous enough to risk the desert mountains. The discovery of uranium in 1947 at a location thirty miles northwest of No Place resulted in a short-lived boom. A heavy duty, two-lane highway, built by the Atomic Energy Commission and maintained by the State of Arizona, which connects to the federal highway in Green Falls, remains a cold-war dividend for the citizens of No Place.

Major Hiram Poole, hero of the fight at Stone House Hill, was called to Washington by the War Department in November 1871. There, he was decorated with the Congressional Medal of Honor at a White House ceremony by President U. S. Grant. Attending this honors formality was the Commanding General of the Army, William Tecumseh Sherman, who had orchestrated Major Poole's public acclaim to assuage the Western clamor for increased, costly, military repression of the hostile tribes.

A few days after the White House honors, Major Poole was called from his round of public appearances to report to the War Department. At this meeting, he was promoted to Lt. Colonel and further assigned to the U.S. Military Academy at West Point as a cavalry tactics instructor.

Brigadier General Hiram C. Poole died of malarial complications, June 1900, while engaged in the Philippine campaign against the Aguinaldo insurgents.

The colonel commanding the 2nd U.S. Cavalry Regiment convened a court of inquiry in answer to the many allegations and rumors surrounding the Stone House Hill fight. All officers and non-commissioned officers were cleared of any allegations of blame in that action. The court's report stressed the positive results of the involved troop. The report did mention that a certain bugler seemed to be in need of additional training. No mention of Major Poole's tangential foray was made in the report, though a footnote by the court's secretary directs attention to the War Department general order awarding the Medal of Honor to Major Poole.

Chief Slit-Nose lived until 1905. During the thirty-four years after his capture at the Stone House fight he was technically incarcerated as a dangerous war criminal. In actuality, he was housed, with a dozen other aging tribal chiefs, in a comfortable brick house on the grounds of Fort Monroe, Virginia. The dozen or so I.I.'s (their keeper's abbreviation for Influential Indians) were well fed and housed, had reasonable freedom of the coastal artillery fortress grounds, and each received a government stipend they could use to purchase tobacco and comfort items. Every year they were measured for a new suit of clothes which were manufactured in a federal prison. Overcoats were issued on a five year basis. Footwear was doled out by the Army quartermaster, although most I.I.'s made their own moccasins.

Many of the I.I.'s chafed under this benevolent restriction. Chief Slit-Nose was one of the I.I.'s who enjoyed the attention and ease. He sometimes was referred to as the "white man's skunk on a string" by his resentful associates, for his ready acceptance of speaking invitations and visits to State Fairs and other public events where Army officials could utilize his notoriety for publicity and recruitment purposes. Dressed in a specially-made costume and carrying his battered carbine, his pose struck the very essence of the enigmatic red man, a role he played to perfection.

Many a white hero had found out to his grief that he could never find happiness at his old home. Chief Slit-Nose, perhaps to his credit, never tried. He was content to be "a skunk on a string" and to enjoy a life of public interest and ease.

Owl-Who-Kills-At-Night, conversely, had a joyless role as a tribal leader. The Indian Bureau officials feared his power and did everything to denigrate his authority. Rival native leaders were encouraged and rewarded in their personal plans of prerogative and avarice. Many times he was arrested and cruelly imprisoned to interrupt Ideas contrary to Bureau policy. During one of these detentions he contracted pneumonia and died after being punished by being chained to a snubbing post in a freezing rainstorm.

Mr. and Mrs. Henry Stultz (she was the former Helen Boorman), settled in San Francisco and quickly plunged into the social whirl fueled by the newly-made fortunes reaped from the bounties of the West. The depression of '73, which devastated the silver market, almost ruined Henry. But he weathered the storm, learning to invest in enterprises other than precious metals. He took to farming, speculating in the agricultural boom in the lush Santa Clara Valley.

In 1877 Henry and Helen began building Stultzhof, their dream mansion in the foothills west of San Jose. Sadly, Helen never saw the completion as she died suddenly of a brain hemorrhage in January of 1879. Henry finished Stultzhof in the summer of 1880 as a memorial to his beloved Helen. Once it was completed he never returned to the love mansion, living out his life as a disconsolate recluse in a suite of hotel rooms in San Francisco.

Esther, the extortionist's daughter, did not communicate with the sheriff or his wife until she reached her majority and came into a sizeable legacy from her uncle. At that time she wrote the Skinners that she could never forget or forgive the sheriff for the killing of her father. This letter caused grievous hurt to the Skinners, especially Gen, as she had felt close to the young Esther at that earlier time. Fortunately, by that period of their lives they were rewarded with the happiness brought them by their adopted daughter, Angelique, who was another rescued waif.

Sheriff Skinner and his loyal staff stayed together for another twenty years, continuing their good work in Green Falls. But although their city began to earn a reputation that would suggest that a criminal would do well to omit Green Falls from his itinerary, such was not the case. Every drifter and law dodger thought that he was unique, faster with a pistol, slicker at thieving and robbing, and smarter than any lawman anywhere. Skinner and company would show many of those who would prey on their fellow citizens the error of their ways.

THE

SHERIFF SKINNER SERIES

by Willie Lynch

The Law in Green Falls
ISBN: 0-9715542-0-X

The Sheriff Gets a Job
ISBN: 0-9715542-1-8

Sheriff Skinner and the Puzzle River Water War
ISBN: 0-9715542-2-6

Sheriff Skinner and the Man from the Past
ISBN: 0-9715542-3-4

About the Author

Willie Lynch, a long-time afficionado of the Western novel, is a retired army engineer sergeant and transportation worker. A widower, he now resides in a senior community center close to his seven children. He uses the "Skinner" name to honor his uncle who perished in the Great War.